THE
BALACLAVA BOY

To Liz,

Richard Parkyn   15th Nov. 08.

Sorry you missed coming !

THE
BALACLAVA BOY

Richard Parkyn

Matador
9 De Montfort Mews
Leicester LE1 7FW, UK
Tel: (+44) 116 255 9311 / 9312
Email: books@troubador.co.uk
Web: www.troubador.co.uk/matador

ISBN 978-1848760-158

A Cataloguing-in-Publication (CIP) catalogue record for this book is available
from the British Library.

Typeset in 11.5pt Sabon by Troubador Publishing Ltd, Leicester, UK
Printed in the UK by TJ International, Padstow, Cornwall

Matador is an imprint of Troubador Publishing Ltd

Thanks to all my family and friends for their support and inspiration, and to my wonderful wife, Lisa, for her encouragement and fantastic cover illustrations.

1

The Dancing Man

Just the other day in a galaxy really really near...

Jack Shillaber somersaulted backwards and drew his Lightsaber. *Pbshursssed* hummed its pugnacious energy. The evil Lord Vader was poised to strike but Jack was ready. He could feel the Force flowing through him. He was a powerful Jedi and Vader could not win. When it came, the attack was no match for Jack's power and agility. The Lightsabers clashed and sizzled like furious hot metal. Jack span, leaped and turned in mid-air drawing his weapon down in a deadly strike.

Silence.

It was over.

Once again, Jack had brought peace and harmony to the galaxy and there were still a few minutes before tea.

'Jack,' shouted his mum from the house.

'Coming, *Aunt Beru*,' he mumbled, dropping his makeshift Lightsaber (a cut-off piece of ash tree). He jogged back to the house. The sky was full of cloud as the evening gloom set in.

'Where've you been, Jack?' his mother asked. 'Dinner's ready.'

'Oh, my watch must be wrong again, sorry.'

'Jack.'

'Yes, Mum?'

'You don't have a watch.'

'Exactly. Not only do I not have one, but it doesn't work anyway,' he said, squeezing around the end of the table to sit down.

'Are you sure you didn't adopt him?' said Jack's older brother, Nigel.

'Sorry, darling,' said their mum. 'He really is your own kith and kin.'

Nigel sneered, 'Is that kin as in – *kin* I hit him now?'

'And is that kith as in – can I give my big brother a sloppy *kith*?' said Jack, pursing his lips in Nigel's direction.

'Carry on like that and we'll put the lot of you up for adoption,' said Mr Shillaber, raising his voice.

The boys' older sister Sarah fumed. 'But I didn't say anything, Dad.'

'Guilt by association, I'm afraid,' said their mum, smiling.

Mr Shillaber divided up the rest of the previous day's roast beef, while his wife dished out the vegetables: potatoes, carrots and greens.

'Why don't they ever help set the table?' said Sarah, glaring at her brothers.

'Don't worry, their turns will come,' said Mrs Shillaber. 'More greens, Jack?'

'No,' he said, solemnly. 'I don't really like them.'

'Well you'll never grow big and strong if you don't eat your greens,' she said.

'But they're all slimy.'

'Well, so are snails.'

'What's that got to do with it? I've never even eaten snails and I'm sure I wouldn't like them anyway.'

'Exactly,' she said, slopping another spoonful onto his plate.

'And I think Sarah's jealous of how much you're giving me – look, she's *green* with envy, get it?'

Sarah shot her brother a withering glance. 'You are so lame.'

Jack was twelve, the youngest of the three children. Sarah, the eldest, was sixteen, and Nigel (Nige to his friends) was fourteen.

Their parents were quite used to all the rubbish spoken in their presence, especially at meal times when they were all together.

They sat at the table in the crowded kitchen – range to one side, cupboards on the other, in front of the cobweb-edged window that overlooked a wildly unkempt garden.

'What on earth's that smell – Jack?' Sarah pulled her jumper over her nose.

'Sorry, there seems to be a gas leak in my central heating.'

'Jack, no letting off at the table or you'll be outside the front door,' said his dad, sternly.

'Sorry. It just came out. Better out than in and all that,' he grumbled.

'Can't we just have him sown up?' said Nigel.

'I think there's a new European law about not having children's bottoms sown up to stop them breaking wind,' said their mum.

'I didn't break anything,' pleaded Jack. 'I just bent it a little.'

'Well please don't bend it back,' said Sarah curtly. 'It may be more than my nose could handle.'

'But your nose is really tough. You're always poking and squeezing it in the mirror and it still stays the same shape.'

Everyone laughed except Sarah. 'Well it's not as tough as your Neanderthal ridge. It's so embarrassing having a family member who's more ape than human.' She smiled an evil smile and stabbed a potato with her fork. Mrs Shillaber glanced at Jack from the corner of her eye.

'Sarah,' said her dad, with a warning tone.

George Shillaber was actually a patient, gentle man – his long face often broken with a broad smile. A practical sort, he could fix anything with a piece of wire or a length of baler cord and like many hands-on farmers he was incredibly strong. When the children were younger they had loved arm-wrestling him, but would always lose, even if they used both arms.

Jack was upset by his sister's insult. He swallowed uncomfortably against the lump in his throat and paused from chewing a particularly gristly morsel of beef. 'What's it like being old, Dad?'

'Well, you ache more and get hairs where you didn't think hairs could grow.'

'Like where?'

'Oh, your lower back, ears... the palms of your hands.' He leaned towards Jack, lowering his voice. 'And sometimes under your tongue.'

'Urgh, Dad, that's disgusting,' said Sarah.

'You see,' said Jack turning to Sarah, 'growing old is uncool, it's something that should be left to... older people. You should try to enjoy your youth.'

'You won't have any youth left to enjoy if you carry on like that.' She glared darkly at him.

Jack ignored her. 'I wonder why Superman never seems to have a problem with hair. If he's so unbreakable, how come he doesn't have a super-beard that he can't shave because nothing will cut it except a razor made from kryptonite. He should have a beard down to his arse.'

'Jack, really.'

'Yes, Mum – really.'

'I wasn't asking a question, Jack, I was – it was an exasperated *really*.'

'Really?'

'Yes, really! George, tell him, please.'

'Well you see, Jack, hair dies soon after it grows out the scalp,' said his dad knowingly. Mrs Shillaber groaned in despair.

'Ah,' pondered Jack, 'but Sarah said she has to have her hair cut to make it grow and that the hair at the root knows when the hair at the end has been cut and that's what makes it grow more,' he said, almost confusing himself.

His dad whispered. 'Well, between you and me, that's just something women say to justify having their hair cut more often.'

'That explains it,' said Jack, putting another oversized forkful of food into his mouth. He chewed and swallowed noisily. 'I wonder what the state of his pubes were?' he said, scratching between his legs.

'*Super*, probably,' said Nigel, through a mouthful of food.

Sarah realised what Jack was doing. 'Will you stop that, you dirty little git,' she snapped. 'It has to be adoption, it's the only way.' She left the table and disappeared upstairs. On her way she brushed passed a pair of jeans hanging from the makeshift drying lines that ran along the beams of the kitchen ceiling. A pair of his mum's knickers fell on Jack's head.

'Think I'll have those thank you, Jack,' said his mum, reaching over and plucking them from his head.

'Don't mind if you do, thanks very much.'

Soon the rest of the family was busy cleaning their plates.

'Mum,' said Jack quietly. 'Can I leave the fat? It makes me feel sick.'

His mum gazed at him with pitying eyes. 'Well, you're the one losing out, but if you can't...'

Jack's heart sank as guilt washed over him. He couldn't help it, he didn't do it on purpose; it was just the way it was.

Nigel stretched across and picked out the tastiest morsel of fat he could see and popped it into his mouth. 'Mmm, delicious.'

'Yee-uck,' said Jack, pulling a disgusted face.

'You need a bit of fat, you runt. Look – nothing to you,' he said, digging his brother in the ribs. There *was* something to Nigel. In fact, quite a lot of something. He wasn't really fat though, more well-rounded.

Jack attempted to wriggle free. 'Hey, get off you big bully. Mum!'

In his best Darth Vader voice, Nigel (still tickling his brother) breathed heavily then said, 'I have you now, young Ape-walker.'

'Argh,' yelled Jack. 'You're just jealous because you haven't got a prominent brow.'

'Prominent,' laughed Nigel. 'You could balance a birthing cow on that,' he said, studying Jack's forehead. 'No wonder you're so good at heading a football – it always reaches you before everyone else. You've an unfair advantage.' Nigel was on a roll. 'There we all were thinking Homo sapiens were the only bipedal primates left and yet here you are – a grunting Neanderthal walking among us.'

'OK, Nigel, enough's enough,' said his dad. 'No harm being unique, everyone is.'

'It's OK, Dad, I don't care,' said Jack quietly. He squeezed out from the table and turned to his brother. 'Oink-oink!' he shouted and ran off to the toilet.

'Nigel, you went on a bit much then,' said his dad. 'You know how Jack is about his brow.'

'But –' began Nigel, then seeing the expressions on his parents' faces. 'OK, sorry. It was just a laugh, you know. I was just trying to – never mind.'

'It's not us you need to apologise to, is it?' said his mum.

Nigel sighed. 'OK.'

A few moments later Jack returned and Nigel apologised.

'Well?' said their mum to Jack.

'Sorry about the *oink-oink*.' Jack scrunched up his freckly nose and took the plates out to the sink. Embarrassed, he let his thick mop of hair droop down over his eyes.

His mum followed him to the kitchen carrying the pans. 'About time you had a haircut, young man,' she said.

'No, I like it like this. It covers this lump,' he said, poking his forehead.

'Don't be so silly,' she said. 'There's nothing wrong with your head.'

Jack went back and got the last dishes from the table. 'Can I go and watch telly?'

'Yes, but not for too long.'

Mr Shillaber was already in the lounge watching the news, sitting as always, at the far end of the sofa, drinking a mug of tea. Nigel disappeared upstairs to do homework as Mrs Shillaber joined her husband on the sofa. Jack slumped down on the comfy chair to the left of the fire.

'Jack,' whispered his father, 'stick another log or two on the fire, won't you?'

Jack shuffled forward on his knees and chucked in a large lump of coal sending a cloud of sparks up the chimney. 'More stars in the sky tonight,' he said, recalling a story his mum used to tell him. He threw a log in and then picked up a second. 'Ow. Damn it,' he cursed, dropping it. 'Ow, ow, ow.'

He raised a quivering hand so his parents could see the deep splinter protruding from his little finger.

'Oh, that is a nasty one, shall I pull it out for you?' said his mum.

'No! No thanks, I'll do it. Damn, why am I so soft?'

'Not enough hard work,' said his dad, grabbing Jack's other hand and rubbing it between his rough palms.

'Ah, Dad, stop it,' said Jack, laughing. 'I need to pull it out.'

Beneath his skin, a bubble of blood darkened the pink flesh surrounding the splinter. He took hold of it between his thumb and forefinger and pulled agonisingly.

'Flipping heck. Look – blood.' He threw the splinter in the fire and held up the bleeding wound.

'Rinse it under the cold tap and I'll put a plaster on it for you,' said his mum.

'Thanks,' said Jack quietly. He got up and left the room, his mum following. Mr Shillaber eased forward onto his knees and carefully placed the dropped log on the fire before settling back onto the sofa. A couple of hours later he started to snore. This woke his wife, who had also been asleep (and also snoring). She gently rocked her husband's arm until his eyes opened. Then she saw Jack.

'Time for bed, young man.' She yawned and sat up.

'But this is my favouritest TV programme ever.'

'And what's this rubbish called?'

'Er, it's called... um, the er...'

'You don't know, do you?'

'No.'

'Have you ever seen this before?'

'Er, maybe.'

'Are you just watching this for the sake of it?'

'Well not –'

'Are you going to bed now?'

'Um... yeah.'

'Goodnight,' she said, and kissed him on top of his head.

Reluctantly he got up and kissed his dad goodnight, then sloped upstairs.

Nigel was fast asleep when Jack entered their shared bedroom. It was a small, cold room despite the thick rugs and heavy curtains. Their beds were set end to end at right angles away from the window, so no draughts could blow around their heads as they slept. Sharing was OK, but as Nigel got older Jack sensed he wanted more privacy than he was getting. Often Nigel would ask Jack to 'Get out and leave me alone.'

Sometimes, it was not much fun. One night, Jack was ill with a bad stomach and in the middle of the night woke with a start. He sat bolt upright in bed throwing up at the same time. The combination of his movement and the powerful muscle spasms from his stomach made his projectile vomit gather enough momentum to reach Nigel's bed. It was not a pretty sight. Indeed, it was not a pretty smell either. Nigel claimed he was emotionally scarred for life.

Jack crept into the bedroom, avoiding the creaky floorboards. He had forgotten about their earlier run-in. He liked his brother, he found something comforting about his happy face and dark, curly hair. He had natural confidence, something Jack could never imagine. He stared at Nigel's bed, thinking how good it was having such a nice brother. A sharp, sucking snore broke the silence. 'Come on pipsqueak, hurry up and get to sleep.'

'OK, calm down, big bro,' whispered Jack, undressing as quickly as possible. 'What's the rush?'

'Rush'll be my fist moving towards your head.'

'Beautifully put. No kiss goodnight then?'

'Only kiss you'll get will be a Glasgow kiss.'

'You wouldn't do that, you'd feel too *kilty* in the morning.'

'Ha ha. Very funny. Good night.'

'Nighty-night.'

In the pitch-black night, far out on one of the most remote parts of Bodmin Moor, an old man danced crazily between a rough wooden bench and a bright, crackling fire. He was waving his arms like a maniac and leaping much further into the air than someone of his age should comfortably be able to manage. The wind swirled and snarled about him as slight wisps of hurricanes spiralled into the air before breaking and dropping their dusty loads back to earth.

The sky was heavy, the clouds low. No stars were visible. A dim glow was the only evidence of the full moon patiently reflecting the sun's rays and transforming them into a brilliant pale-blue light.

On the bench stood a sleek titanium computer, displaying a rotating strand of interwoven, multicoloured particles that looked biological in their make-up. It was repeating the same mechanical animation of joining the particles before flashing significantly.

Over the fire stood a tripod made of branches from a nearby beech tree, below which hung a heavy, black, cast-iron pot. The contents were bubbling away, occasionally popping with brilliant iridescent flashes that momentarily turned the surrounding area into some kind of bizarre bush disco.

'Yes, yes, ye-e-s, you little beauty.' The old man was dressed in modern hiking gear, from his red thermal hat down to his brand new walking boots, and was jumping up and down while screaming out his utter joy. From the surrounding darkness a figure approached. By contrast he was wearing what seemed to be the costume of someone who was auditioning for the part of an extra in a film about life in the Dark Ages. His scruffy, dark brown robes were well-worn but thick enough to keep him warm. He took hold of the oversized hood and threw it back as he drew into the firelight, revealing a friendly, but ancient, face.

'Hello there,' he said in a calm, low voice. The dancing man had not seen the fancy-dress man wander up and almost jumped out of his modern hiking gear. In fact, he almost jumped out of his skin, his flesh, his bones and his modern hiking gear.

'For the love of Uther,' panted the dancing man, holding his hands to his heart. 'You scared the Cheesewrings out of me, Golitha, sneaking up like that.' He was now busy checking his pulse.

'Terribly sorry, Fynn, but if you'd not been making such a racket you'd probably have heard me coming,' said Golitha, once again in his calm, low voice.

'You could've *called*.'

'*Called*? I didn't think you believed in all that rubbish. Aren't you the one who keeps telling all us damned old fools that we need to be a more progressive – try and keep up with the rest of the world and all that?'

'Yes, well –'

'And yet you suggest that I should have *called*.'

'Oh come on, Golitha. Most of them old ways you and the others cling to have no place in the modern world.' He paused. 'But on this occasion, *calling* would have been highly acceptable, thank you very much.'

'Would you like me to go away and *call*, and then come back?'

'Now you're just being ridiculous.'

Golitha shuffled around the fire, staring into the pot and sniffing. 'Those are very nice boots you're wearing,' he said.

'Why thank you. They're modern and they're great – warm, comfortable, waterproof too,' said Fynn.

'They must have been expensive.'

'Yes, well they were quite, they – now hang on just a minute. I see where you're going with this.'

'You know, those funds weren't released for you to make yourself look *cool*,' said Golitha.

'Are you suggesting that I used the research fund to buy myself boots? What kind of person do you think I am?' said Fynn, his voice rising with disgust.

'I know exactly what kind of person you are – remember what happened with Red Ruth?' he said.

Fynn gasped and bit his bottom lip. 'Everyone makes mistakes sometimes,' he said, ashamed.

'Oh come now, Fynn. I'm just joking with you. Ha! Modern humour. You see? Maybe I'm not such an old fuddy-duddy after all. Now then,' he said, turning back to the fire, 'what do we have here? Golitha's friendly face became world-weary, as though he had remembered something quite dreadful was about to happen. He rubbed his short, grey hair and played with the end of his roughly trimmed beard while gazing into the inviting depths of the pot. He sniffed, closing his eyes. 'It almost smells good enough to drink.'

'Well I should think so too. I just hope it's not too...' but Fynn's sentence was lost as his mind wondered over unknown consequences. His face revealed a burden of responsibility. Golitha genuinely felt for him but forced the feelings away – they all had their own part to play and this was Fynn's. He had chosen it willingly and knew what he must do.

'Is it ready?' asked Golitha solemnly.

Fynn nodded. 'Oh yes,' he said. 'It's definitely, absolutely and undoubtedly ready.'

'Did the pom-cuter help at all?'

'It's called a *com-pu-ter* and let's just say getting that was a giant leap forward,' he said, a wry smile breaking over his face.

Golitha eased himself down onto the bench, his joints were stiffer than they used to be and his limbs ached. He'd had troubled sleep lately – maybe the years were finally catching up with him. Unconsciously, he rubbed his right knee and heaved a great sigh. 'It's taken an awful long time – must be several hundred years so far. Has there been any word from Pixash recently?'

'The last *call* we had was a bit garbled. She's finally leaving her post. I don't think we can delay,' said Fynn, grimly. 'The time is close, Golitha, maybe closer than we previously thought.'

Golitha's tired eyes watered from the fire-smoke. Anxiously he asked. 'Is there time enough?'

Fynn nodded uncertainly, slumping down next to Golitha. He pulled off his woolly hat and scratched his head. As he spoke, his voice almost broke under the gravity of his words. 'Only time will tell... only time will tell. This may be our last chance. The evil will not wait for us to be ready. It will come.'

2

Tramp Backwash

Jack was woken the following day by the sound of his mum stomping up the stairs to wake them. Depending on the time of year she would either come in and open the heavy curtains or snap the light on. Thankfully April was a curtain month and as Jack was already awake and it was Friday he didn't mind having to get up and go to school.

He had been dreaming about rabbits but was unable to recall any details. There were definitely rabbits though, he knew that for sure.

'Wakey-wakey, up you get.'

'Morning, Mum,' said Jack.

Nigel mumbled and turned over in his bed.

'Can you put the heater on please?' said Jack as his mum was leaving the room.

'OK, but chop chop, quick quick.' She put it on and went to wake Sarah.

Being an old farmhouse, it had no central heating or double glazing. This made the upstairs particularly cold and was the reason each bedroom had an electric fan heater. At times the bedroom windows even iced over on the inside.

Jack lay on his back cocooned in the warmth of his bed, enjoying its cosiness. When the heater had eased the chill from the room he peeled back the blankets and swung his legs over the side.

'Come on, Nigel, Mum says get up.'

'Yeah, coming in a sec,' said the Nigel-shaped lump.

Jack warmed each item of school uniform in front of the heater before quickly putting it on. When dressed he went over to his still dormant sibling and gave him a gentle shove.

'Come on, get up, sleepy-lump.'

'I'm getting up, lame-brain, now shove off.'

'Charming.' Jack picked up his satchel, made sure he had the right books for the day's lessons and hurried downstairs.

The kitchen was a sizeable room but contained far too much furniture so the table was always left pushed against the wall for breakfast, which was often a rushed affair.

'Morning, Dad.'

'Morning, Jack.'

He carried on through to the bathroom for a pee, returning a couple of minutes later yawning loudly.

'Here you are, Jack,' said his mum, pouring hot milk into his mug.

'There's bubbles on it,' he said, sheepishly.

'Come on, Jack, they're just bubbles,' she said.

'But I can't stand them in my mouth.'

'I'm not going to remove them for you any more,' she said sternly.

Jack's dad swallowed a mouthful of toast and leaned towards him. 'You know, Jack, you could always burst them with the back of a spoon.'

Jack thought for a second, picked up a spoon and tried it. 'Wow, Dad, you're right. Thanks.'

'Well hallelujah,' said his mum.

This seemed to perk Jack up. 'I'm very hungry this morning. For breakfast I would like eggs, bacon, chips, peas, cheese, fleas, bees, beans, waffles, bread, butter... a rudimentary glockenspiel, desiccated coconut, tweezers and some fluff.'

'There's cereal, toast or nothing,' said his mum.

At that moment Sarah and Nigel appeared and sat down to eat. Mr Shillaber poured them tea and passed it over.

'You look knackered, Nigel,' said Jack, chewing a mouthful of cereal.

'That's because you woke me up in the middle of the night talking nonsense, you little git.'

'Nigel,' warned his mum.

'Well that's the second time this week.'

'I can't help it. Sorry, OK?' said Jack. 'I didn't mention rabbits, did I?'

'No, but you kept claiming the *Force* was with you, then you started talking gibberish, don't know what you were saying. I had to throw something to shut you up.'

'Wasn't a rabbit, was it?' asked Jack, casually.

'Yeah, I keep rabbits under me bed in case I need to chuck one at you because you're rabbiting on in your sleep.'

After another ten minutes of petty squabbling they finally set off down the lane to catch the bus for the forty-minute journey to school.

The first spots of rain fell as the bus slowed to a halt and reversed back to stop outside the Games Hall at Launceston College. Dark clouds lingered above and the air smelled of storm. Children wandered in and out of school, meeting friends, playing games and talking. Teachers wandered in and out of school, pretending to be interested in bus duty while nursing hangovers.

Jack headed for the juniors' cloakroom. It was not really a room, more like a large changing room at the intersection of two corridors and some stairs. It had no lockers either, only rows of hangers with open shelves above wooden benches. The corridors were cold and unwelcoming but he had an unsettling feeling of joy.

He saw his friends from way up the corridor. Al was struggling to pack books into his shelf while Luke sat transfixed, playing an electronic hand-held game. Jack smiled as he watched them and decided that school wasn't that bad after all. He jumped down the few steps at the end of the corridor and skidded to a halt, bumping Al in the process. 'How can you be so good at sports and yet so clumsy?' said Jack.

'Unfortunately quite easily,' said Al through gritted teeth while juggling his disobedient books. 'Just get in there, you messed up trees.'

A couple of large books began to slide. He managed to grab one but the other fell and bounced off Luke's head onto the floor. Oblivious to this, Luke carried on destroying the *Swarths of Minghorn*. Jack waved a hand between Luke's face and the game – he inclined one way then the other, like a human metronome.

Jack nudged Al. 'The light's on and there's somebody home, but unfortunately they don't want to come to the door.'

'Yes!' said Luke, triumphantly.

'He speaks,' said Jack.

'Right, gentlemen. I am here. Al, what are you trying to do?' said Luke.

'What do you think I'm trying to do? Count water? Teach cows to line-dance? Knit dental floss into a protective jacket for my teeth? What does it look like?'

Luke stared blankly. 'Looks like you are trying to ruin your school books.'

'Very funny, right comedians, you pair.'

Jack and Luke both grabbed a book and handed them back to Al.

'Talking of books,' said Luke, dropping another of Al's books and rummaging in his bag, 'I purchased this on the Internet, it is quite brilliant – *The Book of Untrue Facts*.' He pulled out a large green book.

'But that doesn't make sense,' said Al.

'Exactly.'

'Is this another of those highbrow intellectual books you love so much, not more cosmology is it?' said Jack.

'No. It is a plethora of the unknown – pick a subject.'

'Education,' said Al, smiling.

Luke flicked through the pages. 'Education, education... ah, here we go. Education... teachers. "Teachers' bad breath is caused by compulsory gargling with a mixture of dung and vomit".'

'Nice. You'll have to show it to Mastermind – he'd love a book like that,' said Jack.

Luke continued. '"By law, teachers can only marry other teachers".'

'Actually that's quite funny because –'

'Morning, ladies.' Al was cut short by the arrival of the most feared school bully, complete with thuggish sidekicks. The unfortunately named Robert Dunce was considered to be the most psychopathically violent child who attended the school. He was not only mad in the head – but also in the legs, arms, lower vertebrate and spleen. In truth, he was pretty livid in all his internal organs. He would fight anyone no matter what size or shape, not caring if he got hurt (if anything, it spurred him on). Even most teachers were scared of him.

'Look at you pathetic creatures – it's like *Dumb, Dumber and Dumberest*,' said Dunce, scratching his frustrated black hair. 'Now I don't want no trouble, but I've forgot me lunch and need a bit of cash to get some. I was hoping you generous people was gonna help me out.' He smiled an evil, gummy smile revealing stubby, yellow teeth before stuffing a half-smoked cigarette behind his ear.

The three boys were petrified and realised that where seconds ago the cloakroom had bustled with activity, now no-one was to be seen. Refusing Dunce's request would end in violence, leaving few options open to them.

Jack broke first, reluctantly reaching into his bag. He opened his lunch box and took out the two rolls his mum had made him, still cold from a night's refrigeration.

'They're egg,' said Jack, handing them over. Dunce passed them to the thug on his right whose left eye was twitching violently.

'And you pair?' said Dunce.

Al quietly handed over his dinner money.

It took Dunce an age to count the one pound eighty. 'Pathetic,' he sneered.

Luke pulled a kitchen-foil-covered lump from his bag. 'It's a home-made pasty,' he said glumly. 'You probably won't like it, it's got swede and peas and too much pepper.'

'Don't look so sad, fatty, not as if you'll starve,' said Dunce, before snorting through a laugh.

Jack hated Dunce and daydreamed that he, Al and Luke were beating Dunce and his cronies soundly, kicking them all the way down the corridor back to the seniors' end. 'Now get lost and take your brain cell with you!' As Jack finished his sentence he realised he had said it out loud, not in his head as intended. Luke and Al glared in disbelief. Dunce casually leaned forward and punched Jack in the stomach. Jack collapsed, the wind knocked out of him. As he lay, silently struggling for breath, Luke bent down to offer awkward comfort. Al tried to make eye contact with anyone, hoping to lure them out to help, only to glimpse heads darting behind coats and bags.

Dunce stood over Jack. 'What did you say, you little git?'

Jack finally inhaled again. 'S... sorry,' he panted. 'D... didn't mean to.'

Dunce poked at Jack's forehead. 'Unless you want me to knock your lumpy head back into shape you'd better –'

'Leave him alone, you big bully,' came a raised voice from behind them. It was Agnes accompanied by Helen, friends of the boys from the same form.

'I said leave him alone, you bully,' she yelled and swung her bag into Dunce. His arms flailed embarrassingly to prevent himself falling over. She swung at him again but his balance regained, he caught the bag and snatched it from her hands, fuming.

'Stupid cow. D'you know who I am?' He ripped open the bag and emptied its contents onto the floor before throwing it aside.

'Oh thanks a lot, idiot,' said Agnes.

'Bovered?' snapped Dunce.

'I suppose you're going to hit me now – think you're so tough, don't you? Why don't you pick on someone your own size?'

The twitchy-eye thug giggled. Dunce's hand shot out, grabbed him by the throat and squeezed. Some rather unpleasant choking noises forced themselves through the crushed windpipe. A few agonising seconds later, Dunce slowly released his grip. Twitchy-eye thug dropped, coughing violently.

Dunce stared menacingly at Agnes. 'I've got to go now,' he snarled, 'but I ain't gonna forget you and your little friends – just watch it, right?'

With a sharp nod his two drones (one still sputtering and rubbing his neck) moved into formation and trailed down the corridor after him. As they rounded the corner, Al, his face tortured with utter disbelief, rounded on Agnes. 'Hello? Are you mental?'

'Well he was hardly going to punch me, was he?' she said.

'I dunno, wouldn't put it past him, he's not exactly sane, is he now?'

'Don't be so melodramatic, he's a silly little bully.'

'With armour-plating and a piston-driven punch,' said Al. 'That's just the kind of excuse he needs to go and break someone's head open. Huh? Luke? Jack?'

'He's right,' said Luke, factually. 'I would expect some kind of revenge to be directed at possibly all of us present. Standard procedure.'

'Exactly. We're dead meat,' said Al desperately. 'We're dead meat that's been processed, packaged and has gone past its sell-by date. We're wearing yellow stickers with fifteen pence scribbled on them. Thanks a lot you, you –'

'Oh shut up, Al, you big baby, if me and Agnes hadn't appeared and she hadn't given him a good belting you might have all been in a far worse state – you ought to be ashamed of yourselves, you bunch a sissies,' said Helen, without taking a breath. She bent down to help Agnes pick up the scattered contents of her bag while Al failed to think of a smart reply.

'You all right, Jack?' said Agnes.

'That's the wrong question,' said Al. 'The question should be what on earth did he think he was saying? One day your little daydreams are gonna get you in serious trouble, Shillaber.'

'Idiot,' mumbled Jack. 'Didn't actually mean to... guess I drifted off. We were – I could see us kicking that lot all the way down the corridor, then...'

'About time someone stood up to them, I say well done,' said Helen.

Jack winced in pain. 'I agree with Al actually. Me and my big mouth.' He saw the disgusted look on Helen's face. 'I mean, don't get me wrong, you're right too, but I just don't think we're the right people to be standing up to psychos like him.'

'Boys,' sighed Helen. 'You're so lame – grow up and make a stand for yourselves.'

'Easy for you to say,' scoffed Al. 'You're a girl – you can get away with things like that against nutters like him – we can't. We're easy pickings. He'll get us at some point and it'll hurt and he'll enjoy it. We'll bleed. They'll –'

Whack.

'Ow,' gasped Al. 'What was that for, you mad cow?'

'You were hysterical,' said Helen.

'I don't believe you. What the – oh never mind,' he said, holding his cheek. Jack and Luke tried not to laugh too much.

'Thanks. Some friends you are,' said Al.

'A slap exerted with that kind of minimal force to the cheek can be nothing except good for the circulation,' said Luke.

'Anyway,' said Agnes, 'we'd better get on. Can't stand round here all day waiting to save you lot again. Hurry up or you'll be late. We're not going to make excuses for you. Can't you just avoid Dunce for a few days?'

'Doesn't really work like that,' said Jack, rubbing his stomach. 'You'd better watch it too. He's bonkers.'

'Are you going to *pwo-tect* us, Jack?' said Agnes.

'Ha ha. Funny guy, hey?' he said.

'Girl. Funny girl,' corrected Agnes and she and Helen set off down the stairs towards the tutor room.

The boys spent the first break in hiding, paranoid that Dunce and thugs would seek swift revenge. They guzzled down their remaining food while Jack and Al formed a plan to head into town for pasties. After scrounging money from sympathetic friends they were all set but Luke was not convinced.

'We are bound to get caught, the statistics are not in our favour.'

'Come on, Luke, chill out a bit, let danger into your life,' said Al.

'I think we had enough danger this morning, thanks,' he said. 'You know if caught, it's detention and a letter home to the olds. We are breaking school rules.'

'Try not to think of them as rules, more as guidelines, you know – "there is no spoon" and all that,' said Jack. 'Anyway, it's not like we're going into town to tear the place up, is it? We just need a bite to eat after having our food nicked – where were the teachers then, hey? Didn't see many racing up to save our stomachs, the fascists.'

'You are quite the anarchist sometimes aren't you, Shillaber,' said Luke. 'They would argue that we could get food from the school canteen.'

'Fo-o-d,' said Al. 'That's not food. It may have been once but once those deranged mutants get their hands on it, they soon cook the goodness out of it. By the time they dish it up, it's just some kind of generic, food-like gloop.'

'Your analysis, though founded largely on hearsay and rumour, is correct,' said Luke, finally relenting. 'OK, let's go and purchase pasties,' he said.

'Northy,' said Jack to Luke, 'have you ever realised that sometimes you sound like Doctor Spock?'

Luke smiled. 'That is illogical, Captain.'

'See,' said Jack.

'And that is Mr Spock to you,' added Luke.

They left the school grounds and hurried through the park adjacent to the school. Luke took *The Book of Untrue Facts* and spent most of the way quoting from it.

'"The only known meat-eating tree is the South African Coniverous Pine".'

'Rubbish,' said Al.

'Yeah, it's true,' said Luke.

'Can't be,' said Jack.

'No. It's true that it's rubbish – that's the point, the clue is in the title *The Book of Untrue Facts*,' said Luke. Al struggled with the concept all the way into town.

Launceston is an ancient settlement. It was Cornwall's capital until Bodmin took over in the 1840s. Its buildings vary from Tudor and Georgian, to gothic Victorian but they are overshadowed by the surprisingly charming presence of the great Norman castle which juts into the sky, towering over the town like a belligerent zit (although not many zits have flags on top). The town has eleven pubs, four estate agents, five banks and twenty-seven locations selling pasties.

The busy town pleased the boys. More people meant they were less likely to be spotted. Al joined the queue at the bakers, while Jack and Luke positioned themselves either side on guard duty.

Herby, the town tramp, stumbled by carrying a tin of *Pickles & Paynes Extra Special Super Strength Brew*, while mumbling to himself in his thick Cornish accent, his voice low and rough. 'Zoapwor', elder, wheat bran, comfrey. Grape, rosem'ry, that'll sort 'em out.'

He was a wretched old man, bent over with a massive tangle of matted grey hair. His mouth was hidden behind a great messy beard (full of unidentifiable small objects). Known for ranting about obscure weeds and herbs, Herby was completely different to the homeless people the boys saw on trips to Plymouth. Many of them were covered in cuts, bruises and open sores – something Herby managed to avoid.

'Mint, carrot, comfrey. Yarrow an' thyme'll do it.' He glugged from the can. Several dribbles rolled down into his beard which he wiped with a crustily stained sleeve as he hobbled away, mumbling.

Jack shivered. Something was not right about Herby. How could he drink so much of that stuff and still be alive? Perhaps he was in league with evil forces.

Thinking of evil, Jack felt his stomach. It was still sore. If only he had been able to draw a Lightsaber and cut off Dunce's arm before the fist had even reached him. It would have served Dunce right. Someone *should* stand up against that bully but *he* was too weedy. It was all right for Agnes – Dunce would never hit a girl. Well, Jack hoped he wouldn't. But Dunce would take revenge and Luke was probably right, it would be on them. Typical.

'There you go, skinny,' said Al, handing Jack a pasty. 'You have the largest one as a treat for being so *bwave* this morning.'

'Ha ha. Very funny,' said Jack.

'May I suggest,' said Luke, 'that we move from this exposed street and head back to school via Western Road?'

'Yes you may, Mr Spock,' said Al. 'Good idea.'

They headed off keeping an eye out for stray teachers. The delicious pasties kept them silent while they ate, which wasn't long for Al (he always finished food first). He pointed to the gloomy sky claiming it was about to rain 'cats, dogs, frogs and clogs' so they quickened their pace.

'Old Herby stumbled by when you were getting the pasties,' said Jack.

'Oh yeah, what did he have to say for himself? asked Al. 'Let me guess, was he ranting on about herbs and drinking a can of super-strength beer?'

'That's about it. He's not right that bloke – something odd going on there,' said Jack.

'Know what you mean,' said Al. 'And he loves getting people drinking from his can. Imagine all that dried spit caked on the edge.'

'Yuck,' said Jack.

'Imagine the backwash,' said Luke.

Al and Jack pulled sickened faces.

'There are more germs in a human mouth than there are in a dog's,' said Luke.

'In a dog's what?' said Al.

'Mouth,' said Luke, tiredly. 'Apparently last year some woman fainted carrying her shopping and Herby appeared from nowhere and sloshed some of that stuff down her throat before anyone else could help her.'

'Urgh. I'm surprise she survived,' said Al.

'Did she catch anything?' said Jack.

'Well, apparently she was OK. Someone chased him off soon as they could but she had to go to hospital to make sure he hadn't poisoned her.'

'And what did the police do?' said Al.

'Nothing. No evidence, so all they could do was follow him around a bit,' said Luke.

'I don't trust him as far as I could throw him,' said Jack.

'You couldn't even pick him up, let alone throw him, Shillaber,' said Al.

'Exactly.'

They arrived back at school as the heavens opened, a minute before the bell went. It had been a successful trip. They had acquired food and managed to avoid any imperial entanglements.

3

Hagar awel war vre meynek

The rain lashed against the oversized windows of the classroom. Physics was tedious enough in dry weather but the continuous deluge and threatening dark sky made it even more dismal. Jack was struggling to concentrate on Mrs Beaks' lecture. She was a small, relentlessly dull, middle-aged lady whose always-short-of-breath voice was irritatingly hoarse. Everyone suspected she had been middle aged all her life and that she spent her evenings screaming at her husband. Sometimes she smelled of cat pee but she didn't even have one. She and her husband were dog people. They had three whippets named Champagne, Livingstone and Cardboard Box, uncommon names in the pet world and another story altogether.

'Settle down... Right... Silence now. So, atoms-and-molecules. Structure-and-weight...'

Jack heard nothing else as he daydreamed about jumping through the rain-washed windows and flying into the driving downpour. '*Au revoir*, Beaky.' He flew up, up, and away towards the darkest, blackest cloud.

'Can we, help you, with-something, Mr Shillaber?' wheezed Mrs Beaks.

'Sorry?' said Jack.

'This is physics, Mr Shillaber, not French.' The class laughed as Jack turned bright red and almost fell off his stool.

'Oi, prat, wakey wakey,' said Al, digging Jack in the ribs with his ruler.

Jack was caught off-guard and unbalanced. Rocking one way then the other, he made a desperate grab for the bench but only managed to drag all his text books off it. As he twisted and clattered to the scratched parquet floor, the books followed.

For a moment, Jack thought he was going to cry but instead he got angry. Even Mrs Beaks was laughing a husky, short-breathed laugh at him. Al was doubled over near to tears, while Luke stared at Jack, trying to understand how someone could be so strange.

As the noise subsided Al whispered. 'Still OK for Roughtor tomorrow?'

'Yeah, fine,' said Jack, annoyed.

'Yes, of course,' said Luke.

Mrs Beaks finally coughed a warning for silence. Al gave Jack another jab with his ruler, although this time only on the leg. He handed him a small piece of folded paper. Jack sighed, took the note and opened it.

"Dear Hero, first your stomach, now your head, you'd better be careful or soon you'll be dead." It was signed by Helen.

'Charming,' whispered Al, his head down to avoid being spotted talking.

'Why's it always this lesson they start with these stupid notes?' muttered Jack.

'Boredom,' said Al out the corner of his mouth.

Mrs Beaks' lecture on the molecular structure of atoms was never going to be riveting stuff, but given a choice Jack felt he would rather hear how many protons a hydrogen atom contained than answer childish notes from the girls.

Al caught Helen's eye and tutted at her. Jack screwed up the note and threw it in the tiny bin next to Mrs Beaks' desk. It struck the metal inside with a satisfying dink. Mrs Beaks whipped around at the noise, narrowing her eyes at the class.

'Nice shot,' said Al, behind his hand.

A few minutes later another note appeared – "You were in my dream last night. Agnes."

'Right. That's it,' said Al, quietly pulling a page from his rough book. Mrs Beaks continued droning on about neutrons, protons and now atomic weights. Al scribbled on the paper, folded it, put Helen's name on it and passed it in her direction.

'What did you say?' whispered Jack.

'Sod off,' said Al, quietly.

'All right – I was only asking.'

'No, that's what I wrote.'

'Quiet please. Talk-at-lunch, not in my class,' rasped Mrs Beaks, her voice raw and shrill. She scanned the class, one eye half closed in focused concentration, searching for guilty faces. 'I hope that, wasn't-you-again... Mr Shillaber? I wouldn't want-to, give you, detention-would-I?'

'It wasn't me, Miss, honest,' said Jack, innocently. He tried to look interested and pretended to make some notes. Mrs Beaks stared contemptuously at him before returning to the blackboard. The chalk-on-board scraping merged with her voice into a scratchy, grating din. Jack wondered how anyone could possibly listen attentively to a word she was saying.

'Matter,' she stated, 'molecular-density – the more dense a substance is, the-heavier-it-is...'

Jack was drifting off again when another note appeared. Al opened it. "Jack. Shut up. Some of us are trying to work. Helen."

A few minutes later a beautifully folded note was passed to the boys. To their surprise it was written on parchment and was sealed with a wax stamp. On the front was written, '*Jack*'.

'That's a bit flash, what are they up to?' said Al.

Jack turned it over, broke the seal and opened it. He read to himself, '*Hager awel war vre meynek*'. As soon as he had read it (and thought 'what on earth?'), the words faded away.

'What the –'

Al peered over to see Jack staring at the blank sheet of paper.

'Mr Shillaber, I will... not tell you again,' called Mrs Beaks, her voice near breaking point.

'Sorry, Miss, but I...'

'Yes?' she snapped.

'Nothing, Miss.'

Jack was mightily confused. Did he really see that? He couldn't even say anything for fear of detention. He sat dumbfounded. When Mrs Beaks was back at the chalkboard he glanced around, hardly knowing what he was checking for. Luke and Al stared at him as if he was mad. He tried to mouth to them that he would tell them later but they didn't understand.

When Physics was finally over, the class bustled out excitedly. As soon as they were in the corridor Jack explained. 'Look, I know this may sound really daft, but you know that last note you passed me?'

'Yeah,' said Al.

'It had this strange writing on it, said something like "Hagger well a war me neck" – what's all that about?'

'Wasn't any writing on it when I looked,' said Al.

'Must've already disappeared, it just faded away on the page, that's why I went all funny, I was freaked out.'

'It sounds highly improbable,' said Luke. 'Unless they were using some kind of special ink. Take it out and let us see.'

Al sniggered.

'The letter,' said Luke, sighing.

'That's the other thing. I put it in my bag, right here,' said Jack pointing to an inside pocket, 'and it's gone. Completely vanished.'

'Who would have stolen a blank piece of paper from your bag?' said Al.

'I don't know, but someone did, all right,' said Jack, getting increasingly irritated. 'And it wasn't blank.'

'Look, you've had a difficult day,' said Al, patronisingly. 'Maybe your eyes have been affected by that punch this morning. 'You must have chucked the paper in the bin with the rest of your rubbish.'

'Oh thanks,' said Jack, who was busy trying to spot Agnes and Helen.

'Oi!' he yelled, jostling passed several children. He reached the girls and ran in front of them. 'What was that last note about?'

'Oh hello, Jack, how can we help you?' said Helen.

'That last note you wrote on the funny parchment paper, what did it mean? And how come it disappeared after I read it?' He paused briefly, expecting a reply. 'Well? And anyway, where did you get a seal from?'

'Make your mind up, Jack,' said Agnes. 'Which question would you like us to answer?'

Jack sighed. 'The note on the parchment – what did it mean?'

'What note on what parchment?' said Helen.

'The last note you sent,' said Jack.

'We didn't send any more notes, you pillock,' said Helen.

'Oh come on, don't be so annoying. It had funny writing on it. Some foreign language.'

'Nope, don't know what you're on about,' said Agnes.

'Come on, just admit it,' said Jack.

'OK, it was us,' said Helen.

'Now you're just saying that,' he said.

'Yep,' said Agnes. Jack contorted his face in frustration. 'Well we told you the truth and you didn't believe us, so we may as well tell you what you want to hear.'

'Well thanks a lot, some friends you are,' said Jack.

'OK,' said Agnes, relenting. 'What did it say on the paper?'

'It said... it said... Har... no. Something, ugly neck... no. Hang on. Something about... I can't flipping well remember.' Jack was so frustrated he put his head to one side and started hitting it, trying to jog the memory back, but it was useless.

Al and Luke arrived.

'Hey, do either of you remember what I said was written on that last note?' asked Jack.

'Er, no,' said Al.

'You said something about... oh, how peculiar,' said Luke.

'Damn it,' said Jack. 'It was on the tip of my tongue a minute ago.'

'Only thing on the tip of your tongue is a white spot, you little fibber,' said Helen.

'I'm not lying, you – if that's what you think, you can all sod off.' Jack stormed down the corridor bumping several children as he went.

'What got in to him?' said Al.

'I blame the parents,' said Helen. 'See ya.'

'Bye,' said Agnes.

'Yeah, bye,' said Al.

'Good-bye. Have a nice weekend,' said Luke. 'See you tomorrow, Al.'

5

A Storm Approaches

Standing side by side at the heart of Bodmin Moor are the two highest points in Cornwall – Brown Willy and Roughtor (Brown Willy edging it by a few metres). This part of the moor was inhabited in the Stone Age and the remains of many settlements are still visible around the edges of Roughtor.

It is a beautiful place that some find eerie, others refreshing – a place to get away and think. The boys loved the moor. It had plenty of rocks to climb and hideaways to explore. They enjoyed it most when no one else was there and they could make all kinds of mischief without the worry of upsetting anyone. On such occasions they had even lit small fires to toast marshmallows over. It would be wrong to say they didn't appreciate the stunning views, they were just far too busy having a good time to discuss all that "rugged beauty" and "beguiling charm".

Jack woke at ten past eight and tried to recall his dream. He was sure it had involved running, but something else had happened as well. Someone tall was in the dream. Yes, that sounded right. Someone tall and running? No. Someone tall and someone else running? But before he could chase the memory down, a particularly cumbersome yawn distracted him and it was gone. 'Damn,' he said quietly.

Jack was looking forward to the day, even though the previous one had ended with him storming away from his friends in a huff.

He couldn't remember what it had been about now. Something happened in Physics, he had fallen off his stool and then... No, it was gone. Anyway, it was the weekend and after he had done the mucking out and had lunch he was looking forward to meeting up with Luke and Al to go up Roughtor.

Nigel was sound asleep, drawing in long sawing breaths before exhaling – his cheeks flapping like the jowls of a sleeping dog.

Jack pulled back the corner of the curtain. It was cloudy but dry and the ivy-clad ash trees standing sentry on the back garden hedge were swaying gently. He wriggled to the edge of the bed to reach the pile of clothes he'd left out the night before, pulling them one at a time under the blankets to warm them before dressing. Finally, his socks went on and he was ready to head downstairs for breakfast.

'Morning, Mum,' he said, entering the kitchen.

'Morning, Jack.'

He smiled. 'For breakfast, I would like toast, beans, eggs, bacon, mushrooms... octopus, some marbles, the Queen of Sheba, tofu, origami, an emerald vestibule, peaches, Botswana and a nosy ocelot. In fact hold the mushrooms.'

'Why?' said his mum sleepily.

'Better leave them or there won't be *mush-room* for anything else.'

'Very funny, Jack, but I'm afraid I have some bad news.'

'Huh?' said Jack, his stomach lurching.

'We've lost your marbles,' she said, smiling.

'Mum! I thought you were serious.'

'You see, mums can make jokes too.'

Jack was lost for words.

'So, what would you really like for breakfast?' she asked.

'Is there enough milk for Ready Brek?'

'Yes, I'm sure you can manage to put that on yourself.'

'Thanks, Mum,' he said and ran off to the loo.

Halfway through his breakfast Jack's dad returned from checking the sheep.

'Morning, Jack.'

'Morning, Dad.'

'Hope you're feeling strong, there's a bit of a build up out there. Been too busy to muck out much this week.'

'OK,' said Jack. His dad was always too busy during the week but Jack didn't mind, most of the time. He knew the more he worked, the stronger he would be.

'Mum, are you still OK for dropping me at Bolventor later?'

'Yes. Soon as you've done the mucking out, I'm all yours.'

'Well, no. I was only gonna go after lunch, I want to see Football Focus first, if that's all right.'

'Oh, yes of course; who's David Beckham playing today?'

'Mum, Beckham isn't a team, you know that. He plays for Man United.'

'I know but it sounds like he beats teams single-handedly the way they talk on TV.'

'No, don't be silly.'

Jack finished breakfast, put on his old coat and wellies and went out to let Dog off his chain. Dog's real name was Dibble and he was the best dog in the world. Jack knew this without a shadow of doubt.

Dibble was a collie and lived across the yard in an old wagon house which still contained an old wagon under several years of built-up mess. The children loved playing football with Dibble. Of course, it was dog-football and the rules were slightly different. There was no offside or referee's assistant (or referee), no game of two halves, no throw-ins, no diving and no substitutions. In fact, the game amounted to nothing more than approximately one and a half seconds of trying to keep the ball away from Dibble, before he clamped the ball firmly in his salivating jaws. This was followed by ten minutes of trying to convince him to let it go. To Dibble, this seemed to be the most important part of the game and involved lots of growling and trying to cover the entire ball with as much drool as possible.

A huge pile of dung had built up in the cow shed and Jack had to work fast to get back in time for his programme. If Dibble had supported a football team it probably would have been Dibble United but Jack's team was Plymouth Argyle.

Cornwall is really a rugby county and though Jack loved rugby, football had the edge. Despite supporting Plymouth, Jack also supported Manchester United, the team his Uncle David had supported. Jack claimed Plymouth was his domestic side and Man Utd was his European side.

The show started with a review of the previous week's Premiership games, then went to a preview of the Champions League fixtures for the following week, which included the highly anticipated match of Man Utd vs Deportivo La Carunia. The show included an interview with Gary Neville which was very dull. They finished the programme with a World Cup preview discussing the England team – who would make it in, who was on the fringe and a look at the teams England would face.

After lunch Jack's mum drove him up to Bolventor. She turned into the car park of Jamaica Inn and Jack immediately spotted Al leaning against his dad's car. They pulled alongside.

'Thanks, Mum, should be back here at five-ish if that's OK?'

'Yes, fine. Have a good time, be good and be careful up there. Got your bag and snacks?'

'Yep. Later,' he said, hopping out and jumping in the back of the other car. Jack's mum waved politely to Al's dad and then drove off. She glanced up at Brown Willy and began worrying about the weather. Windy drizzle at Bolventor meant it could be a lot worse up on the high moor. Then again, it could be bright and sunny.

'Hello, Mr Fry.'

'Hello, Jack, how's farm life?'

'OK thanks, Mr Fry. All right, guys,' said Jack.

Al's dad was short and plump with dark tufty hair, a bald patch and a lively moustache. 'Well, Man United are definitely going to win the title – no doubt,' he said.

'No, Dad,' said Al, 'Arsenal all the way. United have still got a few defeats in them this season.'

'No,' drawled his dad, 'Arsenal will have Champions League distractions – it'll cost them the title for sure.'

'I agree with you, Mr Fry,' said Luke. 'If you take all competitions into consideration the odds are stacked against Arsenal on current form. The statistics point to a United title, with Arsenal coming away with nothing. However, I think this will help the

England team as those Arsenal players will be extra keen to prove their worth after a disappointing domestic run.'

'Interesting point, Luke,' said Mr Fry. 'You may well be onto something there.'

Al and Jack were staring in disbelief. 'Did you swallow a football magazine or something, Northy?' said Al.

'I may have glanced at one of those monthly journals in the newsagents the other day while I was waiting for Mum.'

'What, had they sold out of *Quantum Physics Monthly* and *Geek Weekly*?' said Jack.

'They do not sell those magazines... I was expanding my mind – it was quite interesting, actually.'

'Well, I'm glad for you,' said Jack. 'So d'you think we'll win the World Cup then?'

'No, I'm afraid not. England will go out in the quarter finals, probably against Brazil who will go on to lift the trophy.'

'Well, thanks for your optimism,' said Jack.

'You're welcome,' said Luke pulling out *The Book of Untrue Facts* from his bag. 'Listen to this – "Football will be renamed Fallball before the next World Cup. Goals will no longer determine the winner of a match. This will be decided on points awarded for diving. The referee will score dives with one, two or three points depending on the complexity and artistic interpretation in relation to the position of the ball and the opponent. If a referee is unsighted and his assistant also missed the dive there will be a third video referee on standby with instant review".'

'Rubbish,' said Mr Fry.

Twenty minutes later they pulled into the car park across from Roughtor. The drizzle had cleared and the sun was shining. The remaining clouds reflected a lazy vanilla glow as if seen through a photographic filter.

'Weird,' said Al, getting out of the car.

'Right, said Al's dad, 'I'll see you back here in about three, three and a half hours. Make sure you're here, Al.'

'No worries, Dad, we'll be here.'

'And don't do anything silly up there.'

'Dad – this is us.'

'Exactly.'

They checked their bags and made sure nothing was left in the car except Luke's book which was too heavy to be lugging up the tor, then set off.

'What does that mean anyway?' asked Al. '"Don't do anything silly". What does he think we're gonna do?'

'Well,' said Luke. 'Knowing you two – probably climb rocks dangerously, run recklessly over stony ground, leap from rock to rock without due care for your own safety, light a fire, wander off by yourselves, get lost, fall in a bog, drown, come back from the dead, form an axis of evil, invade Devon, enslave the English, start a nu-metal Morris-dancing troop, eat banana skins, knit trousers for chickens and play the eyeball game.'

'Yeah, fair point,' said Al laughing, 'but what the hell's the eyeball game?'

'You've never played the eyeball game?' asked Luke indignantly.

'No. What are you gonna do – report me to the eyeball-game police?' said Al. 'What is it?'

'It's not so much a game, more a challenge. What you have to do is put your thumb on your cheek just under your eye and your index finger on your eyebrow. Then pull your eye wide open.' Luke demonstrated while he explained. 'The person you are challenging also does this. Then you simply move closer and closer until your eyeballs touch, which of course will never happen because ultimately someone will get the heebie-jeebies and pull away. That's it.'

'That's disgusting,' said Jack.

'And what if neither person gets the heebie-jeebies?' said Al.

'I don't know, never heard of a challenge that went that far. Someone always blinks or gets freaked out. If eyeballs touched you would be breaking new ground, you'd be a *p-eye-oneer*,' said Luke, rather disturbingly.

'You know, sometimes, Northy, you can be really odd,' said Al.

'Thanks.'

'That's not really a compliment, Luke,' said Jack.

They splashed through the freezing, crystal-clear stream that gurgled joyfully as it snaked its way over the moor, and diverted to visit Charlotte's stone.

'Wonder if we'll see wee Charlotte today,' said Al, mournfully.
'I doubt it,' said Jack. 'She's been dead for over a hundred years.'

'I mean her ghost, melon-head.'

'The chances of seeing a supernatural being on a Cornish moor are probably more than a million to one,' said Luke.

'Melon-head?' said Jack.

Al ignored him. 'It does feel a bit spooky today though, check out the sky – it's really strange looking.'

Near the footbridge leading to Roughtor is a stone monument to Charlotte Dymond, a young woman murdered on the moor in circumstances that have never been fully explained. Her crippled boyfriend, Matthew Weekes, was later hanged for the murder at Bodmin Assizes in front of a large crowd of onlookers in 1844. Her tortured ghost is said to roam aimlessly, searching for rest.

The ground was damp beneath their feet but as they climbed higher it became firmer and the squelching ceased. After forty-five minutes of walking and messing around, they reached the top. They stared at the massive rocks set in piles like giant play-stones, then slumped down on a chair-high boulder to admire the view. It was (and still is), a breathtaking panorama. Beautiful yet austere – an unforgiving landscape in a land full of memory.

'That rock looks like a knob,' said Jack, pointing. They laughed childishly until their giggles faded and turned into synchronised deep breathing. As one they held their breath, staring at each other. Twenty seconds passed, thirty, forty-five. After about a minute, their oxygen all used up, they exhaled and gulped fresh air into their chests. When their breathing returned to normal they got up and wandered about, finding to their great joy they were alone.

Back at the rock seat Jack asked. 'Did you remember them?'

'Oh damn, knew there was something,' said Al, his face a forlorn picture of despair.

'But I reminded you fifteen times yesterday,' said Luke.

'If only I'd written it down on my hand,' said Al, revealing the word "marshmallows" written on the palm of his hand, in green ink. 'Damn!' He threw his bag down in disgust and out fell two bags of marshmallows. 'It's a miracle.'

'Git,' said Jack.

'So childish,' added Luke.

They collected all the wood they could find, paying little attention to the slight breeze. The wood was stacked into a pyramid over some kindling. Luke was about to light it when a sudden gust of wind swept the whole lot away.

'Interesting,' said Luke. 'That was unpredictably strong.'

'Yeah, I should say,' said Jack.

A ghostly-voiced Al said, 'Like the moor's a-tellin' us not ta lay fire upon its ancient curves.'

'I very much doubt that,' said Luke.

More wind swirled from all about and within seconds they were struggling to stay upright. Their coats flapped like flags as their bags tumbled away, lodging against the bottom of a large boulder nearby. The bitter wind stung their faces. Gusts crashed like waves, hitting them again and again. Luke was floored. Al grabbed him and shouted to Jack but his voice was robbed by the snarling gale. Jack was swept backwards into Luke and Al, knocking them all to the ground.

The wind howled around them and they were bullied backwards, rolling and falling over each other as they tried to stand, a jumble of arms and legs. Luckily their bags acted like cushions as they piled into the bottom of the boulder. Firmly pinned against the great rock, they struggled for breath.

'What... the hell's... going on?' screamed Al.

'Dunno... but I wish it would go... somewhere else,' Jack shouted back.

'I have a very bad... feeling about this,' yelled Luke.

A strange sucking sound filled the air around them, tugging at their clothes. As abruptly as the typhoon had started, it stopped and was replaced by eerie silence.

'What now?' whispered Al.

'Why, what do you want to do – have a picnic?' said Luke. 'Because I am finding shelter.'

'Didn't think Vulcans practised sarcasm,' said Al.

'There's a time and a place for everything,' said Luke, picking himself up. Jack and Al followed. They ran through a gap between rocks to their favourite hideaway. As they reached the shelter, the wind picked up once more with a vengeance. It screamed, twisting and coursing through the nooks and crannies of the tor. From their partially protected hiding-hole they watched airborne debris carried on the invisible arms of the gale – grass, sticks, plastic bottles... a sheep.

'That wasn't what it looked like was it?' yelled Luke.

'Can't have been,' Al shouted back.

'I'd swear it was,' said Jack.

'Thought it was pigs that were meant to fly,' shouted Luke.

They never did find out what had resembled a flying sheep because it blew over Roughtor and far away. Maybe it was some kind of plastic sack or large chunk of polystyrene, washed up on one of Cornwall's many beaches and blown all the way inland, or maybe it was an old sheepskin jacket turned inside-out by the wind that an employee from the Stannon China clay works had thrown away the previous week... or maybe it really was a sheep.

The three boys crouched within their rock shelter, backs against the worn stone, staring out in amazement and with growing fear.

After twenty minutes of "Hurricane Marshmallow" the wind began to slow and as abruptly as it started, it stopped, as though a giant fan was shut off. The eerie stillness descended once again. In a matter of seconds it had gone from utter mayhem, to deathly silence yet they could not hear themselves breathe. When they realised this was because they were all holding their breath, they exhaled with a communal gasp. No one spoke.

After thirty seconds, Al cleared his throat. 'Hu-hum. What on earth –'

'Shh,' said Jack, 'Listen.'

Phut... phut... phut, phut-phut. At the entrance to their shelter raindrops the size of large marbles splattered down onto the hard, bare earth – water bombs made with invisible paper. Jack stuck an arm out to catch one. It whacked into his palm.

'Ow. That really hurt,' he said.

Phut, phut, phut. Thicker and thicker, wetter and wetter, harder and faster – a maelstrom of torrential rain. Calling it rain did it no justice. This was super-rain, rain plus, a mega-deluge. The drops got bigger – enormo-drops the size of eggs. Later they would recall the day they saw "Egg-rain".

Within seconds a strong stream flowed passed the entrance of their rock prison. Water seeped in around their feet, slowly at first, then with more strength.

'Oh no,' said Al.

'Try to block it with your feet,' said Jack, trying to do exactly that. It was no good. Seconds later the water was up to their ankles.

The sound was chilling, like being stuck behind a waterfall, only everywhere they could see was water falling. They were trapped. A head outside the cave would surely have been knocked off and washed away in seconds. They trembled, wet and fearful of what may happen. The liquid terror seemed to last hours (though in reality it was minutes).

Once again, as rapidly as it had started, it stopped. The sluice-gate was closed.

Over.

Gone.

They waited fearing the worst, but when it came, they realised that what they had been fearing was not the worst because what they got was actually much worse. They got the dinosaur of worst, they got tyrannosaurus-worst.

It started with the gentlest of rumbles, faint... almost friendly. Al's first thought was that his stomach was complaining at the lack of sustenance. The rumble gathered pace then additional hellish instruments were introduced. Soon it was a turbulent mix of thunderous cracking whips, breaking clouds and heart-stopping lioness roars. A deep growling, sonic tremor that surrounded them and penetrated their very souls. For several minutes the horrifying crescendo was their entire world and they were convinced that world was about to end.

A blinding, pure white flash was followed by a deafening crack that ripped through them, leaving their ears ringing with pain. Somewhere, something exploded and bits of burning, black rock smashed and clattered around the doorway of their hole, splashing water at them from a hot cloud of sizzlingly violent steam. Any remaining composure they had deserted them at this moment. Their screams turned into puppyish whimpers, followed by shouts of sheer panic. More flashes and ear-pounding blasts followed.

Then silence.

Crouching and shaking with fear, they wrapped their arms around their petrified legs, remaining huddled and whimpering.

'What the hell's going on?' whispered Al finally. 'I'm too young to die.'

'Huh?' said Jack.

'Maybe it's a military exercise,' said Luke.

After a few minutes they gathered enough nerve to leave their refuge. The water outside had gone. Carefully, they stepped over the steaming debris. The sun was shining weakly but the odd haze remained. They wandered like zombies, staring inanely, their steps confused and silent. More by chance than any kind of plan, Jack found himself back at the rock where they had all been sitting earlier. It had taken a direct hit and now resembled a smouldering lump of shattered coal – smoke curling and snaking from every jagged crack. He turned to shout for the others but as he did, a murky, dense cloud dropped like a dead weight from the sky.

'Luke, Al,' he shouted, but his cries were lost in the mire as if shouting into a pillow. The fog was so thick he could actually feel it when he moved, like being under water.

Jack froze, expecting Luke and Al to appear any second. As he stood contemplating what on earth was going on, something scurried past his foot.

'Hey! What was that?' he asked himself, trying to catch a glimpse of it.

'I think you call them Piskies.'

Jack gasped and stumbled backwards, his heart pounding against his ribs. The thick fog had withdrawn, leaving a clear circle. Opposite him stood an old man wearing shabby brown robes tied with a rope around his middle.

'Hello, Jack,' he said, brightly.

'Huh?' said Jack, loudly.

'My name is Fynn, Fynn Garr.'

Jack felt his stomach churn with fear. He desperately wanted to run but the fog seemed to be alive – wisps of it curled and licked in his direction like some phantom reptile, tasting the air. He preferred his chances with the old man.

'What do you want?' said Jack.

'I'm not going to harm you, Jack. You are perfectly safe and so are your friends.'

'How do you know my name? Who are you? What is going on?'

'Jack. Please, it's OK.'

'What's OK? What do you want?'

'Please calm down and I'll explain.'

'I am calm!' said Jack, his voice still raised. 'What do you want?'

'Jack, you know there comes a point in stories where the potential hero discovers his true calling?'

'Huh?'

'Oh dear. I was afraid this may happen.'

'What may happen?'

'That it would be difficult to explain.'

'What would be difficult to explain?'

'Who I am and why I need your help.'

'Huh?'

'Jack, could you please try to stop shouting?' asked Fynn, a little sternly. This verbal slap seemed to snap Jack out of the shouting rut he had been in.

'Oh. Sorry. Was I shouting?'

'A little,' said Fynn, visibly relieved.

Jack felt his fear subside. He checked the wall of fog from the corner of his eye. It seemed to look back at him and wave. He quickly moved his eyes back to the stranger standing opposite. His appearance was how Jack imagined a monk would have dressed hundreds of years ago (not like the present day ones at Buckfast Abbey, who looked like extras from a film).

'Did you say you needed... my help?' said Jack, a little perplexed.

'Yes,' said Fynn matter-of-factly. Then realising what Jack had asked, more excitedly continued. 'Yes, yes I do, I need your help. Well, in fact, everybody needs your help.'

'Really?'

'Yes,' said Fynn, smiling nervously. 'It took us a long time to find you, Jack. We've watched you closely and we're sure you're the one... we've seen the heroic characters you keep locked in your heart.' Fynn tried an encouraging smile. 'But this isn't a story. This is real and there is a need for someone to take a stand.'

'And that's me, is it?'

'Yes!' shouted Fynn.

'OK, no need to shout.'

'What?' said Fynn, before realising Jack was getting his own back. 'Look, Mr Finger, I don't really understand what's going on. It feels like some kind of dream, especially now you're going on about heroes and stuff.'

'Please, just call me Fynn.'

'I mean look,' said Jack pointing at the fog wall (for a second he thought it pointed back), 'it's hardly everyday stuff, is it?'

'No, it is not, but... it is real, I assure you,' said Fynn waving his arms around, inviting Jack to examine it all. 'See?' He stepped to the side and swished an arm through the fog, displacing a large chunk. The mottled dark lump glimmered as it fell to the floor like a heavy cloud. It hit the ground with a soft thud and spread out in a circle, curling at the edges like a wave of dust from a collapsed building. 'Have a go!' he said.

'How do you do that?' asked Jack poking a finger at the fog, which this time quite clearly pointed back. 'In fact, how do you do any of this? It is you, isn't it?'

Fynn smiled. 'My little special effects, what do you think?'

'To be honest, that weather stuff scared the hell out of me.'

'Oh. Terribly sorry.' Fynn twitched with shame. 'There were reasons. You've been very difficult to get on your own, for a start. And it's not very easy for someone like me to get to talk with someone like you.' Fynn paused checking Jack's reaction to this news. 'But the big raindrops were pretty impressive, weren't they?'

'Very,' said Jack sarcastically. 'OK, Mr Finger, I'm sure I'm dreaming, so you may as well tell me what all this is about.'

'Well, this may sound rather odd but I think you will understand better than most. Let me start from the top, or the side, at least.' Fynn paused thoughtfully. 'If I told you that your race is only one of many that walk upright on two legs, would you believe me, Jack?'

'Er, probably not.'

'Good. You see, Jack, your race – What?'

'Well what do you expect?' said Jack.

'Oh. Well, never mind about that. Anyway, your race – humans – are so frighteningly clever in many ways but when it comes to observing the world, you're lazy. After tonight, I hope and expect that your eyes will be wide open. You may see many things that you've always wanted to see or thought you have seen.'

'O-K,' said Jack, slowly.

'Humans used to see everything – all the creatures of the world – forest dwellers, sea-people, even the wispy bog-dwellers that smell something rotten. But as you developed tools, machines, engines, you neglected many of the old traditions. Pretty soon, some races started to feel scared. Humans were losing interest and getting full of themselves and how clever they were. That's when some started hiding. Almost immediately, humans thought they'd died out. If you don't look, you won't see. And because you didn't see them no more, you started to question whether they ever existed in the first place. Thought it was all myth and legend. Course, there are some who still see, but only every now and then – and the rest of you think they're bonkers!'

'I can't believe it,' said Jack. But even as he spoke the words he started recalling times he thought he had seen movement from the corner of his eye, only to investigate and find nothing.

'I'm talking about Piskies, Spriggans, even Faeries – the old folk who've been around longer than humans. Oh, and of course, my people – the Celts,' said Fynn, beaming.

'You are joking, right?'

'No,' said Fynn, amused. He turned, surveying the living fog. 'Look at all this, Jack. What I'm saying feels right, doesn't it? I made that weather, with a little help from my friends.'

'But it's... just so... unbelievable. This kind of thing just doesn't happen does it?' Jack laughed.

'I come from a different race than you, Jack. I'm so old, I've almost forgotten how old I am. I go back so far I'm in front of me. One of your lifetimes is the blink of an eye to me, and as for the Piskies – they make me look young. They are as old as the rocks themselves.'

'So you're saying we're not alone here after all?' said Jack.

'Far from it. Humans are an odd bunch, you hunt animals to extinction, you wage wars on each other and sometimes you make life a misery for those trying to peacefully co-habit with you. And yet, these other races are always so patient with you. You get away with so much stupidity,' he said, nodding.

'Weird.'

'Not really, but everyone has their own opinion.' Fynn must have realised he was sounding a little negative. 'Though I must say, you've some incredible achievements – flying machines, ships, roller-skates... balm tissues – brilliant. And I love computers. If it weren't for them, I might not be here talking with you now.'

'Why?'

'A little project. Well, big project actually. Brings me back to why I'm here.' Fynn ambled to an intact rock within the clearing and sat down, rubbing his knees. 'Look, I have to get going soon but I need to ask you something first.'

'OK.'

'I'd like your help, Jack,' said Fynn, scratching his chin. 'But for you to help us, you'll need to be a lot stronger, so I need to give you a tonic, a little boost, so to speak. What do you say?'

'Well... seeing as I'm pretty certain this is a dream, that you don't exist, and I'm actually safely tucked up in bed, sound asleep...why not.'

'What about your friends?' said Fynn, sounding shocked.

'They're probably asleep too, I should imagine. Come on, give me your worst.'

'Well, I don't really know what –'

'Come on, Mr Finger, what is my... destiny?'

'Well, it will be dangerous.'

'Uh huh.'

'And may get a bit complicated.'

'OK.'

'And... I can't go into all the details now – time is short. I think you should have the tonic now, tonight, right here.'

'What will it do to me? Will it hurt?'

'Oh no, it won't hurt. May make you drowsy for a while, but there won't be any pain. In fact, if you drink this, pain will become a thing of the past.'

'Yeah? OK.'

'And you'll find you're much stronger than you are right now.'

'Will I be able to beat up the bullies at school?'

'Yes. I mean no. No, no, no! You can't, I mean, you mustn't and you shouldn't.'

'Why not?'

'Jack,' said Fynn, lowering his tone. 'You mustn't let anyone know that you're strong. You'll have to keep that to yourself – it is imperative that you tell no one, not even your friends. This is the one condition that I must place on you. Do you understand?'

'No, but I don't really care anyway, so that's fine. Dream, dream, dream.'

'So – do we have an agreement?' Fynn gave Jack his best friendly, not-too-desperate smile.

Jack thought for a few seconds. 'I know this is a dream, but I'm going to ask this anyway, just because I can. If I say no, will people get hurt?'

'That, I cannot say.'

'Typical. You know all this and that, but the really important questions you just can't answer. What about my family?'

'It's impossible for me to tell. There is a danger to all mankind as there is to all other life forms too.'

'Why me?'

Fynn sighed. 'The very quick answer would be – it's down to a combination of your personality, your temperament and a gut feeling I have.'

Jack looked all around him, it was an incredible amount of detail for a dream. He couldn't think, couldn't remember if he had been awake and doing something, or if he had recently said goodnight to his mum and dad.

'OK, Mr Finger, I'll give it a bash.'

'Great,' said Fynn, excitedly. Then realising the tone of Jack's response his excitement dulled. 'Oh. Well, thank you, Jack, I think. You're very nearly our last hope,' he said. 'And by the way, my name is not Finger, it's Fynn, Garr – two words.'

'Whatever you say, Mr Finger,' said Jack, nonchalantly.

Fynn evidently decided against correcting Jack again. Instead, he stood up and rummaged under his robes, eventually pulling out a brushed, stainless steel flask. 'Another great human invention,' he muttered, unscrewing the lid.

When Fynn removed the stopper his face was lit up by shimmering blue and red lights from within the flask. He gently manoeuvred the lid and poured. The liquid reflected all the colours in the world as it popped with fitful, fizzing flashes.

'Don't worry,' said Fynn, passing the cup to Jack. 'I put a lot of fruit juice in – it shouldn't taste too bad.'

Still convinced he was dreaming, Jack downed the lot in a couple of large gulps. 'Mmm. Not bad. Now what happens?' asked Jack, eagerly.

Fynn sheepishly averted his gaze to the ground before mumbling, 'Well now, you may fine tha yo fel la blih flan-naw flo shlor weel...'

Jack did not catch a word of the rest of Fynn's sentence. A second after he swallowed the contents of the cup his world transformed into a psychedelic swirl of blurred shapes and sounds.

Fynn continued talking, his head down, explaining minor concerns and possible side effects in quasi-scientific language, while struggling to close the flask. He finally looked up just in time to see Jack overbalance and fall, almost gracefully, flat on his face. His head struck a lump of the burnt black rock with a dull thud. The rock broke in two – Jack's head stayed in one piece.

'Oh bugger,' said Fynn.

5

Richie, Dick, Rik and Dickie

The shed was surrounded by a messy tangle of early nettles and brambles. The small square windows had seized shut years ago, the glass in them greening over, allowing little light to penetrate.

A neon strip-light illuminated the damp, dusty inside, humming uncomfortably. Smoke hung in the stale air like a mini pea-souper. Shelves clinging to the rickety walls were stacked with assorted rubbish, from old jam jars containing various nasty liquids, to rusty, lidless tins full of nuts, bolts and nails. A thin layer of dirty oil covered everything that wasn't rusting.

Evidently the shed had once been used as some kind of garage or general rubbish store. Several bits of what appeared to be old vacuum cleaners or washing machines lay under a tool-strewn, metal bench in the corner. Four men sat around a shabby wooden table.

'Right then, now we're all here, we can get started.' Richard Hedman was a tall, thin man with short, sticking-up black hair. His nose was almost three inches long with a right-leaning bend, a third of the way down. He had huge, yellow, horse-like teeth which desperately needed brushing (in conversation people often found it hard not to stare at them with revolted fascination).

The three other men also had varying degrees of dubious oral hygiene (including one who had not cleaned his dentures since they were fitted). They were Rik Marole, Dick Soul and Richie Smythington-Pole. Rik was an ex-banker, Dick had just come back from Sri Lanka (formerly Ceylon) and Richie was an upper-class wangler. None of them had ever met before. They had been hand-picked to do a job that they knew nothing about. Their final contact had been through Richard and it was he who assumed the leadership at this first meeting. He spoke with a nasally South London accent that had been softened by years of living near the Cornwall-Devon border.

Richard continued. 'Afternoon gentlemen, let me introduce myself. My name is Richard, but you can call me Dick. Glad everyone managed to find the place. I know it's a bit out the way.' He sounded nervous. 'You're all used to this kind of fing, so I won't spin you any bullshit, so to speak. I've been asked to make you a very generous offer.' He stopped at some unappreciated sniggering. 'What's so funny...' he glanced down at his notes, 'Mr Smythington-Pole?'

'Oh please, call me Richie,' he said, with a wide toothy grin. 'I was merely savouring your humorous witticism "spin you any bullshit", very fine, very fine.'

'You takin' the mick?' said Richard.

'Not at all, dear chap.'

'Right,' said Richard wearily. 'Let's get on with the business.' Just then he noticed that the other two gentlemen were also finding something amusing. 'Oh cripes, what now?' he said, a little exasperated.

'So you're called Richard and would like to be known as Dick, he's called Richie and I'm Rik.' Rik stuck out a rough, hairy hand and introduced himself as Rik Marole. He shook hands with a reluctant Richard and the delighted Richie.

The fourth gentleman started laughing. When he finally gained control of his mirth, he introduced himself. 'Ha, ha, h-hello... m-m-my name's D-d-dick too,' he said.

'Oh for God's sake,' said Richard. 'Gentlemen please, pull yourselves together. So we share the same name. Ha ha, very funny, but can't we please just get over it?'

'But we have a situation,' said Richie, excitedly dabbing at his forehead with a red silk handkerchief. 'I am Richie, here we have Rik, and you two are a pair of Dicks.'

'What?' said the two Dicks together.

'Right,' said the Richard-Dick standing up and cracking his knuckles. 'Excuse me Mr Soul, but d'you mind being called Dickie?'

'W-w-well, I er, I d-don't –'

'It'll just make fings a lot simpler won't it, if I stay as Dick and we call you Dickie – OK?' said Richard, leaning toward Dick Soul with an intimidating manner.

'No no no! That just will not do,' interrupted Richie. 'Poor Mr Soul here has equal right to be addressed as Dick. Perhaps you could take an alternative humorous sobriquet, Mr Hedman?'

Richard glared at Richie. His face turned a pale red as he forced himself to study his notes and regain composure. 'Solicitor weren't you, Mr Pole?' asked Richard dismissively. 'What did they bang you up for?'

'That's Smythington-Pole,' corrected a shamed Richie. 'And I was callously duped, lulled into a ghastly underhand business, betrayed and left to shoulder all the blame. Where could I go from there? Reputation in tatters.'

'Huh. What-ever,' said Richard childishly.

'I'm just glad Nanna passed away before my troubles, it would have been the end of her.'

'Heart rendering as this is, we do need to get on with business,' said Richard.

'Rending,' muttered Richie, quietly.

'So, Mr Soul, what's it to be?'

'If you w-want to be a D-d-d-dick, that's f-f-fine with m-me. Y-y-you be a D-dick, I'll be a D-d-d-dickie,' said the newly named Dickie.

Dick glared back, his right cheek and eye twitching violently. Then he twitched at the other two men, finding it increasingly difficult to control his temper.

'I know a very fine surgeon who could help you with that twitch you know, Dick,' said Richie, his composure thoroughly regained.

'What... twitch... are... you... talking about?' said Dick, his eye twitching more than ever. He whipped around, anxiously rubbing his face before rifling through his coat. Like giant spider legs, his fingers frantically unscrewed the cap from a small bottle of whisky and he glugged desperately. 'Aah,' he sighed. 'Thank you, gentlemen.'

As the men talked inside the shed they were completely unaware of the child crouched outside under the window, listening intently to every word they said. His legs ached from squatting, but he forced himself to sit there for as long as required. He could hardly believe what he was hearing. The trouble he would get into for being late back would be worth it. This was news, this was big news.

6

Dreams of Posh & Becks

Launceston is not a hotbed of crime and disorder. It has minor problems like any rural town but mostly these do not amount to much. Car-related crime, driving misdemeanours, petty theft and class C drug offences are generally as much as the police ever have to deal with. So when the call about an unconscious boy with his two so-called "mates" needing assistance up on Roughtor came in, it caused more than a little excitement from some of the officers at Launceston police station.

A car was dispatched immediately, although by the time it arrived at the scene the air ambulance had already collected Jack and taken him to Derriford hospital in Plymouth.

The policemen questioned Luke and Al, then marched them up to the top of the tor (to see the exploded rock and where Jack had been found), then marched them down again. But when they reached the top they found no remains of any burnt, smashed rocks or signs of unusual weather conditions, nothing to back up the boys' story. Someone had been cleaning up.

Al wiped his nose across the back of his hand, leaving a trail of shiny snot that made him think briefly of slugs. He inspected it for a second before rubbing it onto his jeans. He sniffed and dried his eyes. He was sitting in the interview room of Launceston police station feeling scared, upset and worried for his friend Jack (who as far as he knew was dead, or busy dying somewhere). Of course, being inside a police station he also felt guilty, though he had nothing to be guilty about.

'Fascists,' he mumbled.

It was a depressing room, painted grey with black plastic chairs either side of a battered table set against the side wall from the door. The grubby blue carpet was wearing thin at the entrance. On the table was a tape recorder, an in-tray, an out-tray, but no shake-it-all-about tray. The thought briefly diverted Al from his misery. A CCTV camera perched on a bracket in the far corner, like an evil police vulture – its beady police eye burning into Al's delicate soul. 'Fascists,' he mouthed to the camera.

The room smelled like a dustbin containing old fish or raw chicken, tinged with a hint of evil. Putrid, thought Al, surely a word derived from puke and hatred. A bitter smell for a bitter place. A large mirror was built into the wall to Al's left which he suddenly realised must be two-way. 'Fascists.'

Not surprisingly, no one believed a word that either of the boys said. They had both recounted the day's events in the same exacting detail. The police suspected the boys had greatly exaggerated the weather conditions they had encountered. Only PC Hoth had any sympathy for them. He was a mature policeman, with bushy, grey eyebrows that curled out at the sides and matching frisky whiskers. Both boys knew PC Hoth as he was the constable that visited local schools to talk on behalf of the police. When the smarmy, iniquitous Inspector Gibson had been interrogating Al as if he were under suspicion of murder, it was PC Hoth who stepped in and calmed the situation down.

'Come on now, Al,' spat Gibson. 'Let's stop telling tales shall we, about time you gimme the truth.'

'I'm telling the truth,' sobbed Al. 'They're my best friends. We wouldn't attack Jack, would we?'

'I dunno. Why don't you tell me?'

'I've told you everything.'

'Rubbish,' shouted Gibson, slamming his fist down. Al's whole body jumped. Gibson knew how to be intimidating, especially to children, though he didn't really look the part. He was short and stocky with a round head and thin brown hair that made a perfect collar for the bald patch sat atop his perpetually sweaty, shining head. A heavy moustache clung above his sour, thin lips, wiggling up and down as he hissed and snarled his way through word after word of petty nastiness.

Al tried to calm himself and as steadily as he could began to speak. 'After that freaky weather stopped, Jack went off to see what was going on. Soon's he disappeared, it went all dark with this weird, black fog. It kind of stole your breath, we couldn't move. Then we seen these creeping lights – all different colours... like tentacles probing the air. Everything went even blacker, couldn't have been more black... That's when I think we blacked out.' Al was embarrassed admitting this, but at least he was telling the truth. Tears ran down his cheeks. He sobbed, his throat tight and aching with the strain of trying not to cry. He coughed to kick-start his voice. 'When me and Luke came to, it was all clear. We got up and ran round to find Jack unconscious with a big lump on his head.' Al half-smiled before quietly adding, 'bigger lump than normal.'

Gibson glowered at the carpet nodding in disappointment. 'And you expect me to believe all that rubbish – do I look stupid to you, Al?' he barked, his beady grey-blue police eyes staring unblinkingly.

'It's... the... truth.' Al breathed out every hard word.

At that moment the door opened and in walked PC Hoth. 'Now then,' he said warmly, in his lilting Cornish accent. 'What's going on here?'

Gibson's face turned sour. 'Hoth, this is my interview so can you kindly leave?'

'Now now, Inspector, you know there's meant to be two of us in here for an interview. Wanna keep it all proper and above board don't we, young Al?' he said, handing Al a cleanly folded white handkerchief.

'Yeah, suppose so,' mumbled Al, feeling somewhat relieved that PC Hoth had arrived. Al blew his nose and wiped his eyes.

'With all due respect –'

'Ah yes. Respect, Inspector Gibson. Very good, yes. We should respect this young man. Sounds like he and his friends had a bit of a scare up there on the moor, in't that right, young man?'

'Yeah, suppose so,' said Al.

'With all due respect, PC Hoth, I think what this "young man" is telling us, is a load of old –'

'Bullocks,' said PC Hoth. Gibson's face cavorted with anger and confusion. 'What?'

'Bullocks, Inspector Gibson. Mr Owen who farms outta Tregoodwell, was feeding his bullocks at the very same time and confirms that conditions up Roughtor were indeed...' he took out his notebook and read, '"vitty strange, even fer moors".' PC Hoth smiled invitingly at Gibson. 'You know, Inspector Gibson, there are many odd things in this world that defy simple explanation. Not everything's black and white, and not all people are born liars,' he paused, turning his gaze towards Al. 'Things aren't always what they seem.'

'You old fool, Hoth,' spat Gibson. 'You should retire before you embarrass us all. I've had enough of this rubbish. You,' he said, pointing a stubby finger at Al. 'I'll be watching you and your mate, and if your other little friend ever wakes up, I'll have some questions for him too.' Gibson stormed out.

PC Hoth stopped the tape recorder and rewound it a little, played it to the point where he had entered the room and stopped it again.

'Thanks,' said Al quietly.

'That's OK, Al. Inspector Gibson can be a bit too keen for his own good sometimes. I think I should apologise on his behalf. He means well, and he's pretty harmless really. I wouldn't worry yourself too much about anything he may have said.'

'What did he mean about Jack – "if he ever wakes up"?'

PC Hoth coughed a little, sat down, and brushed some imaginary crumbs off his legs. 'Ah, well. I'm afraid Jack hasn't woken up yet. The doctors don't quite understand what's going on. They're saying he's definitely not in a coma as such, but he just hasn't come round for some reason, can't seem to work it out. You know what doctors are like, Al – they're not too worried yet.'

'Poor Jack,' said Al, absentmindedly. 'What on earth happened up there?' Al was really speaking to himself more than PC Hoth.

'Well, young man, I've seen a lot of strange things in my time, but what you've told us today is one of the weirdest ever. No wonder people are having a hard time believing you. But you and young Luke don't seem the lying type to me, so I don't know what to think.' PC Hoth stood up and pushed his chair in. 'Now then. I expect your parents have arrived, Luke's too, so you better get your bag and get on home for some rest... Oh, Al,' said PC Hoth, pausing and staring right into Al's eyes. 'If you think of anything or remember any more of what went on up there, you will let us know, won't you?'

'Yeah, course. Thanks.'

They left the interview room and walked back to the reception area. Luke was already waiting by the door with his parents and Al's. They rushed over and hugged him. He felt awkward but was too tired to care about being cool at that moment. Luke ambled over and they had a whispered conversation before being dragged away and taken home.

Luke and Al found Jack lying unconscious exactly where Fynn had left him. Carefully, they hauled him over and got the shock of their lives.

'Oh my God, look at the size of that,' said Al.

'I am no doctor but that cannot be good,' said Luke. Jack had a dark purple golf ball-sized lump protruding from his forehead.

'He is not gonna be happy about that, is he?' said Al.

After some minutes of mild panic they finally gathered enough courage to check if Jack was still alive (something they had learned at school). Struggling to find a pulse, they remembered they could put their faces close to his mouth and see if he was breathing, which he was. This calmed them a little, before they discussed what to do. Al put his jacket under Jack's head. They figured it was best not to move him in case he had a broken neck.

Luke stayed with Jack while Al ran down to the car park (which was unusually empty) to find help. He fell several times on the way and arrived at the car park sweaty, wet and breathless a few minutes before his dad. Mr Fry called the emergency services.

Police, ambulance and air ambulance were alerted immediately. Eight and a half minutes later Jack was carefully lifted into the helicopter and flown to Derriford hospital.

The Shillaber family arrived at the hospital two hours after Jack. They sat by his bed, drank tea in the hospital café, paced up and down the corridor and made phone calls to relatives. Because of the police involvement, Jack was put in a private room and every few minutes an officer would walk by to check on him. Mrs Shillaber gave each and every young officer a hard stare.

Meanwhile, Jack was dreaming. First he dreamed he was David Beckham, out shopping with Victoria. They were in a second-hand charity shop with racks and racks of clothes – he was trailing Victoria around while she inspected every single item. Jack wouldn't remember exactly what he said in the dream, but everyone in the shop kept laughing at it, including Victoria. Then he was farting the tune of the Spice Girls song, *Wannabe*, at Scary Spice's wedding. Jack would not remember this but he found it strangely familiar when his brother swore to him that while he was unconscious he had broken wind to the tune of "zig-a-zig-ah".

In the final part of Jack's dream, he shot over the edge of a jagged cliff and fell towards a rocky, desert-like landscape. This was a recurring dream and he knew exactly how it would end.

Agnes and Helen were convinced all dreams meant something. Helen had a book which listed what anything in any dream meant. Mermaids, lions, knees – "it's all in there" she had said. Luke finally stumped the book when he swore he had dreamed about dirty socks (someone else's dirty socks). The book contained no dirty socks.

'I am not saying dreams don't mean anything. Obviously they must serve some kind of deep psychological purpose,' said Luke, logically. 'But how can you say that if I dream about wombats, that it has the same meaning as if you dream about them?'

'Because we all share the same basic gene pool – we all do the same things, live in the same world and have the same kind of experiences.' Helen was annoyed.

Luke dug his heals in. 'But we are, however, individuals. We have individual feelings. Wombats may mean something different

54

to me than to you.' He was enjoying himself immensely. 'What do wombats mean to you, Helen?'

'I'm starting to think they may mean violence.'

'You see,' continued Luke, 'ultimately someone has just gone and decided that dreaming about wombats means... whatever you said a minute ago. They could have said any old rubbish. How could anyone possibly know what dreaming about an Australian mammal really means? Surely it may mean one thing to one person and something different to another?'

It was at this point that Helen got bored and kicked Luke hard on the shin.

Jack had been unconscious for almost twenty-four hours. He was pale and his head was heavily bandaged. It was clear that under all the padding was a massive lump. The only thing missing from the sorry scene was a machine bleeping at every delicate heartbeat.

Mrs Shillaber was not easily upset but the longer she was witness to this sight, the more helpless she grew. Her youngest child, whom she brought into the world and cared for so lovingly was lying, limp and lifeless, before her eyes – his head bound like a battle-scarred rugby player, and there was nothing she could do.

'Why haven't they plugged him in?' she wailed, wiping her eyes.

'He's not a hair dryer, Mum,' said Nigel, scanning his brother for signs of movement.

'He's only banged his head, Love. He's not in any real danger, just a bit of concussion maybe,' said Mr Shillaber, putting his arms around his wife and kissing the top of her head.

'And let's be honest,' said Nigel, smiling, 'he's spent most of his life concussed.'

Mr Shillaber gave his oldest son a stern glare.

'But shouldn't he have at least one machine?' pleaded Mrs Shillaber. She sat clutching a handkerchief, her eyes glazed with the constant threat of tears.

Every few minutes, she stroked her son's arm or leaned over to examine his pale, expressionless face. It was in one of these moments that in Jack's dream he finally hit the ground, waking with more than a little start.

'Aah!' he yelled and simultaneously bolted upright without any warning.

Thwack.

'Aah.' Jack's mum took a direct hit on the nose from his white-turbaned head. She screamed, careening backwards clutching her bleeding, broken nose. The back of her head smacked into her husband's sternum, knocking the wind from him. He bent double and twisted around as a nurse entered carrying a bowl of warm water with which she intended to bath Jack. What goes down, must come up, which was exactly what Mr Shillaber's head did – right underneath the bowl, which overturned as it flew through the air in a perfect arc, landing over Jack's head.

Splat.

A muted, 'Uh,' echoed from under the bowl as a once more limp Jack fell back onto the bed, unaware of the damp, the bowl or his injured parents.

It was just after nine on the Sunday evening when the Shillaber family arrived back at the farm, tired but relieved. Their neighbours from the lower side of the valley had stepped in to take care of things on the farm after the police had arrived with news of the accident. The Hazel family were the Shillabers' closest friends in the area and the two families always helped each other out.

Mrs Shillaber's nose was not as bad as she had feared, though it was still sore. Jack was fine, except for his thick head, and Mr Shillaber sustained no lasting damage. Sarah and Nigel were just glad to get home.

Jack regained permanent consciousness shortly after his first rude awakening. The doctors were extremely pleased but insisted he stayed until they had the results from some tests due back on Sunday. The family stayed in the charity-run Heartswell Lodge, next to the hospital on the Saturday night.

Inspector Gibson arrived shortly after Jack woke. Against the wishes of Mr and Mrs Shillaber, he insisted on questioning Jack, but being woozy, Jack found it hard to concentrate.

Gibson started off on the wrong foot with the Shillabers and continued hopping on it or placing it firmly in his mouth the whole time he was with them. 'Your son was up to no good with his no-good little friends and I will find out what it was,' he snapped.

Mrs Shillaber was livid. 'Do you know for a policeman you are a complete –'

'Now now, dear, I'm sure the constable, I mean inspector, knows what he's doing,' said Mr Shillaber, although really he felt like giving him a piece of his mind.

They asked what the police knew of the accident but after Mrs Shillaber's outburst, Gibson had refused to tell them anything that Al and Luke had said in their statements.

The car journey home was quiet. Sarah and Nigel fell asleep while Jack rested his bandaged head against the window, staring out into the dark night. He was annoyed that he couldn't remember anything, including being on the moor with Luke and Al.

When they got back to the house Jack said, 'I suppose it's too late to phone them and ask what happened to me, isn't it?'

'Yes, afraid so,' said his mum. 'And I don't suppose they would be allowed to say anyway. Look, you need rest, so it's straight to bed... a-a-a-choo. Aah.' Pain seared through her nose.

'Sorry, Mum,' Jack said, softly. 'But at least you were in the right place to be treated.'

'Oh, ow,' said his mum, holding her hands up to her sore nose. 'That's OK, darling, now off to bed with you.'

'But –'

'No buts, specially head-butts.'

'Mum, you made a joke,' gasped Nigel in tired amazement. Mrs Shillaber tried laughing but it only made her nose hurt more.

'Bed. Everyone. Now,' bellowed Mr Shillaber.

The children kissed their parents goodnight and trooped off upstairs. Jack delicately eased himself into bed exchanging goodnights with Nigel.

Although his head was still sore, Jack had an oddly pleasant tingling sensation throughout his whole body. He soon fell soundly asleep and dreamed of all kinds of pretty coloured flowers with heart-shaped leaves... and socks.

7

School Bus

Jack placed his feet against the wooden slats at the end of his bed and drew his arms up past his head, placing both hands against the headboard. Then he stretched.

Crack – snap – thud.

'Wo-ah,' he yelped as the bed collapsed and sent him tumbling across the floor. He bumped to a halt against the wardrobe, mummified in his blankets.

'Mmm... shurrup,' groaned Nigel.

Jack struggled free from the roll of bedclothes and glanced around the room as if expecting to see something or someone. Walls, floor, brother – everything seemed to be in order, but he knew something was not right. It was Monday morning, after all. He hated Mondays. It meant school and teachers and lessons – the first day of the school week. Normally he started Monday with a heavy heart but after such a shocked awakening he felt surprisingly OK. In fact, he felt good. Spring was in the air. He stretched again, convinced he could feel every fibre in every muscle. He whispered to himself in his Obi Wan Kenobi voice. 'Jack could feel the Force, it penetrated him and flowed through him.'

'Shut up or you'll feel my force,' moaned Nigel.

'Come on, get up, you big twerp. It's Monday.' Jack was embarrassed about how great he felt but he couldn't help himself. He was being swept along on a tide of good vibrations. 'Come on, school today. Exciting stuff.' He started to get dressed. 'What am I saying?'

'Thought you were supposed to be all fragile today? Bang on the head must have done more damage than they realised.' Nigel said as he struggled to prop himself up in bed. 'You're a sad case, Jack.'

'And I love you too, Nigey – now come here and give your little brother a big hug.' Jack jumped on to Nigel's bed and started wrestling him.

'For God's sake, you freak, get off.' Nigel was not impressed. 'We're not in America, you know. Over here you're meant to wait 'til at least your mid-thirties before you can even consider showing any sort of sibling affection, especially the physical kind... now get the heck off.'

Jack suddenly remembered the bandage on his head and without even thinking pulled the whole lot straight off and chucked it across the room.

'What's happened to your bonce, weirdo?' said a puzzled Nigel, blinking.

'Dunno, has it got even more handsome overnight?' Jack tried to pull a cute face.

'No, you'd still make a troll hurl, but that lump's totally gone.'

'Really?'

'Yeah. Hold still, dummy. No, can't see a thing.'

'Always said I was hard-headed,' said Jack, prodding his forehead.

'Maybe its mass has been absorbed by your Neanderthal ridge. Yeah, definitely bigger – you might really be able to balance a drink on it now,' said Nigel.

'Ha ha. Very funny, now excuse me – I think I hear the breakfast bell.' Jack dressed in seconds and ran downstairs.

Mrs Shillaber was pouring herself a second cup of tea as Jack bounded into the kitchen. Mr Shillaber was already out seeing the cows.

'Morning, Jack, how's that head?'

'Morning, Mum, fine thanking ye kindly. I am well. My head is fine, the lump is gone. I couldn't be feeling finer. Dad out seeing the cows already?' said Jack, sitting and smiling at his mum. She stared back at him for a minute as if expecting him to say something.

'Yes, he is, and you'll be pleased to know that my nose is also feeling much better, thanks for asking, Darling.'

'Oh, yes... sorry, good,' he said, ashamed he forgot to ask.

'Are you sure you're all right? Let me have a closer look.' She examined Jack intently but could find no sign of any damage at all. 'Just shows you, those doctors don't know everything. They said you'd be in bed for at least a couple of days.'

'I guess some of us are made of stronger stuff.'

'You're not Spider-man, you know. You just make sure if you do feel funny, you let us, or the school nurse, know. Now where are the others?'

'Nigel's just coming, Sarah's probably making floating candles from her own earwax or delousing her armpits again.'

'Far too early for that kind of talk, thank you.'

Jack ignored his mother's ticking off and proceeded to let her know his breakfast requirements. 'Now then, for breakfast I would like sausage, egg, bacon, beans, pork, cork, a fork, a light slap, coal, Jupiter, a dusky swan, and Uranus. Oh, and a mug of milk please, warm with no bubbles.' He sat and waited expectantly.

'There's cereal or toast, and you can help yourself,' said his mum, before adding. 'But I may be able to rustle up a light slap for you.'

'Thanks, Mum.' He smiled as she came over and gave him a fake slap.

'And as for Uranus – let's not go there, shall we?'

'OK. Probably for the best, I suppose.'

Nigel and Sarah soon appeared and after breakfast they gathered their school bags and packed lunches and walked the half mile down the lane to wait for the bus.

Webbs buses were either super modern, comfy and warm, or ancient wrecks – draughty, falling apart and impossible to do last minute homework on (Jack had tried several times). Sure enough, that morning a tatty, bus-like object creaked its way to a stop before them. It backfired with a loud, smoky bang – the shock causing the front bumper to drop several centimetres forward and hang limply at an angle.

'Look at this. It's not a bus, it's a potential death-trap,' said Jack.

'I dunno, it's better than the one we had last week,' said his brother, 'least this one has wheels.'

'Yeah, but how long will they stay on?' said Jack.

'Well I'm sure it'll get us to school, even if we have to push every now and then,' said Sarah approaching the bus doors. 'Come on.'

'Morning, all,' drawled Mr Squires.

'Morning,' they said.

Sarah and Nigel went to sit near the back of the bus, Jack near the front. The cheap vinyl seats were freezing in the morning and because they were also falling apart, they were particularly uncomfortable.

The bus turned around in the lane and stalled as it was about to pull away.

'Would it help if I got out and pushed?' thought Jack.

'It may, you cheeky little whippersnapper,' said Mr Squires.

'Pardon? Oh, sorry,' said Jack, turning red. He hadn't meant to say it out loud.

As always, Mr Squires' dark, ginger hair was brushed forward and he wore a bright green cardigan. Jack didn't have a clue what colour Mr Squires' trousers were as they never saw his legs. He could have had a skirt on for all Jack knew.

The bus wheezed its way up the higher Drains Valley and turned right at Bolventor, past Jamaica Inn. Jack had been in the famous pub a few times on Bonfire Night because it was the nearest venue that had a firework display. He remembered the peculiar decor inside, including strange stuffed animals in glass cases that he was sure had never existed – like the small dog covered in sheep's wool.

The bus was a world and culture of its own – laughter, fighting, singing, discussion, solitude, sadness – almost every kind of human emotion was on display. It meandered along the A30, picking up more and more children as it diverted through Five Lanes, Polyphant and Tregadillet before nearing its final destination of Launceston College.

Jack preferred to sit by himself. Behind him a year-nine girl was lying on her back across another girl (her friend) and a boy, her head resting against the window. She giggled hysterically as she continually flicked the forehead of the boy on whom she lay. Though obviously intimidated, he did not seem to be trying very hard to stop her.

Sitting at the back of the bus were those children who considered themselves to be ultra cool. They showed this in two ways – either by trying to smoke without being spotted by the driver, or by blowing up different colours and flavours of condoms.

Normally it was a painfully long journey for Jack and always ended with the same depressing conclusion of arriving at school. However, this particular morning he did not care – he was too happy. A broad smile illuminated his face as he watched the countryside roll by, marvelling at the amazing beauty of Cornwall.

Children boarded talking rubbish. Some discussing football, others horses. Even the two boys sitting in front of Jack, arguing over which one of them had invented a particularly irritating sound, didn't bother him (it was a shrieking version of the sound that all Native Americans made in the Hollywood Westerns of the 1950s).

The bus pulled off the A30 at the first Launceston exit and turned right underneath the road towards the Pennygillam roundabout. Second exit from there, up Landlake Road past the school playing fields and Kernow care home, sharp left along by Norman's cash and carry. It was just before reaching the flyover that straddled the A30 (within spitting distance of the school) that disaster struck.

It is not an uncommon occurrence to see empty drink cans discarded on the road in varying states of deterioration. Generally, they are not considered a great hazard and can be driven over quite safely.

On this particular day, Mr Squires saw the soft drink can and thought nothing of it. Unfortunately, he was unaware of two things – 1) the can was only half crumpled which had created a uniquely strong parabolic form with a rapier-like spur that projected at a forty-five-degree angle to the road, which would – 2) strike the recently new (and still perfectly legal) tyre, on its one weak spot.

Bang.

The tyre blew instantly, the bus lurched violently. Mr Squires did the best he could, it was the best anyone could have done in the circumstances, but for a split second, he lost control. It hit the curb with the exact amount of force required to topple it over onto its side.

Children were thrown everywhere, the Shillabers included. Screams pierced the air. The bus scraped along the road with a horrific din of metal and glass on tarmac. Inside, the air was filled with sparks, smoke and the smell of burning rubber. Shards of glass pinged in all directions. An almighty crash added to the cacophony as the bus ploughed through the flyover railings and skidded for what seemed like an eternity before finally grinding to a halt.

A split second of icy stillness ended as the tumult resumed with greater panic. The bus was balanced precariously on the edge of the flyover and rocked eerily like a giant red seesaw. Black smoke bellowed from the back end.

Below on the A30, cars and trucks skidded to a halt in front of the fallen debris. The cars near the front reversed to a safe distance as a dozen mobile phones began ringing the emergency services. At this point there had been no serious injuries, but if the bus fell, that would certainly change.

Jack, Nigel and Sarah scrambled to check on each other first. They were all OK except for a few cuts and bruises on Nigel and Sarah.

'We're sticking out over the edge!' shouted Nigel.

Without thinking, Jack climbed out of the top of the bus (which was actually the side), jumped down onto the road and ran to the rear of the vehicle. Other children were also trying to climb out but struggled in the panic and chaos of bodies.

Jack rounded the back of the bus and paused for a moment, surveying the damage. It was absolutely knackered. With every slow seesaw it creaked further forward and rocked higher into the air. And every time the back rose the wave of screams grew momentarily louder. Smoke poured from the engine. It stung Jack's eyes and he could feel his lungs tighten with each breath. Flames flickered through the smoke behind the grille – not a good sign.

The back lifted again but this time did not stop – the scraping at the edge of the flyover increased – it was going to fall.

Jack leaped up and grabbed the bus. Pushing out the remaining glass from the rear windows, he gripped the edge with his left hand. With the other, he grabbed the metal lip above the number plate. The metal and shards of glass under his hands tried to cut into them but he knew it would be OK (although he didn't know how he knew). His heart pounded with adrenaline as he concentrated on this one moment. Then he pulled. He pulled and strained, and huffed and puffed, and slowly, almost easily, the bus started to move.

The crowd of people gathered below on the A30 saw the bus disappear back over the edge of the flyover. The teachers and children running over from the school saw the bus move but could not see how, as it was directly between them and Jack.

Some children had finally made it out of the bus and jumped down to the road. Jack climbed through the rear window frame and herded the remaining children out the way he had come in. The smoke was now so bad that no one could see what he was doing. He could hardly see himself, his eyes were streaming and everyone (himself included) was coughing violently.

'Come on, this way,' ordered Jack. 'Get away from the bus. Move. Over there,' he shouted at the children and pushed them until he thought they were a safe distance away. The bus was a burning, smoking mess.

Jack was as disorientated and nauseous as everyone else. He bent over, coughing and wiping his streaming eyes. A stinging burn itched in the back of his throat from breathing the acrid smoke. Then, a thought burst into Jack's mind – it was the memory of what happened on Roughtor. There he was in the thick fog, with the old man, Mr Finger, and the colourful potion. 'My God, it's true!' he spluttered, his heart skipping a beat. He fell to his knees, ready to collapse when someone caught him – it was his sister, Sarah. Jack's mind was racing at full speed over what had happened to him and the realisation that everything he remembered must be true. He glared at Sarah, his eyes red with irritation, a shocked, scared look on his face.

'I'm... I'm... it's me...' was all he could manage. An almighty explosion sent a fiery gust of wind, knocking them off their feet, as the back end of the bus was blown to smithereens.

The soft drink can that was largely responsible for the unfortunate incident was later recycled and ended up in four new soft drink cans. Seven months later, one of these found its way back to Launceston and was bought from the twenty-four-hour garage. It was drunk while walking up St Thomas' Road towards the castle. When consumed, the can was carelessly scrunched up by the young man whose thirst its contents had quenched, but a jagged edge ripped into his hand leaving a deep gash. He chucked the can into the road.

The cut became infected yet the young man did nothing about it and a few weeks later collapsed. He was rushed to Derriford hospital but it was too late. This person, David Stroud, was the same individual who had tossed many cans into the road before, including the one that caused a school bus to have a near fatal accident some seven months earlier.

8

Iron Railings

This was a major incident by any standards. Launceston had never seen this number of police, fire crews and ambulances all at once. Most people did not realise Cornwall had that many emergency vehicles (in fact it didn't – some had come from Devon).

'Blimey, Jack, what the hell are you doing? Where d'you disappear to? One minute you were there, next you'd vanished, we thought you were dead or something.'

Jack coughed and tried to swallow some spit to ease the pain in his throat. 'I was just... tried to help some of the others,' he said as Sarah pulled him back up onto his feet.

Nigel appeared. 'Oh there you are. Crikey, Jack, what happened?'

'I was... trying to help,' he said, breathing hard. 'I ended up near the back of the bus, I think.'

'Well we couldn't see you. We thought you must've got out – you just disappeared, you dipstick.' Jack had never heard his brother so angry. 'We ended up climbing out 'cause we couldn't see you.'

'Yeah, OK. Sorry, all right? I didn't mean to... I'm OK, anyway.'

'Good job too,' said Sarah, just as angrily. 'If you'd been hurt Mum 'n' Dad would have killed us.'

'Or worse,' added Nigel. 'Here, have some water.' He shoved a bottle into Jack's shaking hands. He took three large glugs. It was cool and soothing on his throat. He handed the bottle back and wiped his eyes. It was a chaotic scene. People were running around everywhere. Children were trying to find their friends and figure out what had happened, teachers were busy organising help and people from the cars stopped either side of the bus were busy getting in the way.

The school nurse waddled up. 'Oh my heavens. What on earth? Oh dear, oh dear. Are you OK there, Shillaber children?'

'Yes thanks, Mrs Gaunt. Jack's throat's a bit sore from the smoke but he'll be fine in a minute,' Sarah gripped Jack's arm and dug her fingers in, prompting him to answer.

'Fine, Mrs Gaunt, thank you.' Jack coughed.

'Oh heavens. Your poor mother, you'd better phone and tell her you're OK. Dear thing, and after all she's been through what with one thing and another. Any word from your lost uncle? Poor soul. Remember him when he was here. Had a lovely girlfriend, Martha, no Mabel, or was it Mary? Course, her parents moved out to South Petherwin several years back now. They were only there a year when poor Mr, Mr... well, when her father caught shingles. Never recovered fully – complications. Sadly we never saw him again.'

'I think some children over there need treatment, Mrs Gaunt,' said Nigel, pointing to a couple of children on all fours, coughing violently.

'Oh listen to me, yes, yes of course,' she said and waddled away. 'Don't worry, Nurse is here.'

'It's a wonder there aren't more deaths in this school with her as our medical staff,' said Nigel.

'She's very good, it's just a shame she has to talk so much, that's all,' said Sarah.

The first police cars and ambulance crews arrived, adding sirens to an already confusing din. The paramedics hurried the children into the ambulances with cool efficiency, calmly checking them over and administering treatment as required. No one was seriously injured, a few cuts and bruises, but a couple of children did need treatment for smoke inhalation.

The police officers worked with the teachers to push those

children back who had not been directly involved. They put up police tape and ushered everyone outside it including Herby, the town tramp, who had mysteriously appeared from nowhere carrying a tin of *Cripple & Maymes over-strength Scrumpy* (embalmer's grade). He was about to force some down the throat of an unlucky pupil who had fainted on the grass verge when Mrs Gaunt spied him.

'Go away. Shoo, ghastly man,' she shouted. 'Police. Police.'

'Ga-a-d,' hissed Herby. 'Yarrow n' elder, rosem'ry n' mint, stick it in yer gob. Comfrey, carrot, zoapwart n' parsley... up yer –'

'No. Get away,' she cried.

Two young officers shuffled nervously towards Herby, who hobbled away quickly and vanished, magically re-appearing on the other side of the crowd. No one saw him give a swig from his can to a couple of children.

The same two officers who lost sight of Herby then approached the burning bus, cautiously peering through the curtain of smoke to check no bodies were inside. The highly flammable seats had quickly burnt up, along with several school bags full of text books and homework (the silver lining on the cloud of the bus crash for the children concerned).

The first person the police escorted to one of their cars to interview was Mr Squires, the bus driver. They found him transfixed by the burning bus, his normally forward-combed hair sticking up like a peacock's tail feathers, revealing a semi-bald head. On his bandy legs, he wore bright orange trousers.

'Well well well. Look what we have here – young Mr Shillaber.'

'Hello, Officer Gibbon,' said Nigel, stepping between Jack and the policeman.

'What?' said the startled law man.

'Hello, Officer Gibbon,' repeated Nigel.

'That's Gibson.'

'Sorry. Hello, Gibson.'

'That's Inspector Gibson to you. Nigel, isn't it?' sneered Gibson.

'That's Nigel Shillaber, to you.'

'Look, Sonny, don't try and be clever with me or you'll end up in a lot of trouble.'

'It's OK, Nige, thanks,' said Jack. He had just been given the all-clear by the fifth ambulance crew who had arrived at the scene and was waiting patiently in line to speak to the police when Inspector Gibson spotted him and rushed over. Jack had not remembered the few questions Gibson had tried to ask him in the hospital but had heard all about what a fool he was from the rest of the family.

'Well it's so nice to see you up and about for a change, Jack.'

'Thanks.'

'Now then, d'you remember what happened on Saturday?'

'Yeah.'

'Well?' said Gibson, impatiently.

'Yeah, not too bad thanks, apart from a bit of a sore throat from the smoke.'

'Don't push me, Sonny,' snapped Gibson. 'Just tell me what happened.'

Jack coughed and rubbed his throat. Gibson darted off and brought a full bottle of cool water back with him, thrusting it at Jack.

'Cheers.' Jack drank deeply. 'We went up the moors, it was –'

'We? Who was we?'

'Me, Luke and Al.'

'Is that Alex Fry and Luke Northy?'

'Yeah.'

'Then what?' Gibson had taken out his notepad and was writing down everything Jack said.

'The weather turned really nasty. Then it stopped, then it started again. There was lightning, I fell, then it all went blank.'

'What about your friends? Were they bullying you? Were they up to no good? Were you up to no good?'

'The only thing that's "no good",' interrupted Sarah, 'around here, are your stupid questions.'

'Miss Sarah Shillaber, isn't it?'

'Yes. Now he's not answering any more questions about Saturday without Mum or Dad here. Good-bye. Come on, you two, over here.' She pushed her brothers away. 'They just need you to give them your names. I've given them the address and phone number already. Well? Go on,' said Sarah, marching them over to another policeman.

'I'm not done with you yet, Shillabers,' warned Gibson.

'Thanks, Sarah,' said Jack.

'Oh shut up. I'll go and phone home.'

When all the children had finally been examined by the paramedics and interviewed by the police, it was late morning. The first two lessons were cancelled. For Form Y, this was English with Ms French and History with Mr Swift.

Jack wandered into the tutor room mechanically and slouched down onto the chair next to Al.

'Cripes, Shillaber,' said Al, jumping up as if he was going to give his friend a hug. Instead, he patted him awkwardly on the shoulders. 'Didn't think we'd see you today.'

'You almost didn't,' said Jack flatly.

'Your head – where's that bump? We didn't know what was happening Saturday. Tried phoning yesterday but no reply, where were you?'

'Only got home late, Sunday.'

Luke got up and stood over Jack, inspecting his head. 'Remarkable. No sign of damage at all. Would have expected peripheral tissue distress. Even the skin shows no signs of trauma. You do, however, smell of smoke.'

'Oh what,' said Al, the penny dropping. 'That was your bus this morning.'

'Yeah.'

'So, what happened? Why'd it crash? How come your head's OK?' Al couldn't get information quick enough. 'What happened this morning? That was unbelievable. How did it happen? Was anyone hurt? We didn't see a thing – weren't allowed to go and look.'

'They wouldn't let us into the senior end of school, even positioned teachers so we couldn't sneak around the side of school,' said Luke.

'I don't... I'm not really sure... what happened, you know?' said Jack, looking up at his friends with red, watering eyes.

'Must have been mental,' said Al, quietly.

'Are you all right?' said Agnes, from across the room.

'Poor old Jack's been in the wars,' said Al. 'We had a bit of a nightmare up Roughtor this weekend, he smacked his head a beauty. And it was his bus that crashed this morning. Had a couple of bangs on the head.' Al crossed his eyes and made a dizzy face behind Jack, trying to indicate that he was a bit out of it.

'Mr Fry, what on earth are you doing?' said Miss Mount, their form tutor, as she bustled in cheerily.

'Oh nothing, Miss. Morning, Miss,' said Al.

'Oh well, if it was nothing, then you won't mind showing us that little hand gesture again. Fifty times please.'

'Huh?'

'It's not "huh" Al, it's pardon. And I'd like you to show us all that little action where you tapped your finger against your temple, pulling that silly face. Can you oblige by counting, Jack?'

Some of the class started giggling. Al knew there was no way of getting out of it. He sat down and began tapping his temple and pulling the silly face.

'One, two, three...' said Jack, feeling much better already.

'You may stand, Al,' said Miss Mount, a cheeky smile beaming on her face.

'Mi-i-i-ss,' pleaded Al.

'Ye-e-e-s?' she mocked.

Al stood up slowly, the laughter increasing as his face got redder.

'Four, five, six...' continued Jack.

Miss Mount took out the register and arranged her bag and desk.

'...forty-nine, fifty.'

Al looked over to check it was OK for him to sit down.

'Thank you, Al,' she said. 'You may sit.'

He slumped back into his chair and loosened his tie, hot from the shame of his punishment.

The register was called. Everyone was present, though it took Jack two calls of his name before he responded.

'Now then, I'm sure you're all aware of the terrible accident that happened this morning. Just to let you know, no one was seriously hurt, which is amazingly lucky. Jack, Lucy and Stephen were all on that bus. I think that's why Jack appears to be a little hazy, are you all right now, Jack?'

'Yes... Miss.'

'Good. Obviously school will be a lot shorter today, something I'm sure you're all very happy about, but I don't want any of you going off trying to see the accident scene. The police and fire crews are busy cleaning up the place and it may still be dangerous, OK?'

'Yes, Miss,' said the class.

'Good, I know I can trust you. In five minutes we'll be going to the Old Hall for a full school assembly. The head wants to address everyone about this morning's events.' She gazed around the class with a reassuring smile.

'Blimey, I wonder... er... what... old er... Dead-Head's gonna er... say,' whispered Al to Jack and Luke.

'That's quite an accurate imitation,' said Luke.

'Been practising,' he whispered back.

'Luke,' said Miss Mount.

'Yes, Miss?'

'Could you come up here please?'

Luke went red, stood up and walked over, a worried look on his face.

'Nothing to worry about, Luke, you silly.' Miss Mount rolled her big eyes at him. 'I just wanted to ask you if you could take a look at my computer, it's doing funny things again and I know you're good with them.'

Luke smiled, then blushed as he knelt down and smelled Miss Mount's perfume. He glanced out at the class to see some of the boys making suggestive faces.

Miss Mount was attractive. She had long blonde hair, big sparkling eyes and a pretty smile. This, coupled with the fact that she was friendly, made her unique among all the teachers at Launceston College.

Luke concentrated on the computer and it was soon fixed.

'Oh thanks, Luke,' she said softly. 'I'm terrible with these silly things. Maybe you could show me a few things some time, I'm always having to ask people to sort me out.'

'Um... OK, Miss,' said Luke, turning bright red.

'Anyway, off you go, back to your seat. Right, if you'd all like to start making your way down to the Old Hall now please.'

As Miss Mount had advised, the full school assembly was called to let everyone know that everything was all right and that school would continue as normal that day. The huge concertina doors that separated the Old Hall and gym were opened and all pupils and members of staff dutifully filed in.

'I, er... just wanted to... let everyone know, that, er... everything is all right and that school will, er... continue as normal to-er-day,' said the headmaster. Almost as if to avert attention from the unfortunate event of the morning the headmaster (who by this time had had his fill of public speaking) asked his deputy head, Mr Dawg, to announce some "good news".

'Pupils, members of staff, members of support staff. Good news. Exciting news. Really exciting news –'

'What is it?' shouted an unidentifiable pupil.

'Silence that child,' he shrilled. 'The news is, that the World Cup trophy will be coming to Launceston College a week on Wednesday, the seventeenth, I believe. It will be on display for one day, in a special cabinet that has been designed to take it around the country on a tour of schools.'

The whole assembly burst into excited murmuring.

'Of course. That's what they were talking about,' said Al.

'Pardon?' said Luke.

'The World Cup.'

'Shiny metal, moulded into an over-elaborate, quite useless trophy,' said Luke dismissively. 'What is all the fuss about?'

'I overheard these blokes yesterday. We were out visiting Nan at St Giles and I went out for a wander and heard these blokes talking in a shed. That's it. They're gonna nick it.'

'What?' asked Luke.

Jack said nothing, having drifted off somewhere, over the rainbow.

'Jack, are you with us? Can you hear what I'm saying? Hello.'
Al waved a hand in front of Jack but it was no good.

Break time was full of bus talk. Already some children were selling wreckage for five pounds a miscellaneous bag. Jack was still quite remote. After break was French with Mrs English. As always, it seemed to race by (*"Assesez vous! Comment t'appelle tu? Au revoir!"*).

Luke and Al searched everywhere for Jack during lunch break. In French he had been a virtual mute. After the lesson, he disappeared. They finally found him slumped at the bottom of the steps at the lower end of the home economics block, his head against the railings, staring into space.

'There you are, Slim-a-ber, we've been looking all over for you. What are you after here, leftovers? If it's my sister's class I wouldn't bother, you'd be dead before next lesson, she's lethal with her hands, 'specially when she cooks.' Al had never really taken to his sister's unique brand of culinary imagination, which had variously embraced tuna and jam tarts (served with cream), beef meringue soufflé and cat stew (this last description was technically untrue, but it's what Al thought cat must taste like and it wasn't particularly pleasant).

'What?... Yeah,' Jack said, his mind elsewhere.

'Come on mate, just because you've been involved in a near-fatal accident this morning and were saved by some freak miracle, there's no need to be down. Look, there are trees and pretty birds.'

'And you think I'm weird?' said Luke.

'But that's just it, isn't it?' said Jack.

'What, that Luke is weird? Well it's something but –'

'No,' snapped Jack, then dropped his head. 'That wasn't just some miracle – it was me. I pulled the bus back off the edge, with my own bare hands.' He was trembling and although he had fought against it, his eyes began watering. Tears rolled down his cheeks and peppered his faded cords with dark spots.

'Hang on now, Jack,' said Al, feeling somewhat uncomfortable. 'Look, maybe you're in shock or something. You sure you didn't get a second bang on the head this morning? Maybe you need to see Madam Death – I mean, you know, Nurse.'

'No, it's true, it was me,' said Jack, raising his voice, desperate to be believed.

'OK, Jackie-boy, just calm down a bit, we don't wanna scene, do we?' said Al, checking to make sure no one could hear Jack. 'Let's just get the facts straight, shall we?'

'I know the flipping facts.'

'OK, not so loud. Right. You were in the bus crash?'

'Yeah.'

'You didn't hit your head at all when the thing went over?'

'No.'

'And then somehow you hopped out and gave a quick tug on the, what, two-tonne bus, preventing it, several children and one driver from plummeting to their probable death?'

'Yes.'

'How?' Al had nailed him, banged to rights, the facts spoke for themselves. For a split second even Jack was convinced, then he remembered.

Wiping his eyes, he checked to make sure no-one would see, then swung around to face the railings. They had been there for donkey's years and probably painted a hundred times by Mr Watts (the school caretaker) with the same thick, tar-like paint used since Victorian times. Jack grabbed them.

As if drawing a pair of curtains, he pulled the bars wide enough apart to put his head through.

'What on earth? Flipping heck, Shillaber,' said Al.

'Remarkable,' gasped Luke.

'What – I mean, what the – ?' Al could hardly form a proper sentence but was still doing better than Luke.

'Extraordinary.'

Luke and Al instinctively both stepped up, grabbed a railing and tugged firmly at them – they were solid.

'Wow,' said Al.

Jack reached over and closed them back (a little wonkily). His friends stared in absolute wonder.

'Blimey! said Al.

'Incredible,' said Luke, rubbing his chin.

'I mean flipping Nora!' said Al.

'Defies the laws of physics,' muttered Luke. 'Solid iron railings, manipulated like pipe-cleaners.'

'This is awesome, Jack, I mean, d'you know what this means? It's unbelievable,' said Al. 'I don't believe it and I've just seen it for myself. It's like really real. It's too real. You're a superhero. You could do anything. Think of the fame, the fortune. The girls.'

'Can I perform some experiments on you?' said Luke.

'What? No way!'

'Why not? Research, Jack. You are the unexplained.'

'Come on, Dr Freak, leave the boy, I mean superboy, alone for a minute. Give him some room to breathe.'

Jack coughed dramatically. 'Anyway, Spain never do that well, they won't even make it past the group stage.'

'Huh?' shrugged Al.

'Hi, Mastermind, all right?' said Jack. The others twigged and turned to see Magnus Pugh ambling over, laces trailing and ripped shirt hanging over his trousers. He looked like he'd been beaten up.

'Yeah suppose so,' he said. 'You?'

'Yeah, not bad, despite the bus thing this morning,' said Jack.

'Oh yeah, your bus wasn't it. What happened?'

'Dunno, tyre blew or something.'

'Any injuries?'

'Nar, luckily.' Jack saw that Magnus had a graze on his neck and his right hand was red and puffy. 'You sure you're all right? You look like you've been beaten up.'

'Oh yeah. Well. Apart from being beaten up, I'm fine.'

'Let me guess,' said Al. 'Tall, thick, pig-ignorant, couple of years above us, answers to the name Dunce, constantly shadowed by two stooges with a combined IQ lower than half a bag of rotten turnips?'

'Yeah, after money as always. Gave him what I had but he still beat me up anyway. Teachers came along and told me to get down me own end of school. Didn't want to hear that I'd been dragged down the corridor by him and his two thugs in the first place.'

'Someone should make that lot eat their own week-old underpants,' said Luke.

'What, the teachers or Dunce and co.?' said Jack.

'Both,' blurted Al. 'Should be someone else's year-old underpants though.'

'Now that would be disgusting,' said Luke.

'Jack, you could –'

'No I couldn't, Al.' Jack cut him off before he could say more.

'Oh. Right, yeah, course.'

'Only ones who ever stand up to him are Agnes and Helen,' said Magnus, wearily. 'Saw them having a go at him earlier in the corridor. S'pect that's why he wanted to beat someone up. I was just in the wrong place at the wrong time. That and the whole nickname thing.'

'What about it?' said Al.

'Doesn't help does it – "Mastermind". Everyone knows I was named after Magnus what's-his-name that used to present it and that Mum won it answering questions about... well.'

'The history of sewage treatment in Britain from 1850 to 1959. I thought it was fascinating,' said Luke.

'Yeah, but it's still a bit shitty,' said Al.

'You see? Even you lot can't go five minutes without making a joke about it.'

'I'm sorry, couldn't help myself.'

'Magnus, I think your neck requires medical attention, it appears to be weeping watery blood onto your collar. I suggest a visit to Madam Death,' said Luke.

'Oh damn – ow,' said Magnus, touching his wound. 'Well, see you lot later then.'

'Cheers,' they said, as Magnus plodded away.

Jack told Luke and Al the full story of what happened on Roughtor the evening he was knocked out. It was the first time he had discussed it, but even as he told them he scarcely believed it.

'Don't you think it would be wise to inform the authorities?' Luke proposed.

'No. Absolutely not. We can't tell anyone. No one must ever find out about any of this. You must both swear now, on your mothers' lives, that you won't breath a word to anyone. OK?' Jack was feeling pretty confused about most things except the fact that no one else must find out what had happened to him.

'Thing is, I don't know what to do. This might wear off any second, I may drop down dead tomorrow, anything could happen.'

'No way,' said Al. 'This is brilliant. It's better than magic. No, you've been given these powers for a reason. First there was Superman, then Batman, and now –'

'Bantam-man,' said Luke.

'Ha ha. Very funny, chicken licken,' said Jack.

'All right, don't get cocky, kid,' said Al.

'Pardon me,' said Luke. 'But don't you think you have egg-xhausted those jokes?' They all groaned together.

'Seriously though, let's not tell anyone about this. I feel a bit weird,' said Jack.

'You should see how you look,' said Al.

'I don't want anyone sticking their beak in.' Jack smiled weakly.

'Makes my news seem dull in comparison,' said Al.

'Huh?' said Jack.

'Oh yeah. You were a bit lost earlier. I was telling Luke, we were visiting Nan yesterday and I heard these blokes talking in a shed in the middle of nowhere.'

'Yeah, you're right – that is dull,' said Jack.

'No. They were discussing plans to steal something from school. I think it must be the World Cup.'

'You're joking? I take it you haven't told the police?' said Jack.

'No way. Not telling those idiots. Besides, after what they did to us at the weekend I wouldn't tell them even if there was a reward in it. I was trying to think of a way we could catch them ourselves without getting too killed and here it is – your new-found super power. Come on, it'll be brilliant!'

The bell went for the end of break and the boys hurried off to collect their bags and head for Maths with "Digger" Hole, followed by Physics with "Beaky" Beaks.

'Hi,' said Agnes and Helen, rounding the corner of the cloakroom.

'All right?' said Al.

'Well yes, considering,' said Agnes.

'Oh, Mastermind said you'd had another run-in with Dunce. What happened?' asked Jack.

'It was brilliant,' said Helen, talking at a hundred miles an hour. 'We was coming back from the art block and ended up behind him and there was a strap hanging down from his bag and Agnes stepped on it. Whump! Fell flat on his bum.'

'He must have gone mental,' said Al.

'He wasn't exactly happy, stupid git,' said Agnes, smiling. 'You should have seen his face. I thought every blood vessel in his head was going to explode.'

'You'll explode when he straps you to a bomb and lets it off. Have you got a death wish or something?'

'Don't be so dramatic, Al, you pillock,' said Helen.

'He's nuts, Agnes. He will get his revenge – Dunce never lets anyone off the hook. I know he's gonna get us some time.' Jack remembered what he had said to Dunce as he walked off the other morning. 'Me and my big mouth.'

'If only Dunce could see how illogical revenge is,' said Luke.

'Logic doesn't enter his mind,' said Al.

'There're lots of things that don't enter his mind,' said Jack.

'Anyway we'd better get a move on – wouldn't want to keep old Digger waiting,' said Helen.

Maths was never boring. "Digger" Hole walked up and down in front of the chalk board, reading about long division of fractions from the text book. Every few minutes he scratched his bottom. Just like waves, every seventh one was bigger. He dug deeper and scratched harder than before. Lips were bitten. Laughs were disguised as coughs. Silent tears were wiped away. Digger kept walking and talking and scratching.

'Come on, Digger,' whispered Al. 'Come on. Do it. You know you want to. Come on. Luke, what are we up to?'

Luke glanced up from his studies. He never bothered listening to Mr Hole any more as there was nothing he could learn from him. In fact, there was little that anyone could learn from Digger. Luke stopped listening the day he had asked Digger to explain something he had read out, only for him to re-read it more slowly and a little more loudly.

'Well?' said Al.

'Sixteen. Form Z had twenty-three yesterday. We need a bonus to make up the points. My calculations show that if it is going to happen, it will be in the next four and half minutes.'

Jack remained silent, smiling weakly. There was too much on his mind. What was going to happen to him?

'Look, look,' whispered Al, as loudly as he thought was safe. 'He's raising it. Up, up, up. Ye-e-e-s. Bingo. You are good, Northy,' said Al to Luke.

Form Y and Z had an ongoing competition with Mr Hole's maths lessons. Many other forms had similar games too. The rules were simple – one point was awarded for each standard scratch, with an extra three points for every seventh giant scratch. A bonus of ten points was awarded for a special event. Form Y had just witnessed such an event – "Digger" Hole had scratched and then ever so subtly, maybe absent-mindedly, he had raised his hand and sniffed his fingers.

Physics was incredibly dull. Mrs Beaks wheezed. Jack drifted off. Notes were passed back and forth. Mrs Beaks coughed. Al nudged Jack. Bunsen burners were lit. Strange metals were burnt. Luke made sure that his, Al's and Jack's experiment worked OK. Mrs Beaks wheezed good-bye.

The boys huddled outside the Games Hall away from everyone and resumed their discussion about Jack's new-found talents.

'Please expand on your revelations from earlier,' said Luke, then seeing the blank expressions on his friends faces he said, 'What other super powers do you have?'

'Dunno. All I've realised is that at the moment I seem to be really, really strong,' said Jack.

'How strong? I mean could you punch a hole through here?' said Al, patting the Games Hall wall.

'I dunno. All I've done so far is the bus thing this morning and the railings with you pair. I don't really want to try punching a hole through there in front of everyone, I have a feeling it may arouse some suspicion.'

'Any aeronautic capabilities?' whispered Luke, loudly. 'Can you –'

'Fly? Haven't tried. Not too keen on heights, you know. I feel airsick just thinking about it.' Jack turned pale.

'X-ray vision?' said Luke. 'The ability to see through objects?' Jack quite fancied the idea. 'Maybe, I'll give it a go.'

He gathered his thoughts and tried to calm his breathing. It may not actually have made any difference, but it seemed the kind of thing he should be doing if he wanted to see straight through something. His brow furrowed as he concentrated and stared at the side of one of the waiting buses, below the window where Agnes was sitting.

He scrunched up his eyes, opened them wide, then back to normal and stared and stared and stared. His focus on the bus seemed to draw him right up to it, so close he could see the dirt on the paint. A faint flicker of black momentarily saturated his vision, changing his perception. Now, in his mind's eye, he could see molecules of paint. Their fuzzy appearance cleared to microscopic vibrations. Slowly, they started to dissolve. Atoms of metal under the paint appeared briefly before becoming translucent. Fibres of material from the inside of the bus seeped into view. To his left, somewhere in the periphery of his vision, a dark shape emerged, moving closer. He became aware of a voice. He squinted with intent at the bus and then slowly, very slowly –

Whack.

Jack fell back against the Games Hall wall and crumpled to the ground. An irate Agnes, bag in hand, stood over him, threatening to wallop him again.

'That was for staring, you weirdo. Just wouldn't stop, would you? Didn't you see me waving?'

'Well no, I was –'

'I don't care. You deserved it,' she said, storming back to the bus and sitting down on the opposite side.

'I think you upset her, Jack,' said Al.

'Really, Sherlock? Thanks for the keen observation. You'll make a great detective one day.' Jack picked up his bag. 'One of you could've stopped her.'

'We expected your spider-sense to click in,' said Luke. 'Didn't you get a *fowl-feeling*, Bantam-man?'

9

Eminem Comes to School

'"There are one hundred and ninety-six billion, four hundred and sixty-five million, two hundred and eighty-seven thousand, six hundred and ninety-six bones in the human body but only two in a cat. Turnips have no bones as they come from the same genus as molluscs, both being introverts",' read Luke.

'I like bones,' said Al, 'they're good for my posture.'

'And you've got a lot of posture to fill with them. Exactly how tall are you now?' said Jack.

'Dr Spock here reckons I'm growing at two millimetres a week.'

Al's head rose from his book. 'The study was conducted over a period of two weeks in which you grew four millimetres, so logically the data is correct.'

'See?'

'And that's Mr Spock,' said Luke, annoyed. 'How many times do I have to tell you?'

'I'd say about another one hundred and ninety-six billion, four hundred and sixty-five million, two hundred and eighty-seven thousand, six hundred and ninety-six.'

It was lunchtime and they were sitting on a low wall outside Mr Swift's classroom in the junior end of school. Until Luke started reading from *The Book of Untrue Facts* they had been discussing the unusual sequence of events from the previous day.

'That book is nuts,' said Al. 'Does it say that?'

Luke shrugged. 'Let me see,' he said, flicking through to the relevant section. 'Here we go, Books. "Best book ever – *The Book of Untrue Facts*, thinnest – *A Short History of Thin Books (abridged)*".'

'I was right,' said Al. 'It's nuts.'

'Listen to this – "In the whole history of literature only one book has ever ended with the word spatula",' read Luke.

'Go on, which?' asked Jack reluctantly.

'"*Harry Potter and the Spatula of Weevils*",' said Luke smiling.

'You know the rules, Luke, it has to be said in a Welsh accent – '*Arry Potter and the Spat-ula of Wee-vils*,' said Jack, Welshing his heart out.

'You know I don't do accents,' said Luke, seriously. 'You pair always laugh because I only have my generically foreign one.'

'Please do it, Northy, go on,' said Al.

'No.'

Al and Jack stared demandingly at him and eventually he gave in.

'I can nit do zees accents veery well.' Luke stared at his friends with mild contempt at their predictable response.

Al finally stopped giggling and said, 'Hey, what does it say about Man United? Can't wait to see them lose tomorrow night.'

'Very funny,' said Jack. 'Deportivo don't stand a chance. We'll thrash them.'

'Dream on, Stuperman,' said Al.

'Sshhh. Someone'll hear,' said Jack.

'Sport... Football... ah, Manchester United. "Manchester United have more fans in Cornwall and Devon than in the whole of Manchester".'

'Thought it was meant to be a book of untrue facts?' asked Al.

'Ha ha,' said Jack. 'I expect a hat-trick from van Nistelrooy, a free kick from Beckham and a cock-up from Bartez.'

'Why's it you support Man U again?' said Al.

'Uncle David – he went to university there, started supporting them and got us doing the same – ever since the day we were born. Mum and Dad aren't into football. It's a perfectly valid reason.'

'He is the one who disappeared, isn't he?' said Luke.

'Yeah,' said Jack, glumly.

'Do you really suspect he was in the employ of the secret services?' said Luke, then seeing the expression on Al's face explained, 'Was he a spy?'

Al nodded his understanding.

'Dunno,' said Jack, flicking a pebble into a small gap in the paving slabs to his left. 'That's what we always said, but Mum never let on, even if she knew. She doesn't like talking about him now, so we don't ask.'

'D'you think he's, you know...' Al nodded.

'Dead?' said Jack.

'Yeah.'

'He's been missing about five years with no word, so I suppose he must be, but no one really knows, so it's hard to actually think of him as, you know, dead.'

'Hello, boys,' said Helen, brightly.

They mumbled unenthusiastic replies.

'Well don't sound too happy to see us,' said Agnes. 'You'd think someone had died looking at you lot.'

'We were just – never mind,' said Al.

'So,' said Jack, trying to sound upbeat, 'what's going on?'

'Oh, just the usual.'

'Like what?'

'Oh, you know,' said Agnes. 'Brad Pitt called to cancel lunch because he was having his chest waxed, Orlando Bloom can't make afternoon tea because he's had to have an emergency crochet lesson and Jude Law's missing dinner because he's having a manicure and new wig fitted.'

'It's no wonder you two are always getting yourselves into trouble,' said Luke.

'Thanks,' said Agnes.

'We can't help it if we mix in a different social circle to you lot – we've got our own lives to lead away from school and those Hollywood A-list stars can't get enough of us rural types – look at Catherine Zeta-Jones and Michael Douglas,' said Helen, hardly taking a breath.

'I'll look at *her* but I'd rather leave the saddlebag if I may,' said Al.

'Anyway, hope you've been avoiding Dunce,' said Jack.

'Scumbag,' said Helen.

'I was only asking.'

'Not you, him, you divvy. I think he fancies Agnes, won't leave her alone, always seems to pop up wherever we go, sticking his great ugly nose in our business, should be ashamed of himself – and he's got a girlfriend, well a few I reckon.'

'You know, as far as I am aware, under current legislation in this country, it is not illegal to breathe when one is talking,' said Luke.

'What did he say?' Helen asked Agnes.

'He said don't talk so quickly.'

'That's what I thought he said.' Helen walked (in much the same way as she talked) over to Luke who was still sitting on the low wall. 'Luke.'

'Yes?'

'Shut-up,' she said and kicked him hard on the shin.

'Ow.'

'Now didn't we discuss this exact kind of behaviour the other day?' said Al, affronted at Helen's violent outburst.

'Er, yeah and I'll kick you if you want, too. Huh? Huh?' she threatened, pushing her face toward Al's.

'No!' screamed Al, in a slightly effeminate tone. 'Kick Jack, he told me to say it.'

Jack started to plead his innocence but Helen turned and kicked him instinctively. He felt no pain but a split second later his brain reminded him that he needed to pretend that he had felt some. 'Ouch, ow!' he cried, overacting terribly.

'I thought you were our hero, Jack?' said Agnes. 'Come on, are you a man or a mouse?'

'Well actually he's a –'

'Mouse!' said Jack. 'Anyone got any cheese?' He gave Al a hard stare.

'Mice should never eat cheese,' said Luke, still rubbing his leg.

'Why?' asked Helen.

'I had pet mice when I was younger. I conducted an experiment on them, put out a dried apricot, a bit of Weetabix and a piece of cheese for them. First day they ate the apricot. All was fine. Second day the Weetabix, still fine. Third day, they finally ate the cheese.' Luke had a faraway look in his eyes.

'What, so they liked the cheese less?' said Al. 'Big deal.'

'Next day, they were all dead.'

'Let that be a lesson to you, Jack,' said Agnes.

'Uh-oh, what now?' said Al, staring past Agnes towards the music block. Harriet Vernon was hurrying down the path towards them, shouting at someone following her – it was Dunce, half running, half walking, in an intimidating manner.

'He's like Terminator Two,' said Al. 'Look, he's gone psycho.'

'More like Terminator Twit! Poor cow, dunno what she sees in him myself, she should tell him to get lost, heard he was all over that floozy from year eleven the other day, what's her name – Tracy Duck or something,' said Helen.

'Drake. Her name is Drake,' said Al.

'He has got a certain rugged charm,' said Agnes, smiling.

'What!' said Jack with utter disgust. 'You fancy that nutter?'

'No, course not. I'm just saying I can understand why girls fancy him.'

'You're nuts too,' said Al.

'I think she looks scared,' said Luke, quietly. He leaned forward to see the two figures approaching rapidly. 'Hope he hasn't been giving her cheese.'

The shouting grew louder as Harriet darted between meandering children, screaming over her shoulder. As Dunce strode forward, those children that did not get out of his way voluntarily, were skittled sideways.

'Keep your heads down – don't look him in the eye,' warned Al.

'How many heads have you got?' said Luke.

The boys stared intently at the ground, hiding as best they could. Predictably, Helen and Agnes didn't.

'Harriet. Harry. Get back here. Just wait, will you?' pleaded Dunce.

86

'Get lost, maggot,' she yelled, not even looking back. Dunce spotted Agnes and Helen as he approached. 'What the hell are you gawping at, stupid cows?'

'Dunno there's no label on it,' Helen fired back.

Agnes stared right at Dunce, maintaining eye contact with him as he approached. When he was about to pass her, she nudged Al's schoolbag with her foot. She smiled sweetly at Dunce who realised a split second too late that something was wrong. His eyes flicked down, but not in time to speed the message up to his brain, then back down to his legs. The fall was not spectacular – more of a messy, scrambling effort to prevent himself crumpling to the ground, which made him look extremely silly.

He was quickly back on his feet and swung an alien heat-ray of a glare in a large circle, burning through fledgling mirth with efficient ease. 'I ain't not gonna say a word,' he steamed before booting Al's bag into the bushes by the path. He glanced around for Harriet but she was long gone.

'Say that again,' said Agnes, brightly.

Dunce started for her, his right arm drawn back with a clenched fist at the end of it. Jack felt like a frenzied wave of butterflies was flying through his stomach as he darted up and over to Dunce. The next second, their arms were linked. Jack's momentum spun them and he pretended to be dancing, skipping around humming a non-specific tune he hoped sounded like an Irish jig. Dunce was caught off-guard. Normally, no one ever stood up to him, and certainly not in this way. The peculiar dance partners were on their third rotation when Dunce planted his left foot down with determination, stopping dead. He jerked Jack back so they were opposite each other.

As the inevitable punch came, the world seemed to slow down for Jack. If he had wanted, he could have grabbed Dunce's wrist, given it a twist and thrown him flat on his back. Instead, he let the fist plunge into his sternum and folded his body around it (being careful not to injure Dunce's hand). Dunce withdrew his fist and Jack staggered back as if in great pain, wailing with false agony. He was bent over, holding his stomach and could see Dunce preparing a second punch – this time to the head.

He watched the straining knuckles until they were a few millimetres from his cheek. At this point he whipped his head around, making sure that Dunce struck him ever so slightly (so Dunce believed he had given Jack a good clout). The dive was slightly over the top, but this was Jack's first attempt at pretending to be beaten up, and if he overdid it he wasn't going to beat himself up about it. The thought made him smile so he turned his head to the ground, the grass tickling his nose.

Dunce legged it as soon as he had delivered the second punch. Several cries of 'Jack!' and 'Shillaber!' were confirmation that Jack's charade had worked. He opened his eyes and to his surprise, saw a small figure, no more than thirty centimetres tall, disappear quickly behind the bushes near the music block.

'Jack,' shouted Al as he ran over. 'Why didn't you –'

'Ah,' yelled Jack, preventing Al from mouthing whatever he was about to say. Jack grabbed him by the jumper and pulled him close. 'Just play along, OK?'

'Yeah but –'

'No. No one must know.'

'OK. OK, pal, all right, buddy,' said Al, doing as his friend had requested. 'You're all right, pal,' he said, patting Jack on the shoulder as Jack moaned his best moan.

'You idiot, Jack, what d'you do that for? Big loudmouth wasn't gonna do nothing, was he? All mouth, that one – run off like a little baby,' said Helen.

'What is the problem with you two, huh?' said Al, letting go of Jack, who collapsed back to the ground with a bony thud. 'You just couldn't let it lie, could you?'

'We were helping out that poor girl. She was obviously being harassed,' said Agnes. 'I didn't ask hero-boy to step in, did I?' she said, helping Jack up. 'You all right?'

'Ooh. Ah... Yeah, suppose so,' said Jack, painfully.

'Well, one of us had to jump in, didn't we?' said Al. 'Just so happens Jack beat me and Luke to it, this time. Nice one, Shillaber,' he said, patting Jack's shoulder again.

'He looks all right – nothing wrong with him,' said Helen.

'What d'you mean?' said Jack, acting his heart out. 'Look at me, my chin'll probably swell up like a balloon. I can hard-ly ta-l-k.' Jack rubbed his chin gingerly.

'I don't recall asking you to stick your big brow in,' said Agnes. She stopped dead, immediately regretting her words.

Jack felt like his heart almost stopped. He tried to think of something clever to say, but his mind was blank. All he was trying to do was help but now he felt like he was about to cry.

'Well... thanks anyway,' said Agnes, trying to ignore her guilt. 'But please don't worry about it next time. I'm perfectly capable of looking after myself.'

Jack still couldn't think of anything to say except, 'Fine.'

'Good,' said Agnes, angrily.

The bell went and they grabbed their bags (Al struggled to retrieve his from the bushes) and set off for Geography with Miss Arthur.

The first lesson of the afternoon seemed to drag on for hours. Geography was dull and cold. Miss Arthur's classroom was generally considered to be strong with the dark side of the Force, with its icy, dead aura. As she whispered sheepishly away, Jack started daydreaming about plate tectonics. He imagined two huge faces of rock colliding – one forcing the other down through the lithosphere right into the asthenosphere where it melted away. Then somehow the plates turned into rugby players in a scrum, Cornwall vs England – and England was pushed under Cornwall and disappeared. But then England came back as a huge, angry volcano that erupted all over Cornwall and the whole thing started again.

Miss Arthur paused and smiled. Al whispered 'What was that last bit she said, something about butter in the headsock?'

'Huh?' said Jack, who hadn't been paying attention anyway.

'This is geography, Al,' said Luke. 'How many times have you heard the phrase "butter in the headsock", being used in reference to anything that might be covered in a geography lesson?'

'Well, I don't know, how are we meant to learn anything if we can't hear a word she says?' said Al.

'What?' said Jack.

'I said, how are we – hilarious.' Al put his hand up. 'Excuse me, Miss, what was that last bit you said?'

'I said, –'

But all Al heard after that sounded like a drunken Jawa reciting Shakespeare. When Miss Arthur finished, she smiled warmly at him.

'Thanks, Miss,' he said, none the wiser. 'Luke, can I copy your notes please?'

Art with Mr Ford was less dull. Virtually all the girls fancied him. He looked like a rustic, less cool version of George Clooney, only younger, and his clothes were almost always covered in paint (though he never painted in class, other than to demonstrate technique).

The lesson was a straightforward still life of a large bowl of fruit against a colourful cloth background. Mr Ford walked around the class peering over his pupils' shoulders, giving constructive criticism and helpful advice.

'Good, Sarah, melons well defined.' He stopped, eyeing the class but luckily they hadn't noticed. He told himself to concentrate on what he was saying.

The class had noticed but managed to restrain themselves from laughing, as they knew there would be more.

'Maybe some more colour, Stephen, the fruit really isn't that black is it now?... Excellent brushwork, Neil... Nice banana, Jim.' He cursed himself mentally as a few of the class giggled. Recovering composure, he pressed on. 'Good depth in shade, Jack, not bad... Fine proportioning Luke, very precise and mathematical as always... My goodness, Al, what is that?' More giggles went round the class as Al and Mr Ford turned bright red. 'I mean, you know...' said Mr Ford, trying to regain some professionalism, 'it's very interesting in a, in a disturbing kind of way... I hadn't realised you were into surrealism. That's very... nice. Yes. Very good.'

'I can't believe he said that, just can't believe it,' said Al as they walked down the steps from the art block.

'Well he always comes out with something stupid,' said Jack.

'His natural talent for placing his feet firmly in his mouth is uncannily consistent. Maybe he knows exactly what he's doing?' said Luke.

'Maybe,' said Al.

'Aren't you two off that way?' said Jack, nodding in the opposite direction to the car park.

'No way, we're coming to wait with you and discuss plans for our covert operation,' said Al. They passed the maths block and bore right, meandering through the gathering hordes of children, over to the Games Hall. When far enough away so no one would overhear their conversation, they stopped and dropped their bags.

'OK, here's the plan,' said Al, excitedly. 'We hide in school until everyone's gone and it's all locked up, then we set a trap for them and catch them red-handed.'

'And how do you suppose we actually capture them?' said Luke.

'Superboy here —'

'Shut it!' said Jack, checking around nervously.

'I mean Jack here, leaps on them and knocks them all out one after another.'

'That is an incredible plan. You are a tactical genius, like a cross between Bonaparte and Elmer Fud,' said Luke.

'Sarcasm won't get you anywhere,' said Al.

'I would rather *be* anywhere than hiding in school with you and your insane plan.'

'So what do you suggest, Einstein?'

'We could, and should, tell the police.'

'What? You're joking right? After what they put us through – no way.'

'I'm with Al on this,' said Jack, who was constantly peering around to make sure no one was listening in. 'That Gibson's a real piece of work.'

'Something makes me nervous, that's all,' said Luke, concerned.

'Come on, Northy, don't be so... wet,' said Al.

'I am not convinced that this is not an elaborate subterfuge.' Luke realised by the blank expressions on Al and Jack's faces, they had not understood. 'It may be a trap,' he said.

'For what?' said Al.

'Er, let me think... Jack?'

'That's more sarcasm from you, isn't it, Luke?' said Al.

'Well, what if a clinically deranged scientist is already aware of him and would like to ensnare him and... experiment,' said Luke, with jealous eyes.

'Na, I've been super careful,' said Jack.

'Ha, ha. Nice one,' said Al, laughing. 'Good to see you haven't lost your sense of humour.'

'Well,' said Luke, 'don't say I haven't given fair warning.'

Their conversation was interrupted by the screech of tyres and a throbbing engine as a car pulled in to the school grounds.

'Oh joy,' said Al, 'it's Dunce's older, calmer brother... Lucifer. Probably just popping in to place a donation in the charity box and say "hi" to his old teachers, before burning the school down.'

The car sped along the short drive past the car park, scattering children heading for their lifts home, before it skidded sideways to a stop in the no parking zone. The smell of burning rubber filled the air. The engine growled like a lioness protecting her cubs, was revved violently a couple of times then killed. Loud engine sounds were replaced by loud music sounds. The stereo was turned up to eleven and was booming out some expletive-heavy, hardcore rap. An atomic powered sub-woofer (probably welded to the chassis), rocked the gaudily customised 1995 Ford Fiesta.

'One, two, three, cue,' said Luke, before an annoyingly loud horn played the first two bars from the theme tune to *EastEnders*.

The car door opened and out got Eminem... or Gary, as Dunce's older brother was actually named. He was wearing mirror shades, a yellow bandana and a large puffed jacket. His trousers were hanging somewhere near his knees. He ducked back in the car and pulled out a greasy portion of fish and chips. Undoing them, he tossed the paper down by the side of the car and started eating.

'Now just ignore that, OK, Jack?' said Al. 'I know I've been guilty of encouraging you to use your gift, but now ain't the time – we all know how you feel about litter-louts.'

Almost everyone stared at Dunce's brother as he leaned against his car, chewing open-mouthed on his fish supper. Only the teachers chose to ignore him, pretending they had seen nothing. They knew it was unlikely that if provoked he would actually "pop a cap in their ass" but it was not worth the risk to find out. Besides, his brother would arrive any second, and then they would be gone.

'It's like a scene from *Eight Mile*,' said Al. 'Any second, a rival gang may race up in their supe'd up one litre Nissan Micra for a drive-by shooting with some heavy-duty rubber bands.'

'I think you'll find that's crew, not gang. You obviously haven't been reading your *Gangsta's Review* magazine enough,' said Luke.

'Are you dissing my homey?' asked Jack, in as posh a voice as he could manage.

'No, dog,' said Luke, awkwardly. 'I have nuff respec, innit. Big up my good old buddies.'

Al and Jack giggled.

'What?' said Luke.

'What are you on about, Northy?' said Al.

'I was merely replicating the genre's vernacular,' he said, a little offended.

'I think you crossed genres there somewhere, it was kind of gangsta-redneck... it's an interesting concept though,' said Al.

'If Dunce's brother is the Eminem, or maybe that's Enema, of Launceston, what does that make Dunce?' said Jack.

'Fifty Pence?' said Luke.

'You see, if you'd meant that, it would have been one thing, but you didn't, did you?' said Al.

'What?' said Luke, turning red.

'It's Cent, Fifty Cent, not Pence,' said Jack. 'That's like something my mother would say. Any other suggestions? What about Dr Der?'

'Very funny. Well, gentlemen, I think I may have to leave now,' said Luke, starting to look a little serious.

'Oh come on, Luke, we're just joking,' said Al. 'Hang on a minute and I'll walk with you.'

'Yeah, come on, we wouldn't have you any other way,' said Jack, giving Luke a gentle, friendly push on the shoulder.

'Uh-oh,' said Al, spotting Dunce, 'here's Dr Der now.'

Dunce and his ever-present thugs strode menacingly through the crowd of children waiting patiently for their buses. Gary put the half eaten takeaway back inside the car and tried to swagger over with attitude to greet his brother. It looked more like he either had a bad limp or had just soiled himself. 'Dorg,' he said in a thick, Cornish accent.

'Dorg,' replied Dunce, his accent less coarse. They clasped hands and went to bump opposing shoulders. Unfortunately, both leaned the same way, bumping chests, and almost kissing each other in the process. With piercing eyes, they stifled any mirth before it had a chance to begin.

'Word up, bruv,' said Gary.

'Safe,' said his brother.

Above the general murmur of the gathered crowd, some distinctive laughter could be heard.

Al spotted Agnes and Helen, who couldn't manage to keep their amusement quiet. 'Oh no, what are they doing now?' he said.

'*That* is illogical,' said Luke.

'They just can't help themselves,' said Jack, starting to walk over.

'Wait there, Hulk,' said Al. 'I think we should hang here. Remember we've already upset Dunce enough this week.'

'That is a good point, Jack,' said Luke, seriously.

Meanwhile, Dunce marched angrily up to Helen and Agnes. 'I've had enough of you pair. We'll get you.'

'Oo, scared,' said Helen.

'You should be... you should be.' He whipped around and stormed back to the car (Gary limping behind). They dived in. A moment later, the engine roared into life, the wheels span and the car shot forward. As it started moving, Dunce threw the sodden fish and chips out of the window high into the air.

Jack fumed silently. A split second later Dunce's brother slammed on his brakes as a Land Rover (driven by an angry parent) pulled out in front of him. It was a perfect opportunity. Jack imagined himself running over, picking up the thrown-away takeaway and hurling it at the car. He was not the only one.

Agnes darted forward and picked up the discarded food. Jack heard a desperate cry of 'No!' from behind him as Al shouted at her to stop, but it was too late.

94

Her aim was true and the ungainly missile landed with a satisfying splatter on the back windscreen. A muted cheer went up. The engine died instantly as if the direct hit had broken the car. The doors jerked opened simultaneously, the maddened brothers appeared and stalked around to inspect the mess.

'Litterbugs!' screamed Agnes. 'I was aiming for your open window too.' The brothers exchanged a few words then staring at Agnes, drew their hands across their throats before returning to the car and speeding away, filling the air with more wretched squeals of rubber on tarmac.

10

Dickie, Rik, Richie and Dick

The shed was still surrounded by a messy tangle of nettles and brambles, but they had now grown a little taller. The small, square windows remained seized shut, but someone had tried to clean the algae-smeared glass. It had not worked – instead of clean glass or green glass, was merely weirdly smeared glass.

The neon strip light persisted to hum uncomfortably and struggle to illuminate the dusty, damp shed. New smoke hung lazily in the stale air like a mini pea-souper. The shelves against the walls continued to be stacked with all sorts of rubbish, from old jam jars to rusty, lidless tins and a thin layer of dirty oil remained covering everything that was not rusting.

The four men were gathered once again to discuss the dastardly deeds they planned to perpetrate. Dick rolled out a building plan onto the table.

'Everything is in plates,' he snarled.

'Pardon?' said Richie.

'Everything is in plates,' repeated Dick.

'Why is everything in plates? Are we meant to be talking in some sort of fine china code? Do we make our "porcelain vase" on the night of the "teacup" just after the "cutlery" has arrived?' Richie blew his nose on a polka dot, silk handkerchief as Dick stared in disbelief. 'I do require a modicum of clarity from you, Dick.' Richie was exaggerating his upper-class accent and spat Dick's name with a venomous glee.

Dick shot from his seat, sending his chair flying. Leaning halfway across the table, he pointed a menacing finger in Richie's face and through gritted teeth threatened, 'P-l-ace. You trying to be funny, sunshine, 'cause if you are, you've got another thing coming.'

'More crockery?' said Richie. 'A gravy boat and matching cruet set per chance? My gratitude knows no bounds, you humble me with your kindness.'

Dick lunged forward but Dickie and Rik grabbed him. 'My my,' said Richie, calmly, 'did you realise you have a rather dirty fingernail?' He picked a piece of cotton from his tatty, velvet jacket. 'Maybe you should book yourself in for a manicure. While you're there, maybe you should have a pedicure, headicure, smellicure and elocution lessons.'

'Right, that's it.' Dick hurled himself forward, momentarily breaking free from Rik and Dickie. 'Why, you good-for-nothing, toffee-nosed great git,' he yelled, grabbing Richie firmly around the throat with both hands. Rik and Dickie wrestled him away. They righted his chair and forced him back onto it.

'No!' shouted Rik, furiously slamming his fist onto the table (which emitted a dull crack). 'Whatever has gotten into you two gentlemen? Huh? What do you think this is? Some kind of small-time petty theft? This is serious business. The planning that's been put into this. You know nothing, you pathetic morons.' Rik stormed out and slammed the shed door, making the whole structure quiver.

'W-w-well I n-n-never,' said Dickie, bemused. 'D-d-didn't realise it m-meant so m-m-much to him.'

The three remaining men were shocked. Rik had never given them any indication that he was harbouring such strong feelings regarding their nefarious assignment.

Richie's face was bright red. He rubbed his neck, gasping in the musty, smoke-filled room, 'A most... curious turn of events... indeed.'

'Just my luck,' mumbled Dick, fidgeting in his coat. He took out his whiskey bottle and took three swift glugs. 'This whole deal's getting worse by the minute.'

Rik walked back in, a wry smile on his face. 'My apologies for that, gentlemen. I've been – a bit stressed recently. Please, take no notice of me, I didn't know what I was saying. Can I make us all a cup of tea?'

'Now that's a good idea, Mr Marole, ta very much,' said Dick.

'Are there a-any b-b-biscuits? I'd love a r-r-rich tea,' said Dickie.

'Oh yes my good fellow,' said Richie, a little hoarse. 'I do believe I procured a packet of those very same delicacies, along with some chocolate bourbons.'

'L-l-lovely.'

'It's like the bleeding WI round here,' said Dick.

The gang of four drank their tea, ate biscuits and finally studied the building plans that Dick had brought along. Several key decisions were made regarding the execution of the job and it was agreed that they would meet one final time.

11

Breaking of the Second Metatarsal

Wednesday 10th April, a significant day for Sir Alex Ferguson – his 100th European game in charge of Manchester United. Tonight they could clinch a place in the semi-finals of the Champions League (something they had not managed for three years). They had won the away leg 0–2 and history was very much on their side, having never lost a European home game by more than one goal. However, the game would be overshadowed by an incident, the repercussions of which would be reported throughout the world, and it did not involve David Beckham's hair.

Jack had spent much of the day getting more and more worried about how his new super powers may affect his life. Though he tried to avoid the subject as much as possible, conversations with Al and Luke were inevitably drawn back to it. Jack's fear was that someone may overhear, leading to disastrous consequences.

A few things were clear to him – 1) he did not want anyone to know except his closest friends – Luke and Al, 2) although he was incredibly excited about being a superhero, he was equally scared witless about what it may entail, and 3) the reason he did not want anyone else to know, was because if he was identified, he may get locked away in a sanitised, sealed glass bowl in some military laboratory, where he would be poked by mad, evil, "doctors" who wanted to create a race of superhuman soldier clones. The thought of being "daddy" to an army of raging psychopathic desensitised killing machines was not (and never had been) part of the plan for Jack's life. Neither was receiving an anal probe.

'Anal probe, my arse,' said Al. 'No one's going to catch you and stick things up your bum, they can't – you're a super boy and a tight-arse!'

'Easy for you to say,' said Jack, 'but you wouldn't be laughing if it was your arse on the line, or in the line.'

'Is this where I'm meant to interject with another humorous aside about the fact that getting an anal probe must be a real bummer?' said Luke.

'Well, if you must,' said Al.

'Anal probes are useful,' said Luke, pausing. Al and Jack stared expectantly at him. '...if you have a problem that you need to get to the bottom of.'

The boys groaned.

'So, what are we going to do about the old World Cup problem?' said Al. 'We still don't really have a solid plan, do we?'

'No,' said Jack. 'When's it on display?'

'Monday,' said Luke. 'I suggest a more private meeting, how about the weekend?'

'Yeah,' said Jack.

'Sounds good to me. Saturday afternoon?' said Al.

'I'll have to check with Mum to make sure she can run me in OK,' said Jack.

'Surely you could just leap in and leap back without her even knowing?' said Al.

'Mum may not see, but Dad sees everything. Can't even drag your bag up the lane without him spotting you.'

'Fair enough,' said Al.

'There's my bus,' said Jack, as a brand new, luxury bus purred to a stop next to the other, less glamorous ones. 'Funny what a high profile accident can do for a school bus run, isn't it?'

'Looks like some sort of alien insect, with those huge mirror antennas,' said Luke, sounding genuinely interested.

'Well, on that note, I'm going to bug-er off,' said Jack, smiling at his own terrible joke. 'See you.'

'Hope you get thrashed. Come on De Portivo!' shouted Al.

'Goodbye,' said Luke.

Jack found a free seat near the front of the bus. He sat down, relishing the comfort and warmth of the plush surroundings. He had forgotten all about the football that evening until Al had mentioned it. The United players were probably on a bus just like this, he thought, it was certainly posh enough.

'Only one zit in ear,' said a voice. Jack looked up to see Larry, the bus idiot.

'Hey?' said Jack.

'Only one zit in ear,' repeated Larry. What was he going on about? Jack ran the phrase over in his mind, and then realised there was an empty seat next to him.

'Ah, anyone sitting here,' said Jack. 'No, no one,' he said, reluctantly.

'Cheers, mate,' said Larry, plonking his huge frame down next to Jack, who shuffled in his seat before staring out the window.

Larry was only a year older than Jack, but he could have passed for twenty already. Compared to the rest of the pupils he was a foot taller, a foot wider, and many feet thicker. Larry's family were close and somewhere in their recent past, two of them had got a little too close.

'Storm coming zoon,' said Larry, nudging Jack heavily.

'Right,' said Jack, nodding. He thought about giving him an equally hard nudge back. 'You sure? Looks like it's going to be a lovely evening.'

Larry leaned against him and lowered his already low voice. ''Tis coming.' His square face broke into a wonky-toothed, boss-eyed smile. Jack's first thought was "what kind of lunatic is he?", but when he caught Larry's eyes, a pang of sorrow cut through his heart, followed by a severe tug of guilt.

''Spect you're thinking what kind of lunatic is zat next to 'ee?'

'No, I was... dunno.'

'I smell it, zee – the storm. Tis coming. Better watch fut ree.'

'OK,' said Jack, feeling a little spooked and not understanding what Larry meant.

A hand shot over from the seat behind and ruffled Larry's perfectly parted hair.

'Ay, yer numbskulls,' he said, grabbing the hand and giving it a sharp pull. A small mass behind them thudded against the back of the seat with a yelp of someone being winded. The limp hand slithered back and dropped out of sight.

'Huh, huh, huh.' Larry's muted laugh was accompanied by a crazed grin.

'You great big lump of an ape,' screamed the girl sat behind Jack. 'What d'you do that for?'

'He started it,' said Larry.

A boy sat the other side of Larry poked him in the ribs and he bounced across the isle to deal with him. Jack was relieved to see that it was a play fight with a friend.

It was still bright when the bus pulled in at the bottom of the lane to let the Shillaber children off. They said goodbye to the driver (Mr Squires was on sick leave with accident trauma) and headed up the rough track. A minute later the hazy afternoon sun was swallowed by a dark cloud.

'Not again,' said Jack, thinking back to the weekend.

'What's up with you now?' said Sarah.

'This,' said Jack pointing up. 'Reminds me of what happened last weekend.'

'It's April, isn't it?' said Nigel.

'So?' said Jack.

'You know what they say about April, don't you?'

'No.'

'She's a miserable cow.'

'Pathetic,' said Sarah.

A loud crack split the air and shook the ground.

'Wow-we, what a beauty,' said Nigel, gazing up. 'My ears are ringing. Hey, there was no flash.'

At that precise moment a red flash scythed through the air, blinding them all. It was accompanied by an unearthly stillness. A lazy creaking gathered pace before shuddering into the crack of splitting wood. Jack knew exactly what it was. He blinked furiously, impatient for his vision to return. Then something jumped against his leg and a handful of something powdery was thrown in his face. He cried out but immediately his vision returned.

Wood juddered against wood. Sarah and Nigel were stood still, blinking. Jack pushed Sarah hard and she flew into the hedge, screaming. He jumped and caught a thick branch (actually half the tree), deflecting it from crashing onto his brother's head. The half tree crunched to the road landing all around Nigel, who stood between the V of two thick branches.

When Nigel's vision returned a few seconds later, he found himself surrounded by tree while his sister was sitting in a muddy pothole, cursing her youngest brother who was nowhere to be seen.

'Jack,' shouted Nigel.

'Here,' he said, sticking a hand up through the thin foliage. He was pinned down by several branches. 'I'm OK, just a little... stuck.'

'Why d'you push me into the hedge like that, you divvy?' shouted Sarah. 'I'm stung all up my arm.'

'Oh, assume it was me why don't you?' said Jack.

'You were between me and Nigel,' she said.

Jack couldn't think of a smart reply. 'It was an accident. I couldn't see what I was doing,' he said, struggling to free himself.

'Yeah, right.'

'No, don't thank me. If I hadn't *accidentally* pushed you, you may have been brained by this whacking great thing,' said Jack, snapping a twig.

'Awesome,' whispered Nigel. 'What on earth just happened? One minute, fine afternoon, sunny weather, the next – black sky and red lightning bolts. Didn't realise God hated us that much.'

'Crikey!' said Jack, 'Larry said there was a storm coming. He said he could smell it!'

'You what? That inbreed,' said Nigel.

'He's not inbred,' snapped Sarah. 'They weren't first cousins, were they?'

'Bit defensive, not your new boyfriend, is he?' said Nigel.

'Very funny, idiot,' she replied. 'Look, I think we'd better get back. You're bleeding, Nigel.'

'Bleeding what?' he said, then realised the side of his head was stinging. He reached up to find his hair was sticky with blood. 'Oh, bloody head.'

Jack snapped another thin branch. 'And he warned me about the tree. That's just too freaky,' he said.

The rumble of the tractor caught their attention. It was their dad, a concerned look on his face. He pulled up in front of the tree and dropped the revs before climbing down. 'What on earth happened here?'

'Bolt of lightning hit the tree, right as we were walking under it,' said Nigel.

'Look at your bloody head. It's all accidents with you lot lately. I seen the flash from the house, what were you under the tree for?' he said, annoyed. 'You know better than that.'

'But there wasn't any warning,' said Sarah. 'It came from out of nowhere.'

'Poor old thing,' he said, kicking one of the branches. He went to the tractor and unhooked a long chain. 'Here, Jack, take this and feed it through a few branches – better we drag it back to the yard, out the way.'

A few minutes later the children were all back at the house, changing out of their school uniforms. Their mum was busy preparing the evening meal. They were meant to do homework before tea, which allowed them to watch some TV after, as long as something good was on. Often, their version of good and their parents' version of good were wildly different.

Jack took the walkabout phone and slipped out into the garden and dialled Al's number.

'Hello, Mrs Fry, can I speak to Al? Please.' He waited a few seconds. 'Al?'

'No, it's the Queen of Sheba. Yeah, what's up? Last minute bet on the footy?'

'No, the weirdest thing just happened...' Jack told Al all about what Gary had said and the incident in the lane.

'What d'you think?' said Al.

'Dunno. Call me paranoid, but it felt like it was directed at me.'

'What? You're paranoid.'

'Maybe I've done something wrong. Maybe it was that Mr Finger bloke – some kind of warning, trying to keep me on my toes.'

'Why would he do something like that after giving you your powers in the first place?'

'I dunno. You know what else, I swear there was something or someone else there. Something was thrown in my face – that's what made my vision come back so quick.'

'Yeah, that does sound weird.'

'Anyway, better go, we're about to eat, then watch the game. Five – nil, I reckon.'

'Dream on. Right, see you.'

'Cheers.'

After dinner, Nigel and Jack asked their parents if they could watch the match and were granted permission.

Kick off. Not much happened for the first fifteen minutes, then Beckham was recklessly tackled by the Argentinean, Pedro Duscher. Beckham limped off. On came super sub Ole Gunar Solskjaer, who scored within a couple minutes.

Van Nistelrooy had a shot deflected before Solskjaer netted his second, 2–1. Scaloni was dismissed for dissent, then Duscher followed him after a second yellow card. Giggs wiggled his Welsh wizard legs to make it 3–1. Deportivo scored a lucky second, but it was all over, 3–2.

Then, a shock. A suspected broken bone in Beckham's foot. The TV wasted no time in condemning England's chances at the World Cup without Beckham. How bad was his foot? Would he recover in time to face Sweden on 2nd June? How many haircuts would he have while convalescing? Would there ever be a bigger story?

12

A Huge Problem

Jack was alone in school, standing outside the headmaster's office by the Old Hall. It was so quiet he was sure he could hear the goose bumps rising all over his body. He wondered what time it was, as the light was thin and vague. It couldn't be bothered to be bright morning sunshine and certainly wasn't going to attempt afternoon haze – light was being lazy.

'Hello,' he yelled, his voice bouncing off every surface. 'Am I alone?' Nothing but more echoes. 'Spat-u-lars,' he shouted, followed by, 'The-Head-mas-ter-is-a-loony,' to the tune of a famous football chant. 'Where is everyone?'

A massive boulder of granite stood in the middle of the hall like some sort of modern art exhibition. It was approximately three metres tall and the same in diameter. Walking slowly towards it, Jack had the unnerving feeling he was being watched.

The rock was warm to his touch and reminded him of the rough stones buried like dirty icebergs on the Brown Willy side of Roughtor. The texture was like elephant skin, not that he had ever seen it. But what on earth was a massive lump of granite doing in the middle of the Old Hall? As Jack pondered this, a blurred shape darted around the corner of the corridor at the far end of the hall.

'Hey!' he cried. The stone jerked slightly under his hand.

'What the – ?' he said, pulling his hand away sharply. It made the decision to go and find out what the blur was much easier. He jogged across the hall and jumped up the steps, turning into the glass corridor towards the senior end of school. It was empty. Outside, the sky was full of powdery grey clouds.

Again, he saw a shape flash past the end of the corridor. This time, he sprinted straight down, sliding to a stop only to see a figure, a girl maybe, disappear around the next corner.

'Wait!' He pounded down the corridor, skidding around the corner on the polished wooden floor and got the fright of his life. Stood there, calm as anything, was Agnes in her school uniform, pulling an angry face.

'Stop chasing me! You need to go now.'

'What? Where? What's going on?' he said.

'I don't know, just go,' she said, raising a hand to slap him.

Jack woke with a start and immediately put his hand up to his stinging cheek. Apparently, he had been dreaming. But his cheek had definitely just been slapped, yet nothing moved in the bedroom.

The morning gloom was dark and heavy. Even Nigel slept silently in bed and he was aware of no other sound anywhere in the house.

Agnes had slapped him in a dream, but now he had woken with a sore cheek. It all seemed so strange. He examined his pillow with some vague hope that this would explain what had happened but it seemed perfectly normal.

'Weird,' he said aloud. Nigel groaned, wriggled over, snorted a bit then settled back into quiet sleep.

What had the dream meant? A rock in the middle of the Old Hall? Agnes – what had she said? He had to go, but where? Of all the strange things that had happened to Jack over the last few days, this seemed to make less sense than any of them. A chill made him shudder uncontrollably and he realised he was desperate for a pee. Reluctantly, he prised himself out of bed and crept downstairs, gingerly rubbing his sore cheek.

Something was not right but he couldn't quite put his finger on it. Then it hit him, as clearly as Agnes had in the dream. It had hurt. He felt pain. Nothing had hurt him over the last few days until now. It was over. His strength had gone as had he feared. He was back to normal – weak and wimpy. His heart sank and he felt cold and dejected. Just as he had been getting used to the idea, it was gone. A part of him died inside.

What a weird experience it had been. Truly, his eyes had been opened. Life would never be the same again, yet it could have been so much more. That crazy old man, he had got it all wrong. Maybe Jack wasn't the person Mr Finger had thought he was. But to be given a glimpse that he was something different, special, only to have it ripped away, was hard to take.

He flushed the toilet and slipped out into the biting morning air. The cats bolted at the creaking door and a few birds pecking around in the yard flew up into the lightening sky. He welcomed the uncomfortable shivers. Crouching, his back against the side of the house, he began to cry. He sobbed miserably for a couple of minutes, gradually feeling more and more irritated with himself.

'Blinking cry-baby,' he said through gritted teeth. He stood up searching for something to kick. 'Huh,' he mumbled at spying his slippered feet.

Instead, he decided to throw something. At the top of the steps was a lump of coal. He picked it up, and as he tossed it in the air a couple of times his hand blackened. The old barn across the yard made a good target. He aimed for a light-coloured stone in the wall and angrily threw the lump of coal. What happened next both surprised and elated Jack.

The coal shot from his hand like a bullet. He watched it every millimetre of the way as it spun perfectly through the air, leaving a whisper of black dust hanging in its wake. It struck the wall exactly where he aimed and on impact disintegrated with a delightful pop. The grey puff of cloud drifted away, revealing a dark circle on the wall about twenty centimetres wide.

Jack felt like his heart leaped a hundred miles into the air. He was still super-strong. 'Yes,' he shouted, leaping with joy. In his excitement he jumped to the height of the roof. 'Whoops!' he warbled, falling back and landing clumsily on the steps. His head banging against the wall. It didn't hurt, but a small lump of plaster broke off and smashed on the steps. 'Damn,' he said, picking up the pieces and guiltily throwing them over the hedge, behind the goose house. The cats stared with disdain.

He hurried back inside, his spirits soaring, and found his parents eating breakfast.

'Where did you come from?' his mum asked.

'Outside. I came down for a pee and went out for a... breath of fresh air.'

'Oh. Well, wonders will never cease,' she said.

'What've you done to your cheek now?' said his dad.

'Why?'

'It's all red.'

'Oh, that,' said Jack, trying to think of an excuse. 'I was... slapping my cheeks to... wake myself up. Only, I was so tired, I hit myself too hard,' he said, rubbing his face.

'Daft critter,' said his dad, smiling and nodding his head.

'Yeah,' said Jack, casually. He couldn't stop thinking about the dream. It was still odd that someone in a dream could slap him and actually hurt him, but when he was awake, nothing could. Something was very wrong about this. He would have to ask Mr Finger next time he bumped into him.

Mr Shillaber turned on the radio. It was tuned, as always, to Radio Cornwall. What they heard was to change everything they knew as normal. Nothing would ever be the same again for Jack, his family, or indeed anyone in the whole world.

'...emergency. We repeat. Stay away from the Camelford area. Do not attempt to approach the vicinity. Police are at the scene and the Army are on their way. Anyone listening from Camelford is advised to leave the town as quickly as possible. Cornwall is in a state of emergency.'

'Shush now,' said Mr Shillaber. 'What's all this? Poor people, as if they ain't suffered enough.'

'Huh?' said Jack.

'Had their water contaminated, must be several years back now, got sick from it. Terrible 'twas. Whatever this is, must be something bad.'

'Wonder if school's closed?' said Jack.

'Just to repeat,' said the voice on the radio. 'All schools from Launceston to Truro are closed.'

'Yes. Can I go back to bed?' said Jack.

'Don't you want to hear what's going on?' asked his mum.

'No, really tired,' he said, yawning.

'Well OK, but don't stay there too long. I'm sure your father would appreciate a bit of help later.'

'Yeah, no probs. I just need an hour or so.'

'Nighty-night then,' she said, smiling.

Jack had the same feeling in the pit of his stomach as when the school bus had crashed. He knew he had to get to Camelford quickly. Hurrying back upstairs, he passed Nigel and Sarah on their way down.

'No school today,' he said.

'What?' said Nigel.

'Some kind of incident at Camelford. I'm going back to bed, please don't disturb.'

Back in the bedroom, he dressed in a flash and grabbed his balaclava, stuffing it into the large front pocket of his old tracksuit top. He threw on an old coat from under his bed that he had saved to block draughts (shaking it first, in case of spiders). He jumped down from the bedroom window and ran up the lane until clear of the house.

Leaping over the hedge, he quickened his pace, crossing the fields in a north, north-westerly direction. Jack wasn't brilliant at geography but he knew Camelford was somewhere over the top of Brown Willy, so heading to the right of Bolventor was a good start. At this point, he let rip.

Though his legs were a blur, to Jack it was like a light jog. He was running so fast, his eyes watered in the cold air. He had to blink rapidly just to see the ground ahead. Absent-mindedly, he thought about wearing swimming goggles, but they would probably mist up and he would look extremely weird in a balaclava and swimming goggles. There had to be a better way.

The air whistled and swooshed all over and around him. He stumbled and ploughed into the ground, throwing up several large divots, which he quickly replaced. Within seconds he was near the edge of the rough moorland.

The top hedge approached so quickly, Jack could think of only one thing to do – take a running jump. He picked his spot and at take off bent his right knee low like a high jumper, kicking off with as much force as his faltering confidence would allow. For approximately one-point-four seconds, he thought it was a brilliant idea. Within a further one point-six-seconds, he was not so sure.

The freezing air bit into him as he flew up into the sky – ten, twenty, thirty metres, maybe higher. His bowels gurgled uneasily. To be at such altitude with nothing holding him was bad but the thought of hitting the ground really hard was even worse. A nagging doubt in his mind kept suggesting he was about to die a nasty, horrible death.

His stomach lurched at the top of the arcing flight. The momentary weight loss focused all his fear and attention into the long fall to earth. His arms and legs flapped uselessly. What had he been thinking, throwing himself with even mild enthusiasm into such a massive leap.

'No, no, no. Aah –' Jack's scream was cut short as he landed with the kind of sound difficult to describe – part crunch, part crack, with an underlying base of heavy thump.

The more moorish parts of Bodmin Moor are covered in gorse, or furze, as the Cornish say (and would pronounce fuzz). For those unacquainted with this plant, it is an evergreen shrub which has fragrant, yellow flowers and thick green spines instead of leaves. Part of the reason for the odd sound that accompanied Jack's fall was that he landed right in the middle of a massive patch of the stuff.

He was expecting pain and prickles, but to his amazement, neither occurred. It was shock enough hitting the ground, but it was even more shocking to feel absolutely fine. Not a single thorn penetrated his skin.

'Wow,' he said, stunned.

He struggled up and set off, but the watering eyes and rough ground made it impossible to stay on his feet. He spied another launch-pad. He hit it at the same speed as the hedge before and flew up in the same way with slightly more control and a little less fear. It still was uncomfortable and he concentrated so hard on not flapping that he forgot to scream. He landed heavily, crumpling over into himself.

The dual carriageway loomed as Jack donned his balaclava. He crossed the A30 at Palmers Bridge, half a mile down from Jamaica Inn and half a mile above the road. The cars below were like little toys.

Jack landed on all fours – every limb sinking into the soft, marshy earth. He pulled them free, flicked off the dark peaty mud and was quickly up and running. Brown Willy was now in sight. He leaped again and sailed high over the peak of the tor.

'Ye-a-h,' he screamed, hurtling through the freezing air, glad of his coat and balaclava. He realised he was going to land on top of Roughtor which meant he would come down on hard stone. He blinked icy tears away. His landing spot appeared to be a large circular rock to the left of one on the main stack of boulders. Panic rose from his stomach, making his arms flap again, futile though it was.

He screamed and closed his eyes.

Thwack.

Every part of his body bounced on the rock as he tumbled over, ending up facing skyward coughing against the stony dust. Again, he was surprised to find himself unhurt and jumped up quickly. 'Oh no,' he said, turning red with shame – the ancient stone had a gaping crack down its middle. Clumsily he pushed one half trying to close the gap but couldn't get it to stay in place. He ran and leaped away from the scene.

From his aerial vantage point he could see police lights flashing on the outskirts of the town and a mass of people scurrying to and fro like ants from a disturbed nest.

'Blimey!' he yelled into the suffocating air, as he caught sight of the devastation that had been meted out on the town. Several large holes were all that remained where buildings had once stood.

He landed untidily in a field on the outskirts of the town, next to the main road that ran through it. Hopping hurriedly over the hedge he bumped into a sweet old lady hobbling up the road. She was accompanied by a younger woman, probably her daughter.

'Oh, I'm so sorry,' he said quickly.

'Get out of my way, young hooligan,' she snapped, whipping her walking stick up and poking him in his face.

'Ow!' he cried, recoiling with shock, still struggling with the idea that nothing seemed to hurt him.

Through lots of panicked shouting and screaming Jack clearly heard someone scream the word "monster!" which sent a shiver up his spine.

'There. That boy in the balaclava.' A little girl desperately tried to drag her mum towards Jack. She pointed at him, hysterically. 'He was flying through the air. Him, Mum – that boy there.'

Her mother was having none of it. 'Quiet, Emily. Don't be so silly. We have to keep moving.' She dragged her daughter on.

Jack ran to the nearest house, jumping onto the sloped roof like he was skipping up a couple of steps. He landed carefully and peered across the town, ignoring the shocked cries.

All seemed calm and he was wondering what to do when a great crash rocked the whole town. Jack wobbled precariously on his perch. Quickly regaining balance, he saw a dark dusty cloud rising over some half-crushed buildings.

'Oi, you,' shouted an elderly man, his voice undulating musically. 'What on earth d'you think you're doing?'

A large crowd of people had gathered on the road below. They were pointing and staring at him, muttering among themselves. A little startled, he lost balance again and fell, but managed to grab the roof edge and in one swift move, swung himself back up effortlessly. The crowd drew a collective sharp intake of breath.

'There's a great big monster down there, boy,' shouted a grizzled old man. 'No time to be playing up on roofs.'

'I say, you up there. Yes, you,' shouted a tall, horsey woman, her hair clamped in a tight bun. 'Get off my roof. I'll sue you, and that blasted beast.'

Jack did not have a chance to reply to either of them. Another loud crash bellowed from the town. He climbed onto the chimney and sprang away, aiming far down the road that led into town. He sailed over the top of a police car and landed with a stagger.

Ignoring the shouts of a nervous policeman to 'get out of there', he pressed on into the centre of the town. Wrecked cars and debris from broken buildings lay strewn over the road. Curtains twitched anxiously and Jack saw worried faces quickly disappear behind them.

A man limped by, bleeding from a head wound. 'Run, run. It's coming. There'll be no escape – run I tell 'ee.'

Jack continued down the road. Moments later, he rounded the bend into the main stretch of town. Next to the bridge lay a massive boulder covered in dirt and bushes. As he was trying to figure out what it was doing there, it started rolling forward. Then to his horror, a huge head rose up at one end. Accompanying this startling disclosure came a scream so terrible it almost stopped the blood running in Jack's veins. He covered his ears but was transfixed by the colossus standing a mere ten metres before him. It was monstrous – gnarled, ancient, skin like stone, hair matted and filthy. Like the most grotesque homeless person he had ever seen, but it was also a real, live, giant.

With suspicious glee, the massive head turned calmly towards Jack. Muddy water dribbled down its gigantic hairy chest over old festering sores and fresh cuts, sustained from its chaotic rampage of the town.

'Oh cripes,' said Jack, meekly.

A giant. No special effects – a monster giant – alive and apparently taking a little breather from wrecking Camelford. Jack knew several stories about Cornish giants. He grew up knowing Cornwall as the *Land of the Giants*. Well it was true, wasn't it? Here was one to prove it and it appeared as mad and bad as any that he had ever read about.

What could he do? This thing was going to grab him with a huge hand, rip him to pieces and eat him as a light snack. It had probably munched its way through half the town already as far as he knew.

Its stature was difficult to comprehend. The head alone was at least as large as a round silage bale. Grubby ears stuck out at jaunty angles like squashed satellite dishes, ragged bushes of hair sprouting from their centres. Its bloodstained chin rested upon the vast chest (there being little neck between it and the head) giving the creature awkward, uncomfortable movements.

Jack watched as it lowered its silage-bale head and screamed.

A foul gust engulfed him, making him gag. He stared aghast down the beast's throat, its jaw a rotted circle of crumbled teeth and bloodied, swollen gums. It was a violent, terrified roar and it penetrated Jack and strangled his heart. What insanity had driven him to think he could help? This great disgusting hulk that had torn apart half the town was something the police or army were going to have to deal with.

Slowly, he took a couple of small steps backwards – no sudden moves. It was hot under the balaclava and he desperately wanted to remove it, but he feared any change in his appearance may upset the creature, provoking an attack.

On Jack's third step back, his heel came down on a round stone. His leg shot forward, the other crumpled and he fell flat on his back. The crazed beast jerked sharply to its feet, exposing its full height, and the enormity of Jack's predicament.

Not only was this creature massive – thirty metres or more (it would have stood taller had it not been bent over and hunch-backed), but it was naked. Jack found this unbelievably shocking. It was bad enough that such a monster existed in the first place but it seemed incredibly unfair that the thing should also be unclothed. How embarrassing. What a ridiculous situation, thought Jack, to spend the last few seconds of his life in such a way.

As he lay with fear flooding his entire being, a dirty, great, smelly foot smashed down on him, consigning him to darkness.

13

Still a Huge Problem

Jack could hardly breathe. Everything around him was black and stinky. His hands were pinned by his shoulders, his palms facing upward. Amazingly, he was still alive and to his great surprise, was in no pain. A low, mumbling sound crescendoed into another great scream erupting from his captor (though thankfully muffled by the foot crushing him into the ground). It was time to act.

He pushed with all his might and incredibly the foot relented. A circle of light broke around Jack as he clambered to his feet. Standing upright with arms aloft, holding the huge foot, he could hardly believe what was happening. Another roar bellowed out and the giant exerted pressure once more. Jack braced himself and found that, without too much trouble, he could withstand this. It gave Jack heart and new hope that all was not lost.

Then a monstrous hand swooped down, grabbing him tightly. Before he could react, he was discarded with a powerful throw. Several knocks and bumps later, he landed in darkened silence.

Slowly, his eyes grew accustomed to the gloom. He was on the floor of a pub. A trail of broken chairs and tables led back to a bright, Jack-sized hole in the wall.

'Weird,' he said.

'Get off me drink. Who's in here? Away ya devils...' mumbled an old man in the corner, oblivious to the destruction surrounding him. He grunted, took a gulp from his pint and fell back to sleep.

Jack sprang to his feet and ran outside. The creature was

waiting for him and threw a huge lump of rubble. Jack jumped, somersaulted and landed on his back with a thud. A boulder-like fist swung down at him. He rolled quickly and the fist struck the tarmac with a dull thump. Jack grabbed the index finger and pulled it back with all his might – it broke with a sickening crunch and the giant screamed in agony. The injury only served to antagonise his opponent, who now seemed more frenzied than before, unleashing a series of pounding blows. Jack dodged the first two, only to be caught by the third, which flattened and caught him fast.

As the fist lifted, Jack instinctively grabbed it. Up he went, clutching the hand awkwardly. The giant didn't even notice; he was so set on raining down blow after blow. As the giant's hand passed its head, Jack let go and dropped onto the matted hair, scrambling down to the shoulder. The giant was yet to realise it had lost its opponent. Meanwhile, it dawned on Jack that he didn't have a clue what he was going to do next. He felt exposed and rather stupid. The beast finally saw it was hitting nothing but ground and stood as upright as possible. Jack grabbed a particularly grungy clump of sticky, sour-smelling hair and hung on as he momentarily lost his footing.

A jerk of its head and Jack was face to body with his foe. A sorrowful flicker in its bloodshot eyes was quickly replaced with pure rage. What could Jack do? The first thing he thought of – he kicked the drool-covered chin with all his might.

As he fell from the hairy shoulder a huge glob of phlegmy blood erupted from the vile, grubby mouth as the giant's head swung violently to the side. Jack landed heavily on his side and glanced up to see the giant spinning clumsily on the spot before collapsing in a thunderous heap. As quickly as he could, Jack got back on his feet and ran over to its head to check for signs of life. He approached cautiously. All was quiet except his own heavy breaths.

Just as he was beginning to feel the fight might be over, a miserable football-sized eye flicked open. The pupil dilated menacingly. As Jack backed away, the giant coughed a stuttering cough and flung a swinging crane of an arm over, catching Jack in his hand. Another violent cry filled the air and Jack had the feeling his life would soon be over. He was drawn towards its mouth which opened, preparing to bite.

The stench was unbelievable. If Jack wasn't so set on living, he probably would have fainted there and then and been gobbled up. Instead, he frantically pulled his right arm free and punched at the one mouldy, brown front tooth as hard as he could. It cracked off like a splitting tree and shot down the creature's throat. Choking and wailing, the monster dropped Jack, who ran. The giant rolled away but a flailing arm caught Jack unawares, knocking him high into the air.

The world blurred – sky, ground, sky, ground, sky! He smashed through a window in a storm of shattered glass and wood, slamming upside down into an old oak wardrobe. It bounced off the wall behind it then fell forward, crashing to the floor with Jack inside it.

Silence.

He broke through the back of the wrecked cupboard and struggled to his feet.

'Hello,' said a voice, brightly.

'Huh? Ag –' Jack almost said her name. 'Er, ag gotta go.'

Standing either side of the broken window, were Agnes and an old lady.

'Pardon?' said Agnes.

'Ah gotta go,' he said in a deeper voice, sounding much like Mr Bean.

'We've been watching you from here – fighting that monster. What are you?' she asked.

'What?' he said, slipping from his deep voice.

'Agnes, no,' said the old woman, quite fearfully.

'I'm sure it's OK, Gran. I think it's on our side. It's, I mean he's, not doing that well but at least he's trying. You're not going to hurt us, are you?'

'Uh uh,' he said, now sounding like Scooby-Doo. Jack was dumbstruck. He felt silly and embarrassed, but at least his balaclava prevented her from recognising him.

'Well I think you should get back out there. That thing sounds like it's still on the rampage.'

It was true. Now she mentioned it, he could hear distant rumbling and crashing as buildings were torn apart.

He affected his deep voice once more. 'I might not be able to stop it; it's really big and strong. I'm just too small.'

'May I make a suggestion?' said Agnes.

'Uh uh.' Jack scolded himself internally for repeating the Scooby voice.

Agnes laughed. 'Well, whenever I've had problems with big bullies, I find, excuse me, Gran, but in the circumstances I hope you understand, that a good hard kick between the legs works really well.'

'Agnes!' protested her Gran, but at that moment the creature let out another terrifying noise which made them all shudder. She turned back to Jack and said, 'Yes, young man, go kick it in the goolies!'

'Gran!'

'Sounds a bit tricky but I'll see what I can do,' he said, back in his deep voice. He leaped out the window and ran back down the road.

The giant had crashed and bashed itself halfway up the hill that ran out of town and was standing in the ruins of the art centre, which five minutes previously had been a beautiful building with old oak beams. They now lay about like over-sized match-sticks.

Jack approached, picking up a couple of loose stones from the road. He had been thinking back to his coal throwing – how hard and accurate it had been. He was still unsure about kicking the thing between its legs. The problem was that he did not possess the size of foot required to deliver a big enough blow.

He ran past the small car park that separated the arts centre from the next house. The remains of a flattened car lay on its side blocking the exit.

Jack took aim with one of the rocks, pitching it as hard as he could at the creature's forehead. It struck and shattered leaving a red mark and a very irritated giant, which screamed a bloodcur-dling scream and turned angrily towards Jack.

'Oh heck.' Jack rushed forward guiltily, launching the second rock at his enemy's nether-region. The giant grabbed an oak beam and blocked the projectile (which buried itself in the wood, such was the force of the throw), then swung it wildly at Jack who jumped in the nick of time. The weapon whipped under him and crashed into the car park wall. He landed and took a couple of strides forward before the giant's foot tore through the crumbling remains of the arts centre and booted Jack through the air. He thudded through the wall of a house, beneath the chimney stack, bouncing off the ceiling and landing on a Spiderman duvet. Luckily, no one was under it. He scrambled off the bed and peered down through the large hole. As he leaned against the wall it gave way and the whole of the chimney stack toppled off.

The next few seconds happened in slow motion for Jack. The lump of broken house landed on the end of one of the oak beams. Just before this, the giant had climbed out of the art centre building and was standing, hunched and bellowing in the car park. The beam lay across the wreck of the car. The resulting lever action of chimney on beam sent the opposite end shooting up, right between the legs of the poor giant. It was an agonising thud that made Jack wince with empathy.

The giant's blood-red eyes closed in unimaginable pain and it fainted as it stood there within the destruction it created. Swaying first one way, then the other, it fell backwards, its head striking the ground with a mortal blow.

Jack had never witnessed death but his instincts recognised it immediately. It was strange but in death the giant appeared more human than ever before. Jack's throat swelled as he tried to stop the tears from coming. His head felt like it was going to burst. A second ago the creature was trying to kill him and now he was crying over its death.

It even appeared smaller from his high vantage point. He stared in disbelief – it was smaller. It was shrinking! Jack dropped down into the car park and ran over to the now almost man-sized man. Drawing close, he could hear what he presumed must be muscles and bones readjusting to their original sizes – a horrible squelching, crunching sound that made him feel queasy.

The old man stirred and slowly opened his eyes. They were sad and grey, and it broke Jack's heart to see this feeble man stretched before him, dying.

'I'm sorry,' said Jack, pulling off his balaclava, 'I didn't –'

The old man rolled his head from side to side and whispered. 'No. I am sorry.'

Jack could hold his tears no more. He took the old man's frail hand and held it tightly, not knowing what else to do. 'Maybe we can save you,' he said, through the lump in his throat. To his surprise, the old man smiled.

'You already have.' His eyes closed and the hand holding Jack's became limp and lifeless. Jack blinked and several teardrops fell onto their clenched hands.

Anger surged through Jack. 'No! This isn't right. This is –'

He had killed an old man, when all he was trying to do was help. He was so angry, he didn't want to cry. Wiping his eyes, he checked that no-one was watching.

'Sorry, old man.' He carefully placed the hand down and walked over to the far side of the car park, jumped down into the field and ran to the nearest clump of trees. Finally he stopped and, leaning back against a tall, thin tree, tried to gather his muddled thoughts.

'No!' he shouted, kicking back hard. The tree shook violently. He heard what sounded like a scream above him, seemingly getting louder. As he glanced up, a squirrel fell into his arms. It happened so quickly, he had already caught it before he realised what it was. His first thought was that he had never seen a squirrel fall out of a tree. His second was that it was behaving awfully tamely for a squirrel – just trying to right itself while being held in his arms.

On closer inspection it seemed upset. It was surprisingly haggard for a squirrel, not exactly bright-eyed and bushy-tailed at all. To complete the shock, it started unbuttoning its chest and then took off its head.

'Well thanks a lot you gangler, you almost killed me!'

'What?'

'*What?*' mimicked the beautiful, tiny person held in his arms. 'If you had half a brain you'd be dangerous.'

'Oh, moron. I kicked the tree, didn't I? Sorry.'

'You'll be sorry soon, mate.'

'Excuse me, but who are you? In fact, what are you?'

The thing dropped to the ground and started folding up the squirrel suit. 'Name's Pixash. I'm a piskie, not a pixie, not a faerie, not a spriggan or a knocker – a piskie. Got that?'

'Yeah, think so.'

'Good, ignorant twerp.'

'I'm Jack.'

'Yes, I know who you are. What d'you think I'm doing out here? Bird watching?'

'Well, I don't know. What are you doing? There's no need to be so nasty. And what's a gangler?'

'Oh, hark at the long and streaky. Is the lickle human a bit upset?'

Jack didn't know what to do with the feelings inside and this Pixash thing was not helping. He sighed angrily and turned away.

'Oh, for the love of Uther,' muttered Pixash. 'Well 'tis a good job you caught me, could've injured myself real bad. You'd have been in trouble then, you stupid sheep tick.'

'Sorry, OK? I'm just... what happened over there.' He pointed back towards the town. 'That old man's dead because *I* killed him.' Jack slumped down against the tree, his head in his hands, 'What's going on? What was all that about?'

'Oh here we go, "poor little me". You're so petty – only interested in what irks you lot.'

'No but, well, but. Oh, I don't know anything.' Jack sighed again and flopped flat on his back staring up at the trees.

'Get up, you lazy mazed horsefly!' snarled Pixash, kicking him hard on the ankle. He didn't feel it but could tell it had been a hefty kick from the thump it made and the fact that Pixash stifled a cry of pain.

'Sorry,' said Jack, feebly.

'Never mind your sorry. Get up and get on home before someone sees you, or we'll both be in trouble.'

Reluctantly, Jack forced himself up and started walking. The bad-tempered piskie scurried along in front of him. Arrows of light shot through the canopy above, the early spring leaves lending it a green tinge. What contrast it was being surrounded by such beauty, when only a short distance away there was death and destruction.

After some minutes, they left the cover of trees. Jack was drawn from his daze by the bright light. They were at the edge of a field. Some dull-eyed Devon cows stared, chewing the cud nonchalantly. Beyond the field to the left, Jack saw Roughtor's peak. It was such a beautiful day. An odd cloud or two were propping up the sky but the moor was very inviting. Up there, he would feel much better.

'Thanks, Pixash,' he said, but she had already disappeared.

He hopped over the electric fence and was about to break into a run when a thought entered his mind. Crouching down, he picked a blade of grass, held it by the end and touched it onto the plain wire fence. Nothing. Slowly he moved the grass forward so the wire drew nearer his hand. Normally, he would have felt the pulse of the electric current. Dropping the grass, he grabbed the wire fearing a massive shock but all he felt was the faintest of ticks against his hand.

'Hmm.' He had a quick check, ran a few strides and leaped up onto the side of the moor. Landing comfortably, he glanced about and jumped to the top of the moor and sat on a rock to mull over events.

A thousand thoughts ran through his mind. In a few days he had gone through so much – too much as far as he was concerned. Sometimes he was happy because he had such super-strength, but other times it seemed like a curse.

It was ironic that one of the things he loved about Batman was the fact the Bruce Wayne was (in Jack's opinion) absolutely bonkers. It didn't seem so cool now he was seeing it from Bruce's side. People would think *he* was mad. Happy, sad, happy, sad, nutter. And what would happen if someone found out that it was him going around being all super?

'Why didn't Fynn tell me it would be like this?' he said.

'Thought I mentioned it, didn't I?'

'Hells bells!' said Jack with a start. Fynn had appeared from nowhere and was smiling at Jack uncontrollably. The monkish robes had been replaced by shorts and a fleece and he was wearing some smart hiking boots and carrying a backpack.

'No. It's me, Fynn.'

'Yes, I can see it's you, Mr Finger. But why d'you always have to creep up on me like that? You scared the life out of me.'

'I am sorry,' said Fynn, but Jack was not convinced that he absolutely meant it. 'I understand that you're feeling a little... confused?'

'Confused? Just a lot.' Jack got up. 'I think maybe you've got the wrong person. I just don't feel... I don't know.'

Fynn rubbed his chin. He was not good with situations like this. 'Hmm. Jack, you did a very brave thing in Camelford. I can see that it wasn't easy for you. We live in a different time from your...'

'What?' said Jack.

'Oh, nothing,' said Fynn, continuing quickly. 'Several hundred years back, things were done differently in the world. It was a wilder time, there was more... freedom.'

'What does that mean?' said Jack.

Fynn paused and scratched his head through his breathable, thermal-composite woolly hat. 'Ah, now I'm the one who doesn't know,' said Fynn.

Jack had not properly looked at Fynn until now. Though he had seemed so happy at first, Jack thought the lines on Fynn's face seemed more pronounced than the last time they had met. He seemed even older now.

'Nice boots,' said Jack.

Fynn glanced down at his excellent footwear before continuing. 'Back then, law and order weren't what they are today. If someone or something dangerous was about, then folk would band together and either scare them off, or finish them off.'

'Blimey,' said Jack.

'That's the way it was done. It was right for them times. Now you have laws and people whose job it is to make sure other people abide by them. And of course, punishments for those that break them. It all seems terribly complicated.'

'I'm sorry, Mr Finger, but what are you trying to say?'

'The giant you defeated may have killed several of your fellow humans already, but if you had not stopped it, it would certainly have continued destroying anything and anyone that it came across. You chose to try and stop it, which was a courageous decision on your part and one that gives me hope. But you were unable to best it without killing it, which if I'm right, is why you now feel so terrible now.'

Jack had tears in his eyes. He wiped them and bowed his head. 'Maybe,' he said quietly.

'You must learn to accept your power. Your feelings are right, they serve you well, but I would ask you to try and see this from a different point of view.'

'A different point of view?' said Jack, indignantly.

'The world as you know it has changed,' stressed Fynn. 'But after today, the world as the rest of your race sees it, has also changed, forever. New rules begin. What good are laws against giants?'

'I dunno.' Jack slumped onto a rock. 'But when he was dying – died, he shrunk back to the size of a man and seemed normal again. It was like he'd been possessed. What was all that about?'

'Oh dear. I had not foreseen this.' Fynn joined Jack on the rock. 'Wrath is pure evil. He must have created a monster from a broken man. A cowardly and manipulative act.'

'What? Who is Wrath? What are you talking about?'

Fynn stroked his beard, scratched his neck and stood up slowly, both knees cracking loudly. He circled the rock with a silent sigh. 'Wrath has been the cause of much pain and suffering in this part of the world. He's twisted and evil, capable of anything that causes destruction, misery and death. He's the reason that giant existed.' Another sigh. 'In fact, he's the reason any giants ever existed at all.'

'What?'

'Jack, you know your people gave Cornwall the nickname "Land of the Giants"?'

'Er, yeah.'

'You probably know a few giant stories. I'm sure your parents have read bedtime tales of the like.'

'Well, yes, but –'

'Most of those tales are true, even the very grim ones, I'm afraid.'

Jack didn't know what to say.

'You may not want to believe, but I think you realise it's true.'

This was right. Jack sat listening to Fynn not wanting to believe him, but at the same time, knowing it was real. It made sense. His powers, piskies, giants – everything he had seen and done. He didn't like it, but he did understand.

His brain started racing. So many thoughts, so many questions but finally one clear important one. 'Why me?'

He had asked this before, only this time it was not an open-ended question asked in desperation at the situation he found himself in. This time it was asked with purpose. He knew now that it *was* him and he wanted to know why.

'Jack. Are you asking what I think you're asking?'

Jack nodded slowly. 'Yeah. Yeah, I think I am,' he said, almost reluctantly.

Fynn smiled. 'How do you feel, Jack?'

'I feel OK, Fynn. I think I feel ready.'

14

Worse than the Beast of Bodmin

'For the love of Uther, this is a great day, great day. Where's Golitha now?' Fynn had found a new vitality and was skipping up and down, rubbing his hands and muttering away to himself.

'So, why me?' said Jack.

'It's you,' said Fynn excitedly. 'It's your father, your grandfather, your grandfather's mother and so on and so on. It's your blood, your bones, your DNA, the very molecules that bind your cells. It's every living fibre in your body. You're a freak of nature.'

'Oh thanks a lot – charming.'

'A beautiful freak.'

'Right,' said Jack, still not really convinced.

'Jack. Your cells are basically human but with a slight difference, an anomaly that makes you, with a little help from that concoction you drank, into what you are now. That draught has fused the anomaly and brought out your potential.'

'OK,' said Jack, not understanding what Fynn was babbling on about.

'Your forefather had the same thing. It made him the great warrior he was.'

'Did you trick him into drinking the potion too?'

'No, no, no. He didn't –' Fynn stopped, a frown creasing his brow. 'Jack, I didn't intend to trick you into drinking the – potion, as you call it. I was running out of time. It was my responsibility to ask you, persuade you, but, well – I am sorry. I hope you understand.'

Jack stared at the ground, feeling guilty that he had made Fynn feel bad. 'It's just... a bit scary, I suppose. I don't really know what's happening. I feel – lost.' He rummaged in his pockets, pulled out a dirty old tissue and blew his nose. 'Anyway, what were you going to say about my great, great what's-his-face?'

Fynn smiled at Jack. 'He didn't need his strength boosted.'

'How come?'

'Sounds a bit silly really but giants were smaller back then, easier to deal with, for *some*. A trusty sword and plenty of nous was enough. Wrath wasn't able to make such large, vicious creatures then. The bigger he made them, the stupider they got. But we've been watching Wrath, watching him for hundreds of years. He's got clever, developed new tricks. We thought something like this was going to happen, but we never really knew what he was up to.'

'So what happened back then, with my forefather, this great warrior?'

'Well, like I said, it were hundreds of years back when this whole thing started and we desperately needed help. The world was a different place, as I said, rougher, more isolated.'

'Hang on. Why did it start? Why did this Wrath bloke start making giants?'

'Ah. That's a whole different tale. One I don't think we've time for right now.'

'Why?'

'You'll soon be missed.'

'Oh come on. You can't just say something like that and leave it dangling.'

'Jack, you need to get home. No one must suspect, especially not your family. It is imperative –'

'OK then. Fine. But next time, all right?'

'Well... yes, I – I suppose so.'

'Good. So you were saying, more isolation...'

'Yes. Wrath's monstrous abominations terrorised everyone and every thing, from piskies to humans. Hundreds were slain and thousands lost their homes and livelihoods. We asked for volunteers, spread the word far and wide to all races but we heard nothing. One day, out of the blue, a young boy your age arrived at our settlement. First off we told him to return home to his family but he wouldn't have it. Said they'd been killed by a giant. Told us he wanted to help and wasn't scared, though we all thought he looked terrified.'

'Tell me about it!'

'I am. Why do you ask that?'

'Sorry, just an expression. Carry on.'

Fynn was confused. 'One of our fellows, a young 'un, name of Zenor, tried to remove the boy and a fight broke out. Poor Zenor took a beating that day. And so it was, we took the boy in and he helped us. Did great things. Killed Cormoran just like that. Have you heard of the giant Cormoran?'

'The one who was meant to have built St Michael's Mount? Killed by "Jack the Giant Killer".' Jack suddenly put two and two together and got it. 'No. Are you trying to tell me?...'

Fynn finally said, 'Yes, I am. You are a direct descendant.'

Jack stood open-mouthed. 'No. Uh uh. You must be joking. That can't be true.'

'Search your feelings, Jack. I think you know it's true.' Fynn laughed, 'Oh, listen to me, I sound just like Golitha.'

'What?'

'Oh, nothing. Where were we?'

'You were telling me that I should know it's true.'

'And do you?'

'I don't know. Yeah. No. Does it matter?'

'Well, I suppose not, but it should go some way to explaining why only you could take on this burden of responsibility. You must understand, though you may feel doubtful of your capabilities, you've inherited a natural disposition for this line of work. It's in your blood.'

'What, killing innocent old men?'

'I know it doesn't feel very rewarding for you right now –'

'Not very rewarding? That's putting it mildly.'

'But how would you have felt if you'd stood and watched that monster, created by Wrath, kill your fellow human beings?'

Jack knew Fynn would have an answer. He could never win

this kind of discussion with an adult. Of course he would have felt awful if he had done nothing and people had died, but it didn't make him feel any better. It was hard to accept. He wiped his eyes, wishing it would hurt, but it didn't, which made him even more annoyed.

'Suppose this is where you tell me to watch my anger?' said Jack.

'Well... no.' Fynn studied the young boy before him. 'As long as you understand your anger and can master it, rather than letting it control you, I think you'll be just fine. Why do you ask?'

'Nothing,' said Jack, breaking into a half-smile. He sighed and stood up. 'Guess I should be getting home, before I'm missed.'

'Right. Well, thank you, Jack. We're very proud of what you did today. I'm certain your great-great whatever he was, would also have been proud of you. You've taken your first step into a larger world.'

'Of course I have,' said Jack, smiling reluctantly. He walked off in the direction of home. 'Bye,' he said turning, but Fynn had already disappeared.

Jack wanted to get home as quickly as possible so, checking no one was around, he pulled his balaclava back on and took a couple of huge leaps (landing quite untidily both times) until he was back on the farm.

He trudged down the lane that ran from the highest fields back to the house, kicking small stones as he went, watching out for pieces of flint. It was comforting being back in familiar surroundings. The muddy, rough track was hedged on both sides, making it a perfect place for bilberries (locally known as urts) of which there was an abundance. The birds took most of them, but it was always possible to find enough for a good handful at the right time of the year. And in summer, the abundance of furze filled the lane with fragrant yellow flowers. Jack could hardly believe it when Agnes and Helen had told him (during a discussion they were having about perfume) that furze-scented perfume did not exist. Furze had a much nicer smell than any perfume Jack had ever smelled on a girl.

In places, the furze gave way to tangles of brambles sprouting from between the stony hedges. Their thorny protection was perfect for nesting birds which could be spotted darting in and out with worms or grubs dangling from their beaks.

Jack paused against the yard gate, contemplating what a weird day it had been. All his days seemed strange now, but this one had felt like the hardest so far. He wished he could forget it completely, but doubted he ever would. He kept seeing the old man dying before him, his bruised and bloodied face finally at peace.

'Jack! Jack!'

It was his brother, Nigel, shouting from the front door.

'Coming!' he yelled back, jogging down to the house.

Inside it was silent. He had expected some kind of kerfuffle. Then he heard the TV and realised they were all watching something, it dawned on him what it would be. He took off his coat and stuffed it behind the door in the kitchen, making a mental note to wear a different one if he had to do something similar in the future.

'Look at that. I mean, what on earth? It's unbelievable. I don't believe it,' ranted Nigel.

'Oh no,' said Sarah, wincing.

'It's a hoax, surely,' said their dad.

Jack gawped at the TV in utter disbelief, his stomach doing all kinds of somersaults. There, before his eyes, was some shaky amateur video footage of his fight with the giant. He felt himself turning bright red as prickly sweat broke out on his neck.

'Amazing what tricks they can do these days. Hoax. All computers,' said his dad.

'Looks real enough to me,' said Nigel. 'They're even fuzzing over the giant's giant bits.'

'Nigel, really,' scolded his mum.

Jack watched aghast as he was thrown through the wall of the pub. It was shocking. He couldn't even manage a laugh at the boy-shaped hole he had left.

'Well I never,' said his mum.

'That's it, he's dead,' Sarah said, convinced. 'That must have broken every bone in his body.'

'No —' but Jack caught himself just in time.

'Oh there you are, Jack,' said his mum. 'We were starting to worry. Where've you been? The world's gone mad. There's a giant about. Looks like an April fool, but they're a bit late. We don't know if it's true or not. They're telling us it happened minutes ago, right here in Cornwall, in Camelford. Poor people, as if they haven't suffered enough over the years. Well, come and have a seat.'

Jack was stupefied. The blood drained from his face as he watched himself run out of the pub, have a huge lump of rubble thrown at him, dodge it by jumping and flipping over, only to land on his back and have a series of blows aimed at him. He relived every shocking jolt. 'He'll be fine,' he mumbled.

'What?' gasped Nigel. 'He's getting reamed! My money's on the giant. He's not much of a superboy is he? More like stuper-boy.'

'He looks like he's trying to help,' said their mum.

'Still think it's a hoax,' said their dad.

The footage stopped and they returned to the studio. 'Our exclusive amateur footage captures shots of the giant reeking destruction on Camelford, a town which one would have thought has suffered enough. Eyewitness reports, including members of the military and police confirm the validity of this piece of video. We now go live to Rupert McDougal in Camelford.'

Mr Shillaber tutted in disgust. 'They'd the same film on the other channel a minute ago.'

Rupert McDougal's podgy face filled the screen. 'The footage has been beamed across the world and reaction has been unprecedented. The question most sane people are asking? Is this a hoax?

'Already there is significant police and military presence here and the whole area has been cordoned off. Several people have been taken to hospitals at Truro and Plymouth with minor wounds. Arrangements have been made to house those whose homes have been destroyed. At this point there is still one missing person, but no fatalities have been reported. Fire crews working with the military are searching for the missing man, believed to have last been seen entering "The Hole in the Wall" – the very pub into which our little hero was so violently thrown.

'The Army have placed a no-fly zone over the whole of

Cornwall but before this, we were able to capture footage from a helicopter showing the absolute destructive chaos of earlier events. Events which seemingly prove the existence of a life-form thought to be mere legend – Giants.

'However, this extraordinary incident also seems to prove the existence of something no one could have predicted – a super human, a hero, a child perhaps? It would seem so from height and build, but in stature, also a hero. As I've been walking and talking to residents here on the outskirts of Camelford, we have already heard the nickname *Balaclava Boy*.'

'Unbelievable,' muttered Nigel. 'A real life superhero.'

The helicopter footage was amazing. Camelford was ruined. Several buildings either side of the main through-road were completely flattened.

Jack remained mute as his family exchanged views and theories about it all, but he was finding it hard to pick out anything they said. His vision blurred, he felt oddly light-headed and then everything went reddy-black before his eyes. The next sensation he felt was a little bump on the bum. Vague shapes moved above him and he thought he could hear someone saying "yak".

'Jack,' said his mum. She finally came into focus.

'What?' he asked, vacantly.

'You fainted.'

'Oh.'

'Are you all right, darling? What was it? Maybe we should call the doctor. It wasn't too long ago that you were in hospital.'

'Dunno, I'm OK, Mum, honestly. I feel fine. It was – Maybe I got up too quickly.'

'You were already standing, divvy,' said Nigel helpfully.

'Thank you, Nigel. Come on up now, darling.' She gently helped Jack to his feet.

Jack's mind was foggy. He remembered what had made him faint, but of course, could not explain to his family. It had all happened so quickly. He thought he could help but somewhere along the way his heroic deed turned into a frightening battle of self-preservation and then someone had died. It was the final straw, seeing it all played back on the TV.

'I... I think I'm just a bit hungry, you know? Can I get something to eat?'

'Yes of course. I'll make you a sandwich.'

'Thanks, Mum.'

Jack's gaze reverted to the TV. A piece by piece analysis of the day finished and was followed by a recent history of odd events that were now being linked to the mysterious superhero – Balaclava Boy. It started with the "extraordinary" story of the crashed school bus that mysteriously defied the laws of gravity by not falling from the flyover above the A30 when it appeared about to.

'This is Tanya Hyde. She was on the bus at the time. Tell us what happened that morning.'

'We was just about at school and there was a loud bang and the bus just crashed over on its side. We was thrown all over the place. Lots of screeching and stuff. Then it all went silent and we was swaying up and down and up and down and up and down.' She paused, looking like she was about to be sick. 'Then more crying and screaming and then suddenly something proper grabbed hold of the bus – you could feel it, like. Then we was yanked back across the road. We was trying to get out by then – we was all over the place, all confused, like, so you couldn't tell what was going on but I bet it was him or her or it.'

'Incredible story. Thank you, Tanya.'

The phone rang and was ignored by all except Nigel, who reluctantly went to answer it. After some brief mumbling in the kitchen he returned. 'Jack, it's one of your pathetic little mates.'

'Which one?'

'Dunno, didn't say.'

Jack was relieved that he didn't have to watch any more of himself for a minute.

'Hello.'

'Crikey, Jack, you've been busy. You should've called. Have you seen the news? What was it like? I can hardly believe it. You're so jammy. It must be so cool. Come on, tell all.'

'Al?'

'Yeah?'

'Just checking.'

'Well?'

'I can't say anything now, can I?'

'Why not?'

'Well my family's just next door watching it all.'

'Well, I'll ask and you can give one word replies. Did it hurt?'

'No.'

'Was it scary?'

'Yes and no.'

'What's that suppose to mean?'

'I was pretty scared but to get there so quick I had to do these massive leaps, so I was really on a rush.'

'Can't hear you – speak up.'

'Leaps!'

'How far?'

'A mile, mile and half, don't know really.'

'No way! Flipping heck. And when it chucked you through the wall?'

'Really weird but didn't hurt.'

'What happened at the end when you, you know...'

'What, killed it?'

'Yeah.'

The scene flashed through Jack's head again. 'Horrible.'

'Oh cripes, I gotta go,' said Al. 'You're gonna have to tell us all about it tomorrow. It was pretty cool, Jack. Hey – Jack the Giant Killer. How mad is that? Cheers.'

'Bye,' said Jack, so upset he felt sick. He wandered back into the sitting room where the news was still talking about him and the giant. The presenter announced that due to the events of the day *EastEnders* would follow the extended news.

They seemed to be speaking to hundreds of people about every single detail of what had happened. Every weirdo who had ever written a history book that mentioned giants was interviewed. Scientists discussed the physics of the events. They even had an interview with the UK's leading comic book writer about super-hero powers. The Shillabers sat in silent wonder.

'Think I may go upstairs and do some homework,' said Jack.

'What?' said the whole of his family.

'Are you mental, Jack? Look at this. Do you realise what happened today?' said his brother, astounded that Jack could even consider leaving the TV. 'Giants exist. They're real. It's not all myths and legend. But guess what? As if that weren't enough, it's OK, because there's a ready-made superhero out there to fight them! It doesn't get much more amazing than this, does it? And you of all people, who are into this stuff more than anyone else I know, you want to go and do homework. You're bonkers.'

Jack thought about it for a second. It would be a bit odd if he, a twelve-year-old boy who was obsessed with all things super-heroic, disappeared when something he had always dreamed of was actually happening. His family might get suspicious. He decided to stay and show a bit more enthusiasm.

After several more "exclusive" reports (that were the same on every channel) the media finally seemed to run out of things to say.

'Blinking ridiculous,' said Mr Shillaber.

'What is?' asked his wife.

'All this "exclusive this" and "exclusive that", "our reporter first on the scene", "our helicopter first in the sky". Meant to be news, not a ruddy ratings war.'

'Yes, Dad, we've heard it before,' said Sarah.

'Silly blinkers,' he said.

'I think, just for once, you should try to get past that and let yourself be amazed by the fact that giants are real,' said Sarah, raising her voice. 'And also it appears that there's a superhero in the world!'

'Whatever are they going to do?' said Mrs Shillaber.

'About what?' said Nigel.

'Oh let me see, Nigel – the cost of eggs? The rise in idle chitchat among hairdressers? What do you think? Giants.'

'OK, calm down, Mother,' said Nigel defensively. 'Maybe it was a one-off, some sort of government experiment that went wrong.'

'Nah,' said Jack, sounding vacant. 'There'll be more.'

'How d'you know? Expert on giants all of a sudden are you?' said Sarah.

Jack snapped out from his daze and tried to recall why he had said that. 'Er, well, there's bound to be, isn't there?'

'How come?' said Nigel.

Jack thought for a second. Why was he so convinced there would be more? No answer materialised in his head. Nothing other than the fact that he knew. Or maybe he thought it was just his luck, that there were bound to be more. 'Well, why would there only be one?' he said, hesitantly.

'Why would there be more, dumbo?' said Nigel, flicking Jack's head. 'Anyway, Mother, they said what they were going to do.'

'Did they? I must have missed that bit.'

'The military are going to be on standby in case of more incidents. Police will be on patrol. If you're in Cornwall stay away from Camelford and if you're from anywhere else stay away from Cornwall. And report anyone over seven foot tall.'

'What?'

'Joking.'

'It's going to be horrible from now on,' said Nigel.

'Huh?' said Jack.

'Look,' said Nigel, 'reporters, news teams, support crews, the military, newspapers, police, all sorts of emmets, all right here in Cornwall. It'll be worse than the *Beast of Bodmin* time. That was only a small story, this one's huge – in fact it's giant.'

'Didn't you listen to the headmaster the other day?' said Sarah. 'Remember he asked that everyone stop calling the non-Cornish pupils emmets. It's only meant to be tourists that are known as emmets.'

'Well he would say that, wouldn't he?' said Nigel.

'Why?' said Sarah.

'He's an emmet.'

Sarah tutted and rolled her eyes before getting up and heading upstairs.

'Do you think,' said Jack, as calmly as he could, 'they'll try and find out who that child is?'

'Why?' said his mum. 'Do you know who it is?'

'No. No, not at all. How would I know?'

'I think he protests too much,' said Nigel. 'Come on, little brother, what do you know? Tell us.' Nigel attacked Jack with some gorilla-tickling tactics. It was a struggle for Jack to take it when he could have thrown his brother off without any difficulty.

'Aah, ah-aaagh. Get off! I don't know anything.'

'OK, Nigel. Put your brother down,' said their dad. 'Don't think he knows anything, does he?'

Mrs Shillaber hauled herself up from the sofa and turned the TV off. 'Well, whoever he or she is, they must have come from somewhere, and once they find them, who knows what they'll do to them.'

15

Fee Fi Fo Fum

Peep, peep, peep, peep, peeeeep. 'The time is seven o'clock. Now, the national news with David Beckham.'

'De-a Brit-un,' said David, a little shakily, 'Once upon a time there lived a young boy named Jack, who grew up to be the bravest giant killer in the whole land.'

Jack woke from his dream with a start. His heart was beating fast and he was so hot he immediately threw back his blankets. Downstairs, the radio seemed louder than normal. He knew they were old and their hearing was getting worse, but his parents weren't that deaf, yet.

'Widespread panic has hit Cornwall this morning as thousands are trying to flee the county after the incredible events of yesterday when a giant appeared, seemingly from nowhere, and destroyed half the town of Camelford. The monster was stopped when a small figure wearing a balaclava fought and killed it – our very own superhero – the Balaclava Boy.'

Jack shot out of bed, got dressed in seconds and scrambled downstairs.

'What's going on?' he said to his surprised parents.

'Toast if you'd like some,' suggested his mum. 'Good morning Jack, how's your head?'

'Head, what head?' said Jack, sounding confused.

'The one you keep on your shoulders.'

Jack ignored this. 'I mean what's happening with all this panic stuff and giant stuff they're going on about?' he said, pointing at the radio.

'Oh, you mean the news,' said his mum.

'Yes!'

'Well, it seems there are giants about,' she said. 'As you know, one has torn Camelford to pieces and now a lot of people are leaving.'

Another interview started on the radio with a couple who had stopped in a lay-by for refreshments. 'The Fufkins have been on the road since five-thirty this morning,' said the reporter. 'Mrs Fufkin, your reason for leaving?'

'Well, we're in shock. It's just so utterly terrible. We never imagined when we moved down here four years ago that such a thing would ever happen. We own two properties in Polzeath and don't know what we'll do now. Luckily we still have the townhouse in Reading but our poor friends Sienna and Tarquin – their home in Camelford is gone. So awful.'

'Thank you and good riddance, I mean bye, goodbye.' The reporter coughed guiltily and continued. 'And this has been the story we've heard several times this morning – scared people leaving their dream homes, or worse, their wrecked homes, in fear of their lives. Back to you in the studio.'

'Well, what did they expect, 'tis the Land of the Giants,' said Mr Shillaber, smiling to himself.

'Darling, really,' scolded his wife.

The bulletin on the radio continued. 'However, while many are trying to get away this morning, cars and vans in their hundreds have been pouring into Cornwall. Some curious to study the unknown, drawn here in the hope of seeing another giant, others, it would seem, have arrived for their own economic benefit. It has led to major congestion on the A30 and A38 and – hold on, news just coming in – we've heard that within the last few minutes, military road blocks have been set up at all entrances into the county, preventing unnecessary access. The Tamar bridge has been closed for all nonessential travel.'

'Wonder if school's closed,' said Jack, absent-mindedly.

'Afraid not, young man,' said his mum. 'They said a little while ago that although buses may be delayed, schools are still open in all areas except Camelford. I expect they want to maintain the appearance of life continuing as normal.'

All other news was completely neglected except a ten-second mention that Beckham had broken the second metatarsal bone in his right foot and may miss England's crucial opening game of the World Cup against Sweden. Everything else was about the giant and the Balaclava Boy. The TV was the same, no other news existed. It was an endless stream of footage from Camelford and reports discussing every aspect of what happened. Jack suspected that Beckham could have announced he was giving up football to become a full-time dreamer and still not made the headlines. It was strangely comforting to finally hear the weather report (overcast, with rain later).

'Anyway, Jack,' said his mum, smiling. 'I don't think you should be going to school in your state.'

'Hey? I'm fine, Mum. I've been fine for days. That bump on the head was nothing.'

'It's not that.'

'Well what then?'

'Your trousers and shirt are both on back to front.'

The Shillaber children waited for the bus for over an hour. Twice they almost decided to go home and forget about school, but Jack persuaded his siblings to stay, convincing them that it might be worth the journey alone to see what was going on around the place.

When the bus finally arrived, they were a little surprised to see that it had a military escort – an army truck with a huge battered cab and mottle green canvas behind. The open back revealed two rows of seated soldiers wearing full infantry kit and carrying guns. Their faces were daubed with green and black camouflage paint.

The bus, which was once again a crappy excuse for one, was driven by a serious looking young soldier, also in uniform, but no face-paint. He slammed on the brakes as if marching the bus to a halt. The doors clattered open sloppily.

'Good morning, children!' shouted the soldier. 'Private Privet at your service. Privet, like the bush. I will be your driver today.' He saluted sharply as they warily boarded the bus.

'Someone's taking their job a bit too seriously,' said Nigel, quietly.

'Good morning, Private Privet,' said Sarah, smiling. 'I'm Sarah.' She offered him her hand.

'Morning, ma'am,' he smiled back, shaking her hand vigorously.

'Oh yuck,' said Jack, even more quietly.

Private Privet yanked the gear-stick into reverse and hit the accelerator. The bus jolted back, wheel spinning. Never had a three-point turn been executed so quickly or precisely in the civilian vehicle. When the manoeuvre was complete, the bus shot forward, Private Privet taking it up to warp speed by crunching through the gears at full revs.

The bus was struggling to stay together. It complained bitterly by threatening to fall apart, communicating in a form of sporadic rattles, pleading knocks and the groaning protests of straining metal.

A few minutes later they skidded to a stop in Bolventor. The place was crowded with military vehicles and soldiers. A base had been set up in the playground of the old primary school. Sandbags lined the low wall and inside two massive artillery guns stood ready for action. Three huge tents filled the other side. Behind the middle one, a tall communication tower wobbled in the stiff breeze.

As predicted earlier by the radio weatherman, the day was overcast and chilly. Spits of rain streaked sideways across the grubby windows due to the speed Private Privet hurled the bus around.

The grassy brown and purple of winter was slowly transforming into the green of spring, but to Jack the landscape appeared different for another reason – one he could not explain.

'Crikey!' Jack hopped up and made his way back to where Nigel was sitting. 'Check out the emmets,' he said, pointing at the trail of cars crawling eastbound on the A30. 'We'll never get through that lot.'

'Maybe that's why we've got an escort,' pondered Nigel.

'Didn't realise there were so many.'

'Can't all be emmets. Well, you wouldn't want to be driving to work through all that, it'd be a nightmare.'

'Look. Over there,' said Sarah, who had come forward to sit with her brothers. She was pointing towards Jamaica Inn.

'Bit early for me, thanks,' said Nigel.

'Git. I mean the news crews and reporters, look at them all.'

Vehicles lined the road through Bolventor and more were wedged into the pub's car park. BBC, ITV, Channel 4, CNN, Sky – all present. Each had a news van with satellite dish perched on its roof. Vehicles from several major newspapers were also represented – *The Times, Guardian,* the *Sun.*

'What on earth's that?' said Jack pointing at a shabby estate car wearing a giant pasty (sporting large breasts) on its roof.

'Sadly, it's the *Cornish Sport,*' said Nigel.

'How embarrassing,' said Sarah.

The bus collected a few children in Bolventor and wound its way under the A30 and around to the junction. The army van escorting the school bus turned out to have a siren and flashing light, both of which were switched on as they joined the carriageway. Cars dutifully pulled over to let the convoy of army truck and bus through. It was still a slower journey than normal but quicker than the general public were experiencing.

As the bus crawled up the hill past Palmers Bridge, they saw the lay-by full of vehicles. A huge banner was strung across a van, and in front of it were tables stacked with merchandise.

'Ha ha! Look at that,' said Nigel, pointing. 'Pretty quick work; what does it say?'

'"FEE FI FO FUM",' said Jack. The van was selling tee shirts.

'Look – "Balaclava Boy saves the day!", "Yer be GIANTS!", "Vitty LARGE-UN!". Wonder how they're selling?' said Nigel.

'There's another one,' said Sarah, pointing to a car at the other end of the lay-by. 'They've gone for the more arty approach. Looks like they've used screen-grabs.'

'Blimey,' said Jack. 'Someone's even selling balaclavas.'

As the bus drove by, they heard a man preaching over a PA

system. '...be reborn in the shadow of the wrath of God, for only he can save you now. Heathens, pagans, estate agents! Pray for your lives. Only he who prays shall...'

Across his car hung a banner that read "THE END OF THE WORLD IS NIGH. REPENT BEFORE YE DIE!".

'That's cheery,' said Nigel.

'Look, more shirts,' said Sarah, pointing at ones reading "FIRST BEAST – NOW GIANT", "NO GENTLE GIANT" and "GIANTS R US".

'Must be mental at Camelford,' said Nigel. 'Jack, you all right? You look a bit mazed.'

'Huh?'

'Hello, Earth calling Jack, come in, Jack.'

'Sorry, miles away. Thought I saw someone I know in the crowd.'

As Private Privet thrashed the bus towards school, they passed similar scenes at all lay-bys and large junctions. People were selling all kinds of shirts and memorabilia, while preachers preached, reporters reported and burger vans sold over-priced under-cooked health hazards.

'The whole world's talking about it, Jack,' said Al. The three friends were tucked away in the corner of the cloakroom. 'It was... it was... it was just...'

'Indescribable?' offered Luke.

'Yeah, exactly,' said Al.

'It was scary, that's what it was,' said Jack. 'I thought I was gonna die,' he whispered.

'Actually,' said Luke, 'I thought you were dead when you got thrown through that pub wall.'

'Me too. It went all black for a second. Looking back, it's almost funny now – there was an old bloke asleep in there. When I crashed in, he woke up, had a slurp of his drink, and fell asleep again.'

'But you know, yesterday on the phone you sounded really calm,' said Al.

'Think I was still dazed, I was a bit all over the place.'

'Emotional disturbance is a tricky customer,' said Luke.

'Huh?' said Al, but then continued. 'One thing though, Jack, you didn't really look the part. A dirty old jacket and that mangy balaclava of yours – hardly Captain America, is it?' said Al.

'More like Cruddy Corn-walla,' said Luke.

'Ssh, not so loud. Suppose you think I should prance about in a body-hugging, Lycra sock?' They nodded at him, smiling mischievously. 'No way, I'd freeze to death for a start. What about the rain? Think I should carry an umbrella, do you? I can see the headlines now "Super Umbrella Boy stays dry yet again" – sounds really cool, doesn't it?' said Jack. Luke and Al sniggered.

'But all superheroes have costumes,' said Al. 'It's part of the whole scene, man. You're gonna have to make one, it's your destiny.'

'It's impractical. Let's just say, for argument's sake, that I make a tight-fitting super-suit and wear it all the time, under my normal clothes.'

'OK,' said Al.

'What am I going to do when it comes to PE lessons? There I am changing away and suddenly "Whoops, Sir, I forgot to remove my superhero costume". Not very helpful really.'

'He's got a point,' said Luke, deep in thought. 'Then there's the material, where would you get a pattern from? The sewing... mind you, you wouldn't have to worry about using a thimble. And of course, it would be bound to get damaged, then you would have to repair it, or have a spare. I think he's right, Al. Not practical. You never see Spiderman cross-stitching his hem or changing the bobbin on his sewing machine. And you would probably have to hand-wash it yourself.'

'OK, thanks, Spocky, I get the picture.' Al sighed. 'All right, no costume for our superboy here. We'll just have to stick with the whole balaclava thing.'

'Good,' said Jack, relieved.

Al's face lit up. 'What about iron-on patches for each side of the balaclava?' he said, excitedly. 'Please? A lightning flash or something. Go on, you know you want to.'

'Sounds a bit '\Arry Potter,' said Jack. Al's face fell. 'Maybe then, anything to keep you quiet.'

'Yes. You know it makes sense. I'll find something cool, don't worry. Then I promise, not another word.'

'I am curious, Jack,' said Luke, seriously. 'What happened when it died? The amateur footage did not capture that part.'

'It was really horrible. Poor old man.'

'They are still unable to determine his identity, so they say. We will never hear the truth now though. The military took the body for themselves,' said Luke.

'Fascists. I should have taken him and buried him myself. Damn it.'

'You can't think of everything,' said Al.

'Idiot,' said Jack, bashing his head with his fist.

'Careful, you don't know your own strength, remember,' said Al, grabbing Jack's arm. 'Wouldn't want to end your super career when it's hardly started, especially by smashing in your own skull.'

'He is correct, Jack, beating yourself up could be quite dangerous,' said Luke.

'I know.' Jack smiled, half-heartedly. 'But it just feels so much... I don't feel up to it. I know that old bloke explained why it's me, but... I don't know. What should I do?'

'What do you mean? Listen up, you're a lucky git, that's what you are, Shillaber. You're the biggest jammy git there's ever been,' said Al, with mild irritation. 'You've got this incredible super strength, it's a dream come true for you. Don't know about Luke-o here, but I'm more than a little bit jealous, so don't go complaining about it. Just get on with it or I'll become twisted with envy and turn against you.'

'Hey?' said Jack.

Al tutted and smiled. 'Just kidding – but that's what would happen in the film. Anyway, I've said my piece. Let that be the end of it.'

As Al finished his rant, Agnes and Helen strolled around the corner.

'Hey you lot, where've you been? We been looking all over for you, did you see that on TV yesterday about that superboy thing? Agnes was only out at Camelford and actually met the little freak when he smashed through the window of her Nan's house,' said Helen.

146

'What?' said Luke. 'That topic of conversation that everyone is talking about? The subject which has been on every channel, all day since yesterday morning? The revelation that giants and super-heroes exist? The story that is probably taking up more pages in every newspaper than anything ever has before? No. We don't know what you mean,' he said. 'Ow.'

'You should've known that was coming, Luke,' said Al.

You're a bit quiet, Jack, and a bit red. You all right? said Agnes. 'Thought you loved this kind of hero stuff?'

'Yeah, just thinking, you know.' Jack had forgotten all about seeing Agnes at Camelford, and was reliving it. He felt exposed. Did she know it was him? Had she recognised his voice?

'So what do we think – freak or hero?' said Helen.

'To me, Helen, you'll always be a freak,' said Al. Then after the inevitable kick, 'Ow. That really hurt.'

'Good, it were meant to.'

'You know, that's the difference with girls. I've said it before and I'll say it again. If you've made a harmless little joke at their expense, where a bloke will just pretend to give you a knock or tell you where to go, a girl will kick you really hard in the shins, without a care. Wham. Next. So cold, so calculating, so flipping annoying.'

'Thank you, Professor Fry, for your in-depth analysis on the behaviour of girls – I think the world's a better place because of this day. I shall never kick another boy again... unless he happens to be a useless plank which is actually most of you lot, so maybe I will end up kicking a few after all.' She smiled, scarily.

'I fear you most when you talk like this,' said Luke.

'At least I didn't kick him up the bum,' said Helen, eyeing Al with disdain.

'Jack. Hello in there.' Agnes waved her hand over his glazed face.

'What?' he said. 'Just thinking about the question, freak or hero?'

'And?' said Agnes.

'Dunno, really. What about freaky hero?' he suggested.

The bell went and they gathered their books and bags and headed for registration.

'On a lighter note,' said Jack, beaming. 'Man United three, Deportivo La Coruna two.'

'Yeah, but England minus one, rest of World Cup teams, a hundred and fifty-seven,' said Al.

'It's a real sod that, no Beckham, no way we'll reach the final,' said Jack.

'But we have all learned where the second metatarsal bone is,' said Luke. 'Knowledge of skeletal structure in Britain three, ignorance nil.' Al and Jack exchanged a despairing look.

'Luke Northy's weirdness scale one million, friends concern for his mental health, very large indeed,' said Al.

'Talking of knowledge, gentlemen, I have what I am sure you will find a surprising request,' said Luke.

'Sounds intriguing, carry on,' said Al.

'I would like us to steal into town at lunchtime so we can go to the library for some Internet-based research. I am curious about the physiology of giants.'

'*Steal* into town at lunch, definite surprise. Interest in physi-olop-erly of giants, not a surprise,' said Al.

'Will probably need your first-hand knowledge, Jack,' said Luke.

'And what about me?' said Al.

Luke looked him up and down. 'Cannon fodder. I fear town may be overcrowded with police, army and reporters.'

'Charmed,' sneered Al.

They entered the form room and sat down. Miss Mount was already at her desk, arranging papers.

'Why don't we just go to the computer room here and look?' said Al.

'Too many people around, questions may be asked,' said Luke.

'What about one of your homes?' asked Jack.

'Someone'll be at mine, especially lunchtime,' said Al.

'Mine too,' said Luke. 'And we do not have any notes allowing us to be out.'

'You better watch yourself, Northy,' said Al. 'You're becoming a bit of a rebel.'

'Quiet please, you lot,' called Miss Mount. 'Is everybody

here?' She took the register, not surprised at having a few missing children.

'Now I'm sure you are all aware of what is going on at the moment with regards to all things giant.' She glanced around, nervously. 'The police have been in contact with the school, a small team of officers will take over the deputy head's office. If you have any information you think may help them, I'm sure you'll let them know. I would like to think that no-one from this class has got anything to do with this ghastly business.'

Al smiled at Jack.

'Yes, Al, have you got something to tell us?'

'No, Miss.'

'Well it's not much to be smiling about, is it?' she said, seriously.

'No, Miss.'

'OK, anyone else got anything they'd like to smile about?' she said, her voice getting louder. 'Anyone been fraternising with a thirty-metre colossus?'

'She's losing it,' whispered Al.

'You may be right,' said Jack.

'Miss,' said Luke, firmly. A tense silence followed. Miss Mount was startled, but Luke's intervention had brought her back.

'Yes, Luke?'

'Miss,' repeated Luke, his normal scientific logic replaced by a warmer tone. 'Can you tell us about the soldiers?'

'Oh, yes of course I can Luke. The army has also been speaking to the Head and there will be a small unit of soldiers stationed in the car park. You may also have noticed, those of you who come to school by bus, that they were driven and escorted by soldiers. All these measures are just precautionary, so please don't be alarmed. School will carry on as normal. If anything changes, you'll all be informed straight away. OK, Luke?'

'Yes, Miss, thanks.'

'In case any of you were worried, I have been asked to confirm that the visit of the World Cup trophy is still taking place on Monday.' Enthused cheers briefly filled the room. 'There will be a photo opportunity for each class while it's here, though it has to stay in the special secure cabinet thingy, so don't anyone get any ideas about stealing it.'

'It's the only way England'll get hold of it!' shouted one of the boys at the back.

'Thank you, Stephen.' She gave him a hard stare. 'The full details have been posted on all notice boards around school.'

The bell went for the first lesson and everyone scuttled out, excitedly.

At lunchtime the boys took the safest route they could into town – through the park, then over the hedge into Windmill Lane. This way they could avoid the centre of town and cut into Madford Lane to the library.

On reaching the corner of Madford Lane, curiosity got the better of them. An army Land Rover parked at the end of the High Street was surrounded by a large crowd. They sneaked closer to take a look.

'We may as well go down the High Street and check out what the papers say,' said Al.

'That was not the purpose of this venture,' said Luke. 'What about the soldiers?'

'What about them?' said Al, 'They're not gonna be bothered with some kids out of school without permission. Come on,' he said. 'No one's taking a blind bit of notice of us.'

Luke turned to Jack for the final say. 'Well, we've made it this far,' said Jack, 'why not take a peek?'

They slipped past the soldiers among a crowd of pedestrians and scurried along to the newsagent.

'Look at that.' Al pointed to the front cover of the *Sun*. It was a large screen grab of Jack kicking the giant in the jaw. The moment flashed through Jack's mind.

'Check out those headlines,' said Al. They read "Superboy gives a GIANT walloping!". 'This is well mad,' he said.

Every paper had a different picture of Jack fighting the giant, each with a sensational headline. Inside, were pages upon pages devoted to the story – the mythology of giants, the theorising about super strength, aliens, military weapons for dealing with giants. Every single aspect was covered.

'Look at these,' said Luke, kneeling down by the local papers, which had headlines including "Strong as a mad bull!" and "A new Giant Killer!". 'Oh no,' said Luke holding up a copy of the *Cornish Sport*. The headline read "Man eats pasty while juggling one-armed beaver and cheese!".

'That's almost as bad as last week's "Piskie stole my stuffed squirrel" story,' said Al.

'What?' said Jack.

Generally the stories in the papers were accurate (except the "Man eats pasty while juggling one-armed beaver and cheese!" affair) and carried details of the wrecking of Camelford and the ensuing fight between the giant and the superboy. Plenty of pictures were included of the devastation caused and fuzzy stills from the amateur video footage of the actual fight.

The police had issued a statement regarding the affair: "Though we, the police, congratulate the brave person who fought the giant, we can do nothing but condemn this gross act of vigilante action. It is not only foolhardy and dangerous for this young person to involve themselves in this way, it is dangerous for the general public. Anyone who knows this 'person' should come forward immediately and inform the police".

'Fascists,' said Al.

'So are you happy with the name?' whispered Luke. 'Balaclava Boy?'

'Could've been worse, I suppose.'

Al was starting to fidget. 'OK, think we should vamoose to the library now, don't wanna push our luck,' he said.

'Thought I was meant to be the nervous one?' said Luke.

They headed back up the High Street. The crowd had grown so much they struggled to move and had to dodge in and out among the slow pedestrians. Al saw a closing gap and darted through, only to be confronted by a TV camera. Jack was right behind him and ploughed into the back of him followed by Luke, though being a bit slower he only nudged Jack slightly.

'Hello, boys! You're live on *Kids News Extra*! I'm your host-star Katie Lame! Whadda-ya-say?' she squealed, sounding more like a game-show host than a reporter.

Al was back on his feet and brushing himself off. The three boys found themselves standing in front of a strange woman. She smiled inanely and waved a huge fluffy pink microphone to quieten the expectant crowd that surrounded them.

'Let's start with the basics, OK, boys?' She didn't wait for a reply. 'Let's have your names, whadda-ya-say?' She shoved the microphone under each one's nose in turn.

'Al.'

'Jack.'

'Luke.'

'OK, let's have a cheer for our boys, Al, Jack and Luke – whadda-ya-say?' A pathetic ripple of claps was all the apathetic crowd could manage.

'Gr-e-at!' squealed Katie. 'OK, boys. Now, what school are you from?'

They eyed each other in dismay. 'Launceston College,' said Al.

'Wow! Launceston College, right here in town, that's super cool!' She spoke like an idiot, dressed like an Australian's nightmare, and didn't seem to have a clue what she was doing.

'OK now, boys, what do you think about giants?' The microphone was pointed at Al.

'They're ugly.'

'Ye-a-s! They're ug-er-ly, OK.' Next it was Jack's turn.

'It's pretty grim when they die.'

'Oh, you must be the dark one, hey? Well, yes, it's sad when anyone dies.' She even managed to wail this in a cheery voice. Finally Luke.

'They have an unknown physiology.'

'Yes! They are known to be very physical. OK, boys, what about superheroes, huh? We have one somewhere right here in England –'

'Cornwall!' came a shout from the back of the crowd.

'Whatever,' she snapped. 'So, what do you think about superheroes, Luke?'

'A scientific anomaly.'

'Yes, could be a scientific on-ala-my.' This time, the microphone passed over Jack, straight to Al.

'If one hadn't popped up from nowhere and dealt with that giant, we'd all be in the sh –'

'Sharing their views with us, the children of Launceston!' she shrilled. 'I've been Katie Lame, live for *Kids News Extra*! Did we learn about giants, or whadda-ya-say?'

The camera man lowered his camera and Katie whipped around to face the boys, who were in such shock, they hadn't managed to move. Her taut stony gaze erupted into a smile of flashing teeth. 'You were great, guys, thanks so much.' She leaned over and gave each one a kiss on the cheek, leaving a perfect lip-shaped red mark. 'Now, you better run off back to school. Maybe we'll fly up and do a piece live from there. Wicked.' She started jumping up and down on the spot in excitement.

'Bye,' said Al and pushed Luke and Jack into motion. They glanced back before turning the corner to see Katie, all stupid hair and teeth, waving frantically like a child.

'Unbelievable,' said Luke.

'You're not wrong. Where did they get that nightmare from?' said Al.

'One of those drama schools that churns out crap pop stars and crap presenters,' said Jack. 'Whadda-ya-say?'

'It shouldn't be allowed,' said Al.

'It is part of the dumbing down culture that permeates our terrestrial broadcasting,' said Luke.

'Exactly,' said Al.

'And now we have no time for the library. I will have a trawl on the internet tonight and if I find anything interesting I'll bookmark it and show you tomorrow.'

They headed back to school at speed, entering just before the bell rang for the end of lunch.

The last two lessons of the day went quickly, Religious Studies with Mrs Blessed, followed by History with Mr Swift.

'Phone later about tomorrow,' said Al. 'Afternoon's cool for me. What about you, Luke-o?'

'Afternoon is fine.'

'Yeah, should be OK,' said Jack. 'I'll get in somehow. Got to muck out and stuff first though.'

'You farmer types, it's all work, work, work,' said Al.

They meandered through school, Al and Luke once again accompanying Jack to the bus.

'We could go up the castle on Saturday,' said Al.

'Yeah, haven't been up there for ages,' said Jack.

'I see your executive coach didn't last long,' said Luke, spying the mobile wreck of a bus that awaited Jack.

'Yeah, typical. Everyone's forgotten the crash, now there're giants about.'

'How's it being driven by a soldier?' said Al.

'I think he thinks he's in a battle situation and is driving a high-performance reconnaissance vehicle.'

'Oh dear.'

'Goes by the name Private Privet, "like the bush".'

'As opposed to privet – the many-headed carnivorous daffodil?' said Luke.

'And my sister's fallen in love with him.'

'Poor bugger,' said Al. 'The soldier, that is.'

'Yeah, quite.'

'It looks like it may fall apart at any second,' said Luke, squinting.

'The bus, or their relationship?' said Jack.

'Both, probably,' said Luke.

'OK, see you tomorrow.' Jack got on the bus, saluting Private Privet as he went by, who reciprocated, sternly.

16

A Mucky Business

The Shillabers' was a subsistence farm, meaning they farmed to live and lived to farm. They never made any profit and never went on holiday. These kind of farms tend to have old tractors and sheds that are held up with nothing more than baler twine and moss. Though they would like to move with the times, economic restrictions mean they can only do so at the speed of a slug on crutches.

With always so much to do on the farm, everyone in the family had to muck-in and on Saturday mornings Jack had to muck-out the cow shed where the milking was done. Only one cow was hand-milked for the family's own consumption. She was called Arrabella. A beautiful, big friendly Devon cow with picture-book curved horns.

Jack always mucked-out early so he had plenty of time before *Football Focus*. Even with everything that had gone on over the last few days he was still anxious to find out the latest in-depth news on Beckham's foot. The TV coverage of all things giant and superhero had abated somewhat, as no fresh sightings of either had occurred.

He was busy putting on his wellies when his dad entered the kitchen carrying two gleaming stainless steel buckets, full of fresh warm-smelling milk. The frothy tops were dusted with grass from the hay Arrabella ate as she was milked. They looked like two enormous cappuccinos.

'Ah, there you are, Jack,' said his dad, squeezing by. 'There's quite a build-up out there, been no time this week, hope you're feeling strong.' His dad laughed as he placed the buckets carefully on the sink.

'Think I'll be OK, Dad,' said Jack, smiling.

He crossed the yard at a brisk pace humming the theme from *Grandstand*. The sun was tingling Jack's face and the sky was bright blue. A few puffy white clouds lazed around over Brown Gelly, the tor on the other side of the valley. A choir of blackbirds were warming up and the air was deliciously fresh – the smell of spring, bursting forth with unstoppable energy. Jack drew a deep breath.

His dad had not been lying – he could see a lot of dung to shift. It would be a right old ding-dung of a chore, thought Jack, smiling to himself.

The driveway to the house ran directly in front of the cowsheds. Jack would usually heave the muck over the drive into the gap between it and the hedge of the meadow. It would pile up there until there was enough to fill the muck-spreader, when it would be loaded up to scatter over the fields.

Jack grabbed a prong from behind the shed door and gathered his first forkful. Not noticing how light it was, he drew back and launched the unpleasant cargo into the air. It sailed over the lane. It sailed over the small muck heap. It was several feet above the wall when it sailed over that and was still gaining height when a startled rook was forced to adjust its flight path to avoid a nasty collision. It cried 'Kraaad!' angrily.

Finally, the dung-bomb levelled out, arcing beautifully across the morning sky. On its descent it began breaking up, like some sort of muck meteor, re-entering the atmosphere. It landed with the most satisfyingly fragmented sp-sp-sp splat Jack had ever heard.

'Wow, I'm a super-shit-shifter,' he announced.

Mucking out had never been such fun. Forkful after forkful was thrown out onto the field. The dung flew in every direction possible (except the house). He performed little turns and steps before he let fly each load. A one-arm-only shot was delivered under a raised leg like some kind of trick basketball throw.

In no time at all, he was down to the last fork load. He backed out of the shed door, bent his knees and lowered the prong gently to the ground. He paused checking no-one was watching. With one almighty great effort he drew the prong straight up and over his head. He stood motionless, his eyes closed, enjoying the silence. Then splat... splat... splat, splat.... splat.

He opened his eyes to the piercing sky, a bird circled high above him. He thought how cool it would be if he could actually fly. The bird hardly moved, but seemed to be diving as it was getting bigger every second.

'Is it a bird?' he asked himself. It was coming straight at him. 'Is it a plane?' he pondered. 'Oh no, it's –'

Splat.

Just as he realised that it was not a bird or a plane, it landed right on his head. It was, as he had feared in the split second before impact, a lump of cow dung. He wailed to himself in disgust and embarrassment as he ran to the hose, wiping his face and spitting all the way.

Once cleaned up and inside, Jack had a quick bath before sitting down to watch *Football Focus* (which was half an hour later than normal, due to a documentary about the history of giants). It included a heated discussion about Beckham's foot, a piece about that day's Premiership fixtures and a World Cup feature about England's preparations.

Jack had asked his mum at breakfast about dropping him into Launceston. She had said it depended how busy the roads were. Radio Cornwall had been on all day, for the regular travel bulletin. The general consensus was that the roads were now much quieter, and normal journeys could resume. Anybody who had wanted to leave the county had already done so. It was only entry into Cornwall that was still being strictly controlled.

'What time do you want collecting?' said Jack's mum. 'I'll have to come before I put away the poultry. What time is that curfew they've introduced?'

'Oh yeah, forgot about that.'

'Curfew?' said Nigel as he walked through the kitchen. 'Seven o' clock and it's staying until further notice, the sods. It's the pubs I feel sorry for.'

'Well you shouldn't be going to pubs anyway,' said his mum.

'Mother, how could you possibly think I would go to a pub? I'm under age, after all.'

'Mmm, well, just you remember that.'

'Is five gonna be OK?' said Jack.

'Just about I should think. But if it gets dark, I may have to come a half hour earlier.'

'Deal.'

'And?'

'Oh. Thank you, Mum.' He gave his mum a quick hug and kiss on the cheek. She smiled back and went outside to hang some washing.

17

Castle

'Hello, Mrs Fry.'

'Hello, Jack, how're you? Your head better?'

'Yes thanks, Mrs Fry.'

'Well, don't dawdle out there, come in, me lover.'

'All right?' said Al.

'All right,' said Jack.

Instinctively, they disappeared upstairs.

'Hi, Jack,' said Luke, without looking up from Al's computer.

'What? On top of everything else?' said Al. 'Who?'

'What?' said Luke.

'No, who?' repeated Al.

'Who what?' said Luke, annoyed.

'Who's been hijacked?' said Al.

'No one. I was merely greeting our mutual acquaintance, as in "Hi, Jack".'

'What?' gasped Al. 'Who?'

Luke finally tore himself from the screen, his expressionless face saying it all.

Al smiled. 'Just my little joke.'

'Hilarious,' said Luke.

'So, find out anything of interest?' said Jack.

'Not really. It's all a bit traditional – lots of myths and legends of olde Cornwall,' said Luke. 'Actually, most of them refer to the Cornish name, Kernow. It's mostly descriptions of giants, piskies, spriggans and so on, with tales of who killed what, where and when.'

'Nothing about why they exist then? Or how to deal with them in a hand to finger combat situation?' said Jack.

'Afraid not. Though there is one positive point worth mentioning.'

'Which is?' asked Al.

'It would seem that most giants, though mad, bad and generally no good sorts, were eventually despatched in some way or another,' said Luke.

'Well yeah, Jackie-boy's already dispatched one,' said Al, slapping Jack across the back.

'Ah,' said Luke. 'Here's an article regarding Jack the Giant Killer and his trusty sword, bestowed upon him by the grateful folk from the area around St Michael's Mount.'

'I bet that was a cool sword,' said Jack.

'Yes, it says here it was the finest sword ever made – that its maker placed a charm on it that made it unbreakable.'

'Does it say what happened to it?' said Al.

'Listen to you two – anyone would think you actually believe this stuff,' said Luke, rather patronisingly. 'Apart from the fact that it's not real, it says here that the sword was lost after old Jack's death.'

'Of course it's not true,' said Al. 'We were just humouring you. Anything else?'

'Yes,' said Luke, covering his mouth. 'You smell.'

'Sorry, it just kind of crept out,' said Al.

'Do you think you could make it creep back in?' said Luke.

'So, nothing else then?' said Jack.

'Well, there was one other thing,' said Luke.

'Yeah?' said Jack, hopefully.

'Not quite giant related. A news piece regarding security for the World Cup trophy – FIFA have criticised the authorities here for handing over protection of the cup to a private security company.'

'And?' said Al.

'They are claiming it is practically inviting the criminal fraternity to steal it.'

'Why would they be doing that?' said Al. 'Doesn't make sense.'

'Exactly,' said Luke, thoughtfully. 'I smell a rat and I'm not talking about the one that crawled up your bottom and died. Logic dictates that this is a trap.'

'Who for – the people I overheard in the shed?'

'I don't know, maybe. I mean, how could anyone know that Jack would find out about these crooks? Let alone try to stop them.'

'I think it's just the FA or the police being crap. I think FIFA are right,' said Al. 'Someone was bound to have a go. Just so happens I overheard them.'

'Hmm... unlikely,' pondered Luke.

'Well, I don't think there's any harm in us taking a look, is there?' said Jack. 'If it seems a bit dodgy, we'll let them take it. No skin off our noses.'

'Blimey, some hero you are,' said Al.

'I didn't ask for this,' snapped Jack.

'OK, keep your balaclava on.'

Jack laughed despite himself and took out his balaclava.

'Carry it with me all the time now bit of a pain, really.'

'Looks like it could do with a wash,' said Al. 'Yuck, it stinks.'

'Yeah, could do with a wash but I don't have a spare. This is army grade gear, you can't get one of these in Trago. But it wouldn't hurt to get another.'

'You'd better be careful. It wouldn't surprise me if someone is already monitoring sales of balaclavas, in search for you,' said Luke.

'OK, no need to freak the boy out, Luke,' said Al. 'So – what're we gonna do on Monday night?'

'I think I have a cunning plan,' said Luke. 'How about we organise to camp out in your back garden?'

Al peered out his window, over the garden. 'Yeah, should be fine.'

'Good. That way, we can sneak out into the curfewed streets without your parents noticing.'

'Won't they be a bit suspicious if there's no sign of us out there?' said Jack.

'No, leave that to me,' said Luke. 'Then we have to discreetly make our way up to school. Wear dark clothes. Snacks will be essential and anything else you can think of. Probably best we approach school from the pedestrian bridge walk-way over the A30 – it could be a bit tricky – then simply get up onto the roof. We should be able to sneak all the way along, right up onto the Old Hall.'

'Yeah, that may just work,' said Al.

'And we can see anyone coming from up there,' said Jack.

'We'll have to be extremely careful – they may also use the roof,' said Luke, studiously.

'How do we get up on the roof in the first place?' said Al.

'Jack jumps us up there.'

'Yeah, no problem,' said Jack, nodding.

'I know there's slightly more of me than you, Al, but I think Jack can cope.'

'OK, sorted,' said Al. 'Right, what about heading up the castle for a breath of fresh air?'

'Yeah, all right,' said Jack.

'Absolutely,' said Luke.

They went downstairs and were forced into having a banana and drink of juice by Al's mum before leaving. It was still weird seeing so many police and soldiers on every other corner. They walked slowly, enjoying the sunny day, reaching the North gate entrance to the castle twenty minutes later.

Launceston castle started out as an earthwork fort, created after the Norman Conquest. At that time, the settlement was called Dunheved (or Dunhevet). An existing natural mound already overlooked the whole area, and it was too tempting for the Normans not to build a stronghold on top. There it remained, unaltered until the 12th century, when someone got bored and added an inner keep. In the 13th century, Richard, Earl of Cornwall (younger brother of Henry III) overhauled it completely, rebuilding the edifice in stone. He improved the defences by erecting an outer wall encircling the original mound and had the gatehouses rebuilt. He had three pet beetles.

Today, the castle is run as an English Heritage attraction and you have to pay to get in (well, most people do). The children of

Launceston see the castle more as a place to hang out and be cool. This was no different for Jack and friends.

'All clear?' said Al.

'Yeah, let's go,' said Luke nervously, as he put away his small field binoculars.

An easy scramble over the remains of the gate and they were in.

'You could've hopped over the fence, couldn't you?' Al asked Jack.

'Yeah, bit public for that though.'

'S'pose so.'

'If they spot us, meet back here,' said Jack. 'If there's no time to get over the gate, I'll get us over the fence.'

'Hark at you, rebel,' said Al.

'Perk of the job,' he said.

They scurried around behind the castle, out of sight of the entrance building. Rejoining the main pathway, they soon mingled in with the rest of the (paying) visitors.

A couple of performers were dressed in medieval clothes, sitting in front of a group of children on the castle green. The mums and dads were either lying on the grass a few metres away, or walking the grounds.

Al squinted up at the keep. 'Did you hear, apparently Ed and that lot were up here the other evening and he jumped over the railings and walked right around the top. Can you believe it?'

'Must be mental,' said Jack.

'Hang on, what's going on up there?' said Al.

'Don't look happy, whoever they are,' said Jack.

'Just give me a few seconds, gentlemen,' said Luke, focussing his binoculars. 'I believe it is our sociopath-etic friend, Mr Dunce, and his rodent mate.'

'Hey?' said Al.

'Vermin,' said Jack.

'Vernon,' corrected Al. 'What're they up to?'

'Disagreeing in a rather volatile manner, by the looks of things,' said Luke. 'Oh, hang on. Someone is attempting to reason with Dunce. He obviously doesn't realise what he is dealing with.'

'Woh! What happened there?' said Al, straining his eyes against the bright sky.

'Dunce hit him, square in the jaw. I think he fell back down the steps. That must have really hurt,' said Luke.

'Now?' said Al.

'Dunce has thingy-girl pinned against the railings, he won't let her go. I don't like this at all,' said Luke.

'Where's the man now?' urged Al.

'Disappeared. Jack, what do you think?' said Luke, turning to Jack, but he had vanished.

'Where's he gone to now?' said Al.

'I bet...' Luke raised the binoculars once again. 'Yep. There he is, complete with balaclava.'

'Oh no, what's he think he's doing?'

'Trying to help?' suggested Luke, lowering the binoculars. 'Al, that's the man Dunce hit, coming along the path.' Luke nodded the direction to Al.

The man, dressed in jeans and brown leather jacket, marched along talking into his mobile phone, while holding a bloodstained tissue against his nose. 'Yeah, that's right, the kid's nuts. Punched me right in the nose.' After a short pause he continued. 'Nah. Well, what could I do? Exactly. Nah, believe me I wanted to, but you know what *he* said... Yeah.' He hung up the mobile, clearly irritated. 'One lucky kid,' he said, striding by.

'What was all that about?' said Al.

'Sounded extremely unimpressed and extremely American,' said Luke.

'Hope Jack knows what he's doing. Should I go up and warn him the cops may be on their way?'

'No. In fact, I think it is time you and I made a swift retreat. I am sure Jack will understand – he can look after himself.'

'You reckon?'

'Yes. If the police arrive, they'll want to question everyone in the grounds.'

'Oh yeah, we haven't paid.'

'No,' groaned Luke. 'Someone, like the police, may realise we always hang out with Jack, and put two and two together, and get the Balaclava Boy,' he explained.

'Good point. Let's go.'

They casually made their way around the back of the castle to the North gate, climbed back over and hurried away.

Jack left Luke and Al as soon as he realised what was going on. Although the rational part of his brain tried to convince him to stay, he felt he should go and help. He set off up the wooden steps to the outer keep, trying not to draw any attention to himself. When he reached the keep, he waited until no one was around before dashing up one of the dingy, dead-end staircases. He pulled on his balaclava and jumped back down. As he climbed the unlit stone stairs to the top of the castle, he thought about what he could say, but nothing came to mind. Dunce's raised voiced echoed towards him, sending shivers down his spine.

'I dunno what you're talking about!' yelled Dunce.

'Liar!' screamed Harriet.

'What're you going on about, you stupid cow?'

Harriet did not reply. She was staring at Jack, who had joined them at the top of the inner keep. He had been momentarily distracted by the beautiful view.

'Who're you meant to be?' scoffed Dunce.

'What?' said Jack, startled.

'Get lost, you twerp, I'm talking to me girlfriend.'

'I'm not your girlfriend, moron,' she said and went to slap him. Dunce caught her arm, twisting it behind her back. He pushed her forward over the railings onto the unprotected rim of the keep. She landed in a messy heap and burst into tears.

The top of the keep was about a metre wide. The railings stopped four metres around its circumference. Passed them, it was relatively flat all the way to the flag pole, three metres further on. Beyond that, it was uneven and dangerous, especially considering the twenty metre drop either side.

Jack was confused. He knew he should have stopped Dunce from manhandling Harriet over the railings, but he hadn't been able to move.

'I'm wearing a balaclava,' he said, then realised how stupid he sounded.

'Oo – I'm scared,' said Dunce. 'I'm wearing Gucky boxers.'

'What?' said Jack.

'It's Gucci, thicko,' said Harriet. 'I've told you a thousand times. Gucci, with a "ch", stupid great –'

'Shut it,' shouted Dunce. 'Anyway,' he said, 'I don't care if you're wearing a balaclava or the queen's knickers – either get lost or I'll smash your head in.'

'Let her get back over the railings, Dunce.'

'How d'you know my name? Who the heck are you?'

'No one,' said Jack, taking a bold step forward.

'Are you stupid?' said Harriet, back up on her feet and clinging to the fence. 'He's the boy that fought the giant.'

'Don't call me stupid.' He pointed a threatening finger at her. 'Anyway, I don't see no giants here.'

With surprising speed, Dunce threw a punch into Jack's stomach. Not having to pretend, he stood perfectly upright, flexing his muscles a second before he was hit. Dunce's hand crunched into Jack. 'Argh!' he yelped, wincing and recoiling to comfort his sprained wrist.

Jack felt a surge of pride and joy. 'How was that for you, you dunce?'

'Freak,' panted Dunce.

'You're calling me a freak? You're the stupidest, meanest, thickest little twit in the whole school. Everybody hates you, even those two losers that you force to be your bodyguards. Did I mention that you're stupid?' Jack was enjoying himself incredibly. 'You're a petty-minded, evil little coward. You're scum. No, in fact, you make scum appealing, you sadistic, small-minded, no friends, imbecile.'

Dunce swung his left fist at Jack's head. He ducked, effort-lessly missing the punch. As it whipped over his head, he grabbed Dunce's wrist and bent it down, pulling it hard up behind his shoulder blade.

'Hurts, doesn't it?' said Jack, nastily.

'Argh. You're breaking me arm. Please! Stop. Argh!'

'No,' pleaded Harriet. 'That's enough. Don't break his arm.'

Jack had been so engrossed in a couple of years of built-up revenge he had forgotten she was there. He shivered and let

Dunce's arm drop, pushing him away. Dunce doubled over in pain, trying to rub his left shoulder with his injured right hand.

'Thanks,' said Harriet.

Jack started to climb over the railings to help her back. He was half way there when a fuming Dunce charged, thumping into Jack's side with his shoulder. Unbalanced, Jack fell forward, straight into Harriet. Knocked backwards, she tripped and disappeared over the edge. Jack scrambled to reach her hand but it was too late.

An agonising screamed disappeared with her.

Jack darted to the edge, crouched and let himself roll over it. When the soles of his boots were past the vertical, he pushed away. A chunk of ledge broke off and flew back over the other side of the keep, but it had given Jack the purchase he required.

Harriet was already halfway to the ground, still crying out with the terror of probable death and didn't see Jack shoot passed her.

He twisted his body around to land on his feet, but it didn't work. His bottom hit the ground first. He sprang up but Harriet hit him a microsecond before he was ready. Limbs flailed wildly. He flapped uselessly, trying to support her head before they smacked into the ground. A sickening hollow crack was followed by a dreadful, deathly silence.

'Harriet,' whispered Jack. She was lying on him, a dead weight, her sweet-smelling hair tickling his nose. She gave no reply. Carefully, he untangled himself, making sure her head remained still, afraid she had broken her neck. Footsteps and voices approached.

'Please be alive, Harriet,' he begged, unbending her left leg carefully so she lay flat on her back, legs and arms straight by her side.

They had fallen between the inner and outer keeps, onto the gravel-covered ground. Whichever way he ran, he was likely to meet people.

'Help! Help!' cried Dunce from above. 'He pushed me girlfriend off. He pushed her. He's killed her dead!'

Jack ran. Almost immediately he was confronted by several policemen.

'Hey you – stop there, sonny.'

Jack side-stepped the first with ease, brushed passed the next one, and was confronted with a wall of five more.

'Grab him.'

Without breaking stride, Jack ran up the wall and around them, and down the other side, his momentum and strength preventing him from falling. Their shouts died in their throats.

He reached the keep entrance. Soldiers were racing up the wooden steps towards him, guns at the ready. A crowd of reporters and TV crews were down in the castle grounds, their lenses pointing up at him.

'Let's go up the castle, it'll be fun,' he said, absentmindedly. He was going to have to jump his way out of this.

He ran around the path behind the castle, away from the soldiers. Once there, he hopped down the steep bank and ran to the edge of the grounds as an army vehicle skidded to a halt outside the North gate.

The fence wasn't high and Jack leaped it easily, landing in the wooded area the other side. He ran pell-mell through the trees, ripping off his balaclava and stuffing it into the side pocket of his combat trousers. As the edge of the trees approached, the full horror of what had happened dawned on him. He struggled free of his jacket and sank to the ground, his head throbbing, his throat swollen and tight. He closed his eyes and brought his hand up to rub them, but it was no good. The tears came as harsh relief. He cried, stifling any noise by burying his head in his jacket.

Minutes passed and finally the tears stopped. Checking no one was around, he left the trees and crept down the driveway of the hotel nearby. The air ambulance flew overhead, closely followed by an army helicopter.

'Please let her be OK,' he said.

He walked quickly and was soon back among pedestrians. Heading straight for Al's house, he was relieved to find Luke and Al waiting for him at the end of the street.

'What happened?' said Al. 'We heard sirens and saw the helicopters.'

Jack squeezed his eyes against the tears. 'Nightmare,' he

mumbled. 'I just hope she's alive.'

'Harriet?' said Luke.

'Yeah, there was an – accident. Dunce shoved me in the back. I knocked her off the top.'

'Oh no, Jack. How on earth –'

'I know, I know, OK? I'm so stupid. I'm more dangerous than I am useful.'

'I fear nothing good will come of this,' said Luke.

'She may be fine though,' said Al, trying to be comforting. 'Let's go home and have a cup of tea.'

'Al, none of us drink tea,' said Luke.

'Well maybe now's a good time to start.'

18

Dickie, Dick, Richie and...

The shed was no longer surrounded by a messy tangle of nettles and brambles, for they had been strimmed to smithereens. The small, square windows persisted in being seized shut, but someone had finally managed to clean the green, algae-smeared glass.

The neon strip light had been fixed and now hummed comfortably, illuminating the dusty, damp shed with cold, efficient light. Smoke hung lazily in the stale air like a mini pea-souper. The shelves against the walls remained stacked with rubbish, from old jam jars to rusty, lidless tins and the thin layer of dirty oil still covered everything that wasn't rusting.

Dick had sat alone for a long time in the shed, vaguely pondering events that had led him to his current circumstances. Had he made the right decisions in life? Did he feel morally justified for his petty crimes? Would his fledgling guilt eventually grow into an unstoppable monster that would devour him from the inside out? But most importantly of all, did he have enough fags to last him until the morning?

His chaotic introspection was interrupted by approaching voices. He hauled himself up and peered through the small window. As anticipated, it was Dickie Soul and Richie Smythington-Pole. They were engaged in lively conversation, which was throwing up some rather dramatic miming, including grandiose hand gestures and some beaver-like facial expressions from Dickie Soul.

'...and it took us days to wash off all the mud, but it was such good fun,' said Dickie, without a trace of stutter. 'Oh hello, Mr Hedman, how are you?'

'Yeah, not bad.'

'Good day to you, Mr Hedman,' said Richie.

'All right,' he said.

'Where's our Mr Marole?' asked Dickie, once more, stutter-free.

'He's... he's, uh...'

'Cat got your tongue, Mr Hedman?' said Dickie.

'No, I was just... Forgive me, Mr Soul, but didn't you have a stutter?'

Dickie hooted with laughter. 'Me? A stutter? No, not for a long time. Had it fixed when I was young. When on earth did I mention that?'

'You had your stutter fixed?' said Richie, with gentle charm.

'Yes. Hypnotherapy. Doctor Watt – marvellous chap he was. Went in one minute st-st-stuttering, came out the next – not,' he said, pleased at being able to imitate a stutter so accurately.'

'Well, by Jove,' said Richie.

'You're joking, right?' said Dick.

'No. Do you need some hypnotherapy?' said Dickie.

'Course I bleeding don't!' snarled Dick. 'And you definitely had a stutter last time. I'd stick money on it.'

'Nope, not me.' Dickie smiled a genuine smile and gave a little hooted chuckle.

'You calling me a liar, Mr Soul?' Dick clenched and unclenched his right fist.

'Oh do come on now, Dick,' smarmed Richie. 'We're not going to descend into another frightful melee are we? Surely you can keep a firm grip over your uncouth rage?'

If previously Dick had looked daggers at Richie, he was now looking swords at him. As his mind ran over all the possibilities of the violence he would like to unleash on Richie, his eye began twitching. Dickie noticed that Dick's hands were shaking and decided to intervene.

'Well, never mind that. All in the past, isn't it, gentlemen. Job to do and all that. Now, where is our number four, Mr Marole?'

Dick broke eye contact with Richie and reached for his bottle, feverishly unscrewing the cap and gulping a couple of nervous draughts. 'Agh. Right. Now then, Mr Marole,' he said, wiping his mouth with the back of his sleeve. 'He won't be joining us. My contact informed me, he's been pulled off this job. His services are needed elsewhere.'

'Well, how peculiar,' said Richie, somehow looking down his nose, yet up at Dick (who was considerably taller). 'Did you question what dubious motives lie behind this organisational anarchy?'

'No I didn't. S'not my place to question my contact,' said Dick, getting increasingly irritated. 'He orders – I obey. Got it, you upper class plonker?'

'Calm down please, gentlemen,' said Dickie, his voice rising. 'Remember, the job.' He gave a hoot of nervous laughter.

'Plonker?' questioned Richie, ponderously. 'A stupid or useless person, I believe, or slang for a man's private member. You really could have done much better than that, could you not? For a start, there's idiot... fool, twit, twerp... wally and nit... prat and ding bat, dimwit and dope. You rudely neglect nitwit, clot, half-wit and mug, blockhead, dickhead, dunderhead and ass. For plonker? Tut, tut, tut.

'I can absolve you from dolt and dullard, as you are probably unaware of their existence. Chump – a bit American. Ignoramus – too many syllables, ninny – too effeminate for your common use?

'That leaves us with... numskull, simpleton, dunce, and my personal favourites: nincompoop, moron, imbecile and cretin.' Richie stopped momentarily. Once again looking down his nose, yet up at Dick, with a mixture of loathing and pity. Dick was busy building a steam train of fury and revenge inside himself. Dickie had retreated a step or two, without even realising it.

Richie gazed at Dick, as if he was something particularly revolting found on the bottom of a shoe. 'Herewith, I am finding it difficult to decide if you are simply a moron – IQ between fifty and seventy... or an imbecile, at twenty-five to fifty. Or maybe, you wouldn't even score that.'

Dick punched Richie firmly on the nose. Richie's wobbly face whipped to the side, his mind already unconscious. He collapsed to the floor with a wry, satisfying smile creeping at the corners of his mouth.

'Itchy? Mellow. Misty swimming-in-coal. Richie. Hello. Mr Smythington-Pole, can you hear me?' said Dickie. 'Mr Hedman has left. It's all right. You're just feeling a little groggy.'

'Sailors.'

'Pardon?'

'Sailors.'

'Where?'

'In my purse.'

'There are no sailors, or purse.'

'Oh, my nose. Ow.' Richie blinked several times and lifted a hand to his head, slowly smoothing over his greasy black hair. 'He biffed me, didn't he?' he asked.

'Yes, very much so.'

Dickie handed him a glass of water, which Richie sipped tentatively. 'Yuck! Tap water.'

'I'm afraid that's all there is.'

Richie steadied himself and gently touched his face. 'I do deplore violence but it was understandable in the circumstance. Ow, oh. I was somewhat overtaken by a zealous desire to humiliate the poor man. Agh. I believe it is entirely my own fault.'

'Well, yes, I do believe you did bring it upon yourself. Mr Hedman's not a placid man. And I think his fuse is a very short one.'

'You are correct, my friend. You are certainly correct.' Richie struggled to his feet and sat on one of the frail chairs. Dickie had tended Richie's nose as best he could while Richie was unconscious, but it was noticeably swollen.

'And what of our task?'

'He's left us the final details of the job and our rendezvous time and location. I think you'll be completely satisfied. It may even be an education for us all.'

19

History Lesson

'It's Sunday 14th April, 2002. Three days ago our world changed. A giant walked on this land.' The female newscaster spoke in a serious tone. She wore thick-rimmed spectacles, her hair held neatly in place by an ornate gold clip. 'And it was really big. It wrecked a town, injuring several people. But it was stopped by a brave and courageous young boy – a superhero of our time, but was this a mere trick? A stunt, set up to dupe us all? Is the giant really real?' She paused, smiling excitedly.

'Saturday 13th and the so-called Balaclava Boy appears from nowhere at Launceston castle. Why? We don't know. There are huge crowds of people everywhere. Children play, unaware of the danger. Their parents stroll the grounds, braving dark passages within the ancient keep. Why? We don't know. But it all ends in tragedy when a young girl, Harriet Vermin, sorry, Vernon, is violently thrown from the inner keep by our mysterious superboy in a jealous fit of rage and anger. Why? We don't know. But today we're gonna try and find out.' She threw the spectacles aside, unclipped her hair and swept it free. With a grating squeal she cried, 'I'm your host-star, Katie Lame. This is a *Kids News Extra, Extra*! Shall we do it? Whadda-ya-say?'

Nigel groaned. 'I say you're the stupidest, dumbest, irritating cow that's ever hosted a children's news programme in the whole history of television.'

'Couldn't agree more,' said Jack. 'Lying cow.'

'Well,' said Sarah. 'Why doesn't he just come forward and tell the police what really happened?'

'Doesn't wanna be caught, does he?' said Nigel. 'It's Dunce's fault, anyone with a brain can see that. Come on, Sarah, you can't possibly believe *his* rubbish?'

'Course not, but this Balaclava Boy isn't exactly helping himself, is he?'

'Maybe,' said Jack quietly, 'he doesn't know what to do.'

'Oh, but he knows how to push people off castles?' said Sarah, sarcastically.

'It was Dunce,' snapped Jack.

'How d'you know?' said Sarah.

'Cause he's a bullying little git.'

'You're not seriously siding with Dunce, are you?' said Nigel.

'I'm just trying to put a bit of balance against your judgement, OK?' she said and stormed out.

'Boyfriend trouble I reckon,' said Nigel.

'Didn't think she had one,' said Jack.

'Yeah, that's the trouble.' Nigel turned back to the TV. 'Oh, here we go.'

The program cut to a report recorded earlier in the week in Launceston. Katie Lame was walking while talking to camera. 'We've been in Laun-ces-ton all week talking about giants and we've heard some pretty tall stories – ha ha hee.' She laughed so hard, she snorted like a pig.

'Hate to think what sad losers she interviewed.'

Jack flushed with grim realisation. 'Can't we turn this rubbish over? What else is on?'

'Nothing but cartoons and cookery,' said Nigel.

'Anything's better than this,' said Jack, hopefully.

'I'm quite enjoying how terrible she is.'

'But it's really not that –'

'You. And your pathetic little loser mates. Ha ha hee,' he said, mimicking Katie Lame's laughter.

Jack was already crimson. 'It was an accident. We were down town on Friday and literally ran into her. She said it was live too, lying hag.'

The front door closed and a few seconds later their parents walked in with the Sunday papers.

'You just missed your youngest offspring's TV debut on *Kids News Extra, Extra*! Him and his mates, Tubby an' Beanpole got themselves interviewed about giants. So embarrassing.'

'Jack?' said his mum.

'Yes?' he said innocently.

'When was that?'

He sighed. 'We had to go down town on Friday, Luke had to meet up with his mum and he was scared. He had a note.'

'But you didn't, did you?' she said.

'No.'

'Well make sure you don't do it again,' said his dad. 'Specially with all them soldiers and police around.'

'OK.'

Nigel interrogated his parents about the Sunday papers' headlines, which included several damning the Balaclava Boy as a menace to society. Jack grew more and more disheartened but was slightly relieved to find out that Harriet Vernon was alive and only suffered a broken leg but apparently could not recall what had happened to her. All the papers had blurred photos of the incident.

Jack scoured the story in his parents' paper for a reference to the man Dunce had punched and his heart sank when he found it. The "alleged" witness could not be traced. Not even the *Cornish Sport's* headline – "Balaclava Boy steals prize winning stuffed mole" could bring a smile to his face. He traipsed upstairs to stare dejectedly at the bedroom walls, a burning hatred constricting his throat. Wiping his eyes angrily, he decided to get out.

It was dull outside and he trudged to the field behind the house. Walking aimlessly in circles didn't seem to help either. The ground was soggy from rain the night before and his monkey boots were soon clogged with mud. It suited his dark mood. He scraped some off against the hedge, then slumped against it screaming wildly, but quietly, through gritted teeth. Anger got the better of him and he lashed out at an unfortunate ash tree. It wobbled violently.

He couldn't stop thinking about what had happened at the

castle. The newspapers, TV and radio all seemed to have it in for him. He had only been trying to help, yet all they wrote was a pack of lies. Because of that, the police were now offering a reward for any information that may lead to his capture.

Dunce had told them a preposterous story, yet they believed every word he said. What made it worse was the fact that everyone (including the police) seemed to be ignoring the fact that Dunce had hit someone, though the mysterious man's disappearance had not helped. Of course, Al and Luke could have given helpful evidence about the man. Luke especially thought that he should speak to the police but they had decided it was safer not to, in case anyone linked them.

Jack saw his makeshift Lightsaber on the ground. 'Huh, stupid git.' As he picked it up and whipped it through the air, it reminded him of how simple life had been. He stopped, staring at it, then snapped it in two. 'Don't need that any more.' His dreams of being a superhero now seemed so dumb. 'Superhero? More like superzero. What the hell am I supposed to do now?'

Another wave of gloom rippled through his heart and a couple of tears rolled down his cheeks. He sniffed and picked up a rock, rubbing off the dirt. It sparkled in the dull light as he turned it in his hand. Rolling it into his palm, he clenched his fist and squeezed. It gave in his hand like he was crushing a lump of dry soil. The rough debris fell through his fingers like coarse sand. He squished it into the ground with his boot.

For all his strength, Jack couldn't stop his face from scrunching up as he started crying. It felt like he was always crying now. His embarrassment annoyed him. He hated feeling angry which in turn, made him sad. So he did what he always did when he felt this way – he ran.

He hopped over the gate into the lane and sprinted. It was wet and slippery underfoot but he didn't care, he wanted to fall and hurt himself and the fact that he couldn't irritated him even more. He tripped twice, skidding his hands over the muddy rocks. As suspected, it didn't hurt, but his powers couldn't stop him from getting covered in mud.

Jumping the long stretches of murky puddles gave him a spark of enjoyment. It was fun being able to leap so far without trying. He could be world high jump, triple jump and long jump champion all at once. He could be pole vault champion too without even using a pole.

He slowed, dreaming of the Olympics and winning every event. No, maybe only one event. Could he do it? Could he pretend it was difficult to run so quickly or jump so far? He imagined the gold medal being placed around his neck. No, it would never work. Someone would find out or realise that it was all a sham.

Finally he stopped at the far end of the highest field. Lying back against the hedge, he gazed down the valley. It was beautiful. Behind the clouds was a vibrant neon blue. A strange light flooded the valley. He breathed deeply, the air clean and the smell fragrant and friendly – a mixture of wet grass, fresh earth from the molehills and pine from the trees in the gully separating them from next door. Jack smiled as the wind changed and he got a whiff of fox pee.

A slight movement in the grass caught his eye. Moles. The ground broke and was pushed up a little at a time. New earth was visible through the grass. Jack loved to watch the moles burrowing, even though he knew they were pests. The tunnel edged towards him. It was just over a metre away when the forward movement stopped and a mound of earth began to rise from the field.

'Here it comes,' said Jack, quietly. A pink nose popped out though the soil, whiskers twitching, probing curiously at the fresh air. Slowly, the head emerged, checking it was safe with hidden eyes. The rest of the body followed. It scrambled down over the earth, wriggling impatiently.

'You little beauty,' said Jack, forgetting his misery for a moment.

The mole stopped and raised its head toward him, its black fur matted and wet. It stood up on muddy back feet, brushed itself off with its front paws, unbuttoned itself and out stepped a beautiful woman wearing dark brown trousers and a grass-green top.

'Pixash. What are you doing here?'

'Huh,' she said, grumpily. 'Checking.'

'Checking what?'

'Up on you, long-shanks.' She rubbed her eyes and strode over to Jack kicking him hard on the ankle.

'Ow,' he said, though it didn't actually hurt.

'Golitha will be here shortly, now quit your moaning.' She nodded in disgust and hopped over the hedge. Jack leaned over to say goodbye but she had already disappeared.

'How does she do that?'

'Camouflage.'

Jack jumped with fright. 'What is wrong with people round here?'

'Well, all sorts of things,' said the man in a calm, low voice. 'I think it's the multi-surface cleaning products – makes houses too clean, children don't have a chance to build any tolerance. Why do you ask?'

'What are you going on about?'

'I was answering your question,' he said, politely. 'Excuse me, I am being rather rude.' The old man's dulcet tones were already calming Jack. 'Please, forgive me. My name is Golitha. I am honoured to meet you, Jack.' He reached out to shake Jack's hand. A little apprehensively, Jack accepted. The hand was rough and calloused, but the greeting was full of warmth. The old man was dressed in the same robes Fynn wore the day he had given Jack the potion on Roughtor.

'Where's Fynn?' said Jack.

'He's a little busy, I'm afraid.'

'So, who are you? His boss or something?'

Golitha laughed. 'No, no, no. Well, not exactly. I think you would say that we work together.'

'Who for?'

'Well now, that is an interesting question. I suppose we work for everybody – our people, your people, Miss Pixash's people and so on.'

'Did you help Fynn turn me into a freak?'

'A freak?' said Golitha, shocked.

'That's what everyone thinks.'

'Jack, you are not a freak, no.'

'Tell that to the papers,' he said, his calmness deserting him.

'Did you see what they wrote? Or hear the radio, or see the TV? They think I tried to kill Harriet.'

'In time, they will see that you can help. I believe it's what humans call the media backlash.'

'What?' said Jack, his face indicating he thought Golitha was insane. 'You talk about it like it doesn't matter.'

'Well, if you look at it from a certain point of view, it really doesn't.'

'A certain point of view? Flippin' heck. What's that supposed to mean?'

Golitha held up his hands in defence. 'What these people think of you is irrelevant. Humans have lustful eyes. They seek out the unusual, the amazing – that which is not normal.'

'But –'

'They like tall stories, intrigue,' continued Golitha. 'And some love nothing more than to think the worst of their fellows. But they need your help.' He huffed, half-smiling. 'We all need your help. They don't understand that if you don't help them, they may die.'

Jack was dumbstruck. His mouth moved but no words formed. He sunk to the ground, staring out across the field. 'W-o-h,' he said, flicking a clod of mud from his boot. 'Why is all this happening?' He tried to gather his thoughts but they kept getting jumbled and eventually spilled out into speech. 'I mean, there I was – normal boy, going to school... parents, friends, all that kind of thing. Then I get caught in some weird, freaky weather and some old man gives me a potion, which actually works and now I'm super-strong, extremely confused and in trouble with the police. And the papers think I'm some sort of genetic mutation out to rule the world.' He stared at Golitha with scared eyes, his words coming much quicker. 'They'll find me – that's what they're good at. I'll be locked up, prodded, poked and cut up until they've discovered whatever it is they want so they can use my genes to build an army of mutant psycho-warriors. Now you appear out of thin air and you're named after a local beauty spot. I'm going stark raving bonkers. And now you say everyone's gonna die!' Tears rolled down Jack's flushed cheeks.

Golitha remained calm. 'Well, Jack, maybe I can answer some of your questions.'

'Thanks,' he said, quietly.

'For a start, Golitha Falls are named after me.'

Jack gave a stunted laugh. 'Now why doesn't that surprise me?' he said, wiping away the tears with the palms of his hands.

Golitha smiled. 'Jack, do you remember any of what Fynn spoke to you about?'

'He went on about there being other races that most humans can't see and how we've been really selfish but we're not all bad.' Jack found an old handkerchief in his pocket and blew his nose loudly. 'He told me all about my ancestor, the giant killer. I still find that hard to believe, but I guess it's true.'

'It sounds like Fynn gave you quite a history lesson. I'm not sure there's much else for me to say.'

'He was going to tell me about Wrath, but there wasn't time.'

'Ah, I see.' Golitha frowned. 'Wrath... hmm.'

'I may as well know the whole truth. It might help.'

'Huh, just like *him*.'

'Who?'

'Jack – your ancestor.'

'What was he like?'

'He was a great fighter and became a good friend. You remind me of him when you talk like that. There was a certain melancholy that ran through his bravado. But he overcame that, in time.'

'Well, I hope I live up to what he did. It's just so... I dunno.'

'I think you'll be just fine, Jack.' Golitha smiled warmly.

Jack was feeling calmer again. 'Where did he come from, this Wrath bloke?'

'Oh, he's not really a bloke, as you say. He's one of my people, a Celt. Well, he was. I'm not even sure what he is, now.'

'So what made him do all this stuff – create giants and all?'

'Well now.' Golitha massaged his forehead, as if trying to encourage the memories back. 'You're asking me to go back over two thousand years.'

'I think it'll help.'

The old man nodded. 'Back then, Kernow was a wonderful

place, young and fresh. Don't get me wrong, it was a wild, rough land too, but unspoilt. Covered in woodland. All the races of the earth living together.

My people, the Celts, were considered quite a learned lot. We held positions such as teachers and charmers.'

'Charmers?' said Jack.

'Oh, come now, Jack. You know what I mean. Your father still charms the cows when they get an adder bite, doesn't he?'

'Yeah, but... that's just...'

'Is it now?' said Golitha, knowingly.

Jack managed a half-smile. 'Was it all done with charms back then?'

'Charms and herbs.'

'Weird. So what happened, what went wrong?'

'I'm not sure you could say anything went wrong, as such. It just kind of happened the way it happened. Nature will always take its own course.' He paused, studying the sky. 'I remember that humans started breeding like there was no tomorrow, more than all the rest of us. No one really minded at first, but soon there was so many, they had to start cutting down all the woodland, clearing it out so they could build bigger settlements, farms and so on. That's when the friction grew. They ended up clearing places other races had inhabited for thousands of years.'

'What's that got to do with Wrath?'

'The more humans, the more work for charmers. The human charmers were still learning the art, so were less sought after. Wrath was the best around. He could cure anyone of illness or injury, no matter what race. Was always working on new charms, never stopped improving them.' Golitha reached inside his robe and took out a three legged camping stool. 'Borrowed from Fynn,' he said opening it out and gently lowering himself onto it. 'One day, he went to help a young woman who was giving birth, the daughter of a chief from a settlement near Tintagel. There were... complications. Wrath laid on his hands and began his charms, was there for a long time.'

'Let me guess, she died?'

Golitha nodded. 'Saved the child, but not the girl. The chief couldn't accept it and turned the whole village against Wrath. They took him to the cliffs, bound him and set fire to him.' Golitha bowed his head in disgust.

'Crikey, bit much, wasn't it?'

'Then they pushed him off.'

'What?' said Jack. 'Let me guess – he survived?'

'The thing is,' said Golitha, lowering his voice. 'No one really knows what happened. We never saw Wrath again, there were rumours, sightings, but they were never confirmed. People disappeared if they said too much, but most believe Wrath to be responsible for many a despicable terror over the centuries.'

Jack swallowed hard. 'And the giants?'

'Arrived shortly after his disappearance. Vicious creatures they were, indiscriminate. Killed humans, piskies, spriggans – no one was safe. Plundered the land, ate anything and everything in sight.' Golitha smiled. 'Then Jack arrived.'

'So Wrath blamed everyone, all races, for what happened to him, right?'

'Yes.'

'I remember Fynn told me you'd been trying to find out what Wrath was up to. Two thousand years, though, that's a long time to be waiting to take more revenge,' said Jack.

'The time is short for one so old. It's taken us the same time to figure out what we could do.'

'And all you came up with was me?'

Golitha paused, considering his words. 'I think we made the best possible decision we could have, Jack. You are wise beyond your years, though you may not realise.' Golitha lowered his voice and stared into Jack's eyes. 'Your dreams will take you far and your heart will serve you well. Thoughts can deceive.' He moved a hand to his sternum and spoke, his words slow and clear. 'Trust your instincts.'

For Jack, the world stood still for several minutes. He couldn't move even though a dizzying lightness swirled through him. His senses tingled and danced about his body, everything now seeming more real. He heard a sheep chewing in the next field, the wings of a bird flap high above. A rabbit popped its head out from a hole in the corner of the field. A gust of wind carried the smell of cooking from home. Jack felt his hot breath leave his mouth and knew exactly where it blew.

'Jack?' said Golitha, quietly.

S-something's happened. What was that? They were only words, weren't they? You didn't put a spell on me or anything, did you?'

'No, I was just –'

'But your words, they did something to me, I swear. Everything went – all my senses went mad. That was really weird,' said Jack, rubbing his face.

'Words can be more powerful than any weapon,' said Golitha, pleasantly. He stood up and folded away the camping stool. 'Right, well, you probably smelled your dinner cooking then?'

'Yeah. How did you –'

'My favourite – roast chicken, potatoes and greens. Keep eating your greens, Jack, just like your mother says.'

'Right.'

'Now off you go.'

Jack backed away, nodding absentmindedly. Finally he turned and started to jog. 'Bye!' he shouted, knowing that Golitha had already disappeared.

20

Preparations Begin

'Much as I appreciate that thirteen and a half percent of the land surface of the world is covered by masticated chewing gum, that music's louder in the dark and that ninety percent of people can't pronounce the word siphoni-manxi... siphon-inxma.... siphoni-monkey-nactipus, or whatever it was, I do think we need to discuss what we're gonna do tonight,' said Al.

'Knowledge is not a gift,' said Luke.

'No, but this is.' Al lay back on his bed, smiling.

'What?' said Jack. 'Oh yuck – that's disgusting.' He covered his mouth and nose and rolled off the bed onto the deep-pile carpet of Al's bedroom floor.

'An unwanted and unnecessary gift,' said Luke. 'Never mind touching the cloth, smells like you've blown right through it.'

'Actually, I may have to check.' Al pulled the top of his trousers out and peered down.

'Don't let any more stench out, you stink-ass,' said Jack.

'All clear. Do you have super smell, Balaclava Boy?' said Al. 'I mean, is it worse for you? Are you like a dog?'

'Huh,' huffed Luke. 'I for one, do not believe dogs have such amazing smell. If so, surely they would not need to stick their noses right up each others behinds? And if they do possess incredible smell, they must be the most disgusting creatures ever.'

'Thanks, Luke, spoken like a true dog-lover,' said Al.

'And I have never witnessed a dog vacate a room when a human has broken wind.'

'Obviously you feel quite strongly about this,' said Jack.

'I am not what you would call a dog fan.'

'Actually, Luke, that's coming through loud and clear,' said Al.

'Anyway, thankfully I don't have super smell,' said Jack. 'But even normal smell's far too good for what comes out of your backside. Now then, what about tonight?'

The boys had walked to Al's place after school and arranged to camp in his garden that night as a cover, so they could sneak away to try and prevent the World Cup trophy being stolen.

It was still a puzzle to the boys how the gang of thieves thought they were going to accomplish this, as it was guarded and locked in a special cabinet-cum-safe. It also seemed such an odd time to go ahead with the robbery, considering the whole of Cornwall was crawling with police and military. Admittedly, these establishment forces were more interested in giants and super-heroes, but checkpoints were springing up all over the place. Even the harbours were under naval guard.

'I still think we should inform the police,' said Luke.

'No. No way,' said Jack, 'Too risky, they'll ask all sorts of daft questions, 'specially that scumbag Gibson – remember him after the storm?'

'He's right, Luke,' added Al. 'We can do this. We've got super-kid here.' He patted Jack on the back.

'I am not convinced. Look at what happened up the castle. You were extremely lucky Harriet was not more severely hurt.'

'I know,' said Jack, wearily. 'But this is different. These are bad men and we may be able to stop them. If one of them gets hurt, tough.'

'Come on, Luke,' said Al. 'You've made such progress recently, you rebel. I think you're starting to enjoy this wild streak. And we need your brains, you're our plan-man, man.'

'I told you my plan the other day, remember? We're camping in your garden, sneaking out, up on the roof...'

'Oh yeah, course,' said Al, shaking his head. 'Sometimes I'd forget my own head, if it wasn't bolted on. Well I guess that's it then, isn't it?'

'Excuse me,' said Luke, 'but what about weapons?'

'I know I was encouraging your wild side, but I don't think we need weapons, dude,' said Al. 'That's sinking to their level.'

'Not us, dummy, them. Being shot to pieces is not part of my life plan.'

'Oh, right. Good point.'

Jack nodded seriously. 'I think you two will have to be the eyes and ears of the operation and I'll be the er, well, the try-and-not-get-shot-to-pieces type bit.'

'You'll be all right, mate,' said Al, throwing a couple of mock punches. 'Tough as old boots – you.'

Luke raised an eyebrow. 'You have endured and survived some incredible hostility meted upon your physical being, it is true,' he said.

'Exactly as Spocky here says, you've had seven kinds of hell kicked out of you and survived.'

Eventually, they decided to approach school via the playing fields, thinking they would be less likely to run into anyone from that direction. The last thing they wanted was to be bumping into any police or military personnel.

Luke went home for dinner but was back by eight. Meanwhile, Jack ate with Al and his parents.

'Strange old days we'em having lately, Jack, don't 'ee think?'

'Yes, Mr Fry, very.'

'I don't believe there's much in it meself. Lot of special effects and nonsense,' he said, glancing up at his wife.

'Well you won't be saying that when a great big giant's foot stamps on your head and squashes you flat's a pancake will 'ee?' said his wife, smiling. 'Come on now, Jack, eat up. Don't be shy.'

'That's what my dad says too.'

'Wise man your dad. How are your folks?' said Mr Fry.

'Mm-mm,' hummed Jack, chewing quickly.

'Let the boy eat his food, mister,' scolded his wife.

'Fine thanks,' said Jack finally.

'Thank your mother for them eggs won't 'ee, me dear?' said Mrs Fry. 'You sure she won't take no money for them?'

'Mm-mm,' hummed Jack again, chewing quickly again so he

could reply while Mr Fry raised his eyebrows at his wife for doing just what he had done a second ago. 'No, sorry. I'll get in trouble if you give me money.'

'What's for sex, Mum?' said Al.

Everyone froze. Al's parents' faces were aghast. Jack stifled a laugh that almost made him splatter food all over the table. Mr Fry was glaring at her son with bulging eyes.

'Pardon, Al?' she asked, politely.

'What?' said Al, before the penny finally dropped. 'No, I didn't mean... I was asking what's for seconds. What's for secs? You know.'

Jack was chewing desperately while straining not to laugh out loud.

'Shut up,' said Al, nudging him under the table. Mr Fry nodded his head with a disappointed expression.

'Ahem.' Al's mum smiled with relief. 'Well, you can either have fruit or ice cream,' she offered.

The two boys ate their ice cream and had a drink of juice before disappearing back up to Al's bedroom, where Jack could finally let go of his pent-up laughter (which took several minutes). When they finally stopped, Jack was hit by the reality of what they were going to do that evening. 'How are you feeling?' he asked Al.

'What?'

'Well, you know, about tonight.'

'What, you mean tonight?'

'No, I mean next flipping week you divvy. Yes, of course tonight,' said Jack, annoyed.

'Dunno, hadn't actually thought about it much.'

'It could be dangerous – you do understand, don't you? We could all get hurt or arrested or even killed. I might lose the super strength, then we'll be right up shit creek, won't we?'

'What is it with you? Can't do this, can't do that. Why are you so certain you're going to lose it? Come on, Jack, just have a bit of faith for goodness sake.' Al was genuinely angry. 'You're so jammy. Most people would give anything to be a superhero and all you seem to want to do is whinge about it. I thought *you* of all people would be the one who'd most enjoy it.'

Jack had been staring at Al with a blank expression but now had his head down, sitting on the bed, motionless, breathing as calmly as he could. Al saw the first tear hit Jack's trouser leg, followed closely by a second. The silent sadness made Al uncomfortable. This was the second time in the last few days that he had seen Jack cry. The first time was just after the bus crash when he had told them what had really happened. This was different. They were alone and Jack seemed unbelievably sad, considering a minute ago he had been laughing so much.

'I'll be all right in a second,' said Jack, quietly. 'Sorry about this. Just hits me like... can't seem to stop.'

'It's OK,' said Al brightly. 'I need to find some more stuff anyway.' He dived into the bottom of his wardrobe. 'Aha, got it.' He raised his hooded top.

Jack wiped his eyes. 'OK, right. Sorry, Al. I'll try not to do that again. Funny really. Dunno what's going on. Probably just a bit, what's the word... apprehensive.' He glanced at Al who managed to maintain eye contact briefly, before carrying on with his search.

'Scared? You big wimp.' Al pulled out a pair of dark trousers. 'It'll be fine, man. I'm quite excited. You'll be OK. You just need to relax a bit, you're a superhero, remember? It's cool. Nothing's going to hurt you and nothing will hurt me or Luke. We'll be fine. Now do me a favour and lift up my bed, I just need to see what's under there.'

Jack smiled, got up and with one arm lifted the end of the bed.

Al stood, admiring the scene. 'That is just so cool. I'm jealous,' he said, suddenly remembering he was meant to be searching for something. He didn't find what he'd wanted, but he did discover a broken gyroscope, some hairy raisins and his favourite cuddly toy- woodlouse – Ziggy Sowpig.

'Ziggy, there you are. I've been looking everywhere for you.' Al picked up the pink, felt-covered toy and hugged it.

Jack couldn't help laughing. 'I still can't believe you have a toy sowpig.'

'Ziggy's the best. No one else has a giant pink woodlouse, or *sowpig* as you insist on calling them.'

'Are you really that obsessed with them?'

'When I was little, yeah. I loved the concentric legs wiggling away.'

'You sound like Luke.'

'Pardon?' said Luke, entering Al's bedroom.

'Al,' said Jack. 'He's just found Ziggy, his freaky soft toy in the form of a sowpig. In his youth, he was fascinated by their concentric legs.'

Luke pulled a disgusted face. 'Can't stand woodlice. There're always so many of them, hiding under stones and around the drains.' He shivered. 'Not even the mice would eat them.'

'You fed woodlice to your mice?' said Al, hugging Ziggy protectively. 'I wont let him harm you, Ziggy.'

'It was all in the name of science,' said Luke, testily. 'Anyway, are preparations complete?'

'That's a good point, Northy,' said Al, forgetting the whole feeding woodlice to mice unpleasantness. 'Jack, where's your balaclava?'

'Here,' said Jack, whipping it out.

'You still haven't washed it, have you?' said Al, prodding it tentatively.

'No,' said Jack, wafting it at him.

'It stinks.'

'You should know,' said Jack. He had a quick sniff himself. 'It's not that bad.'

'There's only one thing that will make it smell better,' said Al, smiling.

'What?' said Jack.

'This.' Al held up an iron-on patch of a lurid flower. In it's centre was the name of the girls magazine it had come from – *Blossom!*

'You're joking, right?' said Jack.

Luke started chuckling.

'No,' said Al, innocently. 'Come on, it'll be cool... irreverent, dangerous.'

'And what exactly do you mean by irreverent?' said Luke.

'Well, you know – cool, or something like that. Anyway, it's not important. These patches will look fab and that's all that matters.'

'Patches?' said Jack. 'I don't need no stinkin' patches.'

'How did you know?' gasped Al.

'Know what?' said Jack, apprehensively.

He pulled out a second flower patch. 'One for each side.'

'No. No way. Not in a million years,' said Jack, flatly.

'You promised,' said Al. 'Can't break a promise, Shillaber.'

'But flowers?'

'Not just flowers.' Al shoved a patch under Jack's nose.

'Oh phew. That stinks worse than your farts.'

'What? I think you'll find that's the "...alluring fragrance of lilies and geraniums washed through with a summer breeze",' read Al.

'Jack is correct, it stinks,' said Luke.

'Spoilsports,' said Al, throwing them in the bin. He went to his chest of drawers and dug down under his pants. 'I suppose you'd prefer something like this, would you?' He held up two small flag-of-St Pirran patches.

'Now we're talking,' said Jack, grabbing them to take a closer look. 'Yeah, these will do, nice one.'

'OK, give them back, Balsa Boy, and hand us your smelly headsock. I'll iron them on for you,' said Al, with a little disappointment. Jack handed over his balaclava and Al disappeared.

'I brought my programmable Casio SP three for the tent,' said Luke, proudly.

'What use do we have for an electronic organ?' said Jack.

'It's a torch,' said Luke, sighing. 'Good job you have got brawn because if you had to rely on brains we'd all be in trouble. Look,' he said, showing Jack the plethora of buttons. 'It's programmable. You can make it turn itself on and off. It will look like we are still in the tent. I'll set it to switch off for good at ten.'

'I didn't even know programmable torches existed,' said Jack.

Al walked back in and held up Jack's balaclava.

'Yes. Definitely superior to the flower,' said Luke.

Jack nodded approvingly and stuffed it back in the big side pocket of his combat trousers.

'Nice torch, Brains,' said Al. 'Programmable, is it?'

'Affirmative,' said Luke.

'Well,' said Al. 'Let's get out there.'

They said goodnight to Al's parents and trooped off towards the far end of the garden. By the time they had erected the tent and carried all their equipment down, it was almost dark. The sky was mottled with clouds but a little corner to the north was clear. The odd spit of rain hit their faces but it was quite a warm evening for the time of year.

Al's dad popped out of the back door as the boys were nearing the tent. 'And, Al.'

'Yes, Dad?'

'Don't be making a lot of noise.'

'No, Dad, course not. You won't even know we're here.'

They packed everything in the tent, making a thoroughly good job of making it look like they really were stopping the night. Luke had brought one of his electronic games players which they took turns with (Luke getting the highest scores by miles). Al had the official FA magazine guide to the 2002 World Cup which they flicked through, discussing all the stars from every country, always coming back to the fact that England really did have a good chance.

They decided to move out just before nine, when Al's folks would be watching *The 100 Greatest Countdown Shows Ever*. They peeked through the window – number fifty-nine was *The 100 Worst TV Shows Ever* (which was unique among TV countdown shows as it had been voted number one *Worst TV Show Ever*, even before being broadcast).

'You're taking a bag?' whispered Al to Luke who was busy putting on his rucksack.

'Of course,' he said.

Jack and Al stuffed all their snacks into the pockets of their coats.

'I forgot,' said Luke, removing a small pouch from his bag. 'I have liberated my parents' mini DV camcorder for the evidence gathering.'

'Wow, nice one,' said Al, examining the camera. 'You really came prepared, hey?'

'You're a credit to your Vulcan people,' said Jack, earnestly. 'Right, let's go.'

They edged their way up the garden cautiously and ended up bumping into each other and having to stifle potentially loud laughter. Al was particularly pleased that he had remembered to oil the garden gate's hinges (as Luke had told him to the day before). The gate opened slowly, but so smoothly it crashed against the side of the house. They froze for a full minute before continuing.

Al checked the road both ways. No one around. It was the first time the boys had ventured into town since the curfew had been enforced and they were shocked at how quiet it was. No cars were being driven anywhere. Only official vehicles and those who had obtained special permits were allowed to be on the roads. The police had been questioning everyone they found, and if people did not have a permit or a good reason to be out, they were being cautioned or taken in for questioning. Anyone deemed as being in Cornwall for no other reason than curiosity was kicked out, across the border into Devon.

Al paused. 'Weird.'

'Yeah, isn't it?' said Jack.

They ducked and dived in and out of driveways and gardens all the way up Western Road, a couple of times scrambling behind bushes to let police patrols pass by. They pelted through the underpass below the A30 and up to the roundabout. For several minutes they crouched behind some shrubbery on the embankment before sprinting across and into Landlake Road (the same road Jack's bus took in the morning). To the left of the road were the Launceston College playing fields. Hurrying down the steep verge, they hopped over the fence onto the soggy ground.

'My feet are soaked already,' whispered Al. 'What was that? What the hell was that? Something just brushed passed me leg. Luke, where's that torch?'

'Shh!' hushed Jack. 'No torch. Probably your imagination. Either that or a vicious badger about to rip your leg off.'

'Thanks mate, just what I wanted to hear.'

'Hang on,' said Jack, a thought popping into his head. 'Pixash? Is that you?'

'Who?' said Luke.

'She was that piskie in the squirrel suit... and the mole suit, the one I told you about.'

'Oh yeah, likes dressing up, doesn't she?' said Al.

'Oh well, no reply anyhow.'

Luke remained silent.

They pressed on along the fence, stopping every now and then to listen. All was quiet except for the odd police car or army van passing and the squelch of their feet on the sopping ground. At the first hedge they turned left, following it until they came to the gateway into the main field.

'There!' said Al.

'Shh. For crying out loud,' said Jack, annoyed.

'Something brushed my leg again.' Al did not care how annoyed anyone was. They stood in silence hearing nothing but their own breathing.

'Come on, let's go,' said Jack, eventually.

They walked forward, the ground sucking at their shoes.

'There it is again. D'you see it? It went right between me legs,' said Al, his panic rising. 'It's following us. Playing with us, building the fear. Maybe we taste better after we're scared. It's gonna, it's gonna kill us. The evil –'

'Shh,' said Luke as a dim, red glow lit the area. 'Red light, less obtrusive.'

They waited in silence, again only hearing their own nervous breaths. Jack was screwing up his eyes in the hope he would see any slight movement. Still they waited.

'There,' said Al then burst into action with a series of frenetic kicks and aimless swipes into the dark.

'Shut up, you twit,' said Jack, in a whispered shout. 'Grab him, Luke.' They tried to get hold of Al's flailing arms and legs. It was tricky, ducking and dodging his swinging limbs. They almost had him secured when his forearm escaped and struck Luke on the side of the head.

'Aagh,' yelled Luke, falling backwards. 'Ow,' he wailed, hitting the wet ground. This broke the spell of Al's frenzy. His manic limb-flinging stopped and was replaced with concern that he had whacked one of his friends.

'Du-bid moo-merders,' came a muffled voice, clearly not Luke's.

'Who's that? Who's there?' said Jack. 'You all right, Luke?'

'Yes, I am fine, I think,' he said. 'But I landed on something, right under my coccyx. It felt like some kind of animal.'

'Your what?' said Al. 'There's no need to be rude.' He whispered to Jack, 'Why's he talking about his willy?'

'Coccyx, you –' said Luke, irritated. 'The small bone at the end of your spine.'

'Oh right, yeah, course,' said Al, embarrassed.

'Can someone help me up? Whatever I landed on is still alive and wriggling.'

Jack picked up the torch, pointing its dull beam toward Luke. Al helped him up. Jack approached cautiously and shone the light down. To their amazement, lying prone on the grass was a scruffy figure about thirty centimetres long. It was on its back with one leg bent under its body.

'You sure it's alive?' said Jack.

'Dunno,' said Al, bending down and giving it a little shove. As he drew his hand back the figure grabbed it, biting down hard onto Al's little finger.

'Aagh! For crying out loud,' he yelled. The figure let go and Al pulled his arm back to nurse his wound. 'What did you do that for, you little –'

'Whatcha throw that *lump* on me for, great dumb-ass?' said the little man with an unmistakable American accent.

'Verbal communication, impressive,' said Luke.

'Huh?' said the little man.

'Sorry about this. I'm Jack, this is Al –'

'And Luke, yeah, yeah. I got all that. Now give me a pull up.'

Luke and Jack reached down.

'Damn. Back off, clumsy morons. You've gone and broken my favourite leg.'

'Well you scared the hell out of us,' said Al, in a whispered shout. 'We thought you were going to kill us.'

'Kill you? I oughta, you dumb little beaver baiters.'

'Who are you calling little?' said Al.

'Oh, you're a real piece of work, ain't you, kid? You want another bite, huh?'

'You're a piskie, aren't you?' said Jack, trying to change the subject.

'Really, Sherlock? Let me guess, you're a goddamn superhero? Make me laugh. Fynn's really lost it this time.'

'You know Fynn? Where is he?' said Jack, hoping Fynn was nearby.

'What is an American piskie doing here?' said Al.

'American?' Why I oughta...' He clenched a fist at Al. 'Kick a guy while he's down, why don't you? I'm gonna enjoy whopping your hide when I can. I'm Canadian. From Canada, all right?'

'Sor-ry.'

'You will be.'

'So, what're you doing here then?' said Al, still nursing his finger.

'Looking out for your dumb asses.'

'Good job you're doing,' said Al.

'Why I'm gonna –'

'Who are you?' said Jack.

The piskie paused, heavily in pain. 'Name's Zilch.'

'Zilch – what kind of name is that?' said Al.

'What kinda name is Al?' said Zilch.

'It means nothing,' said Luke.

'What?' said Al. 'No, it means helper, or something like that,'

'No,' said Luke, Zilch means *nothing*.'

'It must mean something, Luke,' said Al.

'I just told you, it means nothing,' said Luke.

'It's a miracle your race has made it this far,' said Zilch.

'Did Fynn send you, Mr Zilch? said Jack.

'Just Zilch will be fine,' he said, yanking his leg straight. It made a crunching sound. 'Aagh.'

'Well if it wasn't broken before, it certainly is now,' said Luke, helpfully.

'Yeah... it's broke all right. Damn,' he cursed, breathing hard. 'I'm here at Golitha's request, wanted someone to keep an eye on you.'

'Why?' said Jack.

'Just in case.'

'Of what?'

'Trouble like this.'

Al explained to Zilch exactly what they were doing. Zilch kept interrupting for one reason or another and seemed to get more and more irritated, the more he heard. He produced a small bottle from his scruffy clothes and took several large swigs (not offering any to the boys), smacking his lips with a satisfied sigh after each one.

'What?' said Zilch, defensively on seeing the boys staring at his bottle. 'It's piskie medicine.'

After Al had finished explaining the plan, Zilch sounded genuinely worried. He ummed and ahhed. 'You can't go – too dangerous. Call the cops.'

'No way, bunch of fascists. They hate us and we hate them,' said Al.

'He's right,' said Jack. 'We don't have a very good relationship with the local constabulary.'

'We call them and they'll be down on us like a ton of bricks,' said Al.

'Besides, what's the point in being a superhero if you can't do things like this?' said Jack.

'You ain't no superhero. You're a –'

'A what?' said Jack.

'And that was a double negative,' added Luke.

'Besides, you can't really stop us, can you now?' said Al. 'What are you going to do, hop us into a circle to prevent us leaving?'

'I'm gonna beat your hide if you carry on like that.' Zilch swung out a fist in desperation, but it whistled through the air without striking anything. 'Ow. I need to let Golitha know about this. I have a bad feeling, something ain't right. You're gonna have to get me down to the river.'

'Bit late for a swim isn't it, especially in your condition?' said Al.

'Be a bit cold too, I should think,' said Jack.

'Funny guys, huh?' said Zilch, unimpressed. 'It ain't too late or too cold to drown a bunch of lame-brain little humans. I need running water to call Golitha.'

'There's a tap over there,' said Al, pointing vaguely in the direction of the changing room.

'Oh, I am so gonna kick your ass,' said Zilch.

Luke had been rummaging around in his rucksack and finally produced a bandage. Al found a couple of sticks from the hedge for splints and together they managed to bind Zilch's leg without causing too much pain, mostly down to the effect of his medicine.

'Maple syrup,' blurted Luke. 'That's what that stuff smells like, like a maple syrup cough mixture.'

'Can't bit a beat of old maple bourbon, I mean cough mixture,' slurred Zilch.

'Are you sure it's medicine?' said Al.

Zilch laughed. 'Well, kid, I certainly feel a whole lot better. Huh?'

'Look at him – he's drunk,' said Al. 'What are we going to do with him?'

'I think we should get him down to the river, like he says,' said Jack.

'I agree, it is the logical thing to do,' said Luke. 'I don't mind going. I can empty out my rucksack and we can put him in there – he should be fine.'

'But what about the plan? You've got to film the break-in,' said Al.

'Well Jack can't go, can he?' said Luke.

'I'll go,' said Al, reluctantly. 'After all, it's my fault he's broken his leg. Like Luke says, you can't go, can you, Blunder Boy? And you're the brains behind, well, behind most things, so you'd better stick with him.'

'Ah, moose-burgers. You mean I get stuck with you? I'll be surprised if we make it out of this hog-wallow swamp alive, let alone to the liver, I mean river.'

'So eloquently put, Mr Zilch,' said Luke, emptying out the entire contents of his rucksack onto the ground. He stuffed the various bits and bobs of gear and snacks into his many coat pockets. Carefully, and with much cursing from Zilch, they lowered him in and manoeuvred the rucksack onto Al's back.

'Good luck, guys,' said a deflated Al. 'Meet you back at the tent, yeah?'

'Good luck to you too – you'll need it,' said Jack.

'I heard that,' spluttered Zilch. 'Lazy, good-for-nothing skunk-herders,' he mumbled from inside the back pack.

'Right, see you later,' said Al. 'Anything happens, text me. Luke, you got your mobile?'

'Yes. Good luck.'

Al set off on the journey that would take him and his difficult cargo through town to the river at the bottom of St Thomas' Road. As he disappeared out of sight, Zilch started singing.

'Poor sod,' said Jack.

Luke huffed. 'Which one?'

21

Parting of the Ways

Jack and Luke made their way to the gate and over into the lane that led towards school. They ran as fast as Luke could manage, slowing as they approached the footbridge spanning the A30. On the other side of the bridge was school. They had never seen this side of school at night. Its silhouette was angular and with a fence, it could easily have passed for a prison. Dim security lights high on the walls made the windows invisible in the murk below.

They glanced down onto the A30, ducking back sharply as a spotlight swept above their heads. Cautiously, they peered over the edge again. Military vehicles were visible both up and down the road and four police patrol cars were parked, two on either carriageway, forming road blocks. The policemen were gathered at the central reservation, chatting. An army truck rolled up heavily on the west-bound carriageway, its diesel engine leaving a trail of thick fumes.

'Hmm, love that smell,' said Jack.

'Weirdo,' said Luke, pulling his jumper over his nose.

One of the policemen hopped into his car and reversed to let the truck through.

'Bit risky, isn't it, running right over the top of that lot?' said Jack.

Luke frowned. 'There is a risk but I would say minimal, especially if they are all inside their vehicles.'

'What's the plan?'

Luke rummaged through his many pockets in turn. 'Where are you, my little beauties?' he said, sounding unusually animated. 'Ha.' He produced four small glass phials, shaped like bullets. 'Assault grade stink-bombs. Ordered them from an east European small-arms dealer over the Internet, government-endorsed, of course.'

'Nice,' said Jack, nodding. He stopped, staring at the dark shape of Luke. 'Do your parents –'

'No,' said Luke, 'they don't. Sometimes I think I was adopted.'

'That must be weird.'

'Yeah, anyway, I reckon you can throw these upwind about ten or twenty metres and they will be jumping into their cars quicker than you can say "worst smell in the world".'

Jack took the stink-bombs and stepped back a couple of paces. 'Here goes.' He picked out a glinting cat's eye, drew his arm back and let fly.

'Wow,' said Luke, in quiet amazement. 'That is some throw you have there.'

The bomb hit with precise accuracy. A couple of seconds later the other three phials struck the same spot, unleashing their fetid stench to be gently carried downwind to the policemen.

'Oh my heavens. That you, Perkins?'

'No sir, it –'

'Oh no, that's disgusting.'

By the time the fourth officer heard the second complaint he was already inside his car. Seconds later he was joined by his colleague. The first two officers were now also safely in their car. Jack and Luke sprinted across the bridge and jumped over the wall into the school grounds.

Al was heading back the same way they had come. His feet were soaked, his trousers were wet and his finger throbbed.

Zilch stopped singing abruptly. 'Hey, kid, how's your pinky?'

'Fine. Just great, thanks to you. Real happy about having a bleeding finger full of pesky piskie teeth-marks. Should I be worried about catching any nasty piskie diseases?'

'The old British sarcasm. You were lucky I didn't bite through the bone. Hey, watch where you're going.'

Al had jumped down from the fence and was busy crawling up the bank to the road. 'Here's a thing – why don't you shut your stupid American gob for just one second,' he whisper-shouted.

'Call me Yank again and I'll punch you so hard in the back your heart'll pop out your chest while it's still beating.'

'Charming. Shh – car coming.' Al dived (as gently as possible) down the bank and lay flat on the wet grass as an army patrol rumbled by. 'You OK, Mr Zitch?'

No reply.

'Zitchy?' whispered Al, as loud as he dare. He heard faint snoring from the backpack. 'Thank heavens.'

Jack and Luke crept cautiously around the music block. It seemed so wrong, sneaking into school at night, and the eerie silence played tricks with their eyes and ears.

'Wait,' said Luke, sharply. 'Did you hear that? What was it?'

'My stomach,' said Jack.

'Oh, OK then.'

'Where d'you think's best to get up on the roof?' said Jack.

'Doesn't really matter, what about here?'

'Hang on. Just how are we getting up there?'

'Good question,' said Luke, flatly. 'If only we had the ability to leap up there without any assistance.'

'Hang on... very funny. I may be super strong, but it hasn't increased my brain power, OK?' In the dark, Jack's embarrassment was his own. 'How d'you wanna do this? Shall I throw you up, then jump up afterwards, or d'you wanna hang onto my back?'

Luke was silent.

'Hello?' said Jack.

'Sorry. Just working out the percentages of possible injury, based on the height of the building, visibility, the landing area and how much I trust you.'

'And?'

'Think I'll hang onto your back.'

'OK.'

'But I think you should perform a preliminary investigation.'

'Right,' said Jack, sounding more than a little confused.

'Jump up, take a look around, see how it feels. Hop back down, then we'll go together.'

'Good idea. Thanks.' Jack steadied himself and leaped up into the darkness. 'Wo-ah.' He flew right over the corridor and landed the other side. 'Whoops.' He jumped back, this time landing on top of the corridor. He trod around, making sure the roof was firm enough for the both of them, then jumped down.

'Everything satisfactory?'

'Yep, seems fine to me. Get a good grip and hang on.' Luke awkwardly put his arms around Jack's neck and locked his hands together.

'Oh, hello, darling,' said Jack, putting on a sultry voice. 'I didn't know you cared.'

'Ha, ha, very funny.'

Jack bent his knees and sprang away. Luke's arms tightened around his neck as they took off. He let out a little whimper as his stomach lurched. They landed with a nervous shuffle and the hint of a cracking roof.

'Interesting,' said Luke, relieved. 'Is that how it always feels?'

'Pretty much,' said Jack, smiling.

'OK, let's go before the roof does.'

They crept along on top of the corridor, occasionally stopping to listen. Soon they were confronted by the side wall of the Old Hall. Getting up on this roof would require a bigger leap. They assumed the jump position again.

'Oh, hello, darling,' said Jack again, chuckling. He could sense Luke was not that amused. 'You know what they say about repetition and humour?'

'Something about a bad joke not getting any funnier, no matter how many times you try it?'

'Well, not quite that, no. Another time, maybe. Ready?'

'Yes,' said Luke, sternly. Jack crouched, then leaped into the darkness above.

'String. I need string... and a squeeze of lemon... split your clunge... Aagh. What? Where am I?' Zilch thrashed about inside the rucksack after waking as Al ducked behind a bush in someone's front garden.

'Shh – police,' said Al.

'...well, apparently he's had it done,' said the first policeman.

'What? You're kidding, right? They can't do that. Who said that?' said the second.

'Sally, on Reception. She knows all about that kind of surgery.'

'Gibbo's got a falsey? Who else knows? Huh. Nose – get it? Ha.'

'What?'

'Nose.'

'He didn't have his nose done – it was his moustache.'

'Hey?'

'He couldn't grow one, so he had one implanted. Yeah, apparently they had to...'

They passed on by, their voices fading into the night.

'Hey, what the hell's going on? Ain't you ever used your damn legs before? I've had a smoother ride on the back of a demented groundhog. Hey, kid, you hearing me?'

'Look, Mr Zebody, or whatever your name is, I'm trying to concentrate on not being caught and with all your moaning I'm surprised we don't have half the police in Cornwall chasing us.'

'Bring 'em on. I prefer a straight fight to all this sneaking around.'

Al dashed from garden to garden, ducking into shadows and behind bushes. After what seemed like an hour or more he finally made it to the relative safety of the castle grounds and crouched against an uneven wall.

'I didn't realise avoiding capture would be this stressful,' he said, more to himself than his irritable companion.

'Come on, kid, move your lazy ass. I've seen faster road kill.'

'Oh that's lovely. You've got a real charming way with words, haven't you?'

'Come to think of it, I've eaten faster road kill.'

'Oh come on, you are joking?'

'Yeah, kid, sure. But if you don't shift your backside, I may take a bite out of it.'

Al straightened up, checked and ran off towards the North gate, where he had to stop quickly and back-track, as a police car crawled around the corner.

'Ow – watch it,' snapped Zilch.

'Moan when I'm slow, moan when I'm hurrying.'

Al followed after the police car at a safe distance and took a left down the steps that would bring them out near the top of St Thomas' Hill. Once they got to the bottom of that road they could take a right and be down at the river in no time.

Al glanced both ways and sprinted across the road. As soon as he was over the lip of the steep St Thomas' Hill, he took cover in the first garden, hopping over the low wall. He waited, making sure he hadn't been spotted. A few seconds later, he started down the road. Staying to the right, he let the steep hill increase his pace. He glanced back, hearing an engine somewhere at the top of the hill. Almost there… Almost there…

Whack, bang, whizz!

Al clattered into a soldier, who crashed to the ground noisily. His gun went off – the bullet whirring away into the night sky.

Jack and Luke landed firmly with a hefty thud on the roof of the Old Hall. It felt reassuringly solid. Quietly, they moved towards to the edge of the flat roof.

'Ah –' Jack stifled a cry as he went flying forward.

'What happened?' said Luke.

'Mind the –'

Luke fell with a thud onto the roof.

'…thing,' finished Jack.

'Ow. That hurt. Think I've grazed my knee,' said Luke, rubbing his leg. 'I presume *you* sustained no injury?'

'No, it was just a bit, you know. Now, where's your torch?'

Luke flicked on its red light. Running across the length of the roof was a bunch of cables, all bound together with huge zip ties. Several of the cables alone were two or three centimetres thick.

'What's all that for?' said Jack.

'Not sure. How curious. I can't believe the school's power consumption requires this kind of industrial cabling. And it certainly shouldn't be left uncovered, traversing the roof like this. Very odd indeed.'

They reached the low wall around the perimeter of the roof and knelt, taking a good look around. Directly below them was the higher level of the playground and below that the quad. Opposite and to the left of their lookout was the boarders' building, the tower right in front of them.

'Anyone hanging around in the tower?' said Jack.

'No, not yet. But you know it is true. I have had first-hand experience of the horrors that lie within that building's walls.'

'What?'

'That place is cold, dark. They hear the rope rubbing on the beam, the beam creaking with the swaying dead weight. The hiss of the last desperate gasps for air.'

'Come on, Luke, you're joking, right?'

'No, it's true all right. I've seen it myself.'

'When?'

'I was over there one night, not long after we started. It was a gaming night. Remember I used to be into all that Dungeons and Dragons stuff?'

Jack sniggered. 'How could I forget?'

'Well, some of the older boarders dared us to go up. There was me and two others, both boarders, Daniel something and this boy who was only ever called Left-ears.'

'Don't remember him.'

'He left pretty soon afterwards, no pun intended.'

'What's with the nickname?'

'Some PE teacher was explaining something – he didn't understand so the teacher told him he'd heard of people with two left feet but never of someone with two left ears.'

'That's quite funny for a PE teacher. Anyway, go on.'

'Well, I have never been more afraid in my whole life. There was this biting chill oozing down the stairs like dry ice. It sucked the breath from your lungs. The one time I could find no logical explanation for something.'

'Blimey.'

'Then we heard it, the rope, jarring against the beam.'

'And, the body?'

'We were out of there quicker than I had ever moved before.'

'You didn't even see it then?'

'Didn't need to and didn't want to.'

'Can't believe you've never told us that before, how come?'

'Not sure. I suppose I thought you wouldn't believe me. Seems kind of tame now after everything that's happened to you.'

'Well, I dunno.'

They sat in darkness for a while before taking another look over the edge. They could see nothing except the two guards from the private security company, stationed outside the door that led into school by the Old Hall. An odd light went on and off in the boarders' block. After a thorough inspection they slumped, backs against the wall, to begin their wait. Chatting quietly, they checked below every few minutes. Within an hour they had eaten all their snacks.

'Plastic food always makes me feel sick,' said Luke.

'Umm,' said Jack, picking at his teeth.

The clouds above reflected the streetlights, giving the sky an eerie orange glow. Time passed slowly.

'Sarg. Gotta live one here,' squealed the private. 'Ran straight into Smalls, knocked him clean over. That was his gun going off, Sarg.'

'Ow, that hurts,' yelled Al, struggling.

The jumpy private twitched nervously as he man-handled Al over to the sergeant, sitting in darkness under a truck's awning. He rose, stepping into the dull light of a tired streetlamp. He was tall and wide. Everything from his stomach to his face was wide. Al had never seen such a vast expanse of cheek and jowl.

'Claims he was sleep-walking,' said the private. 'More like sleep-running.'

The sergeant's voice was pure gravel. 'All right, Spiddy, calm down.' It was lower and raspier than any film trailer voice Al had ever heard, only the sergeant spoke with an English accent. It made the sweaty hairs on the back of Al's neck stand to attention.

'All he was carrying were house keys, mobile phone and this rucksack.' Private Spitty held up Luke's bag.

'Go-od,' growled the sergeant, elongating the word in his deathly grating throat. 'Drop it down, Spiddy.'

Private Spitty coughed nervously. 'That's Spitty, Sarg,' he said.

As Al watched the sergeant speak, he realised the craggy face reminded him of a 1:2 000 000 scale map of Norway – all fjords and valleys.

The private chucked the bag down in front of Al. It seemed to take an age to hit the ground and landed lightly.

'Agh,' cried Zilch.

'Al flinched, his eyes bulging with the anticipation of Zilch's discovery.

The sergeant narrowed his eyes to a mere five centimetres apart. 'What are you doing out at this time, boy?'

'I'm a... I'm a...'

'Stop babbling and answer the sergeant,' babbled Private Spitty.

'Yeah, kid, stop babbling and answer the dumb-ass,' shouted Zilch, from the bag.

'B-b-but?' stuttered Al.

'Well?' rasped the sergeant.

'They can't hear me, you doofuss. Now answer him. Tell him you were sleepwalking or something.'

'Just... sleepwalking. I get hot. Really hot, and, hot in the night.'

They may not have been able to hear Zilch but Al knew they would search the bag. And they would find him. How would he explain that? What would Zilch do? Apart from irritating them immensely. They would probably shoot him within minutes. Al's heart was beating furiously.

'Stop lying, b-o-y,' boomed the sergeant. 'What's in the bag?'

'Nothing. There's nothing in the bag. Must have... picked it up by accident when I was sleepwalking out the house.'

Zilch guffawed. 'Wow, you made something up yourself. Shame it was so lame.'

'You... are lying.' The sergeant sounded more like a machine than a man.

'No.' Al struggled in vain.

'Open it, Spiddy.'

'That's a – never mind. Right-o, Sarg.'

Private Spitty let go of Al and knelt by the rucksack. He unclipped the plastic locks and pulled back the top cover. Then he fiddled with the drawstring, finally pulling it out and opening up the bag. Al shut his eyes and prayed. Private Spitty shone his torch inside.

'It's empty, Sarg.' He checked the side pockets but found nothing. 'Not a thing.' He threw the bag at Al, who caught it, his jaw hanging limply. A glob of drool dripped down his coat.

'What are you staring at, gormless?' said Private Spitty, twitching.

'Nothing,' snapped Zilch, kicking Al in the chest.

'Oh, nothing,' mumbled Al.

'When I tell you, run to the bridge and jump over the side,' said Zilch, calmly.

'What?' said Al.

'Wh-at?' The sergeant's voice grated out the word. 'Who are you talking to, boy?'

'What?' said Al, hardly knowing who he was talking to.

'I think he's a bit... mental in the head, Sarg,' squeaked Private Spitty.

'No...' growled the sergeant. 'Something's not right.'

'Ready, kid?' said Zilch.

'The drop,' yelped Al, his stomach churning with fear. 'Too far.'

'You'll be fine. Now go,' ordered Zilch.

'Stop him,' croaked the sergeant, before Al had even moved.

Private Spitty lunged forward. Al ducked backwards and shoulder-barged the soldier who staggered sideways, collapsing at the feet of the sergeant. Al sprinted around the corner to the far side of the bridge. Private Spitty was up on his feet and calling for help. Al peered below into the blackness. He couldn't see a thing, but knew it was a long way down and the soldiers were closing in.

'Jump! Damn it, jump!' screamed Zilch.

'Oh no!' yelled Al.

'And hang onto the bag!'

Al pushed off just as a uniformed arm swiped out at him,

catching his ankle tightly. He fell forwards, pivoting at the clasped limb and smacked into the stony side of the bridge.

'Ow.'

'Kick him, kid,' shouted Zilch.

Al kicked at the soldier's wrist with his free foot. At his third attempt he caught it full on and was released. He dropped, his stomach lurching with the weightlessness and expectation of a crunching fall. But then resistance came from the rucksack – it was moving upward.

'Wha –' Al frantically re-gripped the bag as his legs swung down. His feet juddered over the ground momentarily.

'I said hang on, you goof-ball,'

They lurched one way then the other, careening up and down.

'What's happening?' yelled Al, clinging desperately to the bag.

'What do you think?' shouted Zilch.

'Aagh.' Al wailed as they swung left and dropped, making his stomach lurch again. He was close to tears, but unsure if they were of joy or fear. 'We're flying.'

Al swore he heard Zilch laugh.

The air rushed over them, the cold cutting through Al. On they flew through the black night in their chaotic escape, vaguely following the old steam railway track that links Launceston to the hamlet of New Mills.

'How are you navigating?' yelled Al.

'I'm not,' said Zilch, sounding tired.

'What?' Al felt uncomfortable. His left foot slammed against something, slowing their flight and sending them into a spin. They lost height. Al pulled up his legs but it was too late. They were gripped by a thousand thorns as Zilch flew them into a large patch of brambles. Al screamed as the rucksack tore from his hands and shot off into the dark night. As he writhed in pain, lying half in, half out of the brambles, he heard a heavy thud followed by a weak sigh.

It felt like they had been stuck up on the roof of the Old Hall for hours. Neither Jack nor Luke was feeling the cold, which was surprising in the chill wind. Luke took a break from studying the stars and stuck his head out over the ledge.

'Jack.'

In the murky light three men crossed the quad dressed in identical uniforms to the two guards below.

'Relief guard? Maybe the nightshift,' said Jack.

They watched as the men walked calmly up to the two security guards and exchanged pleasantries.

'Told you,' said Jack, turning back.

'Wait,' said Luke.

The pleasantries had now become less pleasant. Voices were raised, then fists. Seconds later, the three men were busy dragging the two men inside the school.

'Blimey,' said Jack.

'Well, I think we have found our perpetrators,' said Luke. 'We have a problem though.'

'I know what you mean – they look nasty,' said Jack.

'I wasn't actually referring to that. I had always presumed that criminals plotting to steal the World Cup would be nothing less than nasty. They are law breakers, Jack.'

'Fair point. So, what d'you mean?'

'We can't see a thing from here. We need to be over there.' Luke pointed to the roof of the boarders' building.

'Right, yes, well done. I'll go first, shall I?'

'No, it will have to be a one-time effort – no practise runs, they may hear you when you land back here.'

Jack rose and pulled Luke up. 'Grab hold then.'

'Please, not again,' implored Luke.

'As if I would,' said Jack, then slipping into his sultry voice, 'I mean, really, darling.'

'Ha, ha.' Luke assumed the piggy-back position. Jack took a couple of steps then leaped silently into the night sky. They landed and stumbled backwards, quickly crouching to avoid detection. The boarders' building also had a low ledge running around the top of the roof, which they ducked behind. From this viewpoint they could see everything. Almost the entire front of the Old Hall facing them was glass. Luke retrieved the video camera from one of his large inside pockets and started filming.

The three crooks were busy tying and gagging the two guards.

They carried them away, one at a time, disappearing up the few steps from the Old Hall into the gym. They slipped through the tatty vinyl curtains hanging across the wide entrance to the hall then casually strode up to the mobile display case that held the glittering FIFA World Cup trophy, smiling with adoration.

'Well,' said Jack. 'I suppose this is it. Why do I feel so nervous?'

'The unknown is the scariest thing in the world,' said Luke.

Jack pulled out his balaclava and put it on, adjusting it carefully around his eyes and mouth. 'I know I shouldn't be, but I can't seem to help it.' He moved back along the side of the roof and peered over the edge to the darkness below. Even after all the huge jumps he had done, heights could still make his stomach churn.

'I think time is of the essence, Jack.'

'Yeah,' said Jack, absent-mindedly. 'Maybe I should just climb down the drainpipe.'

'Jack, you can leap tall buildings, run faster than a speeding bullet and probably milk a cow quicker than a machine. So why would you want to climb down a drainpipe when you can simply, and quietly, drop off the edge of the building?'

'Because...'

'And besides, it will be very cool on camera.'

'You're right,' sighed Jack. 'I know you're right. It's just. I get... What if I suddenly lose my strength? What if I'm mid-air and run dry on super powers? What happens then?'

'You break both legs.'

'Thanks, but what I was actually after was reassurance and encouragement, not harsh reality.'

'Oh, I see. Well, if you stop and check your powers before every extraordinary thing you do, you're not really going to be much of a superhero, are you? "Oh look, there goes Paranoia Man. He can leap tall buildings, deflect bullets and run faster than a train (but he just has to check first)". Doesn't exactly sound right, does it?'

'No, not really.'

'And besides, don't you think you'll be able to feel if it

changes? There's not much chance that it will just vanish instantly. You have my scientific word on that.'

'OK, I get the message.' Jack smiled weakly and stepped up onto the ledge. 'Can you smell flowers?'

'Go,' said Luke.

Jack dropped over the side, disappearing into the dark. Luke was right, it did look cool. Unfortunately, he had forgotten to film it.

Jack hit the ground with a jolt, having misjudged his landing in the gloom. He ducked down behind the wall of one of the small raised squares of grass that were dotted about the school grounds. Having checked no one was around, he scrambled along and climbed the stairs, approaching the door to the school from the right.

Luke had tried to follow Jack's movement but could not see well even with the camera on night mode. He switched back to standard mode and zoomed in on the fake guards circling the display case. It struck Luke that for people who were about to steal such a famous and valuable trophy they seemed incredibly casual.

The gangly vicious-faced one with the endless nose dug around in his pocket and pulled out a piece of paper. He approached the side of the case and punched in a code on the small keypad. Luke zoomed in. Several lights along the top of the keypad flashed on and off, then they all lit up and stayed on. The whole front of the display unit began to open up like an electric garage door.

'What's going on?' Luke asked himself. 'How could they know the code?'

Then the men all turned to look at something. Luke lowered the camera, searching for what he presumed was Jack, fighting his way through the huge curtain. For Luke, it was like a scene from a silent movie, but he was not finding it funny at all. He brought the video camera back up and resumed filming.

'Zilch. Zilch.' No reply came to Al's whispered cries. He struggled delicately to untangle himself from his prickly bonds. By the faint moonlight he saw a clearing to his left and ahead made out the vague silhouette of a towering tree. The river gurgled away to his right, somewhere beyond the brambles.

'Zilch? Ow!' he cried again. Still no reply. His movement caused the needle-sharp thorns to bite into his flesh. He had never experienced pain like it before. His legs throbbed and his hands burned from a rash of nettle stings. A cut itched on his left cheek. He was cold but sweaty and sticky patches of blood made his trousers cling to his legs.

'Hello? Who's there?' he said, convinced he had heard talking. He cupped a buzzing hand to his ear. Close by he heard short bursts of quick, low whispers.

'Hey, fellas.' Zilch had regained consciousness. 'Hey, over here, damn it. Base of the tree.'

Al clearly heard scuttling whispers replying to Zilch's distress call.

'Yeah, now would be a good time. Get me a shot and a splint. And make it snappy.'

Once again he could hear breathy mutterings.

'Who? Oh yeah, the kid. If you're bothered. Just do me first,' moaned Zilch.

From Al's delicate prone position, he saw five mop-like shapes squelch awkwardly and slowly up from the river into the clearing. Three of them moved with considerable difficulty toward Zilch's cries. The other two approached Al. He was in too much pain to care what they were or what they may do to him.

'Hello,' said Al, feebly. 'I'm Al.'

The creatures muttered away. Al was getting more used to their strange sounds. He was convinced they had started laughing. It took them a while to reach him with their jerky, wet waddling. When they finally did, Al felt ice-cold, slimy limbs reach out and touch his hands. He recoiled, but some throaty cooing relaxed him and the little hands took hold of him once more. They were gently soothing and the pain eased instantly.

Up close, the creatures resembled clumps of weed from the river. Al could make out no clear features. With a moppy flick, one of them leaped in the air and landed on his legs. Al hardly jumped at all. The thing swished up and down spreading cold comfort all over them. He lay back, a feeling of euphoria spreading throughout his body and soon fell asleep.

22

Trapped

When Jack finally managed to stumble forward from the tangle of curtain, he was faced with the uniformed robbers. The tall scary one with the long, bent nose stepped forward a couple of paces, squinting. 'Boo!' he shouted.

Jack jumped, fear and adrenaline coursing through his veins. He tried to steady his breath but it was difficult with a pneumatic drill for a heart.

'Suppose you must be this Balaclava Boy we've all been reading about?'

'Yeah. I – I suppose I am,' said Jack, shakily.

'Look at you, with your pretty patches.' Dick laughed coldly.

Jack felt for the patches. The rectangular flag of St Pirran and – he cursed – the patch on the left was flower-shaped. He blushed angrily. Luckily, he was hidden. The rush of blood made him aware of how hot he was under the balaclava. And of course, the sickly sweet scent from the patch was now all too noticeable.

'Well, my little flower, aren't you gonna arrest us or something?' said Dick.

Jack's mouth was dry. 'No, I'm not the police. Look, just don't steal it, OK?'

'Oh right, now you've put it like that, maybe we won't. Watcha say, lads?' Dick turned to them, but they seemed confused by Jack's appearance.

'Look, Dick,' spluttered Richie, 'don't you think we should

remove ourselves from here? This young chap may have alerted the authorities.'

'I don't think we have to worry too much about that.'

'What on earth are you talking about, Dick? What's going on?' quizzed Richie.

'There're certain authorities gathering right now, all about us.'

'Right. That is it. I have endured enough. I am departing this infernal deed.' Richie launched his security guard's hat at Dick. 'You can take your ridiculous football cup and stick it up your ignorant, cockney-barra-boy-anally-retentive-arse – you *plonker*!'

Dick whirled around to face Richie, pulled out a small handgun and shot him.

Richie screamed as he flew backwards and thudded to the floor. 'You ruddy well shot me, you blackguard.'

'Sh-sh-sh –'

'Shame?' said Dick, smiling. 'Is that a faint stutter I hear, Mr Soul?'

'N-n-n –'

'Now, now, Mr Pole,' said Dick, warmly. 'You shouldn't be using language like that in front of a child. So coarse from a gent like yourself. Surely you could call me something politer than that? What about nincompoop, imbecile or cretin? Huh?'

Jack had never seen anyone get shot before and was starting to feel sick.

Dick swung around menacingly, a smug smile stretched across his drawn face. 'Well, flower, what are you gonna do about that?' He laughed hoarsely.

Dickie sheepishly crept over to tend Richie's wound. The bullet had shattered his humerus just above the elbow, causing overwhelming trauma and suffering. Having a small lump of lead ripping through your flesh, sinew and bone is never going to be anything other than excruciatingly painful and potentially life threatening (even if you are only shot in one of your extraneous limbs).

Dickie bound the wound using some gaffa tape they had brought with them. Richie whimpered in agony and talked nonsense while drifting in and out of consciousness.

'I'm dying,' he mumbled calmly, then his eyes widened. 'Is this a dagger I see before me?'

'N-n-no, it's a D-d-dickie,' said Dickie.

'Nanna, forgive me,' said Richie, before his head flopped backwards.

'C-come on now,' pleaded Dickie. 'It's not that b-bad.'

Richie's head jerked forward. 'Now is the winter of my discontent.'

'Shut up, you toff,' shouted Dick, spitting with anger. 'Or I'll end your discontent forever.'

'Death... It creeps upon me like... a wretched feathery shadow. Clinging... suffocating... writhing with luscious contempt for my puny, frail, flesh...'

'For God's sake, if you're gonna die, do it quietly,' said Dick.

Richie fell silent then coughed daintily, his breathing quick and shallow. He glanced at the bound wound and spoke in a hushed tone. 'The flesh is weak but the will is strong. I shall prevail. The legions of inner strength shall be mustered and sent to battle the ignominies of this misfortune.'

'OK, Richie, you'll be f-fine,' said Dickie, reassuringly. 'He's not talking sense, Dick.'

'No change there then.' Dick narrowed his eyes at Richie. 'Oi, toff, shut it!'

Jack seized his moment. He lunged forward and kicked at the hand holding the gun. Dick's arm flew upward, the gun spun from his hand straight up to the high ceiling. It hit with a muted crunch, embedding itself in a polystyrene tile.

'You little sod,' said Dick, swinging violently with his other hand straight at Jack's head. Jack ducked and kicked Dick's backside. Dick hurtled forward and with a splintering crash smashed head-first into the trophy cabinet and crumpled to the floor.

Jack stood dumbfounded, wondering what the remaining uninjured thief would do. He was expecting some sort of attack, but the man seemed preoccupied with helping the shot one.

Dick was unconscious, lying next to the trophy cabinet, covered with shards of broken glass. A trickle of blood streaked across his forehead. He would wake later with a thunderous headache (mild concussion).

Jack heard footsteps, then was shocked to see several soldiers stream in through the curtains. He smiled with relief and pointed to the crooks. 'Those two and that one,' he said, feeling rather proud.

The soldiers ignored him and kept pouring in. Jack backed away into the middle of the hall. They seemed to be filing in around the edge of the hall encircling him and the crooks. He didn't understand what was going on but knew it wasn't good. He set off towards the far exit but more soldiers jumped down the steps, closing it off. As they took their positions he realised how many guns were pointing... at him. Not normal guns though, they looked more like toy guns with wide barrels and a fat cylinder on top – like paintball guns.

Jack moved to jump through one of the windows at the front of the hall, but huge wire nets dropped down in front of them. His skin prickled under his balaclava. If he had been Spiderman, this would have been one of those "spider-sense going berserk" moments.

'Hi there, little fella. Should I call you, Balaclava Boy?' said an American voice.

An elderly man in a smart uniform had appeared, his hands buried deep in the pockets of his dark blue overcoat.

'We're so glad you could join us.' He stopped and nodded at the soldiers. In unison, they pulled on breathing masks. 'Boys,' he called, smiling cheesily. 'Fire at will.' Then calmly walked away.

There was a metallic swoosh and several strands of silvery wire bound Jack's legs from his ankles to his knees. He forced his legs apart snapping many strands, which pinged off, felling two soldiers. Next he was hit on all sides, not by bullets, but thousands of hollow glass balls. Jack waved his hands frantically trying to deflect them but they broke too easily. And he was feeling so tired... so sleepy.

'Gasss...' he mumbled weakly, as everything around him turned a blacky-red. Still the glass spheres popped against him, tinkling eerily as they broke and hit the floor.

His knees buckled, the final few wires breaking as he dropped to the ground. With one last effort he jumped, convinced he could still smash through the roof and escape. His head collided with something. He threw out his arms to balance, blinking furiously to clear his vision. The roof was dark but something wasn't right.

Shapes... moving above him. He was still on the floor in the Old Hall. He had only managed to jump a few feet before crashing back down. A shadow passed above him. He kicked out and it disappeared with a stunted scream. A few seconds later he heard a loud crash followed by low moaning.

Continuous shouting and weird noises filled the air, and although Jack couldn't tell what was happening he was starting to feel slightly better. After he kicked the one soldier across the hall, the rest had retreated. Now, no one was near him. He rolled over on all fours and shook the fuzziness from his head. Trying to stand, he pulled one leg forward and planted his foot down. It crunched on the remains of glass spheres. He pushed up and whipped the other leg forward, shuffling his feet to stay upright. It sounded like he was walking on a herd of snails, which made him feel nauseous. Cold saliva leaked into his cheeks. He heaved, throwing up the half-digested snacks eaten while sitting on the roof earlier. It stank, but at least he couldn't see the chunks of carrot. He wondered if Luke was all right.

The shouting grew louder. Finally, he drew himself completely upright and tried to get his eyes to focus. The blur in front of him started to clear. He could make out high white walls. The blobs running all about him became visible as soldiers.

'What's that?' he blurted out.

'It's your new ho –'

But before the American voice could finish what it was saying, Jack was chopped down, falling flat on his face, by what appeared to be some kind of floor, sliding under him.

Rolling over, he sat up, his hands pressing down against a cold, smooth surface. With his eyesight virtually back to normal, he watched the bars of a cage descend around him. Electric mechanisms whirred and hummed into life, followed by the buzz of locks thudding into place. His skin tingled and the hairs on the back of his neck stood on end.

'W-w-what's all this about? What's g-going on?' demanded Dickie, still kneeling by Richie, who had passed out. Another man appeared through the vinyl curtain, dressed in a smart blue uniform. Jack recognised him as the man Dunce had assaulted at the castle.

Dick was startled. 'Rik? Is that y-you? W-what on earth –'

'Shut it, Dickie, Dick, Ricky, or whatever the hell your name is,' he ordered. 'You pathetic little morons with your stupid cups of tea and small-time thievery.'

'B-but you're American. You're n-not –'

'That's right. Now get yourself and that upper class fool outta here, now.' He clicked his fingers and three nearby soldiers raced over. Two hauled Richie up and carried him out while the third prodded Dickie along with a pistol. Two more collected Dick from the wreckage of the World Cup trophy cabinet and dragged him away.

Jack watched them disappear, his feeling of dread increasing.

The cage was about three metres high. The floor was like a cross between hard sponge and ceramic tile. It had slight give in it, yet it was cold and smooth. He stood up and approached the bars cautiously, noticing that they didn't butt up to the floor but disappeared beyond it. He couldn't see what the cage was resting on and as he tried, his eye was caught by the surface of the bars – swirling patterns like solid smoke moved all over them.

'Turn on *The Gimp*,' said the drawling accent. A dull buzz filled the hall and the tingling sensation Jack had felt previously returned with vigour.

The bars flickered with a blue, neon glow. Jack lurched backwards, almost falling. He blinked, tears soaking into his balaclava. The bars flickered again, then stayed on and hummed eerily. It was like being trapped in a cage made entirely of Lightsabers.

The blue of the bars slowly changed to pink, then to a light blue, through violent red to dark green, then back to blue.

'Have to keep switching the frequency or it becomes unstable,' said the uniformed man who had been named as Rik by the crook with the stutter. 'And if they become unstable – boom.' He walked away.

Jack wanted to be anywhere else in the whole world but there. What had he been thinking? He wished he was back at the farmhouse, all tucked up in bed, safe and warm, his mum about to kiss him goodnight. He started to sob uncontrollably. It felt as if his whole neck was swelling up, suffocating him. He dropped down onto his knees in despair. The floor was chilling and unforgiving. The soldiers stared in emotionless silence. He curled into a ball, wrapped his arms tightly around his legs and rocked, trying to close himself from the nightmare.

Jack cried until his tears ran out. His balaclava was damp from them (and his running nose). He tried to think clearly and calmly but instead became angrier than he had ever experienced. He sat up onto his backside. The man was still there, sitting in a huge leather armchair in the corner. When he saw Jack, he eased himself up and walked over.

'Welcome to *The Gimp*, son, isn't she a little beauty?'

'Let me go,' said Jack, sharply.

'Well now. Why don't we start by you telling me your name?'

Jack leaped up, his anger welling up like a fifty foot wave, ready to break its wrath over the man standing on the other side of the glowing bars.

'What d'you *want* with me?' demanded Jack, stamping his foot, making the cage shudder.

'Well, I ain't gonna throw you no curve-ball, kid,' he said, almost joyously. 'We're after whatever it is you've got there that makes you so damn strong.'

'Let me out!' shouted Jack.

'I'm afraid it ain't gonna work like that, kid. You see, we have you and we're gonna use you.' He peered at Jack as though he were a freak show exhibit. 'We just gotta find out what makes you tick with such venom. Perhaps then we'll think about letting you go.'

'Huh, right.'

The old man sneered. 'I'm sure they'll be enough of you left for your parents to bury.'

Jack stuck two fingers up, then swiped his arm down, dropping to the floor and smacking his fist into the icy floor. It disappeared inside. He wiggled his left hand in beside the other and pulled them apart.

'Now I don't think you ought to be doing that, kid.' The old man sounded a little unnerved.

A hole started to appear in the floor. Jack worked his hands quickly, making it larger and larger. Outside the cage the old man nodded to a soldier sitting behind a large portable computer terminal near the entrance to the hall. The man rattled away at a keyboard with spider hands.

A new surge of electricity pressed into Jack's face like a ghost. Something buzzed beneath him and more bars, running under the floor he was busy pulling apart, flicked on. The lights in the Old Hall dimmed momentarily.

'Ah!' Jack, let go of the hole and fell back. It reformed leisurely. He dug his hands into the floor and pulled up a chunk of it. Springing up, he hurled it at the old man.

Bang.

Thick black smoke plumed up from the bars, the piece of floor exploding as it passed between them.

'Now now, kid. Don't go throwing all that floor away – you won't have nothing left to stand on. That there's special, designed by NASA for the new shuttle. It can't pass between *The Gimp's* bars.' He scrunched up his ugly wrinkled face and whispered, 'It's not really metal, you see.'

The old man paced outside the cage before facing Jack. 'You know, we've got all sorts of gadgets and gizmos back home. Why, you'd love them!' He stared at Jack with piercing blue eyes. 'We don't have to do this the hard way, kid. You can come on back to the States and we can work this here thing out together, whadda-ya-say?' He raised his wiry grey eyebrows.

'What do I *say*?' Jack's wave of anger finally broke. 'I say you can shove it and sod off back to America. I'm going to rip your head off when I get out of here, you twisted nutcase.'

The old man seemed genuinely shocked but his smugness remained. 'Now, I don't rightly like your tone of your voice, little man. I've tried to be nice about this but I can see I'm wasting my time.' He strode away, shouting. 'Prepare the transport. We'll move out as soon as it's ready. Go!'

Jack yelled. 'If you think I'm going anywhere with you, you're mistaken.'

The old man marched angrily back to the cage, his eyes wet and evil. 'No, kid, I think you'll see it's you who is mistaken… about a great many things.'

A dry swallow stuck in Jack's throat.

The old man's face relaxed, his voice suddenly calm. 'I'm gonna get some shut-eye. I suggest you do the same.'

Jack's tear ducts squeezed the last drops of moisture from his body but he made no sound. He buried his hands in his coat pockets; old tissues, bits of straw, baler cord. Then his left hand closed around a coin. Never had he been happier to see two pence in his whole life. He eyed the soldier in the far corner, sitting at the desk full of computer gadgetry. Jack tossed the coin up, caught it and took aim, waiting for a clear shot. A second later, he threw with lightning speed. A muted flash went unseen as the coin passed between the bars of the cage. It drew a faint trail as it hurtled towards the target, striking the back of a laptop computer with a loud pop, almost cutting it in half. A puff of grey smoke mushroomed over the flaming computer, quickly jumping to other apparatus on the table with a series of electric pops and sparking bangs. The soldier leaped back then got busy putting out the flames and shouting at other soldiers around him.

Immediately the humming that filled the hall stopped. The lights dimmed and the bars flickered and went out. Jack grabbed the bars, his fingers squelching into their soft outer layer. He pulled sideways with all his might and eventually they started to bend.

Orders were being screamed at soldiers.

Then Jack felt the bars began to buzz. Again, he sensed the electricity speeding along heavy power lines to his cage. He let go and fell back on the floor as the bars flicked back on and hummed menacingly.

The chance had gone. A wave of exhaustion washed over him. For the first time in days, he was tired.

The old man swaggered over. 'Kid, you're strong, but you're not that strong,' he growled.

Jack couldn't even muster the energy to insult him. He closed his eyes and fell asleep.

23

Impossible Escape

Spiders, Dracula, Frankenstein's monster, operations, being strapped down, needles, falling, drowning, weird multiple-headed creatures that drool, priests, the sticky, semi-wet sound of someone talking with a dry mouth, eating someone else's old underpants, eyeballs and teachers' putrid, warm breaths. It was Jack's worst nightmare ever, but waking up was little relief.

It was a sudden violent jerk that awoke him. He sat up with a start, his glowing prison rocking gently.

A nearby soldier stood up, startled. 'What the hell was that?' he drawled.

'Beats me,' said another.

The first rays of morning sun had crept into the Old Hall, illuminating the dust in its hazy beams. Soldiers ran to and fro, lugging equipment outside. Soon they would be on the move. The man had disappeared.

Jack's face itched beneath his balaclava. Convinced there would be cameras videoing him, he carefully slipped a hand in under and enjoyed a scratch. A few soldiers stared intently, but he was determined not to let them see his face.

'Hey, kid, you really strong as they say?'

'Let me out and I'll show you,' said Jack, coldly.

'He's strong all right,' said one of the others. 'Kicked Dwaine near enough twenty yards 'cross the hall last night, nearly broke every bone in his body, ripped a hole in that ceramo-carbide floor-block like it was Jell-o. Yeah, he's strong. No wonder Chief's going to all this trouble.'

'I'm scared' said Jack. 'I just want to go home to my mum and dad. Don't any of you have children?'

They laughed. 'Don't think you can appeal to our human side, kid, we don't got one,' said the second soldier, his dead eyes fixed in Jack's direction but not actually looking at him. 'We're the best of the best of the best. We follow orders. We take no prisoners, we have no families. We don't care for anyone and no one cares about us.'

The hall shook violently but Jack hardly noticed. How could anyone be so devoid of emotion or life?

'That an earthquake?' said the first soldier.

'Didn't think they had them here,' said the second.

'Yeah we do, we get them all the time,' said Jack, vacantly. 'Just, most people don't even feel them because they're so small.' Then added. 'The earthquakes that is, not the people.'

'How does a little brat like you know so much?' said another soldier.

Jack was thinking about Luke, stuck up on the roof. 'A friend told me.' He smiled, closing his eyes so the tears wouldn't escape. 'Suppose you don't know what it's like to have friends either?'

'Just shut the hell up,' said the second soldier. 'We don't need friends for our kind of life.'

Jack opened his eyes and spoke quietly. 'What kind of a life is that?'

'No kind of life!' boomed the voice of the man he now knew to be the chief. 'Their lives are mine, just like your life's mine, you better get used to it, sonny.'

'I hate you,' spat Jack.

'Well that is mighty sweet of you, but it ain't gonna do you no good. You're not gonna make this easy for me now, are you?'

'I'd rather die than go anywhere with you.' Jack could hardly think, he was so angry. He clenched his teeth and made tight fists of frustration.

The chief smiled, enjoying Jack's torment, and approached the cage. 'Well, if that's what it takes, so be it.'

Jack lashed out through the bars. The cage shook and blue light flared around his arm which pushed out an opaque, gel-like force field. At first, he felt no pain, only the sensation of intense pins and needles, then it became scalding, burning agony. His outstretched fingers touched the force field edge, it was hot and cold but he knew if he were able to press further he could have pushed his fingers right through. When the pain became too great, he pulled back. By the time he wrestled off his coat to examine his arm, the pain had gone. The arm was fine, though still rather skinny thought Jack, especially compared to the large gap between the bars. An idea began to form in his head.

A distressed soldier bounded into the hall, panting. 'Chief, we gotta situation – another one, bigger than before far as we can tell.'

'Time of contact?' said the chief.

'Ten minutes back.'

The chief led the soldier through the heavy curtains, away from Jack's hearing.

Jack dropped his coat and wriggled free of his long sleeve top, careful not to dislodge his balaclava.

'Sure are a skinny little runt, ain't you?' said a soldier.

Jack paid no attention, his mind racing. He glanced at his arms, the bars, down at his body, then back at the bars he had bent out the previous night. It might just work.

Standing in his favourite orange tee shirt and combat trousers, he tried to gauge how much clearance he would have either side – it would be close. He rolled his clothes into a tight ball and shoved them between the bars. They burst into flames, hissing and sizzling as the soldiers jumped into frantic action. By the time they found a fire extinguisher, all that remained was a black, smoking mess on the hall floor.

Jack kicked a charred clod of burning material from the edge of his prison as another tremor shook the building. A peal of guns and artillery shells followed. Launceston was sounding more like a war-zone than a sleepy market town.

A sharp crescendo concluded with a spectacular crash, blasting debris and clouds of pulverised plaster everywhere as a US army tank smashed through the roof of the hall, landing upside down, crunching into the wooden floorboards, and half burying itself in the process. The engine grumbled as one of the caterpillar tracks derailed and jammed. A desperate screech of grinding metal filled the hall as the track broke and mangled into itself. The engine stalled.

A gaping hole in the roof revealed an overcast sky but, incredibly, the tank had managed to miss everyone in the hall and also the cables on the roof.

'Well?' barked the chief at his sedentary troops. 'Take a look inside.'

The soldiers dashed forward from Jack's cage and prised open the escape hatch on the tank's belly. Immediately pained screams could be heard from within.

A soldier crawled through the hatch bleeding from a cut on his head. 'Giant. Huge goddamn great giant. Must be sixty yards tall. Weapons no good, not even shells. It's wrecking the town. Gotta get outta here, gotta –' But he collapsed into the arms of one of Jack's guards.

The other soldiers from the tank were equally scared and panicked. Two were pulled out unconscious or dead, Jack never found out which.

The sooner he was free, the sooner he could help in some way, even if only to get people away from this new monster. He doubted he would be as lucky as he was against the first giant if he tried to fight this one. No point in thinking about that now, anyway. First he had to concentrate on freeing himself.

Backing away as far as possible from the bent-out bars and with a belly full of nerves, he shuffled a couple of quick steps and kicked off. The floor gave slightly but it was still a solid take-off. He shot between the bars, his arms above his head, twisting his body sideways. Electricity pulled at his bare arms and a membrane of elastic force field closed around him. The pain was instant, like being stabbed with a thousand red-hot and ice-cold needles, it was so intense he couldn't even scream.

The cage's electrical hum intensified. Several fizzing sounds were followed by a small explosion of sparks and fire. As they turned, the chief and his men glimpsed the blur of an object hurtling across the hall and through the large vinyl curtain (leaving a neat tear).

As he bounced off the walls of the corridor, Jack's senses returned. He bumped to a stop in the cloakroom, a mess of flailing limbs – panting but happy to be alive. A book fell on his head, landing open on page forty-two. He smiled. It was *The Book of Untrue Facts*.

"Military... ranks... generals. Generals are soldiers who stay at the back."

'Huh,' said Jack. He picked himself up and raced back down the corridor, knocking a couple of soldiers flying. On reaching the hall he found a wall of men protecting their leader, their guns raised, ready to fire.

'Don't shoot,' bellowed the chief. 'I want him alive.'

Jack ripped out one of the metal poles from the entrance to the hall and deftly swept it through the soldiers' legs, sending them flying. In the same movement, he whipped around, sliding across the floor, and kicked the chief's feet away, knocking him flat on his face. He yanked him up by the belt and hurried over and up the few steps to the level of the gym, dropping him with a thud. He dug his foot under the chief and rolled him over, casually avoiding the wild swing of a fist. Jack caught the hand and crushed it until something snapped.

'Aagh! You little –'

'Now now, Chief, all's fair in love and war. How does it feel, huh?' Jack's face was red with anger. He grabbed the chief by the throat, lifting him up and kicking his feet out over the edge of the stage. They were face to face at either end of Jack's slender, outstretched arm. The chief's legs dangled above the hall floor. Jack was careful not to crush his throat... too much.

'Hurts, doesn't it?' Jack was vaguely aware of gunshots close by.

'Aagh, no... please,' begged the chief.

'You bullying git.'

'N-o-o.'

'I hate you! I hate you!' Jack kicked the chief viciously in the ribs. Another loud crack sounded. The chief gasped for breath and gripped Jack's arm but could do nothing.

'Sorry?' said Jack. 'Didn't get that. Did it hurt? Are you scared? You see, *Captain America*, I may have the strength of a thousand men, and I may be virtually indestructible, but I still have the mind of a child. I'm still learning that two wrongs don't make a right. You kick me, I kick you back.' Tears rolled down Jack's face. 'You scared me to death!'

'Hey, kid,' said a voice. Jack ignored it.

'You're a bullying, evil coward.'

'Balaclava Boy!'

Jack looked up. Several soldiers were standing around him and the chief, their guns pointed down.

The chief could hardly speak, his voice hoarse and strained. 'Sh-oot him.'

'We tried that, Chief – but he didn't even notice.'

'Ag-ain,' spluttered the chief, all the time kicking and punching at Jack.

'No, sir, we're not gonna shoot him again.' It was one of the soldiers who had been guarding the cage earlier. 'What are you gonna do to him, kid?'

'Not sure, throw him through the window, bounce him on the ceiling?' Jack's heart ached with pain and fear. 'Break... his stupid... neck?'

'Don't kill him, son, he ain't worth it.'

Jack could see himself jerking his hand slightly to snap the chief's neck. Just a quick flick of the wrist and he'd be dead. No-one would care, surely. What did death mean to Jack? One second the chief would be alive and evil, the next he could be dead and harmless. It seemed pretty straightforward. But a voice in his head had other ideas. It was busy repeating what the soldier had said, only it sounded like his mum talking. What would she say? His dad too? His whole family? Sister, brother, uncles, aunts, cousins... his friends. They would all be shocked, disgusted... ashamed. Jack wouldn't be able to live with that. Then he remembered the old man who had been the giant and his heart broke all over again.

'We can't stop that giant out there,' said the soldier. 'I believe you've already despatched one monster. People are getting hurt... killed. We sure could use some help – *your* help.'

Jack was shaking – his anger and conscience in their final moments of battle. Finally, he threw the chief down. He landed in a noisy heap of gasps and painful whimpers. High above, the shock of his ample weight hitting the floor dislodged a small piece of metal wedged in a ceiling tile. It fell, spinning through the air with harmless glee, landing a couple of metres from the recovering chief, who by now had rolled over and was on all fours.

The jolt of hitting the floor caused the lump of metal's trigger mechanism to deploy. The bullet it expelled passed cleanly through the fatty part of the chief's right buttock, then through the fatty part of his left buttock, finally lodging in a wooden panel behind him. His screams echoed through the deserted corridors accompanied by some faint laughter.

The giant appeared from nowhere on the outskirts of Launceston shortly after sunrise. It ripped the roof off from Pasty King's factory and peered in hungrily. The nightshift workers ran, screaming in terror. Such easy prey. It reached down with huge dirty hands, searching and grabbing feverishly. The breakfast it craved was raised high into the cold morning air. The messy pit of a mouth opened revealing bloodstained teeth and a tongue crusted with the remnants of its last kill. The enormous slug-like fingers tightened their grip and began to squeeze. The screams grew louder as into its mouth splattered the whole contents of the gigantic cooking pot that would have filled the twelve thousand, five hundred and twenty-one pasties the factory had planned to churn out that day.

It swallowed heartily and gave a huge roar of relief, showering large cow-pat-sized blobs of pasty mix over a thirty-metre radius. One poor employee was splattered with several, felling him instantly. He skidded across the floor, ending up wedged under a stainless steel trolley. An hour later, ambulance crews found him concussed, confused, but alive.

The giant dropped the pot, which landed on the general manager's new Mercedes, crushing the roof and setting the alarm off. The high-pitched squeal aggravated the giant and it roared before covering its dustbin-lid ears and searching out the source of

231

the irritating noise. When it finally pinpointed the car as being responsible, it removed the cooking pot and picked up the car, before discarding it like an unwanted toy. Two and a half seconds later, the car crash-landed in a distant field with a metallic thwack, where it remained for two years, rusting away and providing several new and exciting habitats for various small creatures.

Boom.

The giant staggered forward, crushing six thousand pounds worth of recently refurbished reception with its rugged right foot. The employees had thought the work had been money wasted (which it was) but no one could have predicted it was because five days after completion, it would be obliterated by a giant's foot.

Boom.

This time, the giant did not move. It had the measure of whatever kept poking it in the back and span around to face it (taking the reception toilets out with its heel).

Boom.

The shell struck the giant above its belly-button and exploded, singeing several wiry stomach hairs. The smell was quite pleasant for the giant but it smarted a little and a black mark remained where it had struck.

Boom.

A huge hand darted up and met the shell at a thirty-degree angle, deflecting it and taking out the staff canteen as it exploded.

The giant took two steps forward, leaned down and picked up the tank. It didn't even notice the gun-fire, grenades and rocket launchers that popped against its armour-plated skin as it shook the tank violently. Like a broken toy, it too was tossed carelessly away, somewhere in the direction of the school.

Jack jumped onto the roof of the boarders' building – he had not forgotten about Luke and also knew he would get a good view of the giant. Luke was huddled in the corner wrapped in a silver blanket like a marathon runner at the end of a race. He woke up as Jack landed. 'Hey, Jack, you escaped.'

'Yeah, you OK?'

'My body temperature has dropped a little which has led to

slight stiffening of the muscles, but other than that – I'm OK.'

Jack laughed. 'I've never been so glad to see and hear your logical self.'

Luke started to unravel himself to get up. 'I was confident that you would escape.'

'Oh hell, stay down,' said Jack, nervously. He quickly checked over the edge of the building then darted back to stand a few metres in front of Luke.

'What's up?' said Luke.

'Hold on,' said Jack. The distinct sound of screaming grew louder and louder. Jack stood, arms raised to shoulder height, waiting.

Luke peeked from behind the low wall. 'Ah.' He ducked back as a car shot over his head.

It landed with a rackety thud of creaking metal and breaking glass, but much to Luke's surprise didn't smash into the roof or bounce and skid over the side as he suspected it would in the split second he had to analyse the situation. Instead, the car seemed to stop dead like a javelin – its nose stuck into the roof. The screaming inside the car stopped and was replaced with relieved whimpering.

'Oh crap,' said Luke, hauling himself up. Jack had been standing right where the car landed.

'Help,' said Jack, agonisingly.

'Coming,' said Luke.

'Hurry,' said Jack.

Luke found Jack sat on his bum, his legs stretched out beneath the car. He had caught it with one arm under it, one arm up the side.

'Scratch my nose please,' said Jack. Luke bent down and obliged.

'Oh thanks, that was driving me mad.'

Greatly relieved, Jack raised the car, struggling onto his feet, then gently lowered it to the roof.

'Hello?' said a trembling voice from inside.

'Huh?' They both peered in.

'Nurse De – I mean, Mrs Gaunt. Blimey, are you all right?' said Luke.

'Oh my heavens,' she said. 'Could you please help me out, dear? I feel rather light-headed.'

The building shook as another tremor hit the town.

Mrs Gaunt jumped. 'Oh you poor things, are you all right? Terrible business, another one of those horrible beasts. Picked the car up just like that.'

'It's OK, the Balaclava Boy caught you,' said Luke, impressively.

'Luke,' said Mrs Gaunt. 'It is you. Oh dear me! What are you doing here? Do your parents know? Dear things... Your poor mother, such a lovely girl. You know, my Tom dated her back-along. But they fell out, ever so silly really but that's youth. Course, he wouldn't have met Jill then and I wouldn't have little Willie, but poor Jill, her sister's husband's ill with chicken pox at forty-three. Could be serious at that age and what with his cousin's wife's father being poorly with a virus he caught in hospital when he only went in with an ingrown toenail. Sadly he passed away the next day. Mind you, he was a hundred and three... but so sudden.'

'I've got go,' said Jack, quietly. 'You'll be all right here, won't you?'

'Yeah. Be careful, Balaclava Boy.' Luke smiled, reassuringly.

'Thank you, young man,' shouted Mrs Gaunt as Jack launched himself into the sky, straight towards the giant.

24

More Problems

Helen was ranting. 'If one more emmet asks me where the best place to see giants is or if I know the stupid Balaclava Boy, I swear I'm gonna swing for them – it's the faces they pull when I say I don't know anything about it.' She paused. Agnes nodded. Helen continued. 'You'd have thought I'd just told them their posh car had been filled with fresh cow dung.'

'I agree, it is rather annoying,' said Agnes. 'So, who do you think it is?'

'I knew you were gonna ask that,' said Helen, laughing. 'Actually it's me. I'm the Balaclava *Girl*. Huh, wouldn't be seen dead in one of them things, who wears balalcavas for flip's sake, except those paramilitary types and boys who want to join the army. I'm dying for a drink, me throat's dry as a stick.'

'No wonder, talking so much, you're as bad as your mum. She was hilarious last night, thanks for letting me stay over,' said Agnes. 'D'you want to stay over my house next week sometime?'

'Yeah, thanks my –' Helen stopped, making to zip her mouth shut before she could say anything more.

A car revved by with blaring music, then skidded to a halt. The passenger door opened and out climbed Rob Dunce, smiling.

'Losers,' whispered Helen.

Agnes dropped her school bag to the ground. 'What do you want now?'

The wind rushed over Jack's body. Below stretched a trail of devastation from Pennygillam industrial estate to the centre of town; flattened cars, flattened buildings, people hurt, perhaps dead, cars queuing – their paths blocked by crushed houses, military and police vehicles moving to confront the menace. Yet unbelievably, many morning shoppers crowded the high street, oblivious (or stubbornly ignorant) to the fact that their town was under attack.

Jack didn't see the roof of a house twirling silently through the morning sky, so couldn't even brace himself for the impact.

Crash.

He smashed through it, helplessly showering debris to the ground. Luckily no one was around for it to hit. The collision hardly broke his flight – he was still hurtling towards the giant, which, luckily, was facing the other way.

He landed on its shoulders, grabbing two handfuls of stiff black hair. The stench was unbelievable – a mixture of rotting flesh and cheap perfume. Immediately crane-like hands swung over the formidable back, scrabbling for whatever pest was irritating him so. A guttural snarl accompanied the swift, grasping swipes. Jack rolled to one side to avoid the first, then immediately had to do the same on the other side. The third time he wasn't so lucky and the tree-trunk fingers clamped him tightly. He was hoisted over the shoulder for examination.

The face before Jack was horrific. Originally, it may have been human, but was now a disfigured mutation, hardly recognisable as once being Homo sapiens. The normal proportioning of eyes, nose, mouth and cheeks were greatly distorted. Every feature was bruised and swollen. But this was no old man, subjected to hideous disfigurement. This creature was muscular and vulgar. It made the Hulk look like Arnold Schwarzeneggar's wimpy younger brother. Every aspect of this giant screamed 'raging psychopath'. Nothing human remained in these eyes – just pure hatred.

Its chin was crusted with old food and smelled unmistakably of pasty. The bulbous nostrils flared and blew wagon-ropes of snot over the stubbly top lip every time it exhaled. The stained yellow teeth were caked with the remnants of previous meals.

Sickened, Jack averted his gaze. Not even his perfumed balaclava could mask the stench. 'You stink,' he shouted. 'Could've brushed your teeth at least.'

The beady eyes squinted at Jack as the creature sucked in a great lungful of air.

Jack was unable to bury his head. 'No, not again.'

For a second time in a few days he was caught in a wretched blast of putrid, warm breath accompanied by an ear-shattering roar, before being tossed away like a sweet wrapper. It was all too familiar as Jack span through the air, squirming for control over his chaotic flight.

He could do nothing to prevent crashing through a roof, scattering debris everywhere and landing in a heap. Water sprayed into his face. He lifted his head, wiping the water from his eyes, horrified to see his fall had been broken by a urinal.

'It's definitely not like this in *Smallville*,' he said, panting. 'Still, could've been worse, least it wasn't the Ladies.'

'Wow,' squeaked a high-pitched voice behind him. 'Are you the Balaclava Boy?'

Jack pushed himself away from the foul-smelling porcelain and turned to see a young boy stood by the sinks, his head and shoulders dusted with plaster and crumbs of ceiling tile. 'No,' said Jack, 'I'm Britney Spears – this is a stunt for my new video "Plop till you drop".'

The child's face was unmoved. 'No, you are him, aren't you?'

'There's no fooling you, is there?'

'No, there isn't,' he said, matter-of-factly. 'What are you doing here?'

Jack looked around. 'Just dropped in to use the loo.' He smiled.

'Really?'

'No. Look, maybe you should run off and find your parents. Not sure if you realised but there's a flaming great giant out there trying to tear the place apart.'

'Really?'

'No, I'm making it up to impress you... For crying out loud!' The boy was really irritating. Jack got up and brushed himself off.

Gunfire and explosions started somewhere near the town centre.

'What is that?' whined the boy.

'I really don't know,' said Jack, sarcastically. 'Maybe someone's making popcorn in the car park?'

'Really?'

'No. What does it sound like?'

'Guns and bombs.'

'Yes – because that's what it is.'

The boy stared blankly at Jack. 'You know, for a superhero you're a bit of a ninny-narner.' He off ran.

'Charming,' said Jack to himself. 'For a little boy you're a bit of an irritating, obnoxious pillock.'

Jack followed him out. The toilets were in the car park of the old market, halfway up Race Hill. The boy had vanished. Jack launched himself into the air to the left of the giant, aiming for the roof of the White Hart hotel.

As he landed, an artillery shell exploded under the giant's armpit causing it to throw the Launceston Self-Drive van it was busy crushing, over its shoulder. Jack could tell immediately it would land at the end of the High Street which, incredibly, was still teeming with early morning shoppers. He leaped, keeping an eye on the spinning van as it arced high in the sky.

'Get out the way,' he shouted. 'Move.'

Everyone ignored him. He landed and tried herding the shoppers like sheep but that didn't work either (herding sheep was far easier).

The van would land any second, squashing several pedestrians. Jack half thought to let it. He wondered if Batman ever had ideas like that, then forced himself back to the problem at hand.

He would need to knock the van sideways through the air, away from the people below. Generating that kind of power would be difficult from a standing start and the van was falling rapidly.

A frantic scream signified that someone from the crowd had finally spotted the vehicular meteor.

Whatever Jack was going to do, he had to do it fast. Then he spotted the huge wooded doors of the post office. They were perfect – opened, as always, at a forty-five-degree angle to the street.

He ran and jumped at the left-hand door. When his feet made contact, he bent his knees. The door gave slightly, acting as a springboard. He shot off like a bullet, flying a metre above the heads of the crowd, twisting around so his back was to the ground.

He pummelled against the van in mid-air, like a human battering ram. The force immediately knocking it sideways. He grabbed the side-door handle, his momentum taking him over the top of the van, which rotated under him as he clung to it.

The crowd below him screamed madly.

The van was a metre from the tarmac when it rolled across the shoulders of those pedestrians who had only bothered to crouch, rather than fall flat onto the road.

Finally Jack's feet hit the ground. He stumbled backwards, taking a few stuttering steps while holding the van inches above the heads of the horde of people surrounding him. The screaming stopped abruptly. Jack sighed and carefully picked his way through them. A little wobble brought several sharp intakes of breath. As he placed the vehicle down in the road, the muttering started. Then cameras flashed at him.

'It's him, that Balaclava Boy. Squat little thing, ain't he?'

'Well done, boy.'

'Daft sod's put it on a double yellow line.'

A terrible thumping blasted through the air. Boom, boom, boom, bo-boom. Boom, boom, boom, bo-boom.

Jack feared the worst and spun around only to see the familiar gaudily customised 1995 Ford Fiesta that belonged to Gary Dunce. His brother was sitting next to him and a third person was with them. She was leaning from the back window, her screaming drowned out by the atomic bass. To Jack's surprise, it was Agnes.

'Oh, great, what now,' he said, annoyed.

Running to the middle of the road, he braced himself, intending to stop the car and free Agnes. But instead it screeched to a halt ten metres before him. He relaxed, wondering what they were doing. A panicked scream behind Jack was meant as a

239

warning but didn't work. The Splatts Hardware delivery van landed right on top of him with a terrifying crunch.

It was dark, very dark, and smelled of white spirit. Jack shook his head, waiting impatiently for his eyes to adjust. The thumping bass passed by. A little shaken, Jack fought his way through the mess in the back of the van and kicked at the mangled back doors which dropped to the road, then stepped out and brushed himself off.

He was preparing to leap back towards the giant when frantic waving caught his eye. 'Hey, you're not going to leave that there, are you?' moaned an old woman with lopping lips.

Jack stopped. 'What?'

'It's in the way,' she shrieked.

'Of what?' said Jack, aghast.

'I don't know yet, but something,' she said, childishly.

Jack sighed and reluctantly pushed the van over to the pavement. It grated across the road leaving a trail of broken glass and metal. 'Happy?'

'Better there, than where it was,' she said begrudgingly as a gleefully wicked, but toothless smile drew across her face.

'Can I go now?' he said, sarcastically, and leaped into the sky.

'Aggravating so-and-so,' he heard her say.

Jack landed at the far end of the square. Sink n' Tap's confused head plumber skidded the company's brand new van to a halt in front of the giant. He threw open the door, jumping halfway out before the seat belt jerked him back in. He hurriedly undid it and ran away.

The giant thrust an eager hand down and scooped up the vehicle. With startling speed it hurled it at Jack. He dodged sideways and caught it by the back door, swung it around and threw it straight back. It thudded into the hairy stomach and broke in two. The giant fell backwards and took out half of Barclays Bank with its demolition-ball head. The ground shook. The bank alarm clanged into life with a relentlessly monotonous ring. Swiftly, the giant flicked his fist up and punched what was left of the bank. The alarm stopped but was replaced by desperate screaming.

Soldiers appeared on every street and started shooting at the creature. An armoured assault vehicle edged its way around the corner and fired. The giant hardly seemed to notice.

The source of the screaming was hanging from a door that was suspended from a door-frame, that was protruding from a wrecked wall (the floor no longer there to support any of it). The perilous pendulum swung awkwardly back and forth over an empty space that had been the first floor.

As Jack set off to help the woman, the giant sat up in front of him, its stomach gurgling ominously. It stretched both arms around several cars and swept them towards Jack. He jumped just in time to avoid becoming a car sandwich, glancing down in mid-air and feeling triumphant. But then the giant batted him with a flattened 2 CV, a fine sweep to square leg that any cricketer would have been proud of. He shot straight through the wall of the Nat West, tripping the modern polyphonic and irritatingly loud alarm. After struggling free from his latest destructive sculpture, Jack was confronted by a shaking man in a shiny grey suit with zips on every pocket.

'Take the money but please don't hurt us,' cried Mr Scrimper, the manager.

'Huh?'

'Take it. Everything we've got, just don't hurt us,' he begged.

'I'm going to,' said Jack. He could hardly hear himself over the alarm. 'I'm trying to fight the stupid giant. You lot better get out of here,' said Jack, addressing the crowd of bank staff and customers huddled behind the counter.

'Get out, now!' yelled Jack. They didn't move. 'Any second now, that giant is going to tear this building apar –'

A huge fist smashed through the roof, narrowly missing Jack.

'Fire exit,' yelled Mr Scrimper. They ran.

The other fist then smashed through the roof. Jack dived out of the way then followed the crowd out and down the alleyway that ran behind the White Hart hotel.

The giant clasped its hands over its ears, then pounded away at the bank, but still the alarm kept playing its jolly tune. Then the giant froze, groaned, and clutched its grubby stomach. (Later, Jack swore to Luke and Al that it had almost smiled.) Uncomfortably, it turned and squatted over the broken building. From the passageway, they could see its immense hairy back and the top of its formidably large and naked buttocks.

'It can't be,' said Jack.

'No. Please not...' wailed Mr Scrimper.

'It is, you know,' said a smartly dressed middle-aged bank clerk.

The awfulness of the sound was matched only by the severity of the stench. Mercifully, the ghastly spectacle did not last long. Several people fainted on the spot. Of those that remained conscious, most were unable to hold their stomachs (which only added to the already pungent air).

Jack smiled, thankful for the artificially strong smell of flowers emanating from the patch on his balaclava. 'Were you expecting a large deposit today?' he asked Mr Scrimper, who collapsed like a bunch of broccoli.

At first, the alarm carried on regardless, though sounding like it had been submerged under water (in this case water would have been far preferable). But gradually it lost the will to ring, and stuttered to a silent end.

Between the continuing gunfire, grenades and rockets directed at the giant, Jack again heard the screaming of the dangling Barclays Bank woman. He held his nose and ran back down the alleyway, jumping a five-metre spread of giant-dung leaking from the fire exit of the Nat West (think slow-moving volcanic lava).

The woman was clinging to the door for all she was worth (and she thought she was worth an awful lot).

'H-e-lp. H-e-lp.'

'Hang on, coming,' shouted Jack.

'You're not going anywhere, sunshine,' said a voice.

'Gibson,' said Jack, surprised.

The smarmy lawman was accompanied by two primates in ill-fitting uniforms.

'How d'you know my name? And that's *Inspector* Gibson to you, you freaky little balaclava-wearing weirdo.'

'That's nice coming from a policeman,' said Jack. 'Your name's on your badge,' he said, relieved to have noticed.

'Huh,' scoffed Gibson. 'This whole place is full of freaks and you're the worst.'

'Thought you were meant to be a pillar of the community... more like *pillock* if you ask me.'

'Right, that's it. Grab him, boys.'

The officers darted forward, one from each side. Jack shoved the first one away as the second grabbed him. As gently as he could, Jack stamped on his foot. A week ago he wouldn't have known that he had just broken the second and third metatarsal bones. He smiled as the officer screamed. Poor footballers.

Gibson was deceptively quick and snapped a handcuff over Jack's wrist, the other already around his own. He sneered. 'Where you go, I go.'

'You really are stupid, aren't you?' Jack dragged Gibson a few metres forward to show him the poor woman still swinging precariously above the half-demolished building.

At the far end of the square the giant smashed a fist down onto a tank and kicked it back down the road. Then it swept both hands through the first two shops and flats that backed against the castle perimeter, flattening and spreading them forward into (and all over), the square.

Gibson called for police back-up, the Fire Brigade, and ambulances but was told they were all in the area anyway.

Jack backed away from Gibson and started spinning him around. Ignoring the protests, Jack kept going until the policeman lost his footing and screamed as his legs scraped over the tarmac.

'Let me down,' he ordered.

Jack stopped, letting Gibson smack down onto the road. 'Now get lost,' said Jack, wrenching the handcuff from his wrist.

'Just a few seconds more.' Jack shouted up to the woman.

The entire bank front was gone, the rest of the staff nowhere to be seen. One thing that was intact was the metal frame of the security windows that stood between the bank tellers and the public. Jack yanked it loose. It was a little bashed up but would do the job. He manoeuvred it under the woman, propping it against the back wall.

'Let go,' he called up. 'You should slide down just fine.'

'Are you sure?'

'Just hurry up,' he called.

She let go, bumping and bouncing all the way down the makeshift slide. Jack caught her at the bottom.

'OK?' he said.

'Yes, I think so,' she said, smiling wildly. 'Thank you, young man. You saved my life.' She grabbed him, hugging tightly. Jack wished it was his mum.

'My plant!' she cried, letting him go and pointing frantically. 'Please won't you save it for me? Gran gave it to me, just before she died.'

'But I've got to –'

She broke down in floods of tears.

Boom.

A mobile artillery unit had rolled into the square and started firing. The giant was busy digging around where he had cleared the first few houses.

The woman was still crying and pointing at a manky plant lying on its side in one of the ground floor offices (she had been upstairs when the giant arrived and had hid in someone else's office).

'All right,' said Jack reluctantly and ran over the rubble and broken office furniture to the plant. He held it up for the woman to see. She nodded excitedly. He took one step before the whole building fell in on top of him. The stream of bricks, blocks and rafters pouring over the area where he had stood seemed endless.

The woman checked to make sure no one had seen, then sheepishly started edging away. She glanced back, hoping the little superhero would burst from the rubble, still clutching her precious plant.

He didn't.

She was almost at the corner and took one last look at the pile of rubble and noticed slight movement. Creeping back, she kept one eye on the giant, who was still busy digging away.

Something was stirring under the dust and debris, like a burrowing mole. An upright girder creaked sideways like a lazy windscreen wiper before slowly, a trembling hand edged out followed by the other, pushing a broken plant pot, half full of soil – a miserable, bent stalk protruding to the side. Finally, a filthy balaclava appeared accompanied by lots of spitting and gasping for clean air.

Jack crawled forward until he was clear of the wreckage, gathered himself and lumbered over to the woman, thrusting the pot in her hand.

She deliberated whether to accept, her face like sour milk. 'Oh, that's very –'

'My pleasure,' he said, sarcastically, '...think it may need some water.' He tried to give the woman a look, any kind of look, to tell her what he really thought of her, but it was not easy giving someone a look while wearing a balaclava. He gave up and turned back to the giant.

It was digging like a thing possessed. The army were firing relentlessly – guns, bazookas, sheep – anything they could possibly find (well, maybe not sheep). The battle noise could be heard for miles and though the giant flinched at some loud bangs, it hardly noticed the bullets and shells that struck it.

Jack was puzzled. 'What on earth is it doing?' he asked himself.

'Digging, I should say.'

Jack jumped. 'Why do you always have to do that? Why? As if things aren't tense enough around here?'

Fynn's face was shocked. He raised his voice over the din. 'I was... actually, if truth be told, in this particular instance, I was trying to avoid being seen until the very last minute.'

'Well, OK then.'

'I do believe it's searching for something,' said Fynn, removing his hat and scratching his thinning hair. 'Pixash has gone to call Golitha.'

'D'you know if Al is all right?'

'Yes, Zilch gave us word. They reached the river late last night, though not without bother.'

'What kind of bother?'

'An army unit, Zilch exhausted himself during their escape, which ended a little bumpily.'

'Was Al hurt?'

'Hardly.'

'Hardly. What does that mean?'

'Minor flesh wounds, Jack. The water nymphs took care of them and Al returned home first thing this morning.'

'Water *what*?'

'Nymphs.'

'Oh, of course,' said Jack. 'I knew they'd help out.' Then realising Fynn did not understand his sarcasm said. 'Well, as long as he's safe.'

Fynn paced back and forth, muttering away to himself as Jack watched the giant continue to dig.

'How am I supposed to fight it?' he asked Fynn.

Fynn ignored him, continuing to pace before casually walking around the corner of the destroyed bank.

Boom, boom, boom, bo-boom.

The Dunce-mobile. Jack hurried down the street hoping to intercept it. Agnes was still leaning out of the back window. The car sped by as Jack approached and he sprinted after it. Soon, he was within metres of it and shouted to Agnes. 'What's happening?'

'I can't get away,' she yelled.

'I'll help you.'

'Look out,' she screamed.

A massive chunk of wall was falling through the sky.

'Sod it,' he said, stopping.

'Help me,' Agnes shouted as the car disappeared around the corner.

Again he shouted at pedestrians to move away and was largely ignored. Positioning himself under the falling mass, when it was about ten metres from the ground, he leaped up to meet it. They collided and it broke in half. Jack hung on to the one half but the other fell on the road with a bricky clatter, narrowly missing a group of people crowded in the entrance of the Stone Masons' Arms.

Jack landed and dropped the rest of the wall safely on the pavement. A head of blonde hair caught his eye. 'Arse,' he moaned, spotting the TV camera pointing at him.

The laugh was controlled but seemed a little scared. 'There he is in action, our very own Balaclava Boy.' She darted around the smashed wall with incredible speed for someone wearing such high heels. 'So, why did you push Harriet Vermin off the castle?' She shoved the microphone into his face.

'Her name's Vernon, and I didn't push her. It was an accident. Dunce pushed me and I bumped into her. I was trying to help.'

'Are you in love with her?'

'What? Are you mental?'

Katie Lame's eyes flashed with rage, her face twitching momentarily. 'Who are you working for and why do you keep destroying things?'

'What?' said Jack. 'I haven't destroyed anything. It's that flipping great giant, you idiotic numbskull.'

'There's no need for such rudeness, young man. I'm just doing my job.' Her head span robotically back to her crew. 'We'll cut that,' she snapped, whipping back with a false smile. 'What do you know about the giants, my dear?'

'Nothing.'

'But you know how to fight them, right?'

'No.'

'You don't seem to know much all of a sudden, do you?'

Jack didn't know what to say. 'I'm going. If I was you lot, I'd get as far away as possible.'

'We can look after ourselves, right, boys?' she said, nodding her head at the trembling crew. They mumbled incoherently. 'Well, this has been Katie Lame, live from Laun-ces-ston, talking to the Balaclava Boy for *Kids News Extra, Extra!* Is there a battle on, or whadda-ya-say?' Her smile was so ridiculously large it almost hurt Jack to look at it. 'Cut,' she snarled, her smile vanishing. She narrowed her eyes at Jack. 'We're watching you, little man... every single move you make.'

Jack backed away slowly until he felt safe to turn and run. A shiver tiptoed up his spine. She was scarier than the giant.

Fynn was nowhere to be seen. The giant had given up on digging and was standing erect, scanning the area – its physique lithe and grotesque. The sight disheartened Jack. How could he defeat it? It was a huge, vile, armour-plated monster *and* it was naked.

The army had thrown everything they had at it (which in Jack's opinion, had not been as much as he had expected) and it still stood fast. All it had suffered was mild irritation and a few singed hairs, its body blackened from explosions. Still they kept firing, though it seemed with less enthusiasm.

A small unit of men crouched halfway up the square behind an overturned car. Jack approached and had to shout his 'Hello' several times before they heard.

'Fire!' yelled the sergeant as they let rip another bazooka shell. It deflected off the side of the giant's thigh, exploding in the empty cab of an army truck at the end of the High Street. The soldiers huddled behind it darted for new cover.

'Gordon Bennett,' winced the sergeant nervously. 'For heaven's sake, Smalls, the head. Aim for the flipping head. Well, Balaclava Boy, what are you going to do this time, eh?'

'That's what I was going to ask you lot. Where are all the big guns?'

'Big guns he says, Smalls, big guns.'

'Yes, Sergeant Spitty,' said Smalls, begrudgingly.

The recently promoted Sergeant Spitty ran his hand over his new stripes. 'There are no big guns. None. Virtually everything's been loaded up, on its way to –'

Smalls interrupted with a harsh cough.

'Yes, *Private* Smalls?' said Sergeant Spitty.

'Confidential, sir,' he whispered loudly.

'I know,' squealed Sergeant Spitty. 'Anyway, all you need to know, sonny, is we ain't got no big guns.'

Jack left them. He would have to try and stop the giant by himself, but how? The previous giant now seemed comparatively fragile, but then it had turned out to be a frail old man. Jack imagined that, on seeing this giant in human form, it would resemble a bodybuilding henchman with a taste for horse steroids.

The giant frowned and leaned back, roaring into the sky. It stormed into the square, taking out more of the shops and flats that backed against the castle grounds. Reaching down, it tore the whole roof off St Mary Magdalene's church.

The vicar was at the altar, praying for all he was worth (which by religious terms, was not that much). Having the roof over his head lifted off was not something he was expecting and gave him an almighty fright.

He cowered. 'Jesus Christ!' Then quickly made the sign of the cross muttering, 'Sorry,' before running out the back.

The giant dropped the roof and raised both fists, crashing them down into the middle of the church, destroying the neat wooden benches and breaking up the ornate stone floor. It scrabbled around, digging down... searching.

Jack realised he was shaking with fear. He tried to reflect on everything that had happened to him, especially the positive aspects like the fact that he was still alive. But that was the only positive thing he could think of, so before all the negative points filled his head, he decided it was time to have another go at fighting the giant. He jumped on to a nearby building, hoping for inspiration, but none came. Without thinking, he leaped onto the giant's shoulder. The hideous face raged with anger. Jack kicked it in the chin, his boot crunching against the leathery stubbled skin. It's head jerked violently, then slowly, turned back – the lower jaw knocked out of joint. Jack crouched, ready for action. The giant reached up taking hold of its jaw. With a grind of gristle and a hollow crack it was clicked back into place.

A shell exploded on the other side of its head, filling the air with the foul odour of burning hair. It wailed in pain. Jack screamed loudly in the wax-encrusted ear before him. The creature clamped both hands against its head, pinning Jack against the ear.

Jack shouted. 'Not too keen on loud noises, are you?'

The beast jerked its head from side to side then realised something was trapped under its hand so grabbed it. Jack was shaken vigorously and the giant roared with terrible fury before throwing him into the ruins of the church.

He crashed through the already broken floor of the church, tumbling in darkness, and thumped onto solid ground. A river of dirt and stones fell in on top of him, filling his clothing. Was this the end?

25

Darkness Descends

Jack scrambled backwards so as not to be buried, coughing and spitting out grit while trying to clear the soil from his neck. 'Where... on earth?' he sputtered. 'Or should that be... where in earth?'

The silence chilled him. His grubby skin became alive with sensations as his words were suffocated in the absolute blackness that surrounded him. Even his shallow panicky breaths were mute, every one snatched from his stickily dry mouth. He stretched out shaky arms, fearful of what his nervous fingers might discover.

Earth – damp, sandy earth, full of stones. The side of a chamber maybe? He reached blindly in the opposite direction – more of the same. To his right the way was blocked by fallen debris. He extended an arm sideways to his left – nothing. He was in a tunnel.

Jack forced in several deep, strong breaths and stood up, removing his balaclava and giving his head a relieving scratch. He had one choice – to head down the tunnel. He set off. Even the sound of his wary footsteps was sucked into the earthy ground. He edged forward, hoping for some form of light to appear but it remained absolutely black. The tunnel shook, dislodging small stones over Jack's head as the giant moved somewhere above.

'What are you doing, Jack?' he asked himself. 'Where are you going? Please don't let this be a dead end.' He laughed falsely.

'Dead end, huh...' He stopped. 'Oh no, I've started talking to myself... Have you? Yes... Damn.'

Quickening his pace in frustration, a wave of recklessness ran through him. He yelled and sprinted. 'What... are... you... doing? Running down a tunnel... in the dark.'

The ground disappeared and Jack fell in the pitch black, bashing against jagged rocks as gravity showed him what it was capable of. He twisted one way, then the other, trying to turn himself to land feet first.

Smack.

He landed back first, which knocked his breath out. In the deafening silence his body took stock, before allowing him to breathe again. He sucked in the damp, heavy air, forcing his lungs to fill completely.

Exhaling loudly, he blinked cold tears of relief. 'Wow.'

He was unhurt but shaken from such a shocking twist to this unseen adventure in the dark. A stretched out hand across wet ground discovered a dank wall, which he followed, finding only one way to move forward, touching his toes down first, to avoid further potential falls.

'Light,' he said, squinting to be sure. 'Yes.' Faint light was showing not far ahead. As soon as he was sure, he started jogging, watching out for unwelcome shafts.

'Blimey.'

Before him was a massive circular cavern, roughly fifteen to twenty metres in diameter. The light filtered in at the top from two places on opposite sides of the cavern.

'Must be as tall as that giant,' he said, the words bouncing back to him over and over again.

The rock walls were roughly cut and water trickled over them. Either side of the water, plate-sized lichens and mosses carpeted the rock face. High up, long-stemmed plants bowed out over the cavern like decorated fishing rods. The ground was solid, but the unmistakable remains of ruined wooden walkways and buildings lay all about. Some of the timbers were huge and covered with ornate carvings of incredible intricacy. Jack heard movement against the rock face opposite. 'Hello? Anyone there?'

Nothing.

The sound started again, turning into the rattle of something or someone trapped. Jack was drawn towards it. He stepped over rotten beams and broken joists, carefully edging nearer. The juddering grew louder and more violent. He peered through a length of latticework and saw a rough, wooden trunk, shaking like it was trying to tear itself apart. 'Sod that, I'm gettin' out of here.'

The distance to the light source was one he had easily jumped before, so finding a solid beam, he launched himself into the strangely still air. The gap was not as wide as he thought. He smacked against the rock, sending a stone waterfall cascading beneath him. Scrambling desperately, he jammed his hands against either side of the narrow shaft to prevent himself falling back, before easing forward until lying flat, his heart pounding against the dry ground.

Jack crawled several metres over scattered bones and stale animal droppings before the passage sloped down and opened up. A halo of bright light surrounded a large slab of rock that blocked the tunnel. With no gap clear enough to crawl through, he stretched an arm in and wrapped his fingers around the edge of the stone. It moved easily at first, then stuck against the earth of the passage wall. He heaved until it moved, scooping out a large chunk of dry earth that spewed out a cloud of dust. Past the stone plug, light flooded the tunnel, which began to narrow. Sensing that he may soon be back above ground, Jack put on his balaclava.

The passage was now so small that Jack had to crawl. At the very end were three thick iron bars (too short for bending) set between two heavy lumps of granite. Beyond was a forest of nettles and brambles. He twisted around and kicked the bars. The stones dislodged, the top one rolling forward, neatly crushing the tangle of vegetation beyond. He scrambled away and lay on his back staring into a clear blue sky. He breathed deeply, glad to be above ground among strangely familiar surroundings.

The ground rocked again. Jack jumped to his feet, realising he was in the ruins of the castle's North gate. Behind him, the army were still firing.

He hopped over the wall onto the castle green. Soldiers rushed between various military vehicles parked at the far side. Others crouched by the wall occasionally firing rifles or machine guns. Jack ran to them. 'Hello,' he yelled.

'Oh, there you are. Everyone thought you'd run off,' said a soldier. 'Can't you do something?'

'Give me a chance,' said Jack, annoyed. 'I need grenades... lots of grenades.'

'What for? They don't work, just impact on its surface.'

'You'd better move that thing too,' said Jack, pointing at a big gun near the centre of the green.

'Why?' said the soldier.

'Get me the grenades and I'll show you. *Now*,' said Jack.

The confused soldier ran off, returning seconds later with a small box of grenades. The mobile rocket launcher was moved and Jack ran to the middle of the green. Ripping off the lid of the box, he grabbed a grenade and bounced it in his hand.

'You'd better make them count, we're running low on everything,' said the soldier.

'How many seconds do I have after pulling the pin?' said Jack.

'Five,' said the soldier, running for cover.

'Right then,' said Jack to himself. 'Ready or not, here I come.'

'Wait,' called a voice.

Jack jumped. 'What now?'

Fynn and Golitha lolloped towards him.

'Jack, we think we've figured it out,' said Fynn, excited and breathless.

'Well, possibly,' said Golitha, in his calm, low voice.

'It's searching for something,' gasped Fynn. 'Something that's been lost for over a thousand years,'

Golitha nodded. 'We thought it didn't exist any more – we may just be proved wrong.'

'It must be,' puffed Fynn. 'There's no other explanation.'

'What are you planning to do with those?' said Fynn, noticing the grenades.

Jack smiled. 'Throw them at it. I'm going to –'

Boom, boom, boom.

Three shells exploded nearby hurling earth and stones into the air. Fynn and Golitha charged off in different directions.

Boom.

A fourth shell landed behind Golitha, blasting him high into the air.

'No!' screamed Jack, darting to catch him.

Golitha fell as calmly as he spoke, his robes flapping serenely, but he did not land on the ground. Quite peacefully, he disappeared into it. A muted flare of faint green light rippled across the grass and faded away.

Jack staggered, a suffocating hush surrounding him. Was Golitha dead? Was it a trick? He didn't know what to think.

Boom.

A fifth explosion shattered the quiet and Jack was blown to the ground. Why were shells landing on the green?

He righted himself and dashed back to the grenades snatching one and ripping out the pin. After three agonising seconds he let fly. It exploded behind the giant's right ear. Roaring with pain, it searched for something to throw back.

A car skidded around the corner. It was snatched from the road in a vice-like grip. The engine whined as the driver revved it to no avail, before it spluttered and died.

Jack recognised it instantly – the Duncemobile. That meant Agnes was probably inside. He grabbed two grenades, pulled the pins, counted, then snapped his arm, launching them as the giant prepared to fling the car. Both devices exploded under the giant's hand, causing it to drop the car which bounced heavily and came to rest on the edge of the steep mound surrounding the outer keep.

The giant wrenched off a chunk of castle wall throwing it with violent fury. Jack dodged most of it but one piece knocked his legs away. He sprang to his feet but had to deflect another slab of wall as he dived over to the grenades and grabbed two. He yanked the pins out with his teeth, paused, then threw them one after another. They exploded either side of the giant's head. It roared in thunderous pain like a human volcano.

Jack fumbled for more grenades, again aiming them at its head. The giant retaliated and Jack was floored but righted himself and lobbed more grenades at the beast. Finally, he pitched the last grenade which exploded under its chin, driving the creature into a feverish rage.

Jack collapsed on the grass as the giant swung its arms and launched itself at him. It was a heart-stopping sight – a naked mountain of giant in full flight, its lorry-sized feet descending upon him. He marvelled at the energy required to launch such a mass but was aware enough to leap away in plenty of time.

Easy.

But as Jack moved –

Boom.

He was blasted off his feet and thrown back to where he started from. While spinning through the air, he saw the chief balanced on crutches atop the castle wall, holding a smoking bazooka.

The giant's feet slapped down onto Jack. He shut his eyes tightly before the impact and was squashed with such pressure his breath was forced from his lungs. The ground gave beneath him like a huge block of stony butter. He could taste the fertile soil. The pressure increased. His body ached to breathe and he was starting to panic. His arms wrestled through the sea of soil to his mouth but then the resistance behind him gave way and he fell freely, rocks bouncing off him. He inhaled deeply, his mouth filling with dirt. Coughing violently, he tried to grasp hold of something solid.

His idea had worked almost perfectly, which was nice, except he hadn't planned to be under the giant's feet when it ploughed through the castle green into the huge cavern below. And again, he thought he was about to die.

26

"For the valiant Cornishman who slew the giant Cormoran"

Jack was half woken by a warm, tingling sensation spreading across his back. He wriggled cosily as if waking up in his own bed. But the warm quickly heated up, then soon reached hot. He was properly awake now and remembered his last thought – that he had been about to die.

Was he dead? It didn't feel like it, but then again how would he know? He had never been dead before, so maybe he was. It all seemed too much for his muddled mind right now.

The burning thing against his back was angular and solid. Forcing his hands up, he pushed against what he thought must be the giant's foot, then rolled sideways. Whatever had lain beneath his back shot away, thudding into something behind him. Jack coughed; his mouth was sticky and full of grit, which he spat out as best he could. He clambered to his feet and in the murky gloom made out the silhouette of a sword lodged in a heavy beam, swaying like an malevolent metronome. Confused and somewhat scared, he backed away, slowly raising his hands as protection against the unknown. But as he did this, the ominous weapon unstuck itself and whipped through the air. Jack staggered backwards, ducking away instinctively and stumbling to the ground. Something struck his right hand. Nervously, he opened his eyes to see the sword nestled in his fist.

'Weird,' he muttered, swishing it to and fro, childishly disappointed that it lacked the hum of a Lightsaber. The dark blade was about a metre long – straight and menacing, yet feather-light. A pleasant tremble buzzed through his hands and arms. He rubbed a thumb over the blade edge, catching a few small nicks but it felt like the carving knife after his dad had been at it with the steel – razor-sharp. The hilt was bound with leather and separated from the blade by a round guard – samurai style. Several words were carved around it. They reminded Jack of the writing from the parchment that had disappeared in front of him so many days ago in the physics lesson.

Jack found a scabbard lying nearby. Extracting the baler cord from his side pocket, he tied it through eyelets at the top and bottom of the scabbard and sheathed the sword before hoisting it over his shoulder.

The giant was still. Jack hoped it was dead but, recalling the sickening way in which the first giant had shrunk back to the size of a normal man, doubted it. Soon it would stir.

Seeing no clear way to jump to the surface, Jack began climbing up one of the tree-trunk legs, grabbing handful after handful of bristly hair. It grew lighter as he neared the surface, which was eerily quiet. Finally he squeezed through a gap by the solid mass of the still monster. As Jack lay exhausted on the grass, a murmur spread like a Mexican wave through the crowd that had gathered.

The giant's head was slumped forward, its left arm stretched out in front, the right one, behind, pointing to the castle. Soldiers with linked arms jostled to hold back the multitude, including Katie Lame's news crew. A camera flashed to the side of Jack, then another in front of him. Before anyone could say "cheese" hundreds of cameras were greedily snapping all around.

'Water,' he croaked, crawling forwards. A young private scurried over, handed Jack a flask, then scurried away. He rinsed his mouth several times before drinking the rest.

'Hey there.' Fynn seemed to appear from nowhere, breathing hard.

Jack immediately got up. 'What happened to Golitha?'

'The giant... you must finish it off,' said Fynn, fiercely.

'Where is he? What happened?' demanded Jack.

Fynn ignored him. 'You must destroy it now.'

'I'm not gonna destroy anything until you tell me what happened to Golitha.'

Fynn huffed, checked no one could hear, then lowered his voice. 'Jack, Golitha has passed on... left us... died, as humans say. It will happen to us all at some stage.'

Jack blinked furiously. 'I should have saved him, but I couldn't get... it was –'

'There was nothing you could have done,' said Fynn. 'We didn't realise you would be so sought after by these people.' Fynn gestured towards the soldiers. 'We spoke with young Luke. He told us everything. We just didn't think. Our own silly pride blinded us from the greed of others.'

'That scumbag chief, it's his fault. I should have –' Jack clenched his fist, re-living the memory of when he had him around the neck, only this time, breaking it. 'Golitha would still be alive.'

'We don't know that Jack. No one can ever know that. But killing the military man will not help. Remember what happened with Harriet?'

'I don't care what people think.'

'Maybe not now, but at some point you will. What about your family and friends?'

'Agnes.' Jack ran towards the castle mound.

'Wait,' shouted Fynn, struggling after him. 'The giant – it was searching for the s –'

Fynn was cut short as the giant's arm swept across the ground, launching him into the sky.

Jack span and leaped over the arm. He hit the ground running and half-caught Fynn, landing awkwardly. Fynn bumped his head and Jack's whole body flushed with dread. He stopped, almost expecting Fynn to disappear as Golitha had, but Fynn remained solid.

The giant roared and all Jack's frustration and anger exploded inside him. He twisted around, standing up and drawing the sword from his back in one motion, his face pure thunder. He boomed, 'I have had just about enough of you and your blundering gangly limbs!'

The huge, scabby head lifted and the giant growled malevolently, then snorted and attempted to raise itself up, but it was stuck firm. Jack approached. It smashed an arm down which Jack dodged before swinging the sword and slashing the back of its hand. The sword vibrated excitedly and sent a warm buzz through the hilt. The giant screamed, pounding the ground with its other fist.

Up by the keep, figures stirred within the rocking car perched agonisingly at the top of the slope.

'Gary, get up!' Rob Dunce shook his brother. 'Wake up!'

Gary stirred. 'Mummy, huggies, Mummy.'

'Shut up, bruv,' snapped Rob, shaking Gary more vigorously. 'Mum's not here, it's me, Rob. Wake up.'

'Hey, what? I'm here,' said Gary, finally.

The doors were stuck fast, so they climbed through the smashed windows. The car jerked forward.

'What about *her?*' said Gary.

Rob was lying on the ground, prodding his ankle. 'Stupid cow, leave her. Teach her a lesson.' He tried to stand but collapsed with pain. 'Damn ankle, can't walk on the sodding thing.'

Gary was already up and moving but glanced back at his brother. 'I ain't staying here, bruv, you're on your own, matey.'

'Gary,' yelled Rob. 'Hang on. You wait 'til I tell mum.'

But Gary was gone.

The giant swung an arm, desperate to engage his enemy. Jack somersaulted backwards, gripping the sword tightly. The huge arm swiped back. Jack span low and fast, leaped and turned in mid-air, bringing the sword down with a mighty blow against the giant's arm. It wailed in agony.

Jack ran to the watching soldiers. 'Why aren't you firing?' he shouted.

Sergeant Spitty bustled through the crowd. 'No more ammo. It's all gone.'

'What?' said Jack. 'Since when does the army run out of ammunition?'

'Since now.'

The giant pounded both fists down, struggling in vain to

unstick itself. Jack knew he should finish it off. He jumped, skimming past flailing arms and fists, the creature unable to track him, and landed behind its head. Every awkward punch over its shoulder was met with a swift blade. Again and again he fended off the beast. Finally, exhausted with frustration, it slumped forward, presenting Jack with his opportunity.

Breathing hard, he raised the sword, staring down the filthy blade as it trembled, ready to plunge into the back of the giant's head.

'Help!'

Jack looked up. It was Agnes, still trapped in the car. The giant let an exhausted arm fall to the ground and the car pitched forward slightly.

'Hang on,' shouted Jack, jerking the drooping sword back, ready to strike.

'No,' yelled Agnes. 'What are you doing? You can't just kill it, not in cold blood.'

'What?' shouted Jack.

'It's probably human, just like the last one.'

'But it's —'

'Let it tire itself out, it's not going anywhere, is it?'

Jack hesitated. The giant growled then thrust its calloused elbows deep into the soft ground. The car jerked again then started rolling down the steep bank.

Jack was distracted and a huge hand crashed down on him, catching him fast. He pushed the sword against the leathery palm and was released, falling in a heap. He scrambled to avoid another strike and span like a hammer thrower, flinging the sword at the giant's head. It pierced the temple with a grisly shudder. Jack heard vague cries mixed with rousing cheers that he had no care for. He felt sick. The tension in the thunderous face relaxed and with a dull calmness the giant died.

Agnes was struggling to free herself as she bounced around inside the car. Jack was sprinting but could only watch in horror as the car bumped against a tree stump and rolled over and over. He caught it just before it slammed into a sturdy oak.

He was afraid to look inside.

Agnes lay still on the back seat, a sickening fork of blood running over her forehead and down her pale cheek. Jack swallowed and blinked out hot tears.

'Agnes?' he said quietly. 'Agnes, it's me, Jack. Can you hear me?'

Nothing.

The car was wrecked. The doors that were jammed shut a minute ago were now hanging off. He reached in and ripped the passenger's side seat out. Carefully, he climbed in and picked Agnes up. She was limp. Supporting her neck, he manoeuvred her out, laying her gently on the grass.

'Please wake up, Agnes.' He wiped the blood away with his tee shirt as best he could. She had a deep cut high to the right of her forehead.

'OK, son, move aside,' said a voice behind him. It was an army doctor.

Jack collapsed. 'Please help her, don't let her be hurt.'

The doctor checked her wrist for a pulse, then her neck before pulling up her eyelids. It was agonising for Jack who sat in silence, rocking absentmindedly, tears soaking his balaclava. A second man arrived and helped the doctor. Jack swirled about as his head grew hot and confused. A hundred voices in his head were all saying something different. The scene was a blur before him. He couldn't tell how long he had been sitting there. He blinked and shook his head as the doctor faced him.

'Sorry,' he said. 'She's gone.'

Jack shook his head, swallowing through the lump in his throat. 'She can't be. It's not fair. You must be able to do something.' He was close to choking. 'Please,' he sobbed, clawing out great divots of ground with hands.

The doctor called for help. Several soldiers appeared with a stretcher which they carefully placed Agnes' body on, covering her with a coat before taking her away, leaving Jack sobbing by the car, his head pressed against the damp grass. How could he go on? Now everything seemed pointless. His eyes stung with the tears and exhaustion of crying. He hit himself in anger, closing his eyes only to see Agnes' face – smiling and calm. She said. 'Come on, you can't mope around here all day, you'd better get a move on.' Then she faded away.

Jack's eyes opened wide. He glanced about, not knowing if what just happened was real. Maybe Fynn would know, but Jack couldn't see him anywhere. 'No, not him too,' he said, angrily punching a hole through the car door.

He forced himself up and plodded down the slope to the green. As he approached, people started pointing and chattering. Golitha had been right, humans did have lustful eyes. It had been so dangerous there, yet they remained, gawping at the vulgar spectacle, a visual feast in an otherwise dull life.

A nervous murmur swept across the crowd.

'What do they want?' Jack asked himself.

'To know what is happening to that creature.'

'Fynn,' said Jack. 'I thought you were gone too.'

'So did I for a minute, but never mind that, Jack, look.' He pointed at the giant which was shaking.

'You must fetch the sword, Jack.'

The outline of the giant blurred, then the whole body started vibrating. Slowly, its arms became transparent and shimmered like a swarm of golden bees. The effect spread to the neck, then the chest and down into the cavern below, claiming the entire body. The head became a thick sea of light, formed around the sword which bobbed up and down. It quickly became a mesmerising golden cloud, wobbling like an oversized bubble.

'Fetch the sword, Jack. That's what the giants were sent to recover. Golitha figured it out. We thought it'd been destroyed centuries ago, damned old fools we are.'

'Huh?' said Jack, gawping pathetically.

'Jack! The sword.' Fynn pointed firmly beyond him.

The sword was floating at the top of the vibrating mass of light.

'I don't want it. Let them have it, what good's it to me? What could I do anyway? Look at it.' Jack thought of Agnes and stared down at his bloodstained shirt.

'It's Wrath,' said Fynn, sternly. 'He needs the sword. He knows if you have it, you can fight him, knows you could fight anything.'

But Jack hardly heard a word Fynn said. 'What's the point? Nothing's going to bring her back, or Golitha, is it? I even heard her talking to me a minute ago.'

'Jack, there'll be another time. Save the sword.'

'Why don't you save it?' he moaned.

Fynn stared, open-mouthed at Jack. What could he say? There must be something. What would Golitha do?

'Agnes. You thought she spoke to you,' said Fynn. 'She must be your Key. Of course. Agnes is your Key. Golitha kept that to himself too. But she must be, she can be saved, Jack, I know it.'

'But...' Jack's mind began trying to understand what Fynn was saying.

Then the air was filled with a deafening whine. The golden cloud darkened to blood-red and a point snaked from the floating spectra. It sniffed at the four points of the compass before streaking northwards with a guttural howl, leaving a red scar across the sky, disappearing far into the distance. The sword bobbed in the air as it turned, cradled by invisible hands upon the menacing cushion.

Jack finally realised he must do as Fynn wanted and leaped to grasp the sword, only to bounce off the undulating red matter. He fell back to the green and collapsed in despair. A second later, the sword shot off along the dark vein and was gone.

Herby shuffled past the guards at the South gate, mumbling. They did not see him. He struggled up the tarmac slope into the castle grounds, pausing to crouch and cough volatile fumes over a small girl who had just contracted chicken pox. She burst into tears and grabbed her mother.

He continued into the grounds and slipped inside a makeshift shelter erected by the army. On a table lay the still figure of Agnes. He edged forward and pulled the coat back revealing her lifeless face. Patting at the pockets of his dirty coat, he finally reached inside and pulled out an open can of *Thickle & Blaynes Limping Larger* (one can too many and you'll be limping home).

'Rosem'ry, mint, thyme n' yarrow, knit-bone, knit-bone, right a wrong...'

Carefully, he opened Agnes' mouth and poured in the contents of the can. The liquid gurgled down her throat, seeping into her still body. He closed her mouth gently and brushed the hair away from the deep cut on her head. Awkwardly, he bent over and kissed it, smiling as he drew himself back up. With beauty that filled his heart with rare joy, the damaged flesh began to mend. Every torn fibre knitted itself into place with glorious precision and seconds later the skin zipped together, leaving only a faint white scar.

'Hey you, get lost. Nothing for you here, stinking tramp.' The private jostled Herby from the tent at gunpoint.

'Jack, I must leave. I need to find someone,' said Fynn, spotting approaching soldiers. 'I'll meet you soon.'

'What did you mean about Agnes being my Key?' said Jack.

'It's like a safety check, to make sure you don't lose your head. Agnes will remind you of your own mortality.'

'I had this dream where she slapped me and when I woke – my cheek was stinging.'

Fynn smiled reassuringly. 'Try not to be downhearted,' he whispered quickly. 'All is not lost,' then rushed away.

One of the soldiers cleared his throat. 'The police are asking after you and a unit of American special forces troops too. They've arrested their commander – goes by the name of Chief, they want to court martial him on grounds of insanity.'

'Good. And murder, too. He killed an old man,' said Jack, feeling the lump in his throat.

'You're free to go... wherever that may be. Think we can take care of things from here.'

'Right,' said Jack, though he hardly knew what he was doing. He was hoping for some kind of divine intervention to heal all his pain. Reluctantly, he headed off to the South gate. As he neared, he glanced back to the tent where they had taken Agnes.

A figure hobbling away on crutches caught Jack's eye. It took him a few seconds before he realised who it was, and then his stomach lurched. He marched purposefully in their direction then broke into an angry run.

'Oi,' shouted Jack. 'Oi, Dunce.'

Dunce staggered awkwardly. His face sank at the sight of the Balaclava Boy. Jack reached him and petulantly kicked away one of the crutches.

'Hey,' snarled Dunce, hopping to retain his balance. 'Watcha do that for?'

'You could've helped her out,' said Jack.

'Who?'

'The girl in the car – she died, you moron.' Jack fought the tears.

Dunce's mouth opened. 'I, I –' But he couldn't speak.

'I ought to smash your head in, you miserable scumbag.' Jack sobbed, clenching his fists in frustration. 'I ought to –'

'You're both very silly boys.'

Jack stopped, hardly believing what he thought he'd heard. It couldn't be. But there she was. His heart almost broke with joy. He had never felt anything quite like it. 'Agnes?' he whispered, sniffing.

'Yes?'

'Y... you're alive.'

'Yes, I noticed that. What happened to the giant, where's it gone?'

Jack spoke slowly, still not believing it. 'Yes, but you're alive.'

'Yes, I know,' she said, sternly.

'But you were dead,' said Jack.

'What?' she said, starting to get rather irritated.

'That's what they said. They said you were dead... but you're not.'

'They must have been wrong then, mustn't they? Because here I am,' she said, brightly.

Under his balaclava, Jack's face slowly transformed into the most satisfying smile he had ever managed. He desperately wanted to rip off the balaclava and show his joy, show Agnes who he was, but he knew he couldn't. 'I'm glad... they were wrong.'

'Huh?' Dunce pulled a sick face. 'Guess you owe me an apology then, Bakelite Boy,' he sneered.

'Shut up. Don't even say a word, you pathetic maggot.' Jack went to hit Dunce.

'No,' shouted Agnes. 'He's not worth it.'

Jack stopped, difficult though it was. Dunce spat on the ground near Jack's foot, picked up the crutch and hobbled away through the entrance under the South gate with Jack glaring after him.

Dunce crossed the debris-strewn road. Smashed vehicles lay everywhere – on their sides, upside down, inside out. It would take a while to clear it all up. He stopped by a car and cupped his hands to his mouth. 'Wish she *had* died,' he shouted.

Agnes skipped down to Jack's side. 'OK, now you can get him.'

Within a second Jack had wrenched a tyre off one of the nearest army vehicles, ignoring the complaints of some nearby soldiers. He glanced at Dunce, then up at the remains of the stone wall. 'Stand back,' he said and twirled the tyre around, spinning like a discus thrower. One, two and away it sailed, high up into the air and over the wall.

Dunce heard a whistle on the wind but chose to ignore it. The tyre landed with pinpoint accuracy clamping his arms (with crutches) to his side. He pinballed between three wrecked cars, his screams short and desperate. Eventually his momentum slowed and he staggered, falling to the road, exhausted and dizzy.

It wasn't over.

His whimpering became petrified screams as the oddly balanced tyre-and-boy object rolled down St Thomas' Road. It hit a chunk of rubble, bobbing so Dunce's head nearly collided with the tarmac. Another lump of debris changed its direction and shot him over the low wall to the equally steep field below.

The Fire Brigade recovered Rob Dunce from a patch of nettles and brambles several hours later. They could not be certain, but the evidence suggested that several children had taken a golden opportunity for revenge. They found Dunce blindfolded, gagged and disorientated, his trousers filthy where he had clearly been smacked remorselessly on the behind.

The doctor who pronounced Agnes dead cried out on discovering her body had disappeared. He hurried from the tent and when he saw her with Jack, his face froze as though he had seen a ghost.

Stumbling forward, he clasped her by the shoulders, checking her up and down. Then he fainted.

'Oh dear,' she said.

'Serves him right,' said Jack.

She frowned. 'If you're going to continue being a superhero, you're going to have to improve your attitude.' She prodded him sharply on the arm.

'Ow. That really hurt,' he said, smiling. She was his Key.

27

Spatula

Jack Shillaber really did somersault backwards. He drew his make-believe Lightsaber. *Pbshursssed* hummed its pugnacious energy. The evil Lord Wrath was poised to strike, but Jack was ready. He could feel the Force flowing through him. He was a powerful giant-killer. When it came, Wrath's attack was no match for Jack's power and agility. The Lightsabers clashed and sizzled like furious hot metal. Jack span low and fast, leaped and turned in mid-air drawing his weapon down in a deadly strike.

He smiled, but it was a half-hearted smile. For now, he had brought peace and harmony to Kernow, and there were still a few minutes before tea.

'Jack, telephone,' called his mum.

'Coming.' He dropped the piece of ash tree and ran back to the house. 'Thanks, Mum. Hello?'

'All right, Jack?'

'Yeah, you?'

'Yeah, not bad,' said Al. 'Hey, did you see that *Analysis of a Superhero* special with that Katie Lame last night?'

'No, seen too much of that kind of thing for now.'

'Yeah, was a load of rubbish anyway.'

'Have you done your history homework?' said Jack.

'Damn. Knew there was something I'd forgotten. Due tomorrow, is it?'

'Yeah.'

'Right,' said Al. Then his voice became more casual. 'Have you heard from, old what's-his-name?'

'Fynn?' said Jack, cupping his hand over the receiver.

'Yeah.'

'No. It's only been a few days though.'

'Still can't believe they never mentioned anything on the news about what happened at school.'

'No evidence, was there?'

'Suppose not,' said Al.

'Better go,' said Jack. 'Got to set the table. See you tomorrow.'

'It wasn't your fault, Jack,' said Al, quietly. 'You did all you could.'

An odd silence followed.

'Yeah, OK,' said Jack, unconvincingly. See you tomorrow, cheers.'

'Right,' said Al.

As Jack replaced the receiver the phone rang again. 'Hello?'

'Luke here.'

'Hello, Luke, there,' said Jack, imitating him.

'History homework.'

'Yeah, I know,' said Jack, a little irritated. 'I was just telling Al.'

'Good.' Luke paused, awkwardly. 'I wiped the video, thought it was for the best, seeing as how the media covered it all up.'

'Yeah, probably right,' said Jack.

Another awkward pause. 'In the back of *The Book of Untrue Facts*, there's a postcard you can send off. It says "Tick this box if you do not, not want to not be not on the mailing list".'

'Right,' said Jack, confused.

'Do you think I should send it off?'

'Why not? Nothing ventured, nothing gained, hey?'

'Yes, I suppose so. See you tomorrow, Jack.'

'Cheers,' said Jack, replacing the receiver. He walked to the far end of the table and pulled out the drawer, grabbing a handful of knives and forks. His mum carried through a tray of chocolate buns, fresh from the oven.

'Mmm, smells good enough to eat,' said Jack, stretching out an arm.

'Ah, ah. After dinner, now hurry up with the table.'

Jack dealt the cutlery around the table and snuck out to the conservatory where the buns were busy cooling. He was about to take one when his mum walked in with another trayful.

'Ay, what did I just say?'

'But –'

And she hit him on the head with a spatula.

Epilogue

No more sightings of giants or the mysterious Balaclava Boy occurred during the following weeks. The news stories died down somewhat and once again Beckham's foot became a hot topic as the build-up to the World Cup gathered pace.

The newly discovered cavern under Launceston castle was investigated by the top archaeologists in the world, who came up with all sorts of ridiculous ideas about what it was and why it was there (they all got it wrong).

Rumours circulated about a possible war against Iraq and later it was revealed that troops and equipment had been set aside as early as April, which explained a lot.

When the World Cup finally arrived, England started slowly, then put in some good performances before going out tamely to Brazil in the quarter final (after going a goal up), as predicted by Luke. If Jack had known what was to come, he may not have enjoyed the tournament as much as he did. But ignorance is, as they say, bliss.